CHAOS MAGIC

WHITE HAVEN WITCHES (BOOK 9)

TJ GREEN

Chaos Magic

Mountolive Publishing

Copyright © 2022 TJ Green

ISBN eBook: 978-1-99-004728-2

ISBN Paperback: 978-1-99-004729-9

Cover design by Fiona Jayde Media

Editing by Missed Period Editing

Contents

1. One   1

2. Two   10

3. Three   19

4. Four   29

5. Five   38

6. Six   51

7. Seven   60

8. Eight   72

9. Nine   82

10. Ten   94

11. Eleven   102

12. Twelve   111

13. Thirteen   123

14. Fourteen   133

15. Fifteen   146

16. Sixteen   154

17. Seventeen   167

18. Eighteen   176

19. Nineteen   188

20. Twenty   199

21. Twenty-One   207

22. Twenty-Two   217

23. Twenty-Three   230

24. Twenty-Four   241

25. Twenty-Five   253

26. Twenty-Six   263

27. Twenty-Seven   271

28. Twenty-Eight   279

29. Twenty-Nine   289

30. Thirty   300

31. Thirty-One   311

Author's Note   319

About the Author   321

Other Books by TJ Green   322

                                326

                                327

                                328

                                329

One

A very Hamilton admired Mariah's cottage garden from the garden gate, wishing she was there under better circumstances.

It was a wild tangle of roses, dahlias, delphiniums, and other summer plants. A gardener's paradise, there was order beneath the apparent chaos, and it surrounded a picture-perfect cottage. However, she pushed her admiration aside and assessed whether there were any magical traps hidden on the grounds.

"Well?" DI Newton asked, huffing impatiently at her side.

Avery looked at him, annoyed. "We just got here, Newton! Give me a moment."

It was Saturday evening, and the sun was slanting in low over the garden, casting part of it in shadow. It was the day after their fight with Mariah, Zane, and the pirate spirits in the cave on Gull Island, and Avery had accompanied Newton to Mariah's house in Looe. A Police Constable was guarding the property, and had been standing next to the rough-hewn wall all day, waiting patiently and silently.

Newton bristled with annoyance. "Mariah has been gone for almost twenty-four hours! We need to get in there."

Avery ignored his tone, knowing he was frustrated because he'd been stuck on Gull Island for hours, and had needed to wait for one of the witches to accompany him. "A moment more."

Avery took a few calming breaths to centre herself, then sent her magical awareness across the garden. She could feel Mariah's magic in the garden, but nothing about it was threatening.

"Nothing to worry about out here, but I'll check the house," she said, satisfied. Avery opened the gate and walked down the path, Newton right behind her. "I take it you have no word on her yet?"

Newton cast a wary glance around the garden. "None, but I'm not surprised." He looked tired, his suit rumpled. "She and Zane have obviously planned their escape well. I doubt very much she left any clue as to where she's gone."

They reached the porch, where Avery laid a restraining hand on Newton's arm, and she nodded in agreement. "Unfortunately, I think you're right, but this door is warded. Give me a moment."

Unmistakable power resonated around the entrance, and Avery feared a pulse of magic would be released unless she could neutralise it. She tried a few spells, finally finding one that worked, and with a magical boom that only she could hear, Mariah's ward collapsed. Avery used another spell to unlock the front door, and it swung open into a small hallway with a low ceiling.

Although Newton tried to enter first, Avery pushed him back. "Wait. There could be other traps."

Avery took her time to investigate her surroundings, noting the slightly old-fashioned feel to the cottage, despite its modern furnishings. It was a warm, welcoming place, and Avery struggled to marry the image of frosty, aggressive Mariah with this little piece of heaven. She checked the sitting room to the right, then progressed through to the kitchen on the left that stretched the length of the house, with a dining area at the rear.

"It's all safe down here," she told Newton.

He shook his head. "It doesn't look the house of a murderer, does it? But then again, I've learnt that people present many sides. Nothing remotely smuggling in nature here, though."

"Upstairs, perhaps," Avery said, already heading to the narrow stairs. But after spending a few minutes exploring the small but tidy bedrooms and bathroom, she found nothing there, either.

"Just half-empty wardrobes," Newton mused, checking the drawers with his gloved hands. "Which means she's not returning any time soon."

Avery headed to the window that overlooked the garden behind the house, noting it was also well stocked and maintained with summer plants and shrubs. "She obviously loves this house. I can't believe she abandoned it. Perhaps she's hoping her magic will sustain the place while she's gone."

Newton gave a short laugh. "If she thinks she's coming back after all that's happened, she's mad."

"Or she has a plan that she has complete faith in," Avery reasoned, fearing more violence. She repeated the concerns she'd had after speaking to Dan and Sally in Happenstance Books earlier that day. "There have been a lot of things that haven't made sense. For example, why she or Zane couldn't control the spriggans when we could. It suggests that they let them kill Miles and Jasmine—and that poor man with the dog. That's the only explanation! And they must have been planning to double-cross Ethan all along."

Newton raked his fingers through his short, dark hair, and up close Avery could see how bloodshot his eyes were. "They've got a hiding place."

"And probably allies."

"And a way of getting rid of the pirate gold they've already stolen." Newton's gaze was distant as he studied the garden, and then he focussed with a frown. "There's a garden shed. We should check that."

He turned and marched down the stairs, leaving Avery running after him, frustrated. "Let me assess it first!"

Once in the garden, he let her lead the way. "Perhaps she's planned for a relative or friend to look after the place at some point," Avery suggested to Newton when she finally reached the shed.

"We're checking her family out now, but we need to know which of them are witches."

"I can see if anyone in the Cornwall Coven would know, but let me focus for now." She turned her attention to the rustic building, noting it was a decent size with two small windows. One half was a regular shed, the other side a greenhouse. Now that she was up close she felt it resonating with magic. "Step back, Newton."

Avery scanned the building, noting that the magic felt stronger around the doors and windows. Runes were carved into the door with simple wards, but different to the ones used for the house. After trying a few spell combinations, she disabled the wards and opened the door. It swung open easily on well-oiled hinges. The smell of compost engulfed them, but as she stepped through the door, she saw an area at the other end that wasn't filled with gardening equipment, but looked to have been both a spell room and planning space. Shelves lined the end wall, and although most had been cleared, a few jars of dried herbs remained.

"She's taken herbs for spell work, too," Avery said, studying the remaining bottles and musing on the mostly empty space. "The protection spells weren't as strong as I expected, and I guess that's because she had nothing worth hiding here."

The workbench was clear, but there were a couple of dog-eared books about smuggling on the side. Avery idly searched them, finding nothing other than a few pencilled notes that added nothing to what they already knew.

"What about her coven member, Harry?" Avery had spoken to Genevieve earlier that day to update her and get the details. Understandably she had been furious, but also worried.

"He's married with kids, but there's no sign of him yet. A patrol car is keeping an eye on his place. We'll go there next, if that's okay?"

"Of course. You certainly can't go alone. But although I've met him, I don't know much about him," Avery confessed. Like Mariah, Harry hadn't been friendly towards her or the rest of the White Haven witches.

"That doesn't matter right now." Newton sighed. "And to be honest, all this is what I expected, but we'll get the team in anyway to search it properly. Perhaps Moore and Briar will have better luck at Zane's."

"Are they there now?" Avery asked. She'd been wondering where Sergeant Moore was.

"Should be, but I'll call him with our news."

Briar Ashworth inspected Zane and Lowen's utterly charmless living room while Moore talked on the phone. She had no idea that Zane and Lowen, the other Bodmin Coven member, were flatmates, and it seemed they didn't bother too much to make their house anything more than serviceable. It was depressing. However, she sensed there was something else here they hadn't found yet.

Moore ended his call and turned to face her. "That was Newton. Things are as we expected at Mariah's. Clothes gone and the house spelled with protection. Just like here."

Briar turned, her nose twitching. "I think I'm missing something, Moore. I feel it."

"Magic?" Moore asked, his deep voice resonating around them.

He was a man of slight build with light red hair, and his rich voice was at odds with the rest of him. Briar knew why Newton relied on him, though. He was thorough and observant, and far more patient than Newton.

"Yes. But it's not obvious. More of a prickle between my shoulder blades."

They had already searched the whole house, and Briar found it a gloomy place. It was utilitarian, devoid of artwork or personality. Perhaps they had stripped it all in anticipation of leaving, but Briar doubted that. There were no tell-tale marks on the wall where paintings might have hung. And she found no sign of a spell room, either.

Briar suddenly remembered the creak of the floorboards in the pantry next to the kitchen. This house, although unwelcoming, was a character-filled property that could have been made to be much nicer. "This place is old enough to have a cellar, right?"

"Absolutely. Why?"

"Follow me." Briar led the way back to the pantry where she stamped on the floor, eliciting a squeak. "Hear that? I'm wondering if anything is under here. Zane and Lowen are witches. They should have a spell room, and there's no sign of one anywhere. And Zane's an earth witch, like me." She looked around, frustrated. "He should have plants, and lots of herbs!"

Moore smiled. "Excellent thinking. What kind of witch is Lowen?"

"I'm not sure," she said, annoyed with herself for not checking prior, "but I'll find out."

He gestured to the floor. "Can you detect anything?"

"Not yet." She frowned, perplexed. "And that's odd. I can normally sense space beneath the earth when I focus."

Moore crouched, prodding and pulling the floorboards with his gloved hands, but despite their squeaking, they seemed firmly in place. He looked up at her. "I can look for something to lever them up, or could you move them?"

Briar hesitated. She'd never used magic in front of Moore before... not obviously so, anyway. "Are you sure you're okay with me using magic?"

"I'm fine. In fact, that's an understatement. I'm itching to see you use it." He winked. "Why should Newton have all the fun?"

She gave him a shy smile, suddenly self-conscious—which was ridiculous, considering how often she used magic. "Okay. You'd better stand back."

They exited the pantry, and Briar eyed the worn, wooden floor. She raised her hands, and summoning her power, directed it down to the boards, feeling along their edges and below. She could have just blasted them away, but she hated unnecessary destruction, so she levered up the end of half a dozen planks.

And then power reared outward.

Just in time, she threw up a wall of protection around both of them as a wave of magic blasted out, lifting them off their feet and slamming them into the cabinets behind them.

"By the Goddess!" she exclaimed, both winded and very grateful that her magic had cushioned their landing. "Sneaky bastard! That was unexpected. Are you all right?"

Moore, like her, had hit the countertop, and he put his hand to his lower back. "I'm okay. That could have been worse. You were quick."

"Fortunately." She stared at the newly revealed hole in the pantry floor. "They disguised that well, which means something is down there."

Briar threw a witch-light down the brick-lined steps and, spotting a light switch, flicked it on. The stairs lit up, illuminating the entry to a room below. Briar descended, still on full alert, with Moore hefting a powerful torch as a weapon in his hands. There was no scent of must or dampness, and when they reached the bottom, they entered a large, low-ceilinged cellar that stretched beneath the whole house.

"Oh wow!" Briar exclaimed. "So this is where they spent most of their time!"

Moore gave a low whistle next to her. "This is impressive!"

The space was comprised of perfectly dry brick walls and floor, and arches that split the place into areas, most of which were for spell work, but there was a comfortable sitting area and a TV with a gaming console. The air smelled of herbs and magic, and she made Moore wait while she felt for any more magical traps.

After a few moments, she sighed with relief. "We're fine. The one at the top was it."

Moore prowled around the space with interest. "They did have a personality, after all!"

"I'm relieved," Briar confessed. "This is where they lived—all the time! I guess as an earth witch Zane must have liked being surrounded by it." She headed to the spell room. "I personally like to see the daylight and my garden, but everyone is different."

"Were they both single... Or a couple, together?" Moore asked.

"I have no idea."

He nodded. "We'll double-check all their relationships in the coming days. Today was spent on the cave and Ethan's death." He strode to a far corner and picked up something that twinkled in the light. "A guinea." He grinned at Briar. "So, they stored some of the treasure here."

"Makes sense. It's very secure. But there's nothing to tell us where they've gone." Briar looked despondently at the obviously cleared out sections and missing magical paraphernalia.

Moore patted her shoulder. "Don't worry. It might take some time, but we'll find them eventually."

"But there's a big paranormal world out there, and they're skilled witches."

"But you have contacts, and so do we," he reassured her. "We'll be working with Maggie Milne on this. And we'll be getting a new sergeant to help us." His smile disappeared at that admission.

Briar hadn't forgotten that Inez Walker had died when she was attacked by a spriggan, but it had been pushed to the back of her mind, and now she felt horribly guilty. "I'm sorry, Moore. Another death that is Zane and Mariah's fault."

"Which is why we will find them." Moore's stare was intense and determined. "They have a lot of blood on their hands."

"Why did you become involved in paranormal policing?" she asked, aware she knew little to nothing about him.

"I have a strong sense of justice. Why should people with special powers get away with things? We may approach investigating them differently, but there has to be retribution of some sort. It's not the Wild West! And besides," he added, "it's fascinating."

"But you won't be able to imprison a witch. Not easily, anyway."

"Imprisonment is rarely an option for most of the paranormal creatures we face. As long as the victims obtain some justice, I don't care too much how that happens."

"True." Briar considered the creatures they had faced. Most of those who caused death and destruction met an unpleasant death themselves—or found paranormal retribution. "But I think Newton struggles with the manner of justice sometimes."

"Aye, he does that. And this case makes it more difficult than most. Witches are still people, after all."

"I suppose one of the best ways to stop a dangerous witch is to bind their powers...but that's hard." She shuddered at the very idea. If anyone bound her magic, it would feel as if she'd died.

Moore nodded, a flash of sympathy in his eyes, as if he sensed her horror at the suggestion. "Perhaps that's something you need to consider. Anyway, let's check the garden next and make sure we haven't missed anything."

Two

In a lull between serving customers on Saturday evening, Alex Bonneville joined Zee while he was polishing glasses behind the bar of The Wayward Son. Zee lived with the other Nephilim in the farmhouse above White Haven.

"How is Ash after last night?" Alex asked him as he took a glass from the dishwasher.

Zee laughed, pushing his thick, dark hair back off his face as he straightened up. "He's pretty good, actually. I think he enjoyed himself, despite the risks."

Alex nodded. "Good. I just wanted to check there were no repercussions."

"What about you? I hear you were battling Cruel Coppinger himself!"

Alex shook his head as he placed glasses on the shelves behind them. "Yeah, he was a wily old git. Must have been truly terrifying when he was alive. I had spectral help, though, from my old friend Gil, and Helena, Avery's ancestor."

"So I gather. I also hear that it's not over yet."

"No, not really. Caspian and Reuben broke the curse and the ghosts have gone, but we're left with two rogue witches on the loose who seem to care nothing about their actions, and we have no idea where they are or what their plans are now." Alex leaned back against the counter, frustration and worry passing through him again. "They may not present a threat to us at all, and I really hope no one else either, but I doubt that."

Zee had started to reload the dishwasher with the dirty glasses, but now he paused and stared at Alex. "What makes you say that?"

"They're responsible for at least three deaths, probably four if you count the man walking his dog. There are consequences to those actions, and they know that, and they know that we'll be searching for them. Plus, they'll be trying to sell the pirate gold they stole. They've already proved themselves to be unscrupulous. What if more innocent people are killed?"

"I'm not entirely sure you can call the thieves they worked with innocent!"

Alex rubbed his stubble, suddenly weary. "No. But they didn't deserve to be beaten to a pulp by spriggans, either."

"I guess not. Perhaps you should speak to Harlan about the black market for treasure."

"The idea has crossed our minds. I mean, we know they're not occult objects, but he'll probably have suggestions as to where we can go," Alex admitted. "I'm hoping that will also provide a way to find them. Although, I know Newton is pursuing other leads, too."

"The only trouble is, Harlan is tied up in London right now, and I'm not sure he'll have time to help."

"The job Gabe and Shadow left for yesterday?" Alex asked, remembering what Ash had told them.

"Yep. Nahum and Niel went, too. Early signs indicate this could take a while."

"I honestly think this will, as well." Alex sighed. "I guess we'll see how far our initial investigations take us and go from there. Maybe by the time we need him, Harlan will be free."

"Don't forget, he works with other collectors. Maybe they can help if he can't."

Alex brightened at that suggestion. The whole world of black market deals was far beyond his comfort zone, and something he knew nothing about, and he was certain the other White Haven witches felt the same. Magic was their strength.

"And," Zee added, "surely Newton and Maggie Milne have sources within the police that can help."

"True. And we have the Cornwall Coven who will help, too. Let's just hope there are no other nasty surprises waiting for us," Alex said, before turning away to serve a customer.

El Robinson sipped her beer as she stood next to one of her windows and surveyed White Haven harbour and the sea beyond her flat. The rain that had fallen heavily in the night had washed the town clean, and the sea sparkled in the setting sun.

It was hard to believe that only the night before they had been on Gull Island, battling Cruel Coppinger and his gang's spirits. It was tempting to celebrate after all they had achieved, but with Mariah and Zane missing, there was still danger lurking, and too much to do.

"Cheer up," Reuben Jackson said, when he joined her at the window with his own drink. "We all survived."

She studied him thoughtfully. Although his shoulder had been injured, he looked as if he was recovering well, and he'd certainly had no ill-effects after breaking Seraphina and Virginia's curse. She smiled and kissed his cheek. "You were amazing last night."

He winked. "Thanks. So were you."

"I did my best. It was great that we had Ghost OPS with us, and Ash, but I'm glad Caspian was there to support you. And that you two seem okay now."

"We have to move on. I told him that. And besides, I saw Gil." His gaze turned distant as he looked out to sea. "That was something."

"And it might happen again." He didn't elaborate further, so she decided to change the subject. "Have you arranged any builders for the house?"

"The glaziers measured up today and will be back on Monday, and the builder can make it the week after next. Until then, everything's tarped up and I've reinforced my protection spell—with a new tweak against rain."

"Are you sure you don't want to stay here for a couple of weeks?"

"Positive. I'll just stay tonight. I'd worry too much, otherwise." He leaned against the window frame. "I wasn't in town much today. How does it feel out there?"

El huffed, recalling the conversations that had buzzed in her shop all day. "Excitable. There's a lot of gossip about Ethan's death. Word gets around this place so quickly! Apparently, the queues at White Haven Museum were down the street! At least no one knows we were involved...yet."

The timer pinged on her oven and she headed to the kitchen. Reuben followed, asking, "Any mention about Mariah and Zane?"

"They are named on the news as 'persons of interest.'"

"Wow!" Reuben leaned on the counter. "Newton isn't wasting any time, then."

"He can't afford to, can he? Witches or not, they are prime suspects. And," she mused as she pulled the large tray of lasagne out of the oven to check its progress and then slid it back in again, "it does us a favour."

"How do you reckon that?"

"It means they need to keep their heads down." El had ruminated on their options all afternoon while she worked in her shop. "While it makes them harder to find, potentially, it also gives us some breathing space. And time to consider how best to deal with them."

Reuben nodded. "Time to find any collaborators."

"Exactly." El placed several packs of garlic bread into the oven before turning back to Reuben. "And time to work with the Cornwall Coven."

"Did Avery call Genevieve?"

"This morning, and she's already started to alert the other covens." She noticed that Reuben's beer was almost finished and grabbed them both another from the fridge. "What about your place? I suppose the police are there?"

"And then some!" He shook his head and sighed. "It seems like hundreds of them are trudging through my glasshouse and down to the cave. They've left a couple of officers outside so even I can't get in, and there are police stationed on the island, too." He grimaced. "It was late-morning by the time they fetched Ethan's body out."

"Are you sure you don't want to stay here?" she asked again. "No one will break into your place with hordes of SOCO and police there."

"And miss all the fun? You must be kidding!"

Knowing he wouldn't change his mind, El gave up and checked the clock on the wall. "I'm worried about Briar and Avery. They should be here by now. What if something has happened?"

Reuben squeezed her hand in his large one, brown and rough from all his surfing. "They're with Newton and Moore. They'll be fine."

El nodded, distracted. It was Alex who'd suggested they meet at her place for privacy rather than The Wayward Son, and she had put together a simple dinner. He should be arriving soon, too. Fortunately, they didn't have to wait much longer; it was close to eight when Briar and Avery arrived, and she eyed them with relief. They looked tired, but at least they weren't injured.

"Oh, good! You're both okay!" she said by way of greeting.

"I told you that you were worrying too much," Reuben said, already pouring each a glass of wine. "You've been clucking like a mother hen!"

"Sod off, Reuben," she shot back, before smiling at her closest friends again. "Ignore him."

"We try." Briar laughed, walking over to the open-plan kitchen and accepting Reuben's proffered glass. "He's too big and loud though, most of the time."

Reuben blew Briar a kiss and winked, making her giggle.

"Any news on Alex?" Avery asked, also accepting her wine with a grateful smile.

Reuben nodded. "He'll be here soon. Just wrapping a few things up at the pub. I'm surprised you haven't phoned him."

"Once we'd finished at Harry's I just wanted to get here, so I didn't linger," she admitted. "And I knew I'd be seeing him soon, anyway."

"I take it they've scarpered?" Reuben asked.

Briar nodded, dejected. "The Bodmin Coven has gone. I really had hoped that only Zane was involved. I guess it's not surprising, though. Zane and Lowen lived together. It would be hard to keep secrets."

"They lived together?" Reuben asked, eyebrows arching in surprise. "I didn't know that! Are they gay?"

"I have no idea," Briar said, shrugging. "I gather they were childhood friends, from what Caspian told me, but it doesn't matter either way. Both of their wardrobes were half empty."

El was a realist. "It was inevitable. Look how closely we work together."

"And Mariah and Harry are related," Avery told them. She loosened her untidy bun to let her hair fall down her back, and sat on a bar stool at the kitchen counter. "Newton has started to investigate all of her relatives now."

Briar took a seat next to her. "They'll do the same to the Bodmin Coven."

"They will check Harry too, right?" El asked Avery. "What's his deal?"

"He's married with two young kids, and his wife swears he's away on business."

"I take it she's not a witch," Reuben said, frowning.

Avery shook her head. "Pretty sure not. I think our visit scared her, though. She insisted he was at work, and kept asking us if anything was wrong." She grimaced. "I really hope he is at work and not involved, but I guess Newton will find out. She refused to let us in, so Newton will have to get a search warrant, too."

"I'm sure the police will find out all sorts of things," Reuben conjectured.

El opened the oven to check the lasagne, and satisfied to see the top nicely browned, slid it out and put it on the side. "No stone unturned, then?"

"None," Briar said. "And what about your place, Reuben?"

He grunted. "Inundated with the police."

While they chatted, Alex arrived, and he kissed Avery's cheek as he greeted the others.

"Take a seat at the table," El instructed them. "We can chat while we eat. I'm starving."

When they finally settled with full plates and glasses, El said, "I feel like this should be a celebratory meal after last night's victory. But it's not really over, is it?"

Alex frowned. "I was just saying the same thing to Zee. I don't like the fact that we're fighting other witches. It feels all kinds of wrong to me!"

"We've done it before," Avery said, squeezing his hand. "Remember the Devices from Cumbria?"

"How can I forget?" he admitted. "But they weren't members of the greater coven, and Mariah and Zane are! For all of their antagonistic behaviour, I still can't get over the fact that they tried to kill Caspian and Reuben."

"That's because you're judging them by our standards," Reuben told him. "We can't afford to do that anymore. We have to presume the worst in everyone now."

Avery looked distracted and dejected, and El frowned at her. "What's wrong?"

"Just thinking about a discussion I had with Sally and Dan earlier today about Jasmine and Miles's deaths." She quickly updated them on her theory about Mariah and Zane deliberately not controlling the spriggans, and the table fell silent.

"That's a hell of a theory," Alex eventually said. "That puts things in a whole new light!"

Briar sipped her wine thoughtfully. "But Ethan's death last night was completely spontaneous. No one could have predicted that! The spriggan just erupted from that treasure chest. We couldn't stop it, and neither could they!"

"That's true. It took us all by surprise," El said, remembering Mariah's shriek when the spriggan appeared. And then she thought of how she had been able to control the spriggan in the cave on her own. "But you're right about the other spriggans. The one I encountered was quick, but I managed to subdue it. I had fey armour to tempt it with though."

Avery shook her head, a stubborn expression settling on her face. "You did, but me and Alex didn't, and yet we subdued them, too. If Zane and Mariah were together—and it seems they were—then they should have been able to stop them. I hate to think the worst of them, but I think we have to. Those other deaths were not accidental."

"But they killed a spriggan!" El argued, bewildered at the suggestion. She hated to doubt Avery's reasoning, because it was always normally sound, but this seemed extreme. "That's why the one I encountered was so angry! And how did they get the spriggan out from beneath St Catherine's Castle? And why not take that treasure, if they did? It was still there! You found it!"

All four witches were now looking at Avery, and she tightened her lips.

"I know it seems a leap." Avery's green eyes were troubled. "It was pretty obvious they were targeting Reuben and Caspian, but the other deaths have been niggling me. Mariah and Zane are both powerful witches! Why couldn't they control the spriggans like we could?" She appealed to El. "And you're right. How was Miles killed by one—well, probably—when he didn't even enter that room under St Catherine's Castle? Maybe they lured one out? Perhaps they were intending to go back, but the police presence on the cliff meant they couldn't."

"Perhaps they got too cocky," Reuben mused. "I don't like your suggestion, Avery, but your argument is unnervingly logical."

"But what I don't understand," Alex said, "is why is this all happening now? Is it really just because they found treasure? Or is there something else going on?"

"Like what?" El asked, alarmed that there might be even more subterfuge.

Alex shrugged apologetically. "I don't know."

"That treasure is worth a lot of money," Reuben pointed out. "And money is a big motivator!"

"I can't get over Mariah's lovely cottage," Avery told them. "It seemed so at odds with her actions—weird, I know. Like home décor is a window to your soul!"

"Tell us what you found," Reuben said, addressing her and Briar.

They updated the group on their visits, and then Avery said, "By the way, I spoke to Genevieve again. The Witches Council meeting is tomorrow."

El looked up, surprised. "I thought she wanted to discuss the issue on the solstice?"

"When I told her that all the coven members had gone missing, she decided to bring it forward. We meet tomorrow night." Avery's expression was dark as she looked around the table. "I think she's worried about other coven loyalties."

"With good reason," Briar said, her voice quiet. "Their betrayal is a shock. Let's hope there isn't more to come."

Three

The mood was grim when Avery arrived at Crag's End for the Witches Council meeting on Sunday evening. The day had been hot, and showed no sign of cooling, despite the setting sun. The windows were open wide, ushering in the scent of roses and cut grass, and stiff gin and tonics seemed to be a popular request.

Avery had spent the day relaxing with Alex, catching up on jobs around the house and in the garden, glad for the respite from their current issues. Newton hadn't needed them, instead focussing on gathering background information, and Avery couldn't have been happier. She only wished she didn't have to be at the meeting now. But of course, it couldn't be avoided.

Oswald grimaced as he handed her a drink, the skin around his eyes crimping into a network of fine lines. "A rough few days, I gather?"

"Very. Fortunately we're okay, but it's been odd, Oswald. I can't deny it."

"I never liked Zane, or Mariah, really. They weren't easy people to get along with, although Mariah and I bonded over gardening. However, I am immensely shocked to hear about their exploits."

"I take it Genevieve has told you the latest?"

"She's been phoning all of us during the last twenty-four hours, asking us to remember anything that might shed light on this." His lips pursed in a tight line. "I fear we're going to descend into tittle-tattle and gossip this evening."

Avery loved Oswald's gentlemanly ways and calm demeanour. For the others who had been in the Cornwall Coven for years, this must be a far greater shock to them, the betrayal going deeper.

"I'm sorry. I feel we're somehow to blame. You know, because White Haven is part of the council now."

"Do not be ridiculous," a gravelly voice rasped behind her. *Rasmus.* He sidled next to Oswald, his shock of white hair looking more eccentric every time she saw him. "You have every right to be here. And nothing gives Mariah or Zane the excuse to commit their terrible actions."

"*If* they committed them," another man called Charlie Curnow said, joining their conversation. He was in his thirties, with curly brown hair cut close to his head, but not enough to hide the slight curl to it. Avery had spoken only briefly to Charlie before—polite greetings, either before or after meetings, or at their mutual celebrations—but she knew he represented the Polzeath Coven. She normally found him pleasant, but now she frowned.

"What do you mean, *if*? I was there. I *saw* them—and so did the rest of my coven—along with DI Newton."

"And the paranormal investigators were there, too," Caspian added, breaking off his conversation with Jasper to stand next to her, and giving her a nod in greeting. "Do you think we're lying, Charlie?"

He shook his head, apologetic. "No, of course not. I just find it hard to believe that they were involved in this."

Caspian's voice was tight. "So did we, but there's no doubt about it." He patted his side where he'd been stabbed. "They're responsible for this, too."

"You were injured?" Charlie asked.

"Stabbed by a ghost that Mariah had motivated."

Caspian's eyes were hard, and Charlie faltered. "Sorry. I had no idea."

Avery felt compelled to spell it out, annoyed that Charlie seemed to think them liars. "Charlie, I know this is a shock, but Caspian could have died. Several nasty spirits have attacked all of us, and Reuben was stabbed, too. We know they're behind it all."

Charlie glanced warily at Oswald and Rasmus. "What do you two think?"

Rasmus's eye's glinted with annoyance. "I know better than to doubt half a dozen witches. And look around the room, Charlie. Where are Zane and Mariah now? They're certainly not here to defend themselves."

Rasmus's words had drawn the attention of the others in the room, and Claudia broke off from her conversation with Eve. "Sorry though I am to admit it, this does not bode well. This is a dark day indeed for our coven."

The other witches shifted uneasily. Genevieve had been listening as she sipped her drink, but now she addressed everyone. "I think there's been enough speculation, don't you? Let's get this meeting underway."

As they made their way to their seats, Avery walked next to Caspian. "I wasn't sure you'd be here. Are you feeling well enough?"

"I'm fine. It still twinges, but I'd rather be here than send Estelle."

He didn't elaborate, and Avery sighed. The last thing they needed now was for Caspian to be feuding with his sister, although she was very relieved that Caspian was there. Estelle's abrupt demeanour made everyone tense.

"But your protection spells are strong enough? On your house, I mean?" Avery clarified.

Caspian smiled and nodded. "They are. I'll be fine."

He sat next to her at the table, and Avery eyed the two empty seats, as did everyone else. Mariah and Zane's absence was ominous, and it was clear that everyone was unsettled. Eve and Jasper gave them reassuring smiles, but Avery could see the worry behind their eyes.

Genevieve didn't waste time, and as usual sat at the head of the table. Her dark hair was swept up into an imperious bun, and her sharp glance travelled over all of them. "It's been less than a week since we last met, and already so much has changed. Mariah and Zane were with us, and their behaviour suggested nothing of their involvement. And I admit, I discerned nothing. Now..." She trailed off and took a deep breath, as if to fortify herself. "Well, now we know the full extent of their actions. I have spoken to all of you individually, but I'm making it clear right now—Mariah was seen by Avery and Alex leaving Ethan James's house, and both Zane and Mariah were seen in the cave at Gull Island by many people. Last week we discussed Cruel Coppinger and the spirits, but," she turned to Avery and Caspian, "I suggest you two bring us up to date."

Between them both, they related the most recent events, finishing with how Zane and Mariah had openly attacked them and then fled.

"Essentially," Avery said, her gaze travelling around the table, "Newton needs to find them. *We* need to find them. We have no idea where they are or what they're doing, or whether they still seek revenge on us. Newton is doing background checks on both covens right now."

Caspian added, "It takes a witch to fight a witch. We all need to support each other."

"Of course we do," Claudia said without hesitation. Despite the gravity of their meeting, Claudia was dressed in one of her usual voluminous, patterned dresses, and her attire made Avery smile, despite everything. "It is unacceptable that a witch should attack anyone for personal gain. And to kill and maim, or allow something else to kill when we could stop it..." she said, referring to Avery's suspicions about the spriggans, "well, it just makes my blood boil!"

"Agreed," Genevieve said. "And may I add, this is not a debate about *whether* we should help, but *how* we can help. I don't care how well some of you may have got on with the Bodmin and Looe Covens. I also don't care about personal friendships. This is about bringing people to justice—difficult though this may be."

Eve spoke up quickly, glancing around the table. "I have no problem with that. They must be found."

Jasper nodded, too. "Unfortunately, in my experience, when someone, witch or not, behaves like this, it is unlikely to stop."

"Absolutely," Rasmus and Oswald added together.

Another woman named Gray Pengelly who represented the Bude Coven said, "I hate the thought that we are tracking down other witches, but clearly we must." Gray, Avery estimated, was in her forties. She had a wild mop of curly red hair and hazel eyes, and Avery had always found her friendly but reserved. She never made waves at the meetings and merely listened, added comments when needed, and participated in all the events. However, she gave Avery and Caspian a warm smile. "I'm sorry you've had such a bad experience, but I assure you that my coven will help in any way we can."

Hemani Dutta, a young Indian woman with lustrous black hair who represented the Launceston Coven quickly followed suit. Avery knew she had three other coven members, but didn't know them well.

"Excellent," Genevieve said, and then stared at Charlie. "You are suspiciously quiet. Do you still have doubts?"

"Yes, I do, actually. Because unlike many of you, I was friends with Zane and Lowen. Am friends, rather." He shuffled in his seat, looking down at the table. "I feel uncomfortable moving against them."

"Despite Zane's actions?" Caspian asked, a dangerous edge to his voice.

"I'm not saying I like what he did!" Charlie's voice rose with annoyance. "And there's no evidence that Lowen is involved, either!"

Avery tried not to snap. "Didn't you hear me? His clothes and personal items are gone, just like the others. They have to be involved —and I'm sure Harry's 'work trip' is a ruse."

Genevieve intervened. "Charlie. Have you heard from Zane or Lowen?"

He hesitated, and then shook his head. "No."

"Don't lie to me, Charlie, or you'll find yourself off the council," Genevieve warned, her eyes flashing with anger.

"I'm not lying!" he shot back. "I've heard nothing. I didn't even know they'd left."

"Have you any idea where they might have gone?" Charlie shook his head, and Genevieve turned to the others. "Anyone? Or Mariah or Harry?"

Eve frowned. "I think I heard Mariah mention that she had relatives in Somerset, but that was a passing conversation from years ago. I could be wrong."

Avery felt Caspian become very still next to her, and he said, "You may have something there, Eve. I also remember her mentioning that."

"I'm sure Newton can confirm it," Avery suggested. "But we also need to know who in their families are witches. Does anyone know?"

Everyone shook their heads except for Charlie. "Zane's mother was a witch, but she is a solitary practitioner, and she and Zane have not been close for years. I don't know about the others."

Shocked he'd offered any insights, Avery said, "Thank you. That's good to know."

Hemani's fingers drummed the table. "But what do we do with them once we find them?"

That was a good question, Avery reflected. Everyone looked uncertain or troubled, even though they had offered their help. But it wasn't as if Mariah and her accomplices would give themselves up easily.

Rasmus grunted. "There is only one option for witches who abuse their power to such an extent, and that is to bind their powers so they are no longer a danger." A collective gasp ran around the room as everyone stared at Rasmus. "I know. It's a terrible thing to do, and very, *very* hard. And we're not talking about one witch, but four."

"But," Gray said immediately, "not all of them have maimed or killed! For all we know, they just collaborated to steal treasure. That option is too extreme for such a crime."

"Agreed," Jasper said, steepling his fingers in a contemplative gesture. "However, the more I think on this, the more I believe that this is the tip of the iceberg. They have risked everything—their lives, families, friends...but for what? Just money?" He shook his head and sighed. "I don't get it."

Avery recalled Harry's tatty house that was clearly in need of attention. "Money is important if you have none—and I'm not sure Harry had much. And Zane and Lowen lived together. That might be for financial reasons. But," her heart sank as she recalled Alex's words from the night before, "Alex also thought there must be something else behind this."

"Are they in need of money for some kind of power grab?" Eve suggested, looking very confused.

"A power grab of what?" Genevieve said, flabbergasted. "There are no hierarchies of power in the witch world. No singular leaders who make rules for all. We manage our own covens and areas, and then live and let live."

"Says the High Priestess who's just threatened to kick me off the council," Charlie scoffed, narrowing his eyes at Genevieve.

Genevieve blanched, and everyone froze as magical energy started to build and an ugly atmosphere threatened to break. However, to her credit, she acted quickly. "You're right, Charlie. I apologise. My role here is to offer magical support and guidance, especially to those less skilled in spellcraft than myself and our older members. And it is my duty, of course, to lead our celebrations." She looked utterly stricken, and Avery couldn't help but feel sorry for her. "I did not mean to overstep my bounds."

"Don't you dare apologise!" Rasmus said gruffly as he glared at Charlie. "Liberal, wishy-washy sentiment only runs so far. We *do* need order, and all groups need a leader. Especially in times of crisis—like now." He glared around the table, eyeing every single one of them. "Because make no mistake. This is a crisis."

The atmosphere felt dire now, and Avery's heart pounded. *What the hell was happening?*

However, Oswald, in a reasoned tone, said, "I suggest we all take a breath and calm down. This is a new situation for the current Cornwall Coven, although not for all of us. Years ago we had a contentious issue which I won't go into now, but we got through it—together." He turned to Charlie. "There are reasons for how we work. Never forget that." A frown creased his brow, deepening his wrinkles. "To return to our earlier discussion, we meet to celebrate the old ways and ancient dates, and to share our knowledge. What would we want with power grabs?"

"And what would we do with it, anyway?" Claudia added.

"Perhaps," Gray said cautiously, as the mood settled once more, "there is something the treasure offers, other than money."

"Like what?" Charlie asked, looking at her as if she'd gone mad.

She shrugged. "I don't know! Does it appease a God? Does it buy them into another coven?" She held her hand up at everyone's incredulous expressions. "I know. Anyone can join a coven. You don't have to buy your way in. I'm just speculating here."

"Actually," Avery said, feeling a spike of annoyance. "Not *everyone* can just join a coven. We were excluded from this one for years."

An awkward silence fell, and Caspian turned to look at her, a mischievous glint in his eye. "*Touché.*"

She gave a dry laugh. "Exactly. Not all witches are created equal, and not all want what *we* want. Some hold grudges." She faced the council. "The Devices in Cumbria held the Cumbria Wolf-Shifter Pack in a tight grip for years, aided by their pack leader. They hated our interference when I inadvertently offered Sanctuary." She gave Caspian a wry smile. "You were right. I had no idea what we'd stumbled into."

Genevieve groaned. "Damn it. We are liberal here, and I forget that others are less so. Perhaps there *is* something else to this." She glanced around the council again, her composure returned. "Have you had a chance to speak to your coven members yet?" There was a mixture of nods and the shaking of heads, as some confessed they had yet to speak to everyone. "Please do so, and soon. Any information is of use."

"I can say," Claudia said, brightly, "that Cornell wishes to be involved. He has taken more of a leadership role in the decisions of our coven, and I want to support that." She eyed Avery and Caspian in particular. "I'll make sure you have his number."

Avery smiled at her, thankful for Claudia's no-nonsense attitude and evergreen support.

"So, what now?" Hemani asked Genevieve.

Genevieve glanced at Caspian and Avery, and Avery thought how tired she suddenly looked. "I suggest," she said to all of them, "that we gather information and think on our discussion today, and then we meet back here on Wednesday evening."

"That's too long," Caspian remonstrated. "Tuesday."

"All right, Tuesday—if that's okay, Oswald?"

"Always," Oswald nodded.

"And we'll continue to work with Newton in the meantime," Avery said. "We can update you with his news, too."

"Wait!" Caspian said, holding up his hand and looking annoyed. "Information is not enough, Genevieve. We need a team who is willing to work with us on this. It might have been Reuben and I who were targeted this time, but I don't see why it's the White Haven Witches and my responsibility to find them with just a bit of help thrown in! This is a greater coven issue!" He stared at all of the members in turn, and then back at Genevieve. "We need a dedicated group to work with us. I suggest that when we next meet we have a list of names—it doesn't need to be many. Maybe another half a dozen?"

Immediately, Eve said, "Absolutely, Caspian. I am happy to put forward my name now, and am sure Nate will agree."

"I've already mentioned Cornell," Claudia added. "I know he will want to take an active role. Perhaps, rather than all of us meeting on Tuesday, only those dedicated few should. No sense in delaying things."

"Excellent plan," Rasmus agreed.

"In that case," Genevieve said, forestalling any other comments, "you must decide quickly. We all have responsibilities—family and otherwise. Make sure those who volunteer can really commit their time. And now," Genevieve smiled, "perhaps we can finish with something more uplifting, and talk about our Litha celebrations."

Four

Newton groaned and rubbed his eyes, pushing away from his desk in exhaustion.

He had all but lost the entire weekend to tracking down the missing witches and following up on the events in Gull Island's cave. The SOCO team were still crawling over the island looking for evidence, and had followed the other passage that Zane and Mariah had escaped through. They found that it exited into another cave on the far side of the island, and Newton presumed it must have been blocked for a long time. There was evidence of fresh earth and rockfall around the entrance, and he guessed they had used magic to uncover it.

Moore also found that Harry, Mariah's cousin, owned a boat, and Newton suspected it was the one they used to flee the island—not that it helped much. The boat was tied up in Looe harbour, and although they'd impounded it, there was nothing to indicate that it had been involved with Mariah and Zane's escape. There was certainly no treasure left on it.

Earlier that day they had been granted a search warrant for Harry's house, and had opted to go there without a witch after Avery's reassurance the day before. Plus, he reasoned, Harry wouldn't have any magical traps in the house that would harm his children or wife. Disappointingly, he had found nothing there. Not even evidence of a spell room, and he wondered if Harry had used Mariah's.

Movement at the door caught his attention, and he heard a light rapping on the frame. Looking up he saw Moore, rumpled and exhausted.

"Hey, Guv. I'm heading home if that's okay?"

"Bloody hell, I thought you went hours ago." Newton felt horribly guilty as he checked his watch. "It's nearly nine!"

"I know," he nodded wearily. "I'm hoping to get home to see the kids before bed."

"Of course!" Newton stood and stretched his legs, feeling every single crunch and groan of his cramped muscles. "Shit. You should have gone before now!"

"It's fine. I was assembling a list of addresses, but I'll have to finish it tomorrow."

"It's not like we're going to go storming in tonight, anyway," Newton said. "I want to do this right. Get our ducks lined up."

Moore pushed his hair back, making it look messier than before. "I agree. They're witches, and anything poorly planned will be a big mistake. They'll have witches in their families, too."

"And friends, no doubt," Newton said thoughtfully. "I'm sure they're hiding with another coven."

"Or another paranormal group."

Newton had already thought of that, but hoped they were wrong. "Yes, it's possible. Let's face it. Anything is possible!"

"Heard anything from Avery?"

They knew she'd gone to the council meeting that evening. "No. She said she'd phone if she heard anything significant, but otherwise I'll speak to them tomorrow."

Moore pushed away from the doorframe he'd been leaning against. "I'll see you in the morning, then. Have you made a decision on the new sergeant yet?"

Something else to worry about. "No. But we'll talk about that, too. I want your opinion."

After Moore left, Newton sat down again, easing back into his chair with a sigh. Pushing away Mariah's file, he rummaged under the pile of paperwork and pulled the three staff files towards him. He'd been recommended three officers to choose from, one man and two women. They all came with good references, and all had some experience with paranormal policing. He really wanted a woman on the team. Women were good at things men weren't, and he wanted some balance. But right now, thinking of replacing Inez was hard.

Her funeral was on Tuesday afternoon, and it promised to be horrible. He wanted to wait until after that to make a decision, but couldn't. Pressure was being applied from above, and besides, they needed help with this case. And who knows what else might crop up.

He pushed the files away again in a fit of annoyance. *It could wait.* He needed a shower, and then bed. He wouldn't even drop into The Wayward Son. Right now, he wanted nothing more to do with anything remotely paranormal.

Alex groaned when the alarm buzzed again and he heard Avery turn it off with a groan of her own, muttering, "Bollocks."

He rolled over and pulled her close, and she snuggled into the crook of his arm. She'd hit the snooze button several times, and it was now close to eight o'clock; she'd be heading into the shower soon, so he enjoyed her curves while he could.

"Bad night?" he asked.

"Not really. I just want to stay in bed and pretend none of this is happening."

He kissed the top of her head. "It's not going to go away."

"I know." She wriggled free and looked up at him, beautiful despite her messy hair and sleepy green eyes. In fact, more beautiful because of it. "I just don't want to spend weeks chasing down scraps of clues about Mariah and the others. Or worrying about imminent attack."

"I would imagine they are just as pissed off at the way things have gone. Think of it from their perspective. We *survived*!" He stroked her cheek where her freckles were starting to become more obvious from the summer sun. "That curse was meant to kill as many of us as possible. We beat it, and now they're on the run. I bet that wasn't their original intent." He flopped back on the pillow and stared up at the ceiling as his thoughts became clearer. "I was thinking on this while I worked yesterday. If they had got away with all this, they wouldn't have needed to hide."

Avery rolled on top of him, her arms leaning on his chest as she stared at him. "You're right. They'd have the treasure and we'd be dead, and there'd probably be nothing to link them to it at all!"

He grinned. "Exactly. We forced them to change their plans. As soon as we started asking questions and Newton began investigating, they'd have known they were in trouble."

"And they didn't expect us to find them on Friday night, either. But," she said, playfully poking him in the ribs, "it still doesn't make the situation any better."

He laughed and flipped her over, making her squeal. "Killjoy! It makes *me* feel better. They're on the backfoot now. And you are just on your back," he teased, nuzzling her neck.

"Oh no, mister," she said, pushing him off with surprising strength. "Shower time now, and then work."

Avery slid out of bed and he watched her shapely hips sway across the room, leaving him with an ache in his loins. "You're such a tease, Avery Hamilton!"

She winked. "I know. So, what are you doing today?"

"I'll go to work later and try to pretend life is normal."

He heard the shower start and she came back to the door to watch him suspiciously. "And what else?"

"See if I can get a lead on our missing witches."

She laughed. "I knew it!"

Forcing himself to be patient, he tidied up the flat after breakfast and then headed to the attic room, throwing the windows open to let in the warm June air. Mariah and the others would be hiding themselves using spells, but it didn't mean he couldn't try to find them. He phoned Newton.

"Please don't tell me something else has happened," Newton groaned.

"Nothing has happened! I just wondered if you had any locations for our missing witches. I thought I'd try some revealing spells, and they might work better if I can narrow down their whereabouts."

Newton's tone immediately brightened. "I like that idea. Let me get my files." Alex grabbed a pen and paper, and started to make notes as Newton said, "Mariah's got relatives in Galway, Ireland, and Wells in Somerset. Zane's family lives in Wadebridge, so that's close. Lowen's family is dead. Natural causes, by the looks of it. He was an only child. Harry's father's family is in Exeter. Don't ask for details because I haven't got any yet. I do know, however, that Mariah's mother and Harry's father are siblings. Her mother divorced years ago, and her current husband is Irish—hence the move to Galway." Newton sighed. "Any idea who of them are witches? I mean, I know it runs in families, but that doesn't always mean anything, does it? Or that they'd approve of their current actions. Look at yours."

Newton was right. Magic could do odd things to families. For some it made them closer, for others it forced them apart. Not everyone coped well with it. His own father now lived in Scotland, and had little to do with Alex's life. The same was true for the other witches. El and Briar had little to do with their immediate family, Reuben's extended family had left White Haven years before, and Avery's sister and mother had moved away, too. She hadn't seen her father in years.

"Sorry, Newton," he answered. "The Cornwall Coven are looking into it. We'll have more answers by Tuesday, but I'll do what I can now."

"Thanks. But be careful."

"You, too. What are you up to today?"

Newton's tone was flat. "Choosing a new sergeant."

"Shit. Sorry."

"It has to be done. We need the help. And then I'm going back to Gull Island, just to check on their progress. I'll look in on Reuben, too." Newton sounded depressed, and Alex knew he still carried guilt about Inez's death.

"Come to the pub later. A pint always helps."

"I probably will. Anyway, I have to go. I've got a ton of stuff to do. See you later."

He rang off abruptly, and Alex wished he could say something to make Newton feel better. However, the only thing that would help would be finding the other witches. They had a stack of maps amongst the books on the shelves, and Alex pulled out one now, deciding to focus on Galway first.

Rather than closing the blinds to work in the darkened room, as often worked well for him, he decided to sit in a patch of sunlight on the rug by the hearth. The warmth would help lull his senses and relax him mentally, allowing him to open up his magical sight. Then he had another thought. He could try to scry, using his silver bowl filled with water.

With what was probably an unreasonable amount of optimism, he prepared his materials and settled into a cross-legged position ready to begin.

Reuben stood beside the glasshouse on his grounds behind Greenlane Manor watching the activities of the SOCO team and trying to keep out of the way.

Despite his best intentions to leave them to it, he couldn't. The whole process was fascinating. Several vans were taking up space on his drive, and a trickle of people dressed in white suits trekked back and forth up the slope of his lawn carrying bagged evidence. So far he hadn't seen anything that might suggest the skeletal remains were being removed, but figured he'd missed that.

He eyed the young female PC who stood at the entrance to the glasshouse. She was studiously avoiding him as she stood guard, but he approached her anyway, his smile broad, and held his hand out. "Hi, I'm Reuben and I own this house. You are PC who?"

She looked startled, but shook his hand anyway. "PC Scott."

"Great. How much longer is this going to take?"

She shrugged. "Sorry. I have no idea. I'm just here to make sure no one goes in who shouldn't. But the forensic anthropologist and his team are in there now. Once the bodies are out, things will speed up."

"They haven't taken those yet?" Reuben couldn't keep the disbelief from his voice.

"No. It's painstaking work, and they arrived later than expected. And besides," she lowered her voice, "I don't think they class this as urgent! The recently deceased take priority."

Recently deceased. What a cold way to now refer to Ethan.

Reuben thanked her and sat on the grass to watch for a bit longer, lowering his sunglasses over his eyes and feeling more and more uncomfortable by the minute. As much as he was trying not to let it bother him, the process inevitably reminded him of when Gil's body had been taken away only one year before. But this was very different. And he had seen Gil's spirit, if only briefly. And that was the other issue. Reuben wanted to see him again, but simultaneously wanted Gil to be at peace.

His whole idea of the spirit world had been upended after his recent experiences. To think that Helena had been restrained and Gil had helped her escape her spirit-shackles was just weird. It meant that there really was a whole other life after death, and he was struggling to accept that it sounded far more active than he'd ever considered. Unless Gil's situation was unusual. *Helena's certainly was.*

His reverie was interrupted by an abrupt shout as an irate man strode towards him, peeling off the top of his white suit to reveal a smart polo shirt beneath. His grey hair was thinning, and he was whip thin with a weather-beaten face. "Are you Reuben Jackson?"

Reuben stood up, puzzled. "I am. Can I help you?"

"I bloody well hope so! I want to know why those skeletons have been moved! Did you do it?"

For a second, Reuben couldn't think what he was on about. "What do you mean, moved? Of course not. I can't even get in the place!

Who are you?"

The man didn't offer his hand. "Dr Adam Hales, forensic anthropologist." He swept on without pause. "My team has started to examine the remains, and they are not where they should be!"

"How do you know that?"

"Because it's my job to know. The soil around them is disturbed, and some appear to have been moved considerable distances!"

Shit. Reuben remembered being told that Zane had animated them, and they had all risen and fought the witches. He fumbled for words, not sure what to say. Newton said it was a paranormal team who were investigating, but did that extend to the anthropologists?

Instead, he answered truthfully and with an appropriate air of outrage. "Of course I haven't moved them! I'm not a ghoul!"

Thankfully a familiar voice called out, "Dr Hales. You're not who I was expecting!" Reuben sighed with relief as Newton appeared next to him. "I'm DI Newton, head of the investigation."

"Someone has moved my bodies!" Hales insisted, not even greeting him.

Newton glared at him. "There was a reason I asked for Bob Durrell."

"He's up north and couldn't come. That's why I'm delayed. He kept insisting he could make it, but now can't, and then this has happened!" He threw his arm wide encompassing the manor and the island.

"Calm down, for God's sake," Newton yelled unexpectedly. "It's not a bloody conspiracy. It's a paranormal crime scene! That's why I wanted him. It's his thing!"

Hales blanched and stepped back as if he might be tainted by the words. "I wasn't aware of that. Why wasn't I told?"

"I have no idea! Don't you know what he does?"

Hales swallowed. "I've heard rumours."

Newton took a deep breath and glanced at Reuben, who tried to look sympathetic but knew it looked more like a smirk.

"The skeletons," Newton continued with forced patience, "became animated and moved themselves. That's what's caused the disturbance."

Hales stepped back again. "That's not possible."

"I can assure you it is. I was there and saw it happen. I'm head of the local paranormal division. I investigate this type of thing with increasing regularity."

"Well. Er, that changes everything." Hales clapped his hands together several times like some kind of mutant seal. "Could you come with me, please, and go over the events?"

"Are you serious?" Newton asked, a frown creasing his brow. "I've got a million and one things—"

Hales stopped him. "Yes, I'm serious."

"Oh, good," Reuben said, unable to keep the excitement out of his voice. He was itching to get back in the cave for another look around. "Can I come, too?"

Hales shouted, "No!"

Newton, however, overruled him, in what Reuben thought was sheer bloody-mindedness. "Only if you put a white suit on."

Reuben grinned. "Of course. Lead the way!"

Five

A very had thought that Saturday in Happenstance Books was busy with gossip and speculation, but Monday was far worse.

She massaged her temple as she waved off another chatty customer, and was wondering if she had time to sneak to the kitchen for five minutes of peace and quiet when Mary, one of her regulars, sidled over. Mary seemed to suspect that Avery was a witch, and she didn't give two hoots about it. In fact, she seemed to love the idea.

"So, Avery," she said, lowering her voice, "you got rid of Coppinger and his band of cutthroats, then!"

Avery stuttered, and then gave up. "Well, without going into too many details, Mary, yes, we banished the spirits."

"I don't need details, dear. Just knowing they can't cause any more trouble is good enough for me." She patted Avery's hand. "Such a shock about that nice Ethan man, though. I knew his mother. She'd be turning in her grave to know he was a thief!"

"How did you know her?"

"She was only up the road in Charlestown. I had a good friend who moved there. You know how these things happen. You meet people, chat..." She shrugged. "Lovely lady. She knew Mariah's family, too. You know her—that young lady who's gone missing."

Avery kept forgetting that Mariah's name was in the paper. "Yes, we found out they knew each other from a donation Mariah made to Jamaica Inn's Smuggling Museum. I didn't know the whole family were friends, though."

Mary huffed in a very unladylike manner. "They weren't friends in the end. Mariah's mother and Ethan's had a massive falling out."

Of all the gossip and endless conjecture that Avery had tried to ignore all morning, this sounded the most intriguing. *Was this the real reason for the double-cross?*

Avery leaned across the counter, hoping no one would interrupt them. "What did they fall out about?"

"Some spat about money, I gather. Don't ever lend money to friends or family, dear—it will always come back to bite you in the end."

"Who loaned who money?"

"Mariah's family gave some to Ethan's family. They never paid it back." She looked sly. "Or so the rumours say. Is it true? Mariah found pirate treasure?"

"It seems so," Avery said cautiously. "Cruel Coppinger had several hoards stashed around. The police have recovered some of it."

"And that madam made off with the rest! Wonders will never cease!" She beamed again, her curiosity seemingly sated.

"Mary, if you can get any details about their feud, will you let me know?" Avery wondered if the root of this issue may give them a clue as to whether there was another reason why the witches stole the treasure. It might even help the group find them.

Mary patted her hand. "Leave it with me and I'll see what I can do."

She swept from the shop, and Avery sat on the stool behind the counter. *Was there really something else behind this, or was she just letting old gossip confuse the issue?*

"Penny for them," Sally said as she deposited a tray on the counter loaded with three coffee cups and a plate of homemade shortbread.

Dan appeared from the stacks, drawn by the buttery scent, and he reached for a biscuit. "Fantastic!"

Sally shook her head in disbelief. "You are uncanny. You were at the other end of the shop!"

"I have my own magic!" he said tartly.

"This is lovely, thank you." Avery took a sip of her drink, sighing with pleasure, before updating them with Mary's news.

Sally rolled her eyes. "Not another old feud. Bloody hell, this place lives on them."

Dan laughed. "'Tis the nature of small towns! Especially locals who've lived here forever. You know everybody knows everybody else's business."

"But that's probably going back thirty years," Sally pointed out.

"Which is nothing around here," Avery said, agreeing with Dan. "One hundred years ago for many seems like yesterday."

"You've had no luck finding them, then?" Dan asked.

"Not yet, but Newton has been following up on family links. It's all very distracting," Avery confessed. "I'd rather be looking forward to the solstice. Well, I am, of course, but—"

"This is detracting from it," Sally finished, nodding with understanding.

Avery sighed. "Yes, But the shop looks lovely—as usual!"

Sally had updated their shelves and main window with brightly coloured fresh flowers, and there were splashes of orange and yellow everywhere to celebrate the sun. The town was similarly bedecked with decorations in shop displays, and the pots of flowers and window boxes in the streets were cheery and bright. Avery was glad of it. It lifted her dark mood a little.

"Where's Alex?" Dan asked with a frown. "I thought you said he was working late. He normally pops in by now, doesn't he?"

Avery checked the time, alarmed. "Shit. Yes. Perhaps he went back to sleep?" Even as she was saying it, she knew he wouldn't have, and was just about to race upstairs, her heart already starting to pound, when she saw him weave through the bookshelves. "There you are! I was just getting worried!"

"Liar," Dan said, grinning. "She didn't even notice, Alex."

Alex laughed as he joined them, but he looked distracted, and Avery frowned. "What's the matter?"

He'd taken a bite of shortbread, and through a mouthful, muttered, "Nothing, why?"

"You look depressed about something."

"She's right," Sally agreed, appraising him. "Not your normal, cheerful self."

"Well," he said, glancing around to make sure the customers weren't too close, "I've done a little scrying, but to be honest, it was a complete waste of time."

"Really? Where?" Sally asked, excited regardless.

"All of the addresses that Newton gave me. It was a complete bust!" He had another bite of biscuit, frustrated. "It was utterly pointless. I hate knowing that they're out there somewhere. All I need is one little glimpse of them!"

Dan sipped his coffee. "Is there another way of searching for them?"

"A finding spell, but you need something of theirs to use, and no doubt they're shielding themselves well." He shrugged, despondent. "I'll keep trying, of course."

Sally shivered. "It's unnerving to know that they're still out there, plotting and planning. They could pop up again at any point!"

"Unfortunately," Alex conceded, "you're right, but I'll keep working on it. However, now I must go to the pub. Are you dropping in after work?" he asked Avery, kissing her cheek.

"Sure, see you later."

Alex sauntered out of the shop with a swing to his step, and Sally turned anxiously to Avery. "Is he right? It's going to be hard?"

She nodded, considering the possibilities. "Oh, yes. This is going to be *really* hard."

The large cave beneath Gull Island was brightly lit with huge white lights when Newton entered it with Reuben and Adam Hales, the forensic anthropologist, at his side.

"Holy crap!" Reuben exclaimed. "This place looks different!"

"Can't carry out a crime scene examination in the dark," Newton told him, scrutinising the team's activities.

A couple of photographers, who he presumed belonged to the anthropological team, were working their way around the skeletons, and a small group of white-clad individuals were huddled together and talking, wild gestures filling the space between them.

Newton turned to Hales. "Do you need me to talk to your team?"

Hales shook his head. "No. A couple of them have worked with Durrell, so I presume they're used to this type of...event."

Newton just stared at him. "There are many types of paranormal events, and this one—in my experience, at least—was bigger than most. But to be honest, I don't need your evidence. I know what happened here, and no one will be arrested for the deaths of these men. You just do what you need to."

Hales huffed. "Nevertheless, this has to be done right. I'm sure we can connect these bodies to Cornish families. And," he added, becoming flushed, "everyone has a right to a decent burial."

"That's not what I meant, and you know it," Newton said, his anger rising. "But they have been dead for a long time!"

Hales just glared and stomped off, and Newton took a deep breath, feeling Reuben slap him on the shoulder.

"Ignore him. Our news really threw him. And he's right. I bet a lot of these bodies have families who are still alive and kicking across Cornwall. Once they start DNA testing, it could reveal all sorts." Reuben's gaze narrowed as he watched Hales reach his team and then turned back to Newton. "How do you know about Bob Durrell?"

"Courtesy of Maggie Milne. She's a font of information. I wish I'd known of him when we followed up on the skeletal remains under West Haven—the vampire's victims." Newton huffed, remembering all the subterfuge he'd used, and the odd looks he'd received. Back then, it had felt like only he and Moore would acknowledge the existence of the paranormal. Now, it seemed there were other professionals he could access. It was like he was playing catch-up. "It would have made my life so much easier." Newton directed Reuben down the stone tiers to the bottom level, skirting well around the skeletal remains. "However, right now, finding evidence of Mariah and Zane's involvement bothers me the most."

Doubt filled Reuben's eyes as he asked, "You still intend to prosecute them in the normal, lawful manner?"

"I'd like to try." In truth, Newton wasn't really sure what kind of justice they could face.

"Who's that over by the shipwreck?" Reuben asked, pointing to a man and woman standing on the narrow strip of beach and readying a kayak.

"They're from The Charlestown Shipwreck Museum. They seemed the best people to talk to about the wreck. They want to salvage it."

Reuben looked shocked. "And you let them in now?"

"They argued that they needed to act quickly, and SOCO have gathered everything they need regarding Ethan. But," he added, steering Reuben to the passage that Mariah and Zane had fled down, "this is what I wanted to look at."

He paused at the entrance and stared into the darkness, then pulled his torch from his pocket. "I walked a short part of this the other day, but I'd like to walk it all now. Want to come?"

"Of course! I presume SOCO have done their thing here?"

"Yep." Newton led the way, the light flashing around the rough-hewn stone tunnel. "They've taken impressions of footprints, but there's little else here. And to be honest," he mused, "I'm not sure if I'll find anything here. I guess I just want to see it all. I'd like your opinion, too."

Reuben looked uncertain. "Sure. But I'm not sure what I'll find that the others haven't. We know their magical 'signatures,' if that's even the right word. But that won't tell me where they've gone."

Newton answered with a grunt as he led the way onward, Reuben's witch-light floating above them for extra illumination. The passage was generally dry and uniform, with hard earth beneath their feet, as well as stones and sand.

"Herne's balls," Reuben exclaimed. "These places were meant to last, weren't they? I still can't get over the smugglers' ingenuity."

"And their need to have several escape routes," Newton added. "They could have lived here for months."

"I reckon many of them did. There's plenty of space. They had tables and chairs, and rudimentary beds—basic cots, really. They even had fresh water. Did you see the stream coming through the back of the cave and running to the beach?"

"Only after the fight," Newton admitted with a wry smile. "I was a bit preoccupied that night."

A faint circle of daylight appeared ahead, and Newton quickened his pace. Soon they emerged at the back of a shallow cave with a sandy floor, the exit affording them a view of the sea and the mainland. He examined the mass of rubble on the ground.

"I see what you mean," Reuben said, crouching to study the rockfall. "This does look relatively new. Which means the map they found was pretty accurate."

Newton nodded and watched as Reuben investigated the space, knowing he was feeling for signs of magic. "Whatever map they found they took with them."

Reuben stopped pacing and stared at him. "We suspect we still haven't found all the places they stole treasure from, right?"

"It's possible there were more, yes," Newton conceded. "I guess they could have found another dozen caves, and we wouldn't know. Although, it's unlikely there are that many!"

Reuben ran his hand across the cave wall and then turned to Newton looking thoughtful. "What if they're hiding in another cave? Something like this that has fresh water and plenty of space. They could be hiding right under our noses."

"You think they're hiding in a cold, damp cave?" Newton said, incredulous. "Are you nuts?"

"No. They're witches. They can make the place comfortable. And they could have stocked it with food and blankets and firewood!" Reuben frowned. "Once they knew that we were on to them, they would have scrambled to prepare. Or, for all we know, this was their plan all along. What if they wanted to continue to attack us? And by that, I mean the entire coven! They could bunker down and attack us by stealth."

"But what about selling the treasure?"

"They could still be doing that!"

"But for what purpose?" Newton asked, exasperated. "If they don't escape with their loot, what's the point?"

"The point is that they hate us! And they'll hate many members of the other covens too, the ones who supported White Haven. Bloody hell! They're still here!"

"Slow down!" Newton said, feeling like Reuben was skipping ahead. "Are you suggesting the attack on you is part of a bigger thing?"

"I'm suggesting that it's *possible*. What if they want to bring down the Cornwall Coven?"

Newton felt dread growing in the pit of his stomach. "You think this is the beginning, not the end?"

Reuben's normally teasing blue eyes were suddenly very serious. "That's exactly what I think."

Caspian Faversham hadn't been planning on returning to work until Tuesday, to allow himself time to fully recover from the horrendous week he'd just had, but as he worked on some files in his study at home on Monday morning, he realised he'd left some at the office. He sighed with frustration. He really needed to get all their files uploaded to the computer—another job he'd inherited from his father, who had been notoriously old-fashioned.

Caspian thought he was recovering well enough, but it was only when he arrived home on Saturday after leaving Reuben's place that his adrenalin finally ebbed, leaving him shattered. It wasn't that he hadn't rested at Reuben's—he had slept well—but he was unused to sharing his space with so many people after being alone for so long.

Although, he'd actually liked it. The White Haven witches were funny and welcoming, and he hadn't been lying to Reuben when he confessed that his own coven—family, really—were much different. And of course, he was mentally drained after breaking the curse and being thrown into some kind of spiritual limbo land.

He was also not looking forward to seeing Estelle. He hadn't spoken to her since their argument the previous week, and his unforgivable actions. *But*, he reminded himself, h*er words had been unforgivable, too.*

Just after lunch, he pushed through the gleaming glass doors of the company headquarters situated in a converted warehouse on the Harecombe docks, greeted the receptionists, and headed to the lift and his own corner office on the top floor.

Edith, the elegant secretary who looked after the senior partners, leapt to her feet as soon as he exited the lift. "Caspian, you shouldn't be here yet!" Her gaze raked over him and she rounded the counter to examine him properly. "Are you sure you're well enough?"

Edith was getting close to retirement, and had been at the company for as long as he could remember. There were times when she was almost like a mother to him.

He smiled. "I'm fine. You worry too much. How are you?"

She brushed him off. "I'm okay, just worried about you. You've lost weight! And you're pale."

"I've been eating plenty, I assure you. Especially at Reuben's." He rolled his eyes. "He eats like a horse!"

A frown creased her brow. "The Jackson boy?"

"Hardly a boy now," he said, hoping she wasn't going to criticise as Estelle would.

Instead, however, she beamed. "Oh, how lovely! I'm so glad you have friends who'll look after you."

"I don't need looking after!"

"Everyone needs someone to look after them!" She patted his cheek. "You go and get settled and I'll bring you some coffee."

"That would be great, thank you. I won't be long, though. Maybe an hour." He turned away to walk down to his office, and then paused, knowing there was something else he should do. "Is Estelle in?"

Edith's gaze clouded. "She is. Are you two okay?"

He knew Edith struggled with Estelle's manner sometimes, and also knew she was extremely perceptive. "We've been better."

She nodded, giving him a wry smile. "She's in her office."

Estelle's office door was shut, but he didn't let that deter him. He knocked and entered. Clearly startled, she looked up, scowling. "What are you doing here?"

"I work here. I'm the CEO, remember?"

"That's not what I meant. I heard you'd be at home."

Caspian shut the door behind him and marched to her desk, where she sat glaring up at him, arms folded across her chest. "I need to apologise for last week. I shouldn't have spelled you. I'm sorry."

"No, you shouldn't have. What you said and did were unforgivable."

She hadn't cooled off, then. "And what *you* said was unforgivable, too. Did you think I would just take it? Let you stomp around in my house yelling insults and sneers? *Wow.* You are really something."

She rose to her feet, her hands clenched and her eyes sparking with fury. "I can't work with you right now."

"I'm not exactly enjoying working with you, either. But we will have to tolerate each other, and try and find our way through this."

"I've decided to go to France."

"You're doing *what*?"

"The Nephilim need help, and I offered."

He stared at her mutinous expression, the way her jaw lifted in a challenge. "Saw your way out, did you? Just when *I* might need your help. I'm still recovering from a nasty stab wound, and Mariah Rowe and Zane Roberts—and their covens—have gone AWOL! And I have given Gabe and his brothers time off to pursue their latest job, which

I'm happy to do, but it leaves me short on support." He was so angry he could barely speak. "At least they show me some loyalty."

"Loyalty! I spend hours working for this company—*hours*! And all I've got to show for it is a very full bank account and bugger all else!"

He stepped back, shocked. *Was Estelle feeling the same way as him? As if he was on a treadmill to nowhere, with an empty house and no life except business.*

He chose his words carefully. "I had no idea you felt that way. I'm sorry. But I understand, because there are times when I feel like that, too. In fact, the last week has been, despite everything, some of the best days I've had in a long time. So, fair enough. Go to France. Help the Nephilim. Get some perspective. I'll see you when you get back."

Something he said must have struck a chord, because he was barely at the door when Estelle said, "Do you think Mariah will attack again?"

"I think there's every possibility. But I'll be fine. And if I'm not, I guess you'll be CEO."

He slammed the door as he walked out.

Ben studied the images that Dylan had put on the computer monitors and frowned. "What do you mean, the magical energies are still spiking?"

"Just what I said, dummy!" Dylan pointed at a night-time view of Duloe Stone Circle. "Look at the energy levels!"

Ben pulled up a chair and stared at the bloom of colour on the ancient stones. "What night was this from?"

"Last night. Don't you remember me saying so?"

"No." But that wasn't surprising. Ben had been tired on Sunday night and had slept well after spending most of the weekend reorganising their office space, which was a monumental effort. He glanced round the large first floor room now, thinking that it could be improved, but it was better than it had been.

Cassie's continued insults of their living space had stung. But he had to admit she'd been right. He and Dylan lived like pigs sometimes. Neither of them liked cleaning, and they were both obsessed with chasing down paranormal sightings, especially now, when things seemed really active.

However, he'd had to concede that if they were going to make the business work, they had to be far more organised. Which they were with their research, to be honest; it just wasn't reflected in their office space. Consequently, Ben had cleaned, changed the desks around, organised their filing systems, and made a welcoming area in the corner with a tidy desk and comfortable seating where they would interview potential clients who wished to come to see them rather than chat on the phone.

He rubbed his eyes and turned back to the screen. "They're glowing!"

"I know!" Dylan looked pleased with himself as he stared at the footage. "I didn't expect that."

"Did it feel odd while you were there?"

Dylan shrugged and gave him a wry smile. "It did. But it was pitch black, and that place is lonely—especially at night. I admit to being creeped out."

Ben knew what he meant. No matter how used to the paranormal they became, being in lonely places in the middle of the night was always eerie. "What made you go there?"

"It was partly to do with our continued mapping of the area. But with the solstice coming up, I thought it would be cool to check out stone circles."

"But why that one?" Ben persisted. "There are loads of circles and ancient monuments in Cornwall."

"It's close to Looe where Mariah is from. It's only a small circle, compared to some." He pointed to another screen. "That's Nine Maiden's Stone Row near Wadebridge—all quartz. Same thing. They are all pulsing with magical energy."

Dylan had a steady hand as he panned around the stones using the thermal imaging camera. And he was right. There was no denying that something was happening.

"Have we got older footage? Something to compare it to?"

"Not of these, but I have some of Hurlers Stone Circles on the edge of Bodmin. They looked pretty normal at the time."

Ben stared at the screen, and then at Dylan. "We need to get a second reading on Hurlers, see if they've changed."

"Tonight?"

"Absolutely. The solstice is coming up. Do you think it has anything to do with that?"

"Maybe. We should run it by the witches."

"Let's check this one first. If it's changed, we'll tell them tomorrow."

"In that case," Dylan said, yawning and stretching as he rose to his feet, "I'm going to get a few hours' kip."

For a few moments after he left the room, Ben studied the images again with a growing sense of worry, and then decided some light reading on stone circles was probably a good idea. And tonight, they'd take along a bag filled with some magical protection spells...just in case.

Six

B riar finished wrapping a box of vibrant orange candles scented with citrus that she'd prepared for Litha, had a final chat to her customer as she took payment, and then waved her out the door.

Her smile slipped from her face as she sat wearily on a stool behind the counter, and she checked her watch. *Nearly four, thank the Goddess.* The day had felt like it would never end, and she didn't often think that. She loved working in her shop, but the weekend had finally caught up with her.

Eli exited the herb room with two steaming cups, and he handed her one as he took a seat next to her. "An energising herbal tea," he told her. "I thought you needed it."

She took it from him gratefully. "Do I look that bad?"

He dazzled her with his smile. "Of course not. You look as good as always. But you are lacking your usual energy, and so am I. This is as much for me as for you."

She inhaled before she sipped, and detected rosemary, sage, nutmeg, lemongrass, and honey. "This is one of your blends, isn't it?"

"One of my favourites."

"It's delicious." She watched him through the fragrant steam. Eli certainly looked fine. His honey brown hair and olive skin glowed with health, and his easy grace and lean, muscled frame looked as fit as ever. "What have you been up to that you need this?"

"It's what I might be up to later that this is for."

Briar recalled how Gabe and Shadow had gone to London on Friday, and suddenly realised she hadn't asked Eli a thing about it. "Of course. You have a new case! I've been so caught up in our business that I didn't ask!"

He laughed. "That's okay. And it's been busy here."

"So," she urged him, curious. "What's happened?"

"The Order of the Midnight Sun, a group of alchemists based in London, employed us to find a missing astrolabe; the Dark Star Astrolabe, to be precise."

"That sounds fascinating! How long will that take?"

Eli gave her a rueful smile. "Well, that's the thing. They've already found it. But a group called Black Cronos tried to steal it back last night in London." Eli's smile disappeared. "They aren't quite human, Briar. In fact, we're not sure *what* they are."

"Not human? But are they okay—your brothers, I mean?"

"It takes more than half a dozen mercenaries to kill Gabe, Shadow, Niel, and Nahum. They're back here now, with two members of the order. But we're expecting trouble. In fact," he glanced towards the window and the street beyond, "they asked me to keep an eye out for anything suspicious around here."

Briar stared out at the street, too, half wondering if she'd see Zane or Mariah. *But of course she wouldn't. They were hiding.* "Wow." She turned back to him. "That's worrying. Do you need help?" She asked it and meant it, but really hoped they didn't.

Eli shook his head. "We'll handle it...I hope. Besides, you have enough to deal with. I have learned something, though—about Estelle."

Briar's thoughts flew to Caspian. She knew something bad had happened between them. "What has she done now?"

"So suspicious!"

"With good reason."

"Most of my brothers are going to France in a couple of days. She's going with them."

"And leaving Caspian alone? *Now*?" She almost spilled her drink she was so annoyed. "That bloody woman!"

"I know. And none of us are at the warehouse, either. He's given us the time to pursue the new case."

Briar had grown very fond of Caspian. She sensed his loneliness beneath his gruff exterior and pride. "I can't believe she'd do that! He's vulnerable."

"He *is* a very powerful witch," Eli reminded her. "And I'm still around. So is Zee. If you need our help, just ask. Promise?"

"Promise. Why don't you come to the pub for a pint with us later? I'm going to Alex's place straight after work."

"I need to get home. Zee's there, too. We need everyone there—just in case."

Briar knew she'd struggle without Eli in the shop. She'd grown so used to having him there, and he was so easy to work with, but... "Do you need time off, too?"

"No. I'll be in tomorrow." He drained his cup and put it on the counter. "And what about you? You should get help. You sleep alone. Can Hunter come down?"

Briar smiled, thinking of the same conversation she'd had with him only yesterday. "He's coming down on Wednesday to stay for a few days."

"The distance can't be easy."

"We make it work. Speaking of which, where are your '*women*?'" She held her fingers up in quote marks. Eli's admirers had been a regular fixture in her shop on most afternoons.

"Ah, those. I've discouraged them from spending too much time here after a certain Friday afternoon when you spelled them all. Unless they want to buy something, of course." He winked, took her empty cup, and rose to his feet. "Anyway, I'll wash up and finish those final herb preparations. You stay here and relax. But be careful, Briar. Strange things seem to be aligning."

"I know. I think it's the solstice, and the moon is waxing, too."

"And there's a planetary alignment I recently found out. There's no such thing as coincidences."

No, there wasn't, she thought as she watched him go, shutting the door behind him and leaving her alone. When she went home later, she'd refresh her altar for Litha and repeat her protection spells, and she was once again thankful that Hunter would arrive soon.

Reuben watched the startled expressions of his friends around the table at the rear of The Wayward Son. "I know it sounds odd," he repeated, "but it also makes perfect sense."

Alex nodded, his dark eyes filled with worry. "I don't doubt you. I honestly feel I should have seen something while scrying earlier. If they're underground, that would hamper me."

Reuben had told them about his belief that the witches were hiding in a cave somewhere in Cornwall, and was relieved when Alex didn't think he'd gone mad. The others, however, didn't look convinced.

"Maybe a couple of them are here," Avery said, "but I still think two of them will have taken the treasure somewhere else."

"That's a reasonable assumption," El agreed. "They must still want their money."

"And," Alex added, "they want to keep it safe."

"Perhaps," Reuben conceded, but still unsure. "However, four witches can wreak more havoc than two."

Briar had been sipping her wine while she listened, but now she said, "I was chatting to Eli earlier, and he said there's a planetary alignment later this week. It's something their latest job revolves around. I was wondering if that could affect our issue, too."

"Planets and their correspondences have always played a part in witchcraft," Avery said, "but I guess some witches use them more than others. You think Mariah and Zane are using the alignment for some spell?"

Briar became more animated, leaning forward, her hands wrapped tightly around her glass. "The moon is waxing, and the moon's phases are always useful in spell work. And the solstice is coming. What extra dimension could this planetary alignment have?"

El shrugged. "It depends on what spell you're using. I use the planets sometimes to enhance my spells when I'm crafting jewellery. The seven planets that the ancients refer to all correspond to metals. My old grimoire refers to them frequently. I guess it's something we should research." She turned to Avery, her eyes widening in a question. "And you're so good at it!"

Avery laughed. "I get it! Don't worry, I'll hit the books. Although, it sounds like you're more familiar with that than me. I'm sure I can wriggle out of work for a few hours tomorrow. It won't help us find them, though."

"It might! And anything's better than nothing," Alex pointed out. "Especially after my failed attempt today. I searched and searched and searched. It was infuriating."

"You said Newton gave you addresses, right?" Reuben asked, deciding to be proactive. "I want to follow up on them."

Alex looked doubtful. "Well yes, but that might not be a good idea."

"I don't care. Where's the closest one?"

"Reuben!" El exclaimed, annoyed. "You were stabbed last week. Shouldn't you slow down?"

"Nope. The best form of defence is attack. And I want revenge."

Alex hesitated, then reached in his pocket and pulled out a list. "Lowen's parents are dead, and we have no leads on friends. Harry's father's family is in Exeter. Zane's is in Wadebridge. Mariah has relatives in Somerset."

Reuben grinned. "Excellent. I'll try Wadebridge first. That's closest. In fact," he checked his watch. "I can go tonight. I've only had a pint."

"You're so reckless sometimes!" El glared at him, her blue eyes flashing with anger. He winced. He knew what that meant. "I'm coming with you!"

"Hold on!" Alex glared at him, too. "What will you do if you see him?"

"Attack the scrawny little shit!"

"And then what?" Briar asked, in her usual calm tone. "It's not like you can put him in witch jail."

Reuben took a deep breath, knowing his friends were right, but there weren't any other options. "They think they're invincible. I want them to know they're not. And even if Zane isn't there, his family will be."

Avery leaned forward, almost imploring him. "Remember what Charlie said. His mother is a witch, and although they aren't close, she may still defend him. We should wait!"

"But," Reuben reasoned, "if his parents were involved, they would have run, too. Have they?"

Alex shrugged. "Newton is playing softly-softly while he gathers information. They haven't been to see them yet."

"Well, that settles it! I'm going. Look," he said, trying to sound less like an avenging nutjob and more like a reasonable man of action, "every moment that we wait gives them more time to prepare what they are doing. I understand Newton not wanting to jump in, but why aren't we?"

"Because," Avery said, snapping, "the Witch Council will provide us with extra witches to make a bigger team to hunt them down—*with a plan!*"

"Which won't happen until tomorrow night! And then how long after that until we act?" The more that Reuben thought about this, the more certain he was. "They've had all weekend to plot their next moves—longer, in fact. We sat back, licked our wounds, and did nothing else apart from bloody fact-finding! Newton gave us those addresses for a reason. We need to start rattling people. Otherwise, all we're doing is reacting to them. They need to know that we're actively searching! And," he added forcefully, "Lowen must have friends! One of them might know something."

El squeezed his arm and smiled at him before turning to the others. "To be honest, he's right. Let's rattle our sabres! I'll go with Reuben to make a sociable evening call."

Avery looked at Alex with a questioning glance. "I guess we could speak to Charlie. He said he was friends with both of them. In fact, he was the one with the most objections at last night's meeting. He might be more approachable without the entire council glaring at him."

"Where does he live?" Briar asked.

"Polzeath. But I haven't got his address," she said ruefully. "And I don't want to ask Genevieve."

"But," Briar said, smiling suddenly, "I bet Newton could get it. And I could come, too." And then she frowned as her phone rang. "Hold on, it's Cassie." She rose to her feet and walked out to the pub's courtyard to take the call.

Reuben was now itching to get started, and he finished his pint as he checked the time. "Right. It's about forty-five minutes to Wadebridge, so we'll be there by eight o'clock or so. Let's get going, El."

But before he could move, Briar returned, a mixture of worry and curiosity on her face. "Well, that was weird. Cassie and the boys are going to check out Hurlers Stone Circle, and she wants me to go with them."

"Is this a part of their paranormal mapping exercise?" Alex asked.

"She was a bit cagey, actually. She stressed it was probably unnecessary, just a precaution." She shrugged and picked up her wine glass. "That's fine, though. I guess we're all out tonight!"

"Good," Reuben said feeling optimistic. "Maybe we'll finally discover something useful."

Caspian studied the number in his hand, wondering if this was a good idea, but to be honest, he didn't have many options available.

After a brief conversation with Gabe earlier that day, he'd found out that Harlan was no longer involved in Gabe's latest case, so in a fit of enthusiasm, he called him for guidance on where to look and who to ask about the black market for stolen treasure. While Newton was probably investigating through a more formal route, Caspian was pretty sure trying another angle wouldn't hurt. However, Harlan had been apologetic, saying that actually he was still caught up in a few things. He'd recommended that his colleague, Oliva, was more likely to be of use, but warned him she was on a case, too.

Caspian sighed and decided it didn't hurt to ask. He punched in the number and then walked through the open patio doors to the brick terrace outside his study with a glass of whiskey, and stared at his garden. The sun had set, and thick twilight blanketed the grounds, accompanied by evening birdsong. It was peaceful and beautiful, but he was unsettled. He'd spent the afternoon seething about Estelle, Mariah, and Zane, and he couldn't shake it.

Olivia answered quickly, her voice warm. "Olivia James, can I help?"

Caspian quickly explained who he was and what he needed.

"You're Gabe and Shadow's friend!" she exclaimed. "I love them. Shadow is so much fun!"

Caspian laughed. "That's one word for her."

"I presume Harlan told you that my specialty, like his, is occult objects."

"He did. But he also said you have good contacts...slightly different ones to his. And," he added, deciding a reasonable amount of honesty would be best, "I'm sick of our rivals having the edge. I want to try to get ahead."

"Oh, I know that feeling." She hesitated and then said, "I'm tied up for a couple of days in Nottingham, but I'll be back in London on Friday, latest. Maybe even Thursday if things go well. We can do this one of two ways. I can make enquiries for you and tell you what I find. Or, you can come to London and make the enquiries with me. But," she teased, "only in exchange for a few more details!"

Caspian felt a stir of excitement as the possibilities unfolded in his mind. "Absolutely. I'll arrive in London on Thursday, just in case you're free, and if not, I have business associates to connect with. You just let me know when you arrive."

"Excellent. I look forward to meeting you."

After he hung up, Caspian stared into the growing dusk, debating whether he should really be leaving with Estelle away, too. However, the other senior partners were well able to deal with any urgent business, and they could still phone him. This was a chance to do something positive, and he might even be able to stop thinking about Avery, for once. And seeing as he'd promised Reuben and himself that he had to move on, and moping about in Cornwall wasn't cutting it, London would be the perfect distraction.

Seven

E l watched Reuben's determined profile as he drove them through the busy market town of Wadebridge, and asked, "Are you sure this is a sensible idea?"

He glanced at her, surprised. "I thought you said it was!"

"I'm having second thoughts."

"It's too bloody late now! Besides, it's a great idea." He looked at her while they waited at the traffic lights. "Come on! You know it is. We can't just sit around waiting for them to attack."

El groaned. "I know. I just wish we knew more about Zane's mother's magic."

"We'll know plenty about her soon. Remind me of their names again?"

She checked the paper she'd scribbled their details on as Reuben pulled away again. "Zane's dad is called Marlo, and his mum is Nancy."

"Nancy and Marlo? I wonder how they managed to produce such a miserable son. Maybe they're miserable, too."

"It's interesting that Nancy isn't a member of a coven."

"Maybe she's dangerous. Unhinged! Like Zane."

El sniggered. "Drama queen! I guess she just likes working alone. Maybe she even had a bad experience in one."

Wadebridge was situated on the River Camel, and Reuben drove them across the bridge to the other half of the town.

"This place is pretty," El said, looking with curiosity at the neat houses and trim shops. "I don't think I've ever been here."

"Me, neither."

Reuben's GPS announced their arrival, and they stopped outside a very ordinary, suburban house.

"Well, that looks harmless," Reuben exclaimed. "In fact, it looks boring!"

"It doesn't mean *they* are!" Although, he was right. Many witches had a flare that made where they lived seem a little different. There was nothing remotely different about this house. Reuben was already exiting the car, but she grabbed his arm. "Just polite questions, remember? They might not know anything!"

He winked and she groaned as she kept pace with him down the path. As they reached the front door, El heard the TV, but when Reuben knocked loudly, it muted, and footsteps sounded in the hall.

The door swung open and a narrow-faced man with thinning hair looked at them suspiciously. "Sorry, we don't do religion here."

"I'm not here to offer you any!" Reuben said straightway, looking baffled.

El wondered what on Earth telegraphed that either of them were there to preach.

The man—she presumed it was Marlo, because he looked very much like Zane—said, "I'm not giving to charity, either," and went to slam the door.

Reuben's hand shot out and held it open. "I need to talk to you about Zane."

He frowned. "Are you the police?"

"No."

"Then I have nothing to say. Move your hand."

Reuben bristled. "Not yet. All I want to know is if you know where he is."

They both glared at each other, one wrestling to shut the door, the other to keep it open, and El used the opportunity to feel for any magic. His mother must be there, somewhere. She saw movement from the window above, and glancing up caught a glimpse of a woman behind net curtains.

El spoke quickly. "Perhaps your wife would know where Zane is."

"She's not here."

"I saw her at the upstairs window!"

A sharp voice sounded from above. "Let them in, Marlo."

Suddenly defeated, he stepped back and ushered them inside, allowing them into a utilitarian but spotless hall. A pale woman with greying blonde hair came down the stairs. She seemed too frail for her years, and lines of deep disapproval were on her face, but even so, El felt a hum of magic around her.

She paused a few steps from the bottom and asked, "Who are you?"

Reuben started to introduce them. "My name's Reub—"

"No. I don't need your names. Who *are* you?"

Rueben and El exchanged wary glances, and then Reuben asked, "Are you Nancy and Marlo?"

"Yes," Nancy answered for them both. "Get on with it." Her stare was unyielding, and as El felt Nancy's power swell, she summoned her own in response. Zane's mother was deeply unpleasant.

Reuben said, "We're with the White Haven Coven. Zane is one of the witches behind the theft of some pirate treasure. He attacked us and might attack others. We need to find him."

"Utter rubbish," Marlo sputtered, but Nancy silenced him.

"We both know it's entirely possible, Marlo. Go and sit down and leave this to me."

Marlo shot her a vicious look, but then marched down the hall, slammed the door shut, and turned the TV up.

Reuben watched Nancy with a wary expression, obviously wanting to confirm what they already knew. "Marlo isn't a witch, then?"

"No. And I think he regrets ever marrying one." A ghost of a smile crossed Nancy's face before she glared again. "I have no idea where Zane is."

"You don't keep in touch?" El asked, thinking that if her mother spoke to her father like that, she probably wouldn't keep in touch, either.

Nancy walked down another step so she was at eye-level with both of them, and folded her arms across her chest. "Zane moved out when he was old enough to support himself. I didn't like the magic he was using, or who he used it with."

"Lowen?" Reuben asked.

"Yes. Sly little bugger. And another boy. Another witch."

El's breath caught. "Charlie Curnow?"

"Yes. That's him. Always up to something. I tried to teach them the right ways, but some people are just born to cause trouble, and Zane was one of them."

"Did he ever harm anyone?" El asked, appalled.

"Oh, no. Nothing so obvious as that. Just subverted things so they went his way."

"You're not surprised about his potential involvement in this, then?" Reuben asked.

"Involvement?" She barked out a laugh. "It wouldn't surprise me if he had dreamt up the whole thing! He always liked to be in charge. That's why he formed his own coven. He liked to boss Lowen around. I think Charlie had enough sense, in the end. But what do I know? I haven't seen them in years."

"But Zane is part of the main Cornwall Coven," El told her. "He's not in charge of that."

"And he wouldn't like that. Especially if a woman was the head. I tried my best with him, but in the end only my magic kept the peace between us. He might have been better with a stronger father figure. But...well, that didn't happen."

El recalled what Avery said she'd seen. "He clashed with Genevieve, I believe."

"He'll have been biding his time."

The more El heard, the more worried she became. "You didn't want to join the Cornwell Coven on your own?"

"That's not my path, girl. I work alone. And it won't be his after all this, will it? Unless he gets his way."

El exchanged another nervous glance with Reuben, whose eyes had turned a stormy grey with anger. He squared his shoulders. "What do you mean, gets his way?"

"He'll want the coven for himself. The chance to wield everyone's power and manipulate it."

"But," El faltered, confused, "he can't do that unless it's given willingly!"

Nancy looked at Reuben. "You said pirate treasure? He stole some?"

"Yes. A lot, we think."

"That money has blood attached to it. It might not be visible anymore, but the treasure will be drenched with it. Gold and blood bring their own power. He must have found a way to use it."

Avery studied Charlie's living room that was full of children's toys, and tried not to raise her voice, knowing that the children were upstairs.

"But you were friends!" Avery insisted. "Zane must have told you something!"

Charlie glared at Avery and Alex. "I told you, I don't know where he is—or where any of them are!"

Avery and Alex had arrived a few minutes earlier, just after receiving a text from El updating them on their visit to Wadebridge, which was closer to White Haven than Polzeath. Although Charlie had admitted them into his living room, it wasn't a warm welcome. Avery tried to be charitable, thinking it was because it was the kids' bedtime. She could hear their chatter now, and the sound of bathroom activity, and she presumed his wife, Hannah, was with them. She was another witch and the second member of the Polzeath Coven.

Alex was perched on the edge of the sofa, and he persisted, undaunted. "Zane's mother said you were childhood friends. You,

Zane, and Lowen."

Charlie shrugged and rolled his eyes. "You have been busy! I admit that we were old friends. All three of us grew up in Polzeath. So what?" He laughed. "We ran wild and had a lot of fun. It was a good place to practice our magic in private, too. But," he sobered quickly, "Zane and Nancy always clashed. She's very headstrong in how she approaches her magic. They never saw eye to eye."

"How come he and Lowen ended up in Bodmin?" Avery asked.

"Zane's parents moved to Wadebridge in his early teens. He still used to come here—it's not that far. But when he could he moved out after finding work in Bodmin. Lowen moved with him. It's nothing sinister!"

"And Lowen's parents? How did they die?"

"His father died from lung cancer when he was young, and then tragically his mother died of breast cancer a few years later. Again," he glared, "nothing sinister. Lowen clung to us more then."

Alex took a deep breath, seeming to relax. "Were your parents in the Cornwall Coven—or one of them?"

"My father is a witch, and yes, he was for a while. Then my parents split up and he moved away. I remained here. *Wow*." Charlie shook his head, his eyes hard. "You two are so suspicious. Happy now?"

Avery couldn't help her anger. "Not really. Zane and Mariah tried to kill us. Until we find them, no, we won't be happy. I don't get why you can't understand that."

Charlie shuffled uncomfortably. "I just find it hard to believe that they would do something like that."

Avery glanced at Alex in disbelief. "Yes. You said that last night, despite the fact that we have multiple witnesses to their actions."

"*Your* witnesses."

Avery felt Alex's magic rise, and in response, Charlie's did, too.

Alex replied scathingly. "I'm sorry we didn't have any adjudicators with us in the cave! When they attack you next, you'll see we're not lying!"

Charlie rose to his feet, and Avery sensed that although Charlie was trying very hard to look angry, he was actually worried—and perhaps wary. But she wasn't sure why. *Had Zane threatened him? Or was he or his wife—or more likely, both of them—involved? And what of the other Polzeath Coven member, Robyn?* Avery recalled she was a young hippy with a sharp sense of humour, but she had spoken to her only briefly in previous gatherings.

Charlie said, "They won't attack me. And I truly don't wish to fight with you on this. I'm entitled to my opinion. I don't believe Zane would do such a thing, or Lowen. Now, Mariah—perhaps," Charlie shrugged. "I don't know her as well. And if they stole some treasure and enjoy the rewards—fine! I'll see you out."

He walked to the door, and Avery and Alex had no choice except to follow him. He nodded coolly to Avery, saying, "I'll see you at the meeting tomorrow," before shutting the door firmly behind them.

Briar drove on to the car park a short walk away from Hurlers Stone Circles, parked her Mini next to Ben's van, and for a few moments studied the brooding landscape.

Hurlers Stone Circles were a series of three circles on the south edge of Bodmin Moor, in a bleak and remote spot with only the small hamlet of Minions close by. But despite that, it was beautiful in its own way. The circles were laid out in a line, all of a substantial size, the furthest a good walk across the uneven and occasionally boggy ground. A short distance away was the small Visitor Centre, but that was locked up for the night. The gathering darkness added to its lonely feel, and while normally Briar would love the chance to explore the ancient remains, she had to admit she wasn't looking forward to it now. But she got out anyway, and the wind that always blew across the moor lifted her hair.

Cassie exited the passenger door of the van and came to join her, securing her hair as she reached Briar's side. "I thought I'd wait for you so you didn't have to walk over alone."

Briar gave her a quick hug. "Thank you. I guess it's warmer in there, too!"

Cassie laughed as she pulled her jacket tighter. "Absolutely! I already walked over to the farthest one, and I'm not looking forward to going back. Bloody wind!"

Cassie often helped Briar in her shop, eager to supplement her earnings until their business, Ghost OPS was more established, and Briar found her to be easy, chatty company.

"I must admit," Briar said, "I'm intrigued as to what's going on that means we need to be here tonight."

"It has to do with our mapping of Cornwall's paranormal activity—especially at ancient sites. Dylan filmed Duloe Stone Circle and the Nine Maidens stone row last night and discovered that they were glowing with energy when he used the thermal imaging camera. This is a sort of test."

"*Glowing*?"

"Yeah. Like you when you use your magic, and how we studied Gull Island."

Briar nodded. "I get it, but I didn't expect stone to glow."

"We didn't expect to see the ghost of a giant walking across a cliff top, either." Cassie shrugged and directed her onto a rudimentary path. "Do you know the myths attached to this place?"

"I know that it's either Bronze Age or Neolithic, but the myths say the stones were men who chose to play hurling on the sabbath." Briar shook her head, perplexed. "Such odd myths!"

Cassie pointed to two standing stones a little further away from the rest. "And they are the pipers. But do you know what's beneath our feet?"

Briar examined the ground, puzzled. "Not really, why?"

Cassie grinned, obviously excited. "A few years ago, they excavated this site and found a path made of white quartz that ran through the circles. They covered it up again to preserve it. It's ceremonial, and they believe it was a sacred pathway meant to represent stars or the Milky Way."

"Wow." Briar stopped and stared, following the faint image of the path through the stones, barely a depression in the grass, trying to imagine it uncovered. "It would have looked stunning in the day or at night, especially under moonlight."

"And torchlight."

"Quartz, like many stones, carries energy. White quartz converts negative energy to positive, and provides powerful healing. It's an interesting stone to use for a path," Briar reflected.

"Would it hold energy, too?"

"Absolutely."

They walked right through the two nearest stone circles and Cassie said, "We thought we'd start at the farthest point and work our way back. It will be dark by the time we return."

Dylan was already filming when they joined the guys, and Ben had turned his EMF meter on.

"Hey Briar, thanks for coming. But," Ben shot Cassie an impatient look, "I think she dragged you out here for nothing."

"Why's that?"

"Because we're just filming. And we've already got some of your spells with us, just in case." Ben looked flustered, but that may have been more to do with the wind and darkening sky.

"If you've brought our spells with you, that means you're worried. What's going on?"

Ben summarised Dylan's findings again. "He came here a couple of months ago. Like many stone circles, it carries power, but the stones looked normal on thermal imaging. I wanted to see if this place had changed."

Briar felt the stir of unease. "Was the energy you saw last night that strong?"

"Unusually so. Stone is cold, Briar. It shouldn't glow."

Briar regarded the pillars standing sentinel around them. "I use crystals a lot when healing. Different crystals carry different energies. It's inherent in their properties, but witches charge them with energy too, and we cleanse them before we work."

Cassie frowned. "So these stones *could* carry energy?"

"Of course. That's probably why stone circles were so prevalent. And they last a very long time. But to charge something as big as these?" Briar studied the circle again. Only a few of the stone pillars were still standing. Some were as tall as she was, others shorter, but none looming anywhere near as large as those at Stone Henge, but even so... "It would be hard to charge these with additional energies—especially *all* of them. What are the depressions in the earth from?"

"Tin mining," Ben said, and pointed to a roofless building across the moors. "And that's a tin mine pumping house. They were prospecting here. The Visitor Centre is an old engine room."

The wind dropped as they talked, and the silence of the moors seeped around them, until Dylan called them over. "Guys, these *have* changed since I last came here."

Dylan was tall and slim, and full of energy and enthusiasm. He held the camera out to show them. "Look at this closest one."

Briar crowded around the small screen with the others, noting the orange light emanating from the closest stone pillar. She had a sudden urge to feel the damp, ancient earth beneath her feet. She pulled her ankle boots off and wriggled her feet into the grass, and with surprise, felt a jolt of power resonate through her. She walked over to the quartz pathway, and immediately the energy felt stronger. She turned to find all three watching her. "I can feel the power of this place coursing through me!"

"Let's check the next circle," Ben said decisively. "It's more intact than this one."

Briar carried her boots while they walked, and with every step she felt the earth resonate beneath her. Her unease grew. Part of her wanted to celebrate the fact that the earth felt so vibrant, but mainly she was just worried.

While the three paranormal investigators started their readings again, Briar tried to discern if there was a certain spot where the energy was radiating from, but it seemed to be coming from everywhere. She gathered her skirt and sat on the damp ground. The dew was heavy, but she ignored it. Digging her hands into the springy grass as well as her feet, she closed her eyes and sent her awareness out. If she remembered correctly, this place was also on St Michael's Ley Line, and it carried power across the country, connecting with Old Haven Church in White Haven as it passed through Cornwall to St Michael's Mount. A witch had drawn on the power of ley line once before— Suzanne Grayling, Avery's ancestor. *Was someone drawing on it again?*

Dylan's shout brought her to her feet, and she headed to his side, throwing a witch-light up above her. It was almost dark now, and the moor felt eerie.

Dylan sounded victorious. "Look! It's more obvious here." He panned the camera. "They are all a faint orange colour—that's energy!"

Cassie, however, just sounded worried. "I don't think this is a good thing, Dylan! It's changed completely in two months! Why's that?"

"Someone is manipulating it," Briar said thoughtfully.

"Why?" Ben asked.

"That's a really good question. And I'm not sure whether it's good or bad. My gut says bad."

"Could it be Mariah and Zane?" Dylan asked.

All three investigators were staring at her, and Briar wished she had more answers. "I think it's more likely them than anyone else right now, but we have zero proof. Did you know that this place is on St. Michael's Ley Line?"

Ben nodded. "Sure. It was something we researched when Old Haven Church was targeted."

"Have you checked any other sites along it?"

"Not for months."

"But we can," Dylan added, with a nod of encouragement at the others. "I can't think of what lies along it right now, but it's easy enough to find out."

"That would be fantastic. And while I'm here," Briar said, striding to the closest stone pillar, "I should feel this, too."

Briar cautiously laid her hands on it as if it might burn her, but the stone was cold, its surface feeling surprisingly smooth beneath her fingers. But she could also feel it almost pulsing with power.

"Well?" Cassie asked, watching her anxiously.

"Oh yes, I feel it." She looked across to the last stone circle. "Come on. Let's check that one, too."

Eight

A lex was lost in his own thoughts after their fruitless conversation with Charlie. He and Avery were barely ten minutes out of Polzeath, traveling along the B3314 on a lonely stretch of road, and Avery was also silent as she gazed out of the window. They were getting nowhere with finding the missing witches, and Alex wondered what they should do next.

Suddenly, the engine of his Alfa Romeo Spider Boat Tail stopped.

"What the hell's going on?" he muttered as he rolled the car to the edge of the lane. "It's just been serviced!"

"Shit!" Avery pointed to the fields on either side. It was a clear night, the sun having not long set, but around them a thick mist was gathering. "This isn't normal."

"That bastard, Charlie, is behind this!" Alex exclaimed. "Who the hell else would know we're on this road? He knew we'd drive home!" Alex kept trying the engine, but nothing happened, even when he used a spark of magic. "Stay here," he instructed, about to get out of the car.

Avery glared at him. "Not a chance."

But before either of them could do anything, the thick mist outside start to seep through Alex's open window, coming in tendrils that reached around his hands, binding them to the wheel. More wrapped around his throat like steel fingers. Alex wrestled to free himself, but they were too strong. Without hesitating, Avery blasted fire right past him, but it disappeared into the mist, swallowed whole.

As the tendrils tightened, Alex started to choke. "*Avery.* I can't breathe," he managed to stutter.

Avery tried to tear the fingers of mist from his neck, but it was as if they'd solidified, and Alex could see the fear in her eyes. "Alex, it won't budge!"

Alex rarely gave in to panic, but as the sinewy ropes of mist tightened their grip, he found it harder and harder to concentrate. Spells raced through his mind, none of them seeming suitable. He struggled to speak, his voice rough. "Avery, how are they doing this? They must be close!"

Avery didn't answer, instead leaping out of the car, and he heard her call up the wind. In seconds the car shuddered as a blast of air hit them, leaving Avery standing in the middle of a mini tornado. It gathered the mist up, but it wasn't dispersing it. If anything, the mist was turning into one big knot made of thousands of whipping tendrils. Avery was keeping it at bay, but she wasn't banishing it, and although the tendril wrapping around his neck wasn't getting any tighter, it wasn't going away, either.

He wasn't sure if he was delusional because of the lack of oxygen, but Alex thought if someone was attacking them from close by, then perhaps he could find them by spirit-walking. He would never normally spirit-walk in this situation; he liked to be safe within his own four walls before leaving his body. But, if someone *was* close, he needed to find them. *Now.*

Already deprived of oxygen, he should be able to slip into the necessary state. He closed his eyes, leaned against the seat, fought back his panic, and slowed his breathing. Within seconds he was floating free of his body.

The magical energy surrounding them was a deep, murky red, and as he rose out of the car, the astral energy pummelled him. He extended his magic, throwing a powerful wall of protection around himself, and spent a few seconds strengthening it before rising higher.

Avery's aura shone with a golden light, her magic vibrant in the murk. The dark magic was desperately trying to engulf her, but couldn't get close. But just as on the earthly plane, he could see that the thick, sticky energy wasn't budging.

Alex shot upwards and emerged into the clear night sky. With a jolt of surprise, he saw a silvery figure a short distance away manipulating the energy, the cord connecting them to their body streaming behind. *It was an astral attack!* Without even knowing who it was, Alex sent a blast of magic which hit the attacker in the chest and spun them away. Using magic on this plane was quite different. It was wilder, more visceral, but he gave chase, releasing another jagged blast of white-hot energy like a spear.

His opponent counterattacked, sending a bolt of energy at him.

Alex threw up a shield, and the bolt struck it and glanced away. He advanced again, desperate to see who his attacker was, and with a shock realised it wasn't Mariah or Zane. It was Lowen, his eyes gleaming with mischief. Alex pummelled him with wave after wave of jagged energy, and under the onslaught, Lowen fled.

In seconds he had disappeared, and Alex knew there was no way he could follow him in his current state. Below him, the dark mass was already dissipating, and he could see Avery lowering her arms. He waited for a moment more just to make sure Lowen wasn't coming back, and then returned to his body.

With a jolt he woke up, and a wave of nausea passed over him. He clutched his neck, but the grasping fingers of mist had gone, and he staggered out of the car and leaned against the door, desperate for air.

Avery ran to his side, her eyes sweeping over him. "Alex! Are you okay?"

"I think so. Are you?"

Her hand stroked his cheek. "I am now. What happened?"

"I spirit-walked. It was Lowen. I saw him." Alex felt suddenly dizzy and took another deep breath. "Remind me not to do it like that again."

"Like you'd listen to me! Although," she added, squeezing his hand, "I'm glad you did. Perhaps I should drive home, though."

As another wave of nausea passed over him, Alex glanced up at the night sky. "They're watching us, and I don't like it."

Avery hustled him around to the passenger door and made him take a seat, and then laying her hand to the bonnet, she uttered a spell and the engine fired into life. "You phone the others and let them know we've been attacked while I drive. They might be next."

Reuben tried to focus on the road, but it was hard after El's news about Avery and Alex. "But they're okay now?"

"They're fine," El said, trying to reassure him. But a quick glance at her face revealed her tight expression. "I feel so helpless! If he attacks us, neither of us can spirit-walk."

"Protect the car, then. It should make it harder to attack us. And," he added as another thought struck him, "let's visit his house. We're almost at Bodmin. I really want to see where these two bastards live."

El shuffled in her seat to stare at him. "But Briar already went there. She said their basement room was cleared out."

"But she was with Moore and wouldn't have had time to search properly. We might be able to find something to point us to where they are."

"You're clutching at straws! And I know you're worried—"

"I am not worried. I'm angry. In fact, I'm pissed off! I spent last week injured and sheltering in my house like it was a prison, and I am not doing it again. I do not want my friends doing it, either." He spotted the sign for the turn off to Bodmin centre. "Phone Briar and get their address."

Reuben was furious and getting more so by the second. He kept thinking on what Nancy had told them, and was beginning to suspect that last week's actions were going to be minor in comparison to what might happen next. "Maybe we should call Genevieve, too. The whole coven needs to be on alert. I can't see why they'd stop at just us."

"I know. Alex is already updating her."

He fell silent while El called Briar, pulling over to the side of the road until they had directions, and not really listening to the conversation as he thought about the attack. It was too convenient that they'd just been to see Charlie. Surely he wasn't that stupid to tell Lowen where they were so soon after visiting him. *Unless, of course, he hoped they wouldn't survive.*

"I've got the address," El said, interrupting his thoughts and ending her call. "But there's something else going on, too. Hurlers Stone Circles are gathering energy."

"What?" he turned to look at her properly, her face striped under the streetlights and her eyes huge with worry. "How?"

"Briar's not sure, but she's there now with Ghost OPS."

"In the open? They're vulnerable to attack if Lowen's still circling like a bloody vulture!"

"I know. She's taking precautions." She squeezed his arm, her expression settling into grim determination. "Let's go and turn their place upside down."

Cassie looked at Briar after she ended her phone conversation and knew something was wrong. Something worse than they had already discovered.

"What's happened?" she asked, not really sure if she wanted to know the answer.

It was cool on Bodmin Moor now, the sharp wind tugging at her clothes. And it was eerie standing in the middle of the stone circles in the dark. There were no warm yellow streetlights, or lights from houses. Instead, there were just endless stretches of darkness until they crested the rise, allowing them to see the scant lights of Minions.

"We need to head back to the cars and go home," Briar said, her lips tightening into a thin line.

Dylan lifted his head and lowered his camera. "Why? I want to get more footage of the final circle."

"It's not safe out here. Alex and Avery were just attacked by Lowen."

"Oh, no!" Cassie clutched her coat to her throat. "Are they okay?"

Briar was already pulling her boots on. "They're both fine, now, but things got a bit hairy. I can't risk us being attacked here."

"But they're miles away," Ben pointed out. "How are we at risk?"

Briar straightened. "Lowen spirit-walked, which means he can cover large distances quickly. Alex struck back, but couldn't pursue him. If he finds us..."

Her words hung between them, and with a worried glance at each other, the team hurriedly packed their gear away, except for Dylan and his camera.

"I'm hanging on to this," he said, catching Cassie's troubled look. "I might be able to see Lowen's energy."

"No, you won't." Briar shook her head. "It's highly unlikely you'll pick it up. It's on another plane—the astral plane."

"Ghosts can't always be seen with the naked eye or your magic, and yet I can pick them up." As he finished speaking, he lifted his camera and focussed above them, sweeping around the sky.

Dylan was very good at what he did, but all Cassie wanted to do was get moving. "Not now, please, Dylan!"

Briar grabbed him by the elbow and steered him across the tussock-filled grass, a witch-light bobbing ahead of them and their own torches trained on the uneven ground. "Come on. You'll have to look and walk at the same time."

However, they were still striding across the last circle on the buried stone path when the air started to shift around them. It was an odd sensation, as they couldn't really see anything, but Cassie felt a brush of energy across her skin.

"Something's happening!" she said, quickening her pace.

"Run!" Briar instructed, picking up her skirts.

But they had only advanced a few feet when the charged air stopped them, and Cassie felt like a fly trapped on sticky paper.

Briar froze, arms raised. "Get close to me, now!"

They didn't hesitate, even Dylan lowering his camera as they huddled around Briar. She had planted her feet firmly, and her lips moved soundlessly. With a whoosh they were suddenly encased within a bubble of protection. The charged air and cool night breeze vanished, replaced by warmth and utter silence.

"Whoa! What's this?" Ben asked, alarmed.

"A protection spell, dummy!" Dylan said, lifting his video camera again. "Bloody hell! We're surrounded by red-hot magic."

On the screen they could see it swirling around them, blocked only by Briar's spell.

"What would that do if we weren't protected, Briar?" Ben asked, fumbling for his EMF meter again.

Briar scanned their surroundings. "Good question. Suck our lifeforce out, perhaps? Or overwhelm us so that we collapse? It's hard to say. Whatever happens, do not move. This protection spell is not as effective as I would like."

She had barely finished her sentence when something hit them from above. It rebounded off the shield, and a bluish-white flash sizzled around them.

"Shit!" Cassie exclaimed, her heart racing. "What was that?"

"Pure energy, I suspect," Briar said, staring above them. "Magic on the astral plane works slightly differently, but I'd guess Lowen is pretty comfortable there. Did anyone see where that came from?"

Cassie shook her head, but Dylan was adjusting his video equipment. "If I can tweak this—make it more refined—I might be able to spot him."

"Nothing yet, then?" Ben asked, peering over his shoulder.

While they conferred, Cassie rummaged in her pack. "We brought some of your spells with us, Briar. Do you think one of them might help?"

Before Briar could answer, another blast hit them, and she again raised her hands. Cassie felt power radiate from her as she strengthened their protection.

Cassie had another idea. "Briar, we're on the ritual path—the one made from quartz. Could that help you?"

Briar grinned. "Yes, it certainly could! That's a brilliant suggestion!"

Briar kicked her boots off again, and as her feet met the ground, it started to churn. In seconds the stones that lay inches beneath the surface were exposed, and Briar stood directly on them.

"I've got him!" Dylan yelled triumphantly. "I see a shape to the north. See?"

He pointed to the screen, where a silvery-blue shape hung in the air like a bird. It swelled, and a jagged burst of energy showered over them, but their safe bubble held.

"Is he still there?" Briar asked, her eyes narrowed in concentration.

"He's moving clockwise above us...trying to spot a weakness in our protection, I suspect," Dylan said, following Lowen's route.

"Show me."

Without taking his eyes off the screen, Dylan angled towards her so she could see the image. "It's faint, but I'm sure that's him."

Briar nodded. "I can't see his cord, but that will be too small from down here. I think you're right, Dylan. Well done! In a second I'm going to drop the protection spell, and I want you all to run to the van."

"Not a chance!" Ben said immediately.

"Trust me! What I'm about to release will knock you off your feet and hopefully catapult him back to his body. Quartz's natural element is aether, and it not only offers protection as part of its properties, but assists in banishing spells *and* projects energy." Briar's eyes lit up with green fire, her excitement palpable. "Hold steady—he's attacking again!"

A white light flashed across the video screen, and simultaneously smacked into Briar's shield. She threw back her shoulders and the circle of protection flashed in response. Lowen, however, hit them several more times.

Cassie winced under the onslaught, but Briar didn't. "Almost time," she said, readying herself. "I'm going hit back hard when he finishes. He'll be temporarily weakened, and you *must* run! Agreed?" she asked, staring at them, especially Ben. They nodded, and after what seemed an eternity, Lowen's attack finally stopped. Briar dropped her protection and shouted, "Now!"

Cassie, Ben, and Dylan raced across the stone circle as an explosion of white light radiated behind them, illuminating the moor with blinding brilliance. Cassie felt a wave of power hit her, knocking her over, and she landed face-down on the ground with Ben and Dylan next to her. Winded, she rolled over to look behind her.

The sight was terrifying.

Briar was lit up in a column of brilliant white light that she directed towards a patch of sky above, and with a shock, Cassie saw the quartz path light up beneath the grass. Fortunately, they were no longer on it, and for a heart-stopping moment, she couldn't work out where she was. But then the light faded, leaving Briar bathed in an unearthly glow.

Briar picked up her boots and ran to catch up, yelling, "Keep going!"

Cassie dragged herself to her feet, terrified that another blast of power would hit them from above, and ran so fast that she almost fell again. She finally stumbled on to the car park, heaving for breath, and leaned against the van. Ben was already fumbling to open the door, while Dylan leaned on his knees, the camera still clutched in his hand.

Briar arrived seconds later, and Cassie stared at her. "Briar! What the hell was that?"

Despite her exertions, Briar looked energised. Her hair was wild, her feet were dirty, and her eyes glowed green. "A mixture of the Green Man and magnified quartz energies! Amazing, wasn't it?"

"That's one word for it," Ben said, chest still heaving. "It was like a bloody supernova!"

"Dylan," Briar said, still smiling, "never let me doubt your abilities again! You made all the difference. Now, go home and stay safe, guys! Although, you don't need to worry. It was me he wanted."

Cassie hugged Briar, feeling the power still radiating from her. "You be careful, too! Will he be back?"

"Not tonight. I set a bomb off under him." Raised voices at the edge of the car park made them whirl around.

"Shit. We've roused the village," Dylan said, straightening up and heading to the passenger door. "Let's go."

With final wave at Briar as she followed them out of the car park, Cassie leaned back in the seat, wondering what response that would elicit.

Nine

W hen Avery woke up on Tuesday morning, the events of the previous night flooded her mind, and she rolled over to check on Alex.

They had arrived home uneventfully after their encounter with Lowen, but Alex had been left with a horrible headache, and she'd prepared a restorative tea for him before bed. For both of them, actually. She had then double checked all of their protection spells. The attack on Briar hadn't helped her mood, either.

Alex stirred as she turned, and he blinked sleepily at her. "Morning, gorgeous."

"Morning gorgeous, yourself. How are you?"

He took a moment to respond. "I'm okay. A slight headache only." He rolled on his side, propping up on his elbow. "Remind me not to do any impromptu spirit-walking again."

"You didn't really have a choice. But yes, I will."

He looked rueful. "I didn't know Lowen could do that. Or suspect he'd be so bloody aggressive."

"The gloves are off now," she mused. "We know nothing about their magical strengths, which puts us at a disadvantage. We need to find out what they're all good at." As soon as she said it, Avery felt more positive. She liked lists and plans. They gave her focus. "I'm going to start on that today. Genevieve should know more than most, right?"

"Right. Or the older members—Rasmus, Oswald, or Claudia. They would possibly have known their families."

"True." She noted the red welts around his throat and touched them gently. "Bloody hell! That mist actually marked your skin!"

"Really?" His hand flew up to feel his neck. "*Great*. People will wonder what the hell I've been up to."

She wriggled forward to kiss him, snuggling into his arms. "At least you weren't badly injured. Unlike poor Inez." She closed her eyes briefly, as if to block out the day ahead. "I'm not looking forward to her funeral this afternoon."

"No. Me neither." He kissed her again and then rolled over. "Come on, time to get up and face the day. I want to get into work early so I know everything's okay before we leave."

"Me too. And then I'm going to start calling people and working on magical correspondences."

As lovely as her warm bed was, Avery dragged herself out of it, and once they'd breakfasted, she headed down to the shop.

For once she arrived before Dan and Sally, and she took advantage of the fact to strengthen the wards on the shop. Her protection spells encompassed the whole building, but she was so paranoid at the moment that she was second-guessing herself on everything. She'd bundled up some protection herbs over the weekend and she used them now, tucking them into odd corners of the shop. She'd also fashioned a new wreath of summer flowers that dispelled negativity, and she replaced the old one above her shop door.

Avery had just finished when Dan and Sally arrived, and Dan cocked an eyebrow at her. "Ah. I see you had an eventful night."

"How do you know that?" she asked, stepping down off the ladder and folding it up.

"Because you're always in here early when you're worried." He walked behind the counter and within moments, Delta blues music flooded the shop. "And this always helps."

She smiled. "You know me so well."

"So," Sally said, absently straightening a pile of books on a display table. "What happened?"

Avery groaned and updated them on the previous night's attack, hating to see her friends' worried faces. "That's why I've increased the protection here. You'll be safe now."

Sally shot Dan an uncomfortable look. "While I'm grateful for that, it's not *my* safety I'm worried about. I know you've been attacked by witches before, but never by your own council...well, not since Caspian, anyway."

"And that's why I'm going to use this morning to find out more about the two missing covens—strengths and weaknesses—and check out some other things. Are you two okay with that?"

"Of course we are," Dan reassured her. "And it's Inez's funeral today, isn't it?"

"Yes, and I feel a mixture of sadness, and..." she struggled for the right words. "Absolute fury that she died so needlessly."

Sally hugged her. "Then take that anger and go do your thing. I'll see you mid-morning, with coffee, if I have a chance. We don't need you in here at all today, right Dan?"

"Right."

Avery felt tears threaten, and she quickly blinked them back, thinking she was turning into a sentimental fool. "Thanks, you two. You're the best."

Alex arrived at The Wayward Son before ten o'clock that morning. He'd already talked to Reuben, who had offered to drive them all to the funeral. They were meeting at one o'clock for a pub lunch, and then would head to Truro after, allowing plenty of time to get to the church for the service. He just hoped that Newton was holding up okay. Alex knew he still carried a lot of guilt about Inez's death.

Alex was the only staff member in the pub, so far, and he opened up the courtyard doors, allowing the warm summer air to circulate. It promised to be another fine day, and only a few clouds marred the blue sky. He adjusted tables and chairs, and polished the long bar, musing on their conversation with Charlie while he worked.

He was still seething about it, unable to understand Charlie's attitude towards Zane. *Although*, he reasoned, *if someone were to accuse any of his coven or friends of those things, he'd be pretty reluctant to believe them, too.* He and Avery had talked about the conversation for hours, both feeling that Charlie knew more than he was saying, but with zero evidence, there was nothing they could do. And there was nothing to link Charlie to their attack either, except for suspicious timing. *Maybe he should spirit-walk to watch Charlie that night, and try to see Lowen again.*

His thoughts were interrupted when Zee came in, and his greeting died on his lips as he took in the bruises on his face. "What the hell happened to you?"

"Black bloody Cronos!"

"Who?"

"The not-quite humans who want the Dark Star Astrolabe." Zee walked around the bar, shedding his leather jacket and revealing bandages on his arms as he headed to the small staff area next to the kitchen.

"They came, then," Alex said as he followed him. He'd let Zee leave earlier the previous afternoon after Gabe said he needed help. "Are you all okay?"

"We're alive but battered and bruised." Zee started to make coffee while updating him on their night. The scale of the attack left Alex horrified, but Zee grinned. "They came off worse. We killed a lot of them. *A lot*! Unfortunately, Newton was not happy."

"Shit." Alex leaned against the doorframe. "I'm amazed he didn't arrest you."

"He fingerprinted us and let me go early." He made Alex a drink too, and crossed the kitchen to offer him his cup. "The place is crawling with forensic experts. We feel terrible because we know he's busy with this pirate-treasure business."

"And the missing witches." Alex sipped his coffee, taking in the grazes on Zee's face. "But it's not like you planned this. Do the others look as bad as you?"

"We're all injured in some way, some worse than others. But look," he said, as they walked back to the bar area, "I'm staying here, and so is Eli, even though the others are heading to France. We'll help if you need us."

"Don't you mind being left behind?"

Zee shrugged, pushing his dark hair off his face with a sweep of his hand, and close up, Alex saw a bruise blooming over his cheekbone. "We'll be involved at some point. Besides, I like working here. It's not like this place is boring. And Eli has no intention of getting more involved than he needs to. He likes working for Briar...and of course seeing his women!"

"No chance he'll settle down, then?" Alex asked with wry smile.

He laughed. "Not bloody likely! Are you going to Inez's funeral?"

"Yes. We'll leave at one. In fact," he said, as a horrible thought crossed his mind, "all of the witches are going. I'm sure nothing will happen here while we're gone, but I'd hate to think that Mariah or Zane might take advantage. We were attacked last night, too." He considered his mild headache and felt ashamed. "Not quite on the same scale as you, though." He updated him on their previous night, telling him about Briar as well.

Zee shook his head. "Don't downplay it, Alex. It might have been a different style of weapon, but you were still targeted. If you weren't such skilled witches, maybe you would be dead or severely injured."

"It's not arrows and swords, though!"

"No, but it's powerful magic that only a few can wield. I can't, for all my skills with a blade and a crossbow. And my wings, of course! In fact," he said as he started to unload the dishwasher and set out the clean glasses, "between the two groups of us, we offer a formidable force. Gabe certainly thinks Estelle will help them in France."

Alex nodded. "Briar told us she's going. I'm worried about Caspian." As soon as it was out of his mouth, he wondered why he'd even said that.

Clearly Zee did, too, because he stared at him speculatively. "I'd have thought you'd like him being vulnerable."

"I guess I do have a conscience when it comes to Caspian, after all. Even though he casts longing glances at my girlfriend."

Zee laughed. "To be honest, quite a few men cast longing glances at Avery. She's very pretty. Lucky bugger."

That lifted Alex's mood. "I know I am."

"And Caspian can look all he wants. She only loves you."

"Do you often offer pep talks?"

"Only to the people I like." He became serious. "About Mariah and Zane. They won't attack here, surely? Killing ordinary folk serves no purpose."

"No, it doesn't. But that again leads us back to the question we keep circling around. What the hell *is* their purpose in all this?"

Avery eased the kink from her back as she stood, pushed her books away, and walked along the gravel path in her garden for a break.

She'd set up a workspace at her garden table, shaded by a large tree, and had been reading up on planets and their magical correspondences. Her head was buzzing with all the information, and for a moment she just took in the bright summer day, wishing she was gardening instead. While she regularly worked with phases of the moon, working with the planets was not normally part of her practice, and after this morning's research, she remembered why.

It was very complicated, and the planets had many correspondences. Like many aspects of magic, it required that you finetune your intuition to find what worked for you. But, if Mariah and Zane were going to use the planetary alignment to enhance their magic, she needed to understand it better. Currently, the waxing moon was close to full—only days away. A potent time. The waxing moon was useful for "creating" and "generating" spells, and the full moon for bringing them to fruition. Once the moon waned, its energies could be used for "destroying" and "banishing" magic.

Avery continued to pace in the sunshine as ideas formed. They needed to find their opponents, quickly, and then work to destroy whatever plans they had—potentially to destroy the Cornwall Coven and all it stood for. But Avery was sure they were still missing something.

A flutter of movement in her peripheral vision had her turning quickly, hands raised, but then she smiled. "Helena!"

She hadn't seen her ancestor's spirit since Friday night when she had joined Gil and battled Cruel Coppinger's ghostly gang on Gull Island, and she walked down the path to her side. Helena looked the same as she always did, wearing her long, black gown with a tight bodice, her dark hair flowing down her back, but she looked even more ethereal in the sunshine.

"I hoped you were okay," Avery told her, feeling a rush of affection. "I was so worried when I found you had been imprisoned."

Helena smiled, her hand reaching out as if to stroke Avery's cheek, but it passed straight through her, Avery feeling only a cool draft on her skin.

"Is Gil okay?"

Helena nodded and laid a hand on heart.

"You like Gil? He's a good man."

Helena laughed, and it made her look like a teenager.

"Thank you for the other night. We couldn't have done it without you. Either of you. And I'm sorry you were imprisoned for so long. I didn't even know that could happen!"

Helena's eyes flashed with anger, but it quickly subsided, and Avery decided to ask her a question, just in case she could point her in the right direction. "The witches who caused this are still working against us, and we have to stop them. Do you know anything about planetary correspondences? We think they might use them in some way."

Helena looked across the garden, her gaze distant as if she was deep in thought, then she beckoned Avery to follow her, returning to the grimoires and witchcraft books on the table. It was to her own grimoire that she turned her attention. She spread her fingers above the pages and they flipped, finally opening to a section on the planets that Avery had examined before. Helena pointed towards the notes on Jupiter. An ink drawing featured the planet, and beneath it was a list of its correspondences in neat but tiny script.

Avery nodded. "I saw these earlier."

Helena extended her finger to the words, *plenty, expansion, wisdom.*

"It's a positive planet, I get that. But how can it help?"

Helena directed Avery's attention back to the grimoire, turning the following pages, and then staring at Avery as if to impress something important. She extended a finger to her own head and tapped.

Avery looked at her, bewildered. "I need to study these spells?"

Helena nodded.

"I wish you could speak. Why can't you, when Gil could?"

But Helena could only offer her a sad, worried smile before she vanished.

Frustrated at the lack of proper communication, but grateful for her help, Avery sat again. Pulling the grimoire towards her, and then all her other books on witchcraft, she searched for all of the references to Jupiter she could find. The more she read, the more intrigued she became. Key phrases jumped out at her: *influencing power, authority, the ruler of the Gods who overthrew Saturn, stability, success, expansion.*

Avery quickly turned to Saturn's correspondences, and realised they were the opposite qualities of Jupiter's: *limitations, boundaries, restrictions, binding.* Powerful words, and powerful spells. If their opponents were planning to use these correspondences against them, they had to hit back hard...and preferably, first. *Was Helena suggesting that using Jupiter's positive energies were the way to do this?*

Avery checked the other planets in the parade, too. Mercury, Venus, Mars, and of course the sun and the moon. So far, she felt as if she had only dipped her toe into the sea of knowledge that existed. Pulling her own grimoire towards her and picking up a pen, she found a fresh page and started to make notes, thinking she could share her findings with the others at lunch.

El collected her pint from the bar in The Wayward Son, and then joined her coven, who were already seated at a table in the courtyard garden.

They were shaded from the sunshine by a large umbrella with drinks in hand, and appeared to be deep in conversation. The heat in the sheltered space was welcoming, and El felt herself relax. She gave her friends a quick shoulder hug before she sat, noting Alex and Avery looked worried, but Briar looked invigorated.

"I'm glad to see you three are okay after last night. Bloody Lowen."

Alex grunted. "Yeah. He had one up on us. I'm planning how to strike back."

"Any ideas?" Reuben asked.

"Yeah. My very own spirit-walk."

El studied his grim expression. "Is that wise?"

"Yes. Although I'll make sure I have a few surprises prepared first."

El spotted the red mark around his neck. "Is that his handy work?"

"Yes. Killer mist."

She laughed, despite the situation. "Unexpected and dangerous, but inventive!"

Avery took a sip of what looked like cider, and said, "Reuben mentioned you didn't find any leads when you raided their house."

"No, and we were very thorough." She looked at Reuben's sly grin and smiled back. "Has he told you what we did find, though?"

"No! What?" Avery asked, eyes wide.

Reuben gave an exaggerated Machiavellian laugh. "Their hair and blood!"

A few startled customers looked around, and he hurriedly lowered his voice. "Oops. Yes. Hair and an old shaver in the bathroom."

Briar grimaced. "Yuck! Were you looking down the plug hole?"

"He was," El admitted. "Their bathroom was not the cleanest, I have to admit."

"I noticed that the other day," Briar agreed. "I should have thought to look for hair and stuff."

"Tricky with Moore though, I guess?" Alex asked.

Briar wrinkled her nose. "He was very relaxed about me using magic, but I have to admit, I wasn't entirely comfortable about it. And collecting bits of their body for spells seemed macabre."

"But they are useful," Alex admitted. "Are you thinking about a finding spell?"

Reuben shrugged. "Perhaps. Or a poppet. Or maybe something more unpleasant."

They all exchanged worried glances at that, but then Avery nodded. "We need to consider everything. I have broadened my approach this morning."

There was something in Avery's tone that intrigued El. "How so?"

"I started investigating planetary correspondences in more depth today." She scratched her head and grimaced. "Not my specialty, but I admit it's interesting. Helena visited this morning and pointed me in the right direction—I think. Jupiter."

"Jupiter?" Alex asked, perplexed. "Why?"

"I think it's the planet's associations that will be of most use to us. It's the planet of wisdom, luck, protection, and abundance, and is the absolute opposite of Saturn—which is binding and destruction, as well as change. But I also looked at the other planets. Mars is in the planetary parade—the planet of war. But, so are its opposites. Venus is the planet of love and harmony, and Mercury rules logic, communication, and intellect."

"So, in theory," El mused, "all of those associations could be harnessed?"

Alex nodded. "As well as the waxing moon."

"And the solstice, of course," Briar added.

Avery leaned forward. "But it's how we use them. We need to be smart. We need to combine their associations with our magical strengths. Mariah and Zane are planning something big. Last night's attacks—on top of last week—are just a taste."

"And we," Reuben pointed out, "have the biggest coven. The Cornwall Coven, I mean. We might doubt the loyalty of some, but surely most are trustworthy."

"Yes," Avery said, nodding thoughtfully. "But I don't want to say too much at the main meeting tonight. I'd rather wait and see who joins the hunting team, as Caspian called it."

"That makes sense," El admitted. "Keep our cards close to our chest."

"Yes. I feel I haven't even scratched the surface, but I have a stack of reading to do, and with luck, other witches that we trust can help."

They paused while Marie, one of the bar staff, delivered their food with a cheery smile, and then Alex said, "Perhaps Helena knows about it because they were used more often back then. Or maybe it was one of her strengths."

"Hopefully, she'll help me again," Avery said. "At least she's back. I just wish Helena could speak like Gil did the other night. I still can't work out why she can't."

"Maybe it's the length of time she's spent in the spirit world," Briar suggested.

While El took a mouthful of her burger, she observed her closest friends, considering how lucky she was. "I wish we were meeting under better circumstances. This afternoon is going to be so sad, but I keep reminding myself that it's also a celebration of Inez's life, too."

Briar gave her a sad smile. "But she was so young. And," she cast a furtive look at Reuben, "it's about a year on from Gil's death, too. It brings back horrible memories."

"It does," Reuben acknowledged, "but having seen him only briefly the other day, and knowing he helped you on Gull Island, I don't feel like he's gone anymore. I just feel that he's living his life somewhere else."

El squeezed his hand. Once again, Reuben had managed to surprise her with his insight. "I think that's a wonderful way to look at it."

"And that's how we need to think about Inez, too."

Ten

A lex felt the potion start to take hold, and he lay back on the rug
in front of the fireplace in Reuben's attic, shuffling to get
comfortable. The room was filled with evening sunshine that bathed
everything in a mellow glow. His windows had been replaced that
day, so at least the space was now sealed from the elements.

It was Tuesday evening, and they were all on edge after the funeral
earlier that day. Briar had been right. It brought back memories of
Gil's funeral only one year ago. All of the girls had been tearful, but
hearing the eulogies about Inez had, however, fired them up, and
they all decided to work together that evening while Avery attended
the meeting. Reuben and El were planning to use some of the hair
they found to try and locate Zane and Lowen, and also, to work
magic against them. Briar was supporting Alex.

A fire burned low in the grate to keep the chill away, and Alex was
surrounded by a protective circle. He ran through the spells he'd
prepared, certain they would be of use in the metaphysical world.

Briar's gentle voice disturbed his final preparations. "Are you sure
there's nothing else I can do?"

He looked over to where she sat cross-legged on the rug, watching
him.

"No. The only thing you can do is protect my body if anyone
breaks our wards."

"You can be sure I'll do that."

Reuben called across the room from where he sat at the table with El. He'd rearranged his space specifically to accommodate Alex. "Are you certain we won't disturb you?"

"No, as long as you don't do anything too loud!"

"As you know, I do sometimes set off violent curses, but I'll try my best."

Alex rolled his eyes with mock annoyance, then closed them, confident that Briar could keep him safe. She'd come armed with quartz, amethyst, moonstone, and obsidian, insisting he hold a moonstone in one hand and obsidian in the other. They were warm in his palms, and as he slipped from his body, he held on to their impressions.

In seconds he was floating above his body, with Briar's calm white aura below him—as sure a sign of her pure spirit as any he'd ever seen. Reuben and El's auras were different, but the sight of all of his friends close by was reassuring, and he soared out of the attic and high over White Haven, turning up the coast to Crag's End. The group had decided earlier that there was a strong possibility that Lowen might attack again, and believing Charlie to be working against them, felt sure he would have told the rogue witches about the meeting. If Lowen didn't appear, he'd search further afield.

It wasn't long before Crag's End loomed below him, nestled within woods on a rise just out of Mevagissey. It resonated with protection spells, as if Oswald had placed a dome over it.

He rose high above it and hung there for endless minutes, scanning the area. Below him the world was mapped in dayglow colours and swirling energies, and for a moment he just drank it in. Perhaps he would do better to settle in amongst the trees. If someone was looking for him, he'd be too obvious out in the open. Alex decided to head up the coast and circle back much lower. *He needed to lure Lowen in.*

As Caspian took his seat at Oswald's table on Tuesday evening, he wished he'd offered to hold the meeting at his own house.

The next one, perhaps.

It wasn't that he had any objection to Oswald, but Caspian sensed he wouldn't be overly involved, so why put him out? There had been very little pre-meeting chatter. Everyone carried an air of nervous anticipation, and Avery looked pale and distracted. As she sat next to him, he asked, "Are you okay?"

"It was Inez's funeral today. It was horribly sad."

Caspian experienced an unexpected jolt of pain at learning this news. "I had no idea, but I would have come. I'm so sorry."

"Would you have?" She looked at him, surprised. "I didn't know you knew Inez."

"I didn't, but I know Newton, and I would have offered my respects."

"I'm sorry. We didn't even think..." she trailed off, obviously upset.

He wanted to squeeze her hand, but resisted. "It's okay. I should have asked. I guess we've all been preoccupied. I take it there were no attacks at the service?"

"No. Just a very packed church, and lots of speeches. Newton and Moore looked awful." Her eyes started to tear up. "I feel so angry...and useless."

"You are far from that. And to be honest, I think we all feel unsettled. Have you had any trouble?"

"We've had issues, but I'll share them with everyone. There's fewer here than I hoped," she added in a low voice.

"It doesn't surprise me in the slightest. This is going to get ugly."

Caspian was pleased to see Eve and Nate from the St Ives Coven, both of them looking as unconventional as usual. Cornell, the rangy witch from Perranporth who Claudia had suggested attend, was there too, chatting to Hemani. Ulysses was also there, looking quietly composed. And for all of his annoyance the other day, Charlie was there, too. Most surprising was that Genevieve wasn't present.

Oswald hovered by the door to the room. "I believe this is it, so I'll leave you to it. Genevieve sends her apologies. She wishes to focus on

Litha, and her young children are also absorbing her time." He shut the door, leaving them in a stunned silence.

Caspian rallied. "Well then, let's get on with it. Does anyone want to lead?"

"It should be one of you two," Eve said immediately, encompassing Avery in that statement.

"In that case," Avery said without hesitation, "Caspian should."

He glanced at her, surprised, but said only, "If you wish. Firstly, I would like to thank you all for coming. I knew this wouldn't be a popular request, but even so, I had hoped for higher numbers. Jasper wanted to join us, but felt he should be providing protection to his young witches."

Nate rested his elbows on the table. "Jasper has a strong sense of duty to his coven, but the others are scared or in denial." He looked at Charlie. "After your attitude the other night, I'm surprised you're here."

"I'm trying to remain objective, despite the desperate attempts of some to convince me otherwise." He shot an annoyed look at Avery.

"Really?" Avery's voice was dripping with venom. "After leaving your house last night, we were attacked on the road by Lowen!"

A chorus of voices rose with surprise, Caspian's amongst them. "Avery, explain!"

Avery was still glaring at Charlie, who now looked utterly shocked, but she gathered herself and related the previous evening's events. "So, Charlie, who else would have known where we all were?"

"You think I had something to do with this?"

"Who the hell else could? In fact, I'm not even sure you should be here! Are you here as a spy?" A wind had whipped up around Avery, lifting her hair as her fury built.

"Of course I'm not! You're being paranoid!"

"Alex almost died last night—as well as Briar! They were both very vicious attacks!"

Caspian had been expecting many things at this meeting, but not this, and he acted quickly. "Perhaps, Charlie, considering your current ambivalence and last night's events, you really shouldn't be here."

Charlie glared at Caspian. "I beg your pardon?"

"You have to understand that what happened looks bad for you."

"It's just coincidence."

"Nevertheless, we can't risk you being here, listening to our strategies. You must leave."

Charlie gave a startled laugh. "You're ejecting me from the meeting?"

"Yes. For your own good, actually. If you don't know anything, you can't be accused of anything."

"I agree," Cornell said. "This is for the best, Charlie."

A flurry of nods ran around the table, and Charlie reluctantly rose to his feet and walked to the door. "As you wish."

"Any last words of advice?" Nate asked.

"Go screw yourselves," he said, slamming the door behind him.

Reuben stared at El sitting across from him, and then looked down at the map between them with disappointment.

"Well," he huffed, "that was a bust."

"We thought it would be. They'll be veiled and well protected from prying eyes."

They had just tried a finding spell, one of many they were planning to use that night, and he refused to be defeated. "On to the next, then." He glanced over to where Alex lay immobile, with Briar watching him. "Everything okay, Briar?"

She nodded, then returned to her quiet contemplation, a couple of books on her lap, and Reuben turned his attention back to El.

She grimaced at the bowl filled with hair on the side of the table. "Some men are disgusting."

"Everyone has hair down their plugholes," he pointed out. "You included. You have *a lot* of hair!"

"At least I use bleach in my bathroom!"

"Some men have different priorities."

"Yeah, like attacking innocent people."

Reuben sighed. "Yeah, well, some people suck."

El squared her shoulders and gathered the prepared ingredients. "If the next one doesn't work, we'll keep going until one does. We've certainly got enough hair."

"As long as we keep some for a poppet."

"I'm not sure I like them. I keep remembering what Genevieve said on Samhain."

Reuben nodded, remembering that night all too well. "I know its limitations. But she used it well in the end. She banished Suzanne to the Otherworld with it."

"Is that what you'll do?"

He smiled. "Not quite so dramatic as crossing worlds, but I'll work something out."

"The thing is," El said, staring at the bowl, "we don't know whose hair this is. They're both fair-haired."

"I don't give a crap. Either works for me."

"All right. Let's move on." El turned her grimoire's pages to the next spell on their list, and then pulled the next bowl to her. They had spent time preparing ingredients for several spells so they could strike one after another. "A spell for confusion and delirium." She gave Reuben an anxious look. "Are we sure we should do this? It goes against everything we hold dear. And we might experience karma."

Reuben leaned forward to emphasise his point. "This *is* karma. We are merely delivering it. Begin."

Newton studied the list in front of him and shoved his grief aside. The witches may be looking for Mariah and her companions through magical means, but he had the police force at his disposal.

Over the last few days, they had worked hard compiling lists of friends as well as family. He had photos of all of the witches and had distributed them widely, with a caution to inform only Moore or Newton if they were spotted. They were also keeping a discreet watch on Harry's house. He didn't want anyone taking chances by approaching them, but he wanted to know where they were.

He'd also been thinking about what Reuben had said, and after consulting the expert who'd led them down Wheal Droskyn, had assembled a list of mines that their group might have hidden in. Caves, however, were a harder issue. They weren't as well mapped as the mines were, and smugglers' tunnels were well hidden for a reason. But part of him thought they would have found somewhere close by to shelter in.

He stood and examined the map on the wall of his home office, focussing on Polzeath. If this had been a childhood home for Zane and Lowen, they would have known it well. And now they lived in Bodmin. God knows what maze of tunnels and cave systems were under there. *And didn't Cruel Coppinger have another well-known cave?*

Last night's attack on Alex, Avery, and Briar confirmed that at least one of them was close. A rush of anger overwhelmed him, and he leaned against the wall taking deep breaths. Hearing that Briar had been threatened had affected him more than it should, and he broke out in a cold sweat just thinking about her being attacked while on her own. As far as he was concerned, Ghost OPS didn't count as help.

His head swam and he sank to the floor. *What was the matter with him? Was it tiredness? Grief? Anger?* All three were swirling in one big mess in his head. And then another wave of *something* hit him so strongly that his vision flickered, and he blacked out.

El finished the spell, knowing as she always did when something was successful. It was palpable as her intention resonated out, sure and true.

She smiled at Reuben. "Bingo."

"You're sure?"

"Didn't you feel it?"

"Oh, I felt it. I mean are you sure it's found its mark?"

Silly Reuben. For all of his success lately, he still had his doubts. She grinned impishly, and then instantly felt bad about it. She had just caused someone harm, after all. "I'm sure. One of them is going to start to feel weak, as if their magic has been muted. It will start slow, but it will build." She held his gaze. "It *will* happen. But I want to try another."

He looked startled. "If you're so sure of that one, why cast another?"

"Because I can. What about a spell to incite paranoia?"

"You want them to distrust each other?"

"Yes. Or at least one of them to distrust the others. We need to split them up. It will make them weaker. And," she nodded at the cloth on the side. "You're right. While I do this spell, you make a poppet. Let's hit them hard! They need to know that we mean business."

Eleven

A s soon as Charlie left the room, Avery subdued the wind she had whipped up subconsciously, and felt the tension in the room ease.

"I'm sorry," she said, "I didn't mean to lose my temper."

"You had every right to," Hemani reassured her. "Charlie should not be in this group, and his behaviour *is* suspicious. It may be bad timing, but we can't dismiss it. So, Caspian, I presume you have some ideas about how we proceed next?"

Caspian nodded. "We need different forms of attack. The use of spells to find them or undermine them, and then once we find them, we need to catch them." He groaned, rubbing his forehead. "I can't even believe I'm saying this."

Avery shot him a sympathetic smile, and then addressed the group. "Reuben and El broke into Zane and Lowen's place last night. They found some hair," she grimaced, "in the plug hole, and they're using it right now. I didn't mention it while Charlie was here...just in case."

Eve looked impressed. "Good. I like that we aren't waiting around. Let's search Mariah's place, too."

"And Harry's," Ulysses added, speaking for the first time.

Avery shook her head. "I'm afraid we can't. Harry is married with kids, and they're still at home. But searching Mariah's home is a good idea. I was there on Saturday," she confessed. "I should have thought to do that then."

"Let's go after this meeting," Caspian suggested. "I used witch-flight to get here, and presume you did, too. We can be there in seconds."

"Yes, okay," she agreed, startled at his suggestion. It was better than going alone, or waiting to drive there with someone else.

Eve played absently with the ends of her dreadlocks, her expression bleak. "It's the *what then*, that worries me. I think Rasmus is right. We have to bind them. But that takes time, and a lot of magic. They need to be temporarily bound first in order to do the full binding." She stared around the table. "I think perfecting binding spells will be very useful."

Nate nodded. "Agreed. I'm happy to work on some. However, we'll need the Cornwall Coven in order to fully bind their magic forever." He looked across to Avery and Caspian. "Hair will be useful in some spells."

"Or personal objects," Hemani added. "Mariah will surely have left behind jewellery or clothes that we can use."

"But we need to protect ourselves, too," Cornell said. "They will be well aware that we're searching for them."

"What are their magical strengths and weaknesses?" Avery asked. "Knowing that will help us target them more effectively."

"And," Ulysses added, his deep voice rumbling around the table, "using our own strengths. As you all know I am a sea witch, with strong elemental water magic. It's more potent than most." He smiled almost shyly, as they all knew his mother was a mermaid. "The water speaks to me. I can see if it has knowledge of their whereabouts."

"Seriously?" Nate asked, eyes wide.

"Oh, yes. We have many interesting conversations. I'll call you, Caspian, if I have news." He shrugged, a mischievous glint in his eye. "And I can use my mother's Siren song when needed. It's not as strong as a full mermaid's, but I can be very persuasive when I have to be. I'm physically strong, too."

There was no doubting that, Avery reflected as she took in his enormous build, thankful that Ulysses was on their side.

Eve nodded. "That's good to know, Ulysses. I am a weather witch, as many of you know. It means I can harness large amounts of energy for long periods, and gather your energy, too. It could be very useful, depending on what we do. Nate?" she said, turning to him.

"Telekinesis, potions, heat. I'm a fire witch. And I cook a mean chilli if that helps," he said, grinning.

A ripple of laughter ran around the table.

"What about you, Cornell?" Avery asked, taking in his edgy appearance. His short, dark hair was ruffled, shaved above the ears, and he had a rakish grin. "I've worked with some of the other witches before, but not you. Claudia, however, speaks highly of you."

"Claudia is very kind. I'm a cosmic witch. I work my magic with the stars and planets. At the moment, there are many powerful planetary aspects."

Avery gasped. "I know! I've been researching them, and if I'm honest, I'm finding it all quite overwhelming." She quickly summarised what she'd been reading, and their thoughts on what the other witches' plans might be. "We think they might be using the upcoming planetary parade in some way."

Cornell nodded. "It was something I wanted to discuss with you, and why I particularly wanted to be involved, because unfortunately, cosmic witchcraft is Harry's strength, too."

A groan filled the room, as Caspian asked, "Explain how this works for those of us less familiar, please."

"It sounds more complicated than it is," he told them, smiling. "Much as many of us use phases of the moon to enhance our spells, the planets do much the same. Yes, there are many correspondences, some with conflicting attributes, but the more we experiment with them, the more we understand what works for us as individuals. This practice is much like any spell that we finetune as we use it. Rising energies and conjunctions enhance magic when used correctly."

Avery felt a wave of relief wash through her. *Someone who actually understood planetary energies was a huge bonus.* "Cornell, you have no idea how happy I am to hear that."

"And what about your strengths?" Caspian asked Hemani.

"Crystal magic. I use stones in my work all the time, along with kitchen witchcraft." She smiled. "I'm a great baker."

"And what about the others' strengths?" Avery persisted. "We know Mariah is a hedge witch who raises and walks among spirits, and Lowen spirit-walks and has strength on the astral plane. They must have other powers!"

"I'm sure they do, but I don't know what they are," Eve said, apologising.

A flurry of shaking heads and collective murmured apologies followed, and Avery had to accept that was all they knew. And then a wave of guilt raced through her. "That reminds me of what else I need to tell you." She recounted what Ghost OPS had discovered about the stone circles.

Hemani immediately looked at Cornell. "Harnessing the power of standing stones at such auspicious cosmic times would be incredibly powerful."

"Dangerously so," he agreed. His gaze shifted to Avery. "Any idea how they're raising the stones' energy?"

"Zane's mother mentioned something interesting last night that we hadn't considered. She said the pirate treasure would be associated with blood, and that gold and blood was a powerful combination. We thought they stole the treasure to sell it, but what if it they had another purpose for it?"

"Shit," Cornell said, dropping his face in his hands for a moment. When he looked up again, his face was grim. "Litha is when the sun is most powerful. It also associates with gold. And yes, gold connected with blood makes a potent combination." He glanced around at the staring witches. "The planetary parade will add power to this, but overall this suggests to me that they are planning something for the solstice. Something big. *Very* big."

"To what end?" Caspian asked, leaning forward, his hands clenched.

Cornell shrugged. "Sending out a powerful magical wave? It could wipe us all out for a while—sort of squash our magical powers. Or maybe harness a binding spell to target one of us or several. Or maybe the plan is just to super-juice their own powers. They'd be virtually untouchable." He looked around at their stunned faces. "We are talking about a lot of cosmic energy here. I wouldn't take anything off the table."

"Holy shit," Nate muttered. "I didn't imagine anything this big."

"And," Eve added, "on the solstice we will all be together to celebrate. The entire coven in one place. Suddenly, that doesn't seem a good idea anymore."

"Or," Cornell said eagerly, "it's the perfect time to mount our own attack!"

As he finished speaking, a massive jolt shook the whole house, quickly followed by several more. The dark sky beyond the long windows was shattered with crackling energy that burst like lightning across the grounds, and they raced to the windows.

"Someone is trying to break Oswald's protections spells!" Eve shouted to be heard above the noise.

And then there was another boom that knocked them all off their feet.

Alex had seen Lowen approach, a cloud of murky red energy surrounding him, and he waited and watched, curious as to his intent. He was sure Lowen hadn't seen him. He had veiled himself, tricky though it was on the astral plane, by hiding within the raw energy of the trees in Oswald's grounds. Lowen's silvery form was resonating in an unnerving fashion, and the red cloud around him was growing. *Was Lowen there to spy, or do something else?*

And then with unexpected speed, Lowen sent out a wave of rolling energy at Oswald's house, striking with such force that it rebounded off Oswald's protection spell and rolled across the spectral plane, catching Alex in its wake. Fortunately, his own protection held, and although he was buffeted, he held his position and struck back with a spell designed to repel Lowen.

At the same time, Lowen struck Oswald's house again, and his protection wavered. On this plane Alex could see tiny fractures like stress lines spreading, and then they vanished again. Oswald must be acting quickly.

Alex's spell hit Lowen, but bounced off as if Lowen was wearing armour plating, and unfortunately, he spotted Alex. His next attack was aimed at him. Alex thought he was prepared, but he wasn't. The energy caught him in a maelstrom, turning him end over end. When he finally stopped spinning, Alex found that he was far out to sea, and land was barely in sight.

Reuben looked at his poppet with satisfaction. He had used the rudimentary gingerbread man shape and sewn basic crosses for eyes and a line for a mouth.

"Not bad for a first attempt."

El smiled, her jewellery glinting in the candlelight that alleviated the twilight gloom. "I guess until you use it, we won't know. Are you ready?"

Despite his earlier bravado, Reuben felt nervous. "What if it's not their hair? What if I cause harm to an innocent person?"

"There was no evidence of anyone else in that house, Reuben. This hair belongs to one of them, or both." She gave an impish grin. "With luck, we'll strike both of them." She became serious. "I'm actually uncomfortable with this, too. I've never knowingly harmed anyone like this. Fighting someone one on one with fire or balls of energy is one thing, but this seems underhanded. But I keep reminding myself of the damage they've caused...and the deaths."

Reuben took a deep breath and exhaled slowly. "True. Okay. I thought I'd use this spell." He pulled his grimoire towards him and picked up the grey ribbon curled on the page. "I thought rather than using a pin, I would bind the poppet, as if binding their magic. What do you think?"

"I think it sounds perfect."

Reuben summoned his water magic, feeling the strength in its fluidity. It would work well for binding. Before he could back out, he started the spell.

Caspian spun around in alarm as the door flew open and Oswald rushed in, his eyes wild.

"Is everyone okay?"

"We're fine—for now," Caspian reassured him, noting his dishevelled appearance. It looked as if Oswald had raced from one side of the house to the other. "Your wards are holding up well."

Oswald wiped his forehead with the back of his hand as if removing sweat. "So far. But the attack is astonishingly strong. Would you all please lend your power to mine?"

Caspian nodded, noting the other witches did the same. They were still clustered around the long windows, watching the crackling energy assaulting the house.

Cornell was furious. "Is this Charlie's doing? Because the timing is suspicious—again!"

Hemani's dark brown eyes looked almost black in the low light. "We shouldn't jump to conclusions, but it is worrying."

Another rumble shook the room as the air outside fizzed.

"We haven't got time to debate this now," Oswald said, organising them into a circle. "Join hands with me now. One more blast could shatter my protection completely."

Caspian placed his hand in Oswald's, feeling its bony, dry fragility, but the magic he emanated wasn't weak at all. Hemani was on Caspian's other side, her hand warm in his, and within seconds they had opened up their magic to Oswald.

The rush of mixing powers was heady. No one held back, all willingly sharing with Oswald. If anything, this attack had strengthened their resolve. Caspian felt Hemani's magic, unfamiliar to him. It was sure and potent, and then he felt Avery's energy, familiar and comforting. The different threads were bewildering, but then he detected Ulysses's magic. It was deep and dark, full of a wild but tightly harnessed power unlike anything he had felt before. It carried the ocean within it, and a deep, rolling energy that threatened to unseat Caspian's equilibrium. He saw the other witches stare at Ulysses too, but he focussed only on Oswald.

As Oswald started his spell, another boom shook the room, and darkness fell as if a blanket had been thrown over the house. Caspian hoped their combined powers would be enough.

Alex sped across the sea, furious with himself for having been so easily disarmed.

The magical storm brewing above Oswald's house drew him like a magnet, visible even from a distance. His main worry was Avery, and even though he knew she was strong, Lowen's magic was potent. *Perhaps he was already accessing the power of the standing stones?*

As Crag's End came into view, Alex faltered. The magic surrounding Lowen was like a thunder cloud. It should be impossible to amass such energy on this plane, and yet...

Alex launched a volley of astral fire spears at him. The first couple disappeared into the murk, but one hit its mark, and the cloud of energy wavered.

Lowen spotted him, and in seconds Alex was engaged in a furious battle, close enough to see that Lowen's astral body was mottled black and green, and his face was twisted with rage. He looked demonic. He shot a bolt of lightning at Alex's cord, fortunately missing it. Alex couldn't afford to lose. Lowen was trying to kill him. Alex counter-attacked, drawing attention away from Oswald's house.

And then Lowen faltered, his rage-filled expression changing to bewilderment. The cloud of potent astral magic started to shrink, and Lowen writhed as if something had caught him.

This was the chance Alex needed, and he unleashed his most powerful spell. He conjured a lasso of pure energy, so strong that it sparked like a live wire, and getting as close as he dared, threw it around Lowen and pulled, snapping the lasso tight. Simultaneously, he uttered a binding spell.

With a flash, Lowen's magical storm vanished, and terror spread across his face before streaking back towards his body. Alex raced after him.

Twelve

A very broke away from the circle at the same time as everyone else and walked to the window. The clear twilight returned, and calm descended.

"I'm pretty sure I didn't do that," Oswald said, staring at the sky.

"Perhaps your spell deterred them, Oswald. *Something* certainly did," Caspian mused.

"Well," Eve said, watching the sky anxiously, "that's as clear a sign as any that we are *all* under attack."

"I'm hoping that El and Reuben were successful," Avery said, wondering what spells they'd been using. "And maybe Alex, too. Do you think that was Lowen?"

"Surely that couldn't have been an astral attack?" Cornell asked, alarmed.

"It's possible," Nate said. "Someone skilled enough in spirit-walking could manifest that much energy, but perhaps he had support."

Hemani nodded. "Magic to draw on, just as we have done."

Eve crossed her arms and stared at Caspian and Avery. "If whatever happened out there was stopped by a spell using the hair you found, you two should act quickly, before Mariah works it out and tries to stop you."

Caspian turned to Avery. "She's right. We should go now." He stared at the others. "Let's end this meeting now, and get planning. Cornell, can you work on a strategy to use the planets in a counterattack?"

"Of course." Cornell's eyes flashed with pleasure, and with the thrill of the challenge, Avery suspected. "The planetary parade is only two days away, and the full moon is on Friday. I can work something out for then. But of course, it's almost a week until Litha. That still allows them plenty of planning time."

"But the same applies to us," Ulysses pointed out. "Unless Litha is not their intent. There are many options at their disposal."

"Then we have to be prepared for all of them," Hemani stated, before turning to Cornell. "I'll help you. I'm intrigued that planetary magic could be coupled with the stone circles' energy. I'd like to explore that."

Nate turned to Eve. "What if we work on the binding spells we talked about earlier?"

She nodded. "Absolutely."

Oswald had staggered to a chair, and Ulysses sat next to him. "Are you all right, old friend?"

"A little shocked at the strength of the assault."

"Perhaps I should stay here," he offered. "In case he comes back. Two witches are stronger than one."

Oswald gave him a grateful smile, and Avery thought he'd aged years in mere minutes. "I would like that. Thank you."

"Can I suggest," Caspian said, "that we keep our plans to ourselves, for now? We are the team that volunteered to deal with this, and that means no one else is privy to what we do. I'll be in touch about when we next meet, and we'll do that at my house...thanks all the same, Oswald."

Oswald nodded, a flash of relief on his face.

"Avery," Caspian turned to her, holding his arms out wide, ready for her to step into them. "Are you ready?"

If she was honest, Avery would rather return to her friends and Alex to check that they were okay, but they couldn't waste time, so she nodded. "I'm ready."

In seconds, Oswald's house had vanished, and they stood in Mariah's living room in the dark. They waited for what seemed like a long time, ensuring there were no sounds around them. Finally satisfied, Caspian threw a witch-light above them, and walked out of the living room and up the stairs, with Avery following behind him.

"Have you been here many times?" she asked him, thinking he seemed to know the layout well.

"Once or twice, but it was a long time ago now."

Was it Avery's imagination, or did he sound regretful? She'd never asked, but now it struck her that they might have had more than just a friendship. "Were you close?"

"Only as friends, and seemingly not as well as I thought." As soon as Caspian was in the bathroom, he squatted down by the sink and started to dismantle the plug. He glanced up at her with a wry grin. "I'm glad I'm not wearing my suit."

"And I'm glad it's you doing that and not me," she confessed. "I'll look for jewellery."

The silence of Mariah's comfortable cottage wrapped around her as she hurried along the landing and into her bedroom. A chest of drawers stood under the window with a pretty jewellery box on it, and Avery slid open the drawers to see a selection of necklaces, bracelets, and rings. Once again, she was struck by how normal everything seemed, and she felt sad that she hadn't known Mariah better. Or rather that Mariah hadn't let her get to know her better. She had tried—at first, at least—until her effort was met with a wave of animosity.

Uncomfortable with the fact that she was stealing with the intention to harm, Avery took one necklace and bracelet and put them in her pocket, and then decided to search the bedroom again. She opened the drawers, filtering through the few items left behind, and then searched under the bed and in the wardrobe. Frustrated at finding nothing more of use, she headed back to the bathroom to find Caspian rising to his feet by the shower.

"Success?" she asked.

He grimaced as he held a ball of hair in his fingers. "I guess you could say that. The sink proved clean, but I found some in the shower."

"Good. I have jewellery, too." The noise of a car pulling up had them running to the bedroom window, and they saw Mariah exit a car with Harry.

Caspian pulled her away from the window just as Mariah looked up. "Time to go."

"Let's go to Reuben's," Avery suggested, eager they discuss their options once more before separating, "and see how Alex got on."

Caspian nodded, wrapping his arms around Avery once more, and they vanished just as the front door opened.

Briar studied the sweat on his Alex's brow and his eyes moving rapidly beneath his closed lids, hoping that he was staying safe. A cry of success had her twisting around to look at Reuben and El.

"Everything okay?" she asked them.

Reuben winked. "You betcha! I felt this bad boy resonate like a bow string. Whoever is affected is hit big!"

"Good, I guess. But I still feel uncomfortable about this."

El gave her a twisted smile. "I understand, but you were attacked and could have been killed."

"I know."

Briar turned back to Alex, unable to forget the huge jolt of power that she had accessed the other night. She was familiar with using stones in her work, they were a useful addition to her healing spells, but standing on the quartz stones had been entirely different. She'd felt like a conduit of magic. For some reason, it made her feel both incredibly powerful and horribly alone. Now she couldn't wait for Hunter to come. She just wanted to be held within the strong arms of a vibrant man who could make her feel lots more than just being a witch. She rubbed her face with her hands. *What was the matter with her? She should feel energised by her power, not exhausted by it.*

A displacement of energy in the middle of Reuben's main attic made her lift her head, alarmed, but Avery called out, "It's just me and

Caspian." They appeared at the brick archway, both looking flushed with victory, until Avery's gaze fell on Alex. She lowered her voice with a trace of anxiety. "He's still gone?"

"For some time now, but there's nothing happening to suggest anything is wrong."

"Have a seat," Reuben said, gesturing to the spare chairs at the table. "How did the meeting go?"

"It was eventful," Caspian said, accepting his offer, "but I've brought you a present." He placed something on the table that Briar couldn't see from her spot on the cushion.

"Ugh!" El said, her face wrinkling with disgust. "Not more hair!"

Caspian laughed. "Sorry, but we're going to need it."

"I have some jewellery, too," Avery said, placing the pieces next to the hair.

Reuben was more enthusiastic. "Good. I think we may have achieved something tonight."

"Well," Caspian said as he picked up the poppet and examined it, "someone attacked Oswald's place this evening, and then it stopped, abruptly."

Alex's groan had them all turning around, and Avery hurried to his side as he croaked, "It was Lowen."

"He was spirit-walking again?" Avery asked.

Alex nodded and sat up, rubbing his hair and his face as if he'd woken from a long sleep. "Yep. I chased him from Oswald's place. He was heading to the north coast, but he disappeared quickly, and I didn't linger." He finally seemed to focus on the fact that Caspian had arrived. "Are you two okay? Lowen was throwing a lot of power at Crag's End."

"We're fine," Avery reassured him. "But it was pretty hairy for a while."

Alex squeezed her hand, and gave El and Reuben a wry smile. "Something completely stopped Lowen...absolutely strangled his power. Was that you two?"

"I bloody well hope so," Reuben said. "Three spells aimed at whoever's hair we have. We're hoping we hit both of them hard."

For the first time since he'd returned to his body, Alex appeared to relax, and Briar handed him the cup of restorative tea she'd kept warm at her side. "There you go. You'll soon be feeling better."

"I feel better just knowing that something we did worked really well." He gave short laugh. "*Really* well! I threw a binding spell at him, too. *Bastard.*"

"But," Caspian pointed out, "somehow they knew that we would be at Oswald's tonight. That suggests it's either Charlie passing them information, or someone else in the coven is a mole."

"Which means," El said, "we need to keep a tight circle."

Briar's phone buzzed in her pocket, and she quickly answered when she saw it was Newton. "Hey, Newton. How are—"

But she couldn't finish her sentence. "Briar, something is wrong. I feel weird."

"What?" Her voice rose with shock. "What kind of weird?"

"Weak...dizzy. Can you come? I'm at home."

"I'll be there as soon as possible. Stay put!" She had stood as they spoke, and now everyone was looking at her. "Newton is hurt. I have to get to him!"

Avery was about to stand, but Caspian urged her to sit. "No, let me. I've never been to Newton's, but I could get you close if you can give me a landmark."

"But I..." Avery started, casting an anxious look at Alex.

"No. You stay with Alex," Caspian insisted, extending his arms. "Briar, just stand next to me, and I'll transport us."

As anxious as she was to go, Briar had never used witch-flight before.

"Are you sure? It's just a short drive."

"This is quicker." He met her eyes with his calm ones. "We can bring him back here."

"But you've just got here. Aren't you tired?"

His eyes were kind and amused. "I'm strong enough to do this. Come on."

She pushed her hesitation aside. "Thank you."

In seconds, Caspian's arms were around her, and the room vanished into swirling blackness.

Dylan studied the map with interest, then tucked it in his pocket, ready to exit the van. "You know, it hadn't really registered just how many stone circles are on Bodmin Moor. It's uncanny."

Ben nodded in agreement. "I know, but it's a moody, lonely place, so it's not surprising."

"And," Cassie added, "the tip of Cornwall is the same. There's something about these out of the way spots that encourages these monuments to the Gods and the elements. And this one is pretty big."

They were on the lane that led past Stannon Stone Circle on the north side of Bodmin. After their experience the night before, they were all worried about being attacked again, but Dylan didn't care; he was determined to get plenty of footage.

Cassie hesitated before getting out of the van. "The witches' spells won't be of much help if there is a repeat of last night's attack."

"I know," Ben admitted, exchanging a worried glance with Dylan, "but we need this information."

Cassie sighed and exited the car, aiming her torch across the moor. "At least I've got wellies on tonight. I think it could be boggy."

Dylan checked his backpack to ensure he had plenty of batteries, and holding the camera, set off towards the stone circle, the others striding next to him. "You know," he said, chatting to take the edge off the vast silence that surrounded them, "this circle and Fernacre are thought to be the oldest on the moor, and Fernacre is bigger than this one."

"I noticed," Cassie said. "I was reading about them this afternoon. There's evidence of stone age settlements around here, too. This was an important place for our ancestors."

"I think it's an important place for some current witches, too," Ben reflected, the EMF meter in his hand.

They reached the edge of the circle without incident, Dylan almost banging into one stone in the dark, and he wished they'd set off earlier. The twilight would have offered better visibility, but all three of them felt safer in the dark, out of sight of prying eyes—or so they hoped, at least. He also wondered if the readings would be stronger at night, so they had avoided going in the daytime. Plus, there were less likely to be visitors than in the day. He paused and let his eyes adjust, and out of the sea of grey, he made out a few of the standing stones. It was large circle, but the stones were barely knee-height.

Ben's meter emitted a low whine. "Wow. This is starting already." He panned it across the closest of the stubby stones and it rose in frequency. "Cassie, can you take some notes?"

She hurried to his side, while Dylan looked at his own screen with a mixture of dismay and excitement. These stones were showing signs of building energy too, and even the stones on the far side of the circle were visible from here. He could definitely make out the circular alignment. He huffed. "Bollocks. It's happening here, too."

Cassie and Ben huddled closer to him, Cassie holding her hair back as the wind ravaged it, and he caught a whiff of her perfume as she said, "There's no doubt that this is a *thing*, then."

Dylan could only just see her expression from the light of the screen, but there was no doubting her concern because it echoed his own. "Yep, it is most definitely a *thing*. Let's cover this place quickly. I want to investigate Louden Stone Circle on the way to Fernacre." He checked the sky, seeing only scudding clouds and an expanse of stars. "It's relatively clear. What do you say we do an all-nighter, and cover Trippet, Stripple, and Craddock, too?"

"Absolutely," Ben agreed. "Cassie, let's get temperature readings and the works. If all of these circles are lighting up, we know we're in trouble. I want to give the witches as much info as we can."

And with that, they scattered, and Dylan focussed on his recordings. This was going to be a long night.

Newton had managed to drag himself to his desk chair, and he flicked on a lamp and checked his watch. *Crap.* He'd been out for over an hour.

He heard someone knock on the door downstairs, and then a click as it unlatched, and Briar called up, "It's just me, and I'm with Caspian."

"I'm up here!" He had barely time to wonder how she arrived so quickly when they were at the doorway, Briar looking queasy, and he said, "You look ill, too."

"That's just the witch-flight," she explained, heading to his side.

Caspian looked sheepish as he followed her in. "Sorry. It was quicker, though."

"I always thought Alex was exaggerating, but he wasn't," she admitted, already holding her hand above Newton's body and scanning him. "Your energy does feel low."

Newton closed his eyes and took deep breaths, willing that he should feel normal, but it felt as if there was a weight on his chest. It was odd; even though he wasn't watching Briar, he could feel where her hand passed over him. It felt like a caress. A feeling he could have been more familiar with if he hadn't rejected her. *Idiot.*

He opened his eyes again to find her staring into his face. "I'm not sure it's a spell, and the protection on your house feels strong. I'm wondering if it's tiredness and grief."

"Great. Now I sound like a sissy."

She straightened and tutted. "Don't be an idiot! Look at the week you've had. And I heard about today at the farmhouse. You were up early."

He flopped back in his chair. "Shit. That feels like a week ago."

"Exactly. You've been doing too much!"

Caspian was staring at Newton's massive pinboard that was filled with notes on the current case. He'd barely got around to Black Cronos yet, but Caspian said, "I heard about the Nephilim's place being attacked. That's bad timing."

Newton grunted. "Hardly their fault. Eli apologised, but they had to call me. Bad timing for me, but worse for them."

Briar's hands were on her hips as she regarded him. "Have you even eaten?"

"Snacks at the wake."

Her forehead wrinkled with annoyance. "Herne's horns, Newton! Now I'm pretty sure you are just rundown. I was going to suggest you come back to Reuben's with us, but after my unpleasant experience, I'm going to cook you something light, and then you're going to bed."

Despite his nausea and pounding head, he couldn't help laughing. "Sorry, Briar. Obviously, paranoia has got the better of me, but I can manage that. You should get back to Reuben's place. You're holding Caspian up, too."

She swung around to look at Caspian. "You don't mind, do you?"

"Not at all. But I suggest we strengthen Newton's protection when you're done—just in case."

Her eyes flashed with a ring of green fire. "There, Newton, you see!"

"Yes ma'am."

"Don't *ma'am* me! You should look after yourself better." She strode from the room, her skirts flouncing. "And don't you dare follow me."

Newton waited until she'd gone before speaking to Caspian. "For a tiny woman, she's very bossy."

Caspian smiled. "She has a good heart, and she's generous to her friends. I'm very fond of her. I can't help but feel she's like a little sister."

Newton was about to bristle with annoyance until Caspian added his last statement, and he softened his response. "She's fond of you, too. I don't think she's in touch with her family, and as far as I know, she has no siblings."

"Good. Then she needs a big brother." A cheeky grin crossed Caspian's face. "I don't think you fulfil that particular quality."

"I don't fulfil any other quality, either," Newton said, surprising himself. "That bloody wolf does."

Caspian's head dropped and he stared at the floor for a moment. "Yeah, I know how that feels." Surprised at his admission, Newton was temporarily silenced, and Caspian studied Newton's notes again. "You've got Moore helping with all this?"

"Yes. We have no news on anyone's whereabouts yet. They're keeping a very low profile, but I'm convinced some of them are still here."

"They definitely are. Mariah and Harry were outside Mariah's house earlier, and —"

Newton interrupted him, his thoughts racing through possibilities. "They were? Bollocks. Then where the hell are they?"

"No idea. But Lowen attacked again tonight, too. Don't worry, we're all okay."

"Attacked how?"

"An astral attack."

Newton closed his eyes, feeling exhausted. After the funeral, he'd heard about all about the previous night's attack, but had tried to banish it from his mind during the wake. Everything felt like too much.

When he opened his eyes again, Caspian was watching him. "You've heard about the activity at the stone circles?" He leaned against the wall, arms folded across his chest, looking very different with his casual clothes on—less authoritative—and Newton wondered if this was a conscious effort to be more approachable.

"Yes," he nodded, wondering where Caspian was going. "It's concerning."

"It's possible the blood-soaked treasure—and I mean that metaphorically, of course—is helping to raise the energy of the circles in some way, but I remain convinced that Mariah and Zane will still try to sell it on when whatever they have planned is done. I'm going to London on Thursday. Why don't you come?"

"London?" Newton was so startled it almost dispelled his headache. "Why there?"

"I'm meeting Olivia, Harlan's colleague. You could meet her too, and the famous Maggie Milne I've heard so much about."

Newton could only stare at him for a moment, fearing he'd lost his marbles, and thought honesty would be the best option. "I'm surprised you want me to go."

"I think looking at this from another angle will be useful. Have you replaced Inez yet?"

That was something else he didn't want to think about. *No wonder he felt like shit.* "No, I'm putting it off, but I'll have to do it tomorrow."

"Good. Whoever you choose can help Moore. Nothing like getting thrown into it."

"If I can get them transferred that quickly. What's in this for you?"

Caspian shrugged with a rueful smile. "Nothing. I just thought some company would be good, and you need to get away. And I gather Hunter arrives tomorrow."

Newton tried not to groan, but it escaped anyway. "Of course, he does." He heard Briar coming up the stairs and knew that seeing her with him would be horrible, and even though he'd still be around when Newton returned, maybe he should go. "How long are you planning on staying?"

"Just a couple of days."

"All right, then. I'll organise things tomorrow and call you about a time to leave."

Thirteen

Compared to how Avery was feeling, the atmosphere in White Haven was bright and cheerful as she strolled back to Happenstance Books on Wednesday morning, carrying coffees and cakes.

She'd volunteered to do the mid-morning coffee run, needing to stretch her legs and experience normality after what felt like a crazy few days, and walking along the town's festive streets always restored her good mood. She looked around now with pleasure. The sun was shining, the seagulls called overhead, and the breeze carried the scent of the sea. The hanging baskets and planted pots were full of summer colour, and the shops' Litha displays looked amazing.

There were green wreaths on doors and in windows, as well as huge displays of flowers and images of the Goddess in various shapes and forms. Locals and visitors alike were dressed in summer clothes, and there was lots of chatter about the upcoming solstice celebrations on Saturday that would be held on the beach. The witches' own celebrations would take place a few days later, on the actual solstice. Well, they hoped they would, but those plans might change depending on what happened over the next few days.

Avery's shop door was wide open as she entered, allowing the warm summer air to circulate, and she headed to the counter where Dan was changing the music and Sally finished serving a customer.

"Hey guys, coffee and cake time."

Sally reached for her latte and then studied Avery's face. "Thank you. You look brighter."

She nodded. "I needed that. The town looks lovely, and I'm feeling positive. I presume you two will go to the bonfire on the beach?"

"Sure," Dan said, pulling a cream donut out of the bag. "I'm going with Caroline." He looked at Avery suspiciously. "I presume it will be safe?"

"I'm pretty sure it will be. Whatever Mariah and her gang are planning is aimed at us. In fact, we're planning on going, too." She sipped her coffee, thinking how much fun it would be just to enjoy a party without fear of attack. "Yes, it will be fine."

"Good," Sally said, looking pleased. "I'm taking the kids, and of course we'll watch the parade. However, something *is* bothering you. Come on, spill."

Avery hadn't shared the latest news as the morning had been too busy, and if she was honest, she wanted to put it from her mind, but now she updated them on the events of the previous evening.

"Wow," Dan said, shocked. "Reuben and El spelled them?"

"Yes," she confirmed, still feeling uncomfortable about it. "It's weird for all of us, but it's a good job they did."

"So, say Lowen is bound in some way," Sally ventured, lowering her voice. "What does that actually mean? Is he physically ill?"

"It means that his magic is bound and that he can't spirit-walk... well, that's how it should work. It's not a full binding because that's a huge thing to do, but it means that he's restricted, for now."

"And you'll do the same with Mariah's *things*?" she asked, alluding to the items Avery and Caspian had stolen.

Avery nodded, thinking on their discussion the night before. "We're considering our options right now."

Dan wiped some cream and sugar from his lips, and said, "So, this alignment is tomorrow, right? Does that mean something will happen then?"

"Good question, and the answer is that we're not sure. Cornell is working on a strategy for us with Hemani." Avery frowned as she thought through the possibilities. "We probably can't stop what they're doing, but we can perhaps counter it—or harness the energies, too. The thing is," she added, growing more worried, "Caspian and Newton will be in London, so we won't have Caspian's power to use. Not that I know if Cornell will even need us."

"London?" Dan asked.

She updated them further on their plans, admitting, "I was surprised, too, but he's right to speak with Olivia, and Newton meeting Maggie is a good idea, too."

A knock on the window had them all looking outside, and they saw Ben and Dylan grinning before they strode through the door and to the counter.

"Dan, my man," Dylan said, shaking Dan's hand with pleasure. "You won't believe what we've found out!"

"I gather it's something to do with stone circles?"

"And then some!"

Avery groaned. "Don't tell me you've found more that are affected!"

Ben looked like he would burst with excitement. "Every single stone circle on Bodmin Moor is lit up like a Christmas tree!"

His excited voice carried across the store, and Sally shooed them away. "To the back room, all of you—that means you, too, Dan. Don't worry, I'll watch the shop."

Shooting her a grateful smile, Avery led them all to privacy, and had barely closed the door when Dylan pulled his backpack off and started to rummage in it. "I think Bodmin is supercharging!"

"And Hurlers Stone Circles look even brighter than they did even a couple of nights ago!" Ben added. "It's crazy!'

Avery groaned, wishing she could feel as excited. "I'm not sure we should be celebrating this!"

"Sounds bloody ingenious to me," Dan said, heading to Dylan's side. "Have you brought your footage?"

"Dude! Of course! Well, some of it." Dylan turned his camera on and searched through the footage. "I had hours of film, and have downloaded most of it, but this is Hurlers largest circle."

Avery stood on Dylan's other side, squinting at the screen. At first all she saw was a flicker of darkness, and then as the camera panned around, she watched flickers of golden light like fireflies. "Bloody hell."

"Like an alien landing pad, right?" Ben said, his eyes shining.

"No, do not say that," Dan remonstrated. "There's enough going on without aliens."

"So, this circle is on St Michael's Ley Line," Dylan said, turning the camera off. "But the others look the same."

Dan sat down, putting his feet up on the next chair. "And there's six or seven stone circles, right?"

"Nine," Dylan corrected him. "And I've checked them all. Six on the north, three on the south."

"What about King Arthur's Hall?"

"Bollocks. I didn't think to check *that*."

"Hold on," Avery said, slowing them down. "There are nine stone circles on Bodmin? That's mad! And what is King Arthur's Hall?"

"Take a seat," Dan said, lifting his feet and gesturing to the empty chairs, "and I will educate you."

"Good grief. Will this take long?" she asked, teasing him. He looked like he was settling in for a long tale.

"How dare you. Sit."

Avery smirked and sat, and Dylan and Ben followed suit. "Go on, then," she said, knowing Dan was going to regardless.

"Bodmin Moor is stuffed full of Neolithic remnants of settlements and ritual sites. Not far from Hurlers is Trevethy Quoit, a portal tomb, and there's the Cheesewring, a pile of flat boulders that legends tell was the result of a fight between saints and giants." He shrugged, amused. "Weird, I know. Anyway, the whole place may be a lonely, windswept area now, but history suggests it was once bustling with activity."

"And King Arthur's Hall?" Avery asked.

Dan winked. "You can't leave him out of anything around here. Although it's called a hall, it's actually another stone circle."

"More like an enclosure, really," Ben said, butting in.

"Fair enough. It's a rectangle—hence the hall—and the stones look like chair backs. No one knows what purpose it served, but it was probably ceremonial."

Avery leaned on the table, chin in her hands. "Something to do with solstices or equinoxes, right?"

Dan nodded, and Dylan said, "Some of the circles align with sunrises, but I'd have to check the details."

"And," Ben added, "some of them share alignments with other local structures—other circles, stones, or Tors. You know, significant landmarks."

"Like a giant game of connect the dots," she mused.

"That's probably a good way to put it," Dan said, watching her. "This is important, isn't it?"

"I think it is. And it makes me surer than ever that they are in Bodmin somewhere. Or beneath it. Any issues with the ley line?"

"Initial inspections say not. This is a Bodmin thing. Although, we shouldn't forget Duloe Stone Circle and Nine Maiden's Stone Row." Ben stood, his chair scraping along the floor. "Come on, Dylan. Let's head to King Arthur's Hall. I'm not trekking across the moor again in the dark. I almost broke my bloody neck!"

Avery stood as well. "Be careful, and keep us informed. I think I'll call Cornell, and you should avoid the circles tomorrow night, during the alignment...just in case."

Newton assessed the young woman in front of him, sure he'd found Inez's replacement. She was thirty-four and lived in Truro, and had spent most of her time on the force in Devon, only transferring to Cornwall a couple of years before. Her previous superiors spoke highly of her, and she was apparently very committed to the job.

Her dark, almost black hair was styled in a pixie cut, framing a pale-skinned, heart-shaped face, and it make her dark eyes look even larger.

She was tall, and he guessed she used the gym from the appearance of her toned arms visible below the sleeves of her summer shirt.

He'd just interviewed her with Moore, and glancing at him now, Moore raised an eyebrow, a sure sign of his agreement. They'd chatted before she arrived, both certain that as long as she interviewed well, they'd appoint her quickly, and so far, things were looking good.

Newton turned back to her, finding her dark eyes on him. "You've got an excellent record, Sergeant Kendall, but are you sure you want to work with us, chasing down the paranormal? It's not for everyone."

"I like a challenge, and I've experienced a fair number of odd things in Devon. Things the other officers would rather ignore."

"Like what?"

"Poltergeists and restless spirits, mainly. A couple of haunted houses and an unexplained death that I'm sure was spirit related."

"Have you come across any witches?"

"A few Wiccans. Some psychics who claim to be able to find the missing—but didn't."

"Well, I can assure you there's a lot more than that going on here."

"I suspected as much," she said, trying not to look too excited. "I keep an eye on the news and hear the rumours in the station. I'm looking for a challenge."

"Ha." Newton couldn't help his snort of derision. "You'll get that, and more. You know, of course, what happened to my colleague, Inez Walker." It wasn't a question; he knew she did. He'd seen her yesterday at the funeral, as well as most of the force. It was a huge turnout.

"Of course."

"It hasn't put you off?"

She swallowed. "No. There are always risks in this job."

"Then welcome to the team." He reached across the table and shook her hand. "I want you transferred ASAP," Newton told her. "Do you think your DI will object?"

She looked surprised, but pleased. "I have a few cases, but I can transfer them easily."

"Good. I'll phone her now, and with luck you'll be with us tomorrow." He grinned, feeling hopeful and relieved that he had made his decision. "Cheeky, I know. I have to go to London tomorrow, but I can catch you up on current events now, and Moore will help you acclimatise. He's very comfortable with all this."

Moore shook Kendall's hand too, being his usual, loquacious self. "Welcome."

"Moore, show Kendall to her desk while I make the call, and then we'll discuss our current cases."

Newton watched them leave the room, heading to the office next to him that he often wished was connected. *Maybe he should press his own superiors for that.* He massaged his temples, hoping his headache would ease now that he'd made this big decision. He was sure having that weighing on him had contributed to his collapse the night before. Briar was right; he'd needed food and sleep, something he'd been in short supply of the past couple of days. He just hoped that Black Cronos wasn't about to make another appearance. One bloodbath at the Nephilim's farmhouse was more than enough.

He nodded to himself, reaching for his now cold coffee. Yes, visiting Maggie Milne would be a good thing. He had plenty to ask her, so he better phone her and arrange that, too.

El finished buffing her latest piece of jewellery and examined it in the afternoon sunshine that streamed through her window and onto the workbench in the studio behind her shop.

It was a stylised sun pendant, part of her new Litha collection, and the gemstone in the centre was topaz. *Yes, that would do nicely.* And it was charmed with positivity and strength, too.

She placed it to the side with the matching bracelet and earrings, and then stood and stretched, rolling her neck. She'd been sitting for hours, and now her eyes felt dry and her shoulders ached. She turned her coffee pot on and walked into her courtyard, lifting her hair to catch the breeze on her neck.

Something was bothering her, but she couldn't work out what. It was like a tickle at the back of her brain. She'd made a list of things she'd needed to do in her shop, wondering if she'd forgotten something, and every now and again she leapt to her feet to add something else to her whiteboard on the wall. But she'd also been methodically ticking things off, and she was sure there was nothing she'd forgotten.

Maybe she was just worried about the spells they'd cast on Lowen the previous night, because from all they'd discovered, he was the main recipient. She couldn't shake her guilt over her and Reuben's actions, even though she knew it had helped stop Lowen's attack.

She huffed, annoyed with herself, and walked back inside to pour her coffee, making one for Zoe too, and then stuffed a pack of shortbread into her waistband. She headed into the shop, carrying the drinks to the counter, and was surprised to see Zoe in conversation with Stan, the town's pseudo-Druid.

He gave a welcoming smile. "El! I was just wondering where you were."

"I was putting the finishing touches on one of my new collections." She handed Zoe her coffee. "Would you like a coffee, Stan?"

He waved it off. "Oh no, I'm fine. Just doing my rounds to see everyone's Litha decorations." He glanced around, nodding with approval. "As usual, The Silver Bough looks lovely, but then again, so many shops do. Everyone makes such an effort!"

El exchanged a grin with Zoe, who said, "We wouldn't dare not to, knowing that you inspect us!"

He flashed them a guilty smile. "Well, it does help to keep everyone motivated. I'm running a Best Decorated event too, you know. You could be in with a shot."

El laughed as she glanced around at the flower-filled room. "Maybe, but I think other shops do far more than us." She shrugged. "That's okay, though."

"I have high hopes for this celebration. The weather is good, the crowds are building, and the museum will be displaying the pirate treasure in time for Saturday."

El had a moment of confusion as she studied Stan's excited face, thinking they had found the treasure that Mariah and Zane had stolen. And then it struck her. "Ah! The treasure found on Gull Island."

"Of course. The police—that nice Newton man—have worked quickly to allow us to have it so soon." His chest and large stomach swelled with pride. "I helped lobby, you know, argued that to have it on display for Litha would be marvellous. To increase the visitors to the museum, you see. Such tragic business."

"Ethan's death, you mean? Yes, of course." El didn't think she'd ever forget seeing his broken body propelled across the room.

Zoe lowered her coffee cup. "Do you mean the treasure will be on display in the Cruel Coppinger exhibition? Won't that need a lot of security?"

"We have it all in hand. It will be in a locked display cabinet, and there'll be plenty of security personnel around. It will be fine," he reassured them. He nodded to the local paper on the countertop. "It even gets a mention in there. We'll unveil it on Friday."

The thing that had been niggling El suddenly became very clear. "Where is it now?"

"In the museum's basement. Again, very secure!" He looked amused. "You two are a pair of worriers! Anyway, I must get on," he said, turning to the door with a wave. "I'll pop in later in the week!"

As he left, El pulled the newspaper towards her. On the front page was an article about the treasure being added to the display. "Bollocks!"

"Problem?" Zoe asked, edging closer to read the article.

"I just think broadcasting where the treasure will be could be an issue for us." Zoe knew all about the recent events. "What if Zane and Mariah decide they want it to add to the rest?"

Zoe stared over her steaming cup. "If they need to enhance their spell with more blood-soaked gold? I guess it's a possibility. And if your friend is working out a counterattack, wouldn't it be—"

"Yes," El interrupted. "We might need it, too. I wish Newton had mentioned this." El's phone rang, and she knew who it would be before she'd even looked at the screen. "Avery. I think we have a problem."

"I know we do," she answered immediately. "Have you seen the local paper?"

"Yes, and Stan's just been wittering on about it, too."

"Cornell wants us to get the treasure—tonight."

El started to pace as her adrenalin soared. "I had a horrible feeling you were going to say that. And if we don't get it, there's every chance Mariah and Zane will. Can Newton delay it?"

"I've already asked him, and unfortunately he can't – not with all the arrangements and publicity. It never even crossed his mind it could be an issue."

"Not surprising considering the speed of the recent developments."

"Let's meet at mine to discuss options. Eight this evening?"

"No, at mine," El suggested. "I'm closest. Same time, though."

"Fair enough," Avery agreed. "See you then."

As El pocketed her phone, she caught Zoe's amused expression. "I take it you will be busy tonight?"

"Just pretend you know nothing."

Zoe snorted. "I always do."

Fourteen

A lex popped the cap off his beer bottle and leaned against the kitchen counter in El's flat, watching Avery argue her point and failing.

"But it *will* work," she insisted. "I can fly into the museum, find the treasure, and fly it back here. Easy!"

El's arms were crossed, and she stared at her with incredulity. "You know the museum well, then?"

"Not really," Avery admitted, "but I know the entrance well enough to fly into it."

"The entrance by the big doors that everyone can see through? With the alarm that you could set off just by arriving there? That could trigger a police car or security to arrive in seconds?"

Avery pouted. "I could shut off the alarm!"

"*Before* you arrive? I know you're a clever witch, but tell me how that works again?"

Reuben strolled over to join Alex, grinning, and with a low voice intended not to disturb the argument, said, "This is fun! Avery's tough, but I'd put money on El winning."

The sound of raised voices covered Alex's response. "I know better than to bet against Avery, but it is one of her madder ideas." He lowered his voice even further. "The very fact that she's still here means she knows it's nuts."

"Why aren't you involved in this—" Reuben gestured wildly, "heated chat?"

"I have already expressed my disapproval." He winced as he thought of Avery's annoyance when they had walked down the street. Most of the time she was mild and rational, but there were other times when her feisty nature reared its head. Like a viper. "I've learned to let her cool off."

"Great make-up sex, though, right?" Reuben said with a wink.

"I will not dignify that with a response, you randy goat."

They both became aware of sudden silence, and looked around to see Avery and El staring at them.

"What was that, Alex?" Avery said, her eyes narrowing.

Aiming for breezy insouciance, he said, "Nothing! Just chatting with my mate while you two locked horns. Anyway, El," he cleared his throat and smiled, "have you talked Avery out of her mad scheme yet?"

El shot them both a suspicious look, but then stared at Avery again. "I believe so."

Avery huffed with annoyance. "All right. I was just trying to avoid too many of us going. I thought it would be safer!"

"How dare you try to deny me my ninja witch night!" Reuben said, teasing her. "I'm already dressed for it!" He gestured to his completely black clothing. "I live for this shit."

"You're an idiot!" Avery shot back.

"And the wolfman is here now! You know he'll want to be in on the action!"

"Did I hear my name?" Hunter said, grinning broadly as he stepped through El's front door. He tipped his head back and howled, and then said, "So good to be here!"

Reuben howled too, enveloping him in a hug. "Wolfman! Good to see you!"

Alex laughed. "Since when do you call Hunter 'wolfman,' you tit?"

"Since now!"

Hunter howled again and hugged Alex in a fierce grip that crushed his chest before turning to El and Avery and sweeping them in hugs, too. "Ah! The lovely ladies."

Briar had followed him in, and she was laughing as she watched him. "He's been like this since he arrived. He assures me it's nothing but excitement."

Hunter looked lean and ready for action. It had been a few weeks since Alex had seen him, and he'd almost forgotten the wild energy that Hunter exuded. He was dressed in his habitual worn jeans and a faded leather jacket, and oozed self-assurance.

"I'm excited to see you, my sweet," he said to her with a wink.

Briar rolled her eyes. "He was so much more excited when I told him about tonight."

Hunter was doing some weird jig in the middle of the room, and he caught Alex's bemused expression. "It's my happy dance!" He looked around the room. "No Newton?"

"Absolutely not," Avery said. "I told him our plans on the phone, and he was apoplectic. And guilty. I think he's been so busy that he didn't consider there'd be any consequences to releasing the gold. I suggested he stay away tonight, so he is."

Alex was pretty sure that if it wasn't for Hunter, he'd be here regardless, waiting for when they returned, but perhaps it was for the best. "He's got other plans, anyway," he said, by way of explanation. "He's going to London tomorrow."

Hunter nodded. "Oh yeah, Briar said. With Caspian!"

"And he's not coming, either," Briar told them. "He wanted to, and I know he's recovered well from his stab wound, but it was only a week ago!" She shook her head, lips pursed. "I told him he shouldn't risk it, so he grudgingly agreed."

Alex gave a silent cheer of joy. "That's sensible." He grabbed Hunter a beer from the fridge and poured Briar a glass of wine. "You might as well have a drink while we wait. We are."

"Cheers, mate," Hunter said, accepting the bottle. "So, what's the plan?"

"Well," El said, shooting Avery a sideways glance, "we are entering the museum through the back door, and making our way down to the basement. Then when we find the treasure, Avery brings it back here using witch-flight, and the rest of us make our escape." She turned to Avery, puzzled. "Didn't Cornell want to come?"

"Yes, he did actually, but I talked him out of it, too. As much as I trust Cornell, I don't know him well enough to want him involved in this. And besides, he did say he was tied up with his big spell."

Hunter swigged his beer. "Is it likely we're going to run into the others? Your witch nemeses?"

"It's possible," Alex said. "The news about the treasure was everywhere today. Of course, they might have enough. We have no idea how much they found."

Reuben shrugged. "Or they might want to stop us from doing a counter-spell. We should go as soon as it's dark."

"The pubs won't have closed! There'll be too many people about," Alex said, already feeling edgy.

"Is there a pub close by?" El asked. "We could go there, keep an eye on the place. Swoop in after closing."

"The Hollow Bole," Reuben said. "It has a green tree on its sign. Nice little pub, just across from the museum. We go there sometimes after a surf." He rubbed his hands together and grinned. "Shall we?"

El led the way up the dark, narrow passage at the rear of the museum, pausing as she reached the door that led to the loading bay, and turned to Reuben, Avery, and Alex.

"We should check this place out. If the treasure was delivered today, it could still be in here."

"Agreed," Alex said, already opening the door and heading inside, "but I think it's doubtful."

The loading bay was a big, square space with a large roller door, accessed from the car park behind the building that was for staff only. A drive ran down the side of the building from the main street, and the staff entrance was only a short distance from the roller door.

They fanned out, searching the few crates that were there, but most proved empty. "Ah, well," Reuben said with a sigh, "it was worth a shot."

Avery led the way further into the main museum, a witch-light bobbing along the ceiling as she navigated a series of turns, muttering, "This place is a maze."

"Old buildings," El answered, sticking her head in a room as she passed it. "Another office. I guess we're in what would have been the servants' quarters, or something of the sort."

Reuben nodded. "The murky back rooms that no one else saw." He looked into another room, but backed out quickly. "According to Newton, the basement is accessed from a door in the main foyer. That's where Ethan's office was."

They soon entered the reception hall, the wide glass doors offering them a view of the street, and Avery stopped, throwing her hand out and making the rest of them stop, too. She pointed to a figure in the adjoining hall wearing a uniform. *A security guard*. Low lights illuminated the displays, and his back was towards them as he patrolled, his torch playing around the room.

El felt Avery's magic flare and the security guard stumbled and fell, landing heavily on the floor.

"What have you done to him?" Alex said, racing to his side.

"Just a sleep spell!"

"What if there are more?"

"Perhaps we should shut up, then!" Reuben suggested in a low voice. He gestured to the next hall and disappeared into it.

El waited, watching the stairs that led to the first floor, but all was silent. She hung back in the shadows and looked through the main entrance, but there was no sign of Briar or Hunter, who were patrolling outside and keeping watch.

Eventually the others returned to her side, and Alex said, "I've dragged the guard to the corner. Let's go."

El nodded and led them through the ticket area with the gift shop on the side, and found the door marked *Private* that Newton said led downstairs. It had a keypad on it, and she quickly disarmed it and opened the door.

A flash of light on the street made El hurry inside and down the stairs, Alex following them last.

"It was the security van doing a routine patrol," he told them. "Let's hurry up!"

El picked up the pace and arriving at the bottom saw the passage stretching ahead, multiple doors and corridors leading off it. "Bollocks!" She turned to see the others looking just as dismayed. "Let's split up."

Briar stood in the recess of a shop's doorway, draping herself and Hunter in a veil of darkness as she watched the security van slow and then take off again. While they paused, she used the opportunity to use a spell to urge them on their way...and to stay away.

"Bloody hell. I thought they were about to stop," Hunter said from behind her, whispering in her ear. He was encircling her with his arms, and she leaned against him, loving the feel of his arms around her and his muscular physique at her back. It sent shivers down her spine.

"I've spelled them. It should give us time." She fell silent as a couple strode past, laughing as they walked, and she was grateful the museum wasn't on one of the more main roads. When it was finally safe, she said, "They'll be as quick as they can."

A few cars passed them, but one was slow, too slow, and she tried to see the occupants. With a feeling of dread, she noticed one of them had blonde hair. "Bollocks! I think that's Mariah."

They watched the taillights round the bend, and Hunter asked, "Are you sure?"

"No, but I don't want to take any chances. Let's head around the back now, just in case."

Briar darted over the road and down the drive at the side of the building, and spotting a huge wheelie bin and a couple of vans at the rear of the compound, pulled Hunter to them. "Let's hide here."

"And if it's them?" he asked, settling into position.

"We have to stop them from going in."

He gave her feral smile. "Good. I'll change shape."

He whipped his clothes off and Briar took a moment to steal a kiss before she called Avery, hoping to warn her. But the phone kept ringing, and she tried the others, one after another.

"They must be out of reception—no one is answering!" Briar thought through her options. If it was Mariah and they couldn't stop her, she'd soon be inside, and the others would be cornered. They needed to be warned, and she was better able to defend the entrance than Hunter. "Will you find them and let them know, and come back when you're done? I'll hold them off."

He shook his head. "I don't like leaving you alone."

"You have to—just be quick! But change inside and make sure you shut the door behind you!"

He leaned down and kissed her, his eyes full of desire and worry. "Be careful." In seconds he ran across the car park, opened the door, and slipped inside.

Briar only had to wait a short while before her fears were confirmed, and she saw Mariah rounding the corner of the building. But it wasn't Zane who was with her. It was Harry. He was a tall, broad man, with a shaggy mane of hair and an imposing presence. As they approached the entrance, Briar struck, opening the ground beneath their feet. The concrete surface cracked and pitted, swallowing them up to their waist.

Both reacted quickly. Mariah whipped her arms up and sent fire around the car park in a whirling blaze, forcing Briar to dive for cover. She knew she'd given away her position, because Harry yelled, "There she is!"

Briar leapt to her feet, ready to strike again, but the huge wheelie bin next to her took flight and hit her, pinning her to the wall behind, and crushing her so badly that she felt ribs crack and could barely breath. Acting out of pure instinct, she struck back with a ball of energy. The bin rocketed across the ground, heading straight for

Mariah and Harry. But they were both out of the hole she'd made, and the bin crashed into it, upending rubbish everywhere.

While Mariah stood her ground, fire balling in her hands and her lips moving with a spell, Harry ran inside the building.

Avery heard the patter of paws before she saw Hunter, but in seconds he was in sight, racing down the corridor.

She had just emerged out of a storeroom with Alex, having found plenty of interesting artefacts but no treasure, and he muttered, "This can't be good news."

Hunter skidded to a halt and changed form, standing naked in front of them. Usually there was wicked glint in his eyes, because he knew it made Avery uncomfortable, but there was no glint this time. "Mariah and Harry are outside. I have to get back to Briar."

He shifted and ran back up the corridor, and Avery turned to Alex. "I'll go, you help find it. They *cannot* win!"

"Avery, you're the one transporting it out of here. *I* should go!"

She was about to argue, but knew he was right, so while he ran to help, she shouted, "Reuben! El! They're here!"

She heard a muted cry and ran to the top of another corridor, seeing El halfway down, looking at her with a puzzled frown. "What did you say?"

"They're here! Hurry!"

She ran back the way she'd come, leaving El to tell Reuben, and threw doors open in increasing annoyance. This place was huge, and she had never imagined there could be so much stuff stored down here. There were endless boxes and crates of a bewildering array of sizes, and shelves stacked with objects and books. *But where was the damn treasure? What if it wasn't here, after all?*

A yell caught her attention, and she ran to the top of another corridor to see Reuben running towards her. "Last door on the end. I'll help the others. And Avery," he paused, his eyes intense, "the treasure comes first. Get it to safety."

Without waiting for her response, he took off, and she heard several bangs and muffled shouts from above. Ignoring them, she had just arrived at the door when Reuben yelled and she saw him flying backwards, past the top of the corridor. A ball of fire followed him, with Harry in its wake.

Alex dragged himself out of the shattered glass case, wondering what the hell Harry had hit him with. His ears were ringing, and his vision was black at the edges, but he shook himself like dog, trying to decide whether to turn back or head to Briar.

A howl drew his attention, and he saw Hunter emerging from behind the reception counter, blood matting his fur and limping badly. The others temporarily forgotten, he ran over to him. "Hunter?"

He changed form, and Alex could see an ugly cut down his thigh. "I'm okay. Bastard caught me by surprise, but I took a chunk out of his leg. I'll survive."

The sound of an enormous bang drew both their attention, and as Hunter shifted again, Alex ran to the rear entrance, cursing the twisting corridors. As he rounded the final one, he saw Mariah framed in the doorway, as what appeared to be a cloud of flashing white light lit up the space in front of her. And with horror, he saw Briar suspended in it. Alex hurled a searing ball of energy and hit Mariah in the back, pitching her forward and on to her face. He followed it up with another, feeling a sharp sting of satisfaction as he saw her body twitch on the ground. The white light dissipated, and he heard a thud as Briar hit the ground.

Hunter streaked past him and jumped on Mariah, his huge jaws settling around her throat as he lay fully on her, pinning her to the ground. Alex yelled an incantation, binding Mariah's tongue, and then followed it up with another spell that bound her with runes. He wove them around her, thick and strong, seeing the terror and fury in her eyes, and it was only when he was satisfied that she couldn't break free that he nodded at Hunter. He gave her a final, vicious nip, drawing blood, and then both turned to Briar, looking like a ragdoll on the ground.

Reuben felt the ache deep in his injured shoulder from where he'd landed on the floor of the passage, the ball of fire sailing overhead and striking the far wall.

With a grunt, he leapt back to his feet in time to see Harry run down the corridor where the treasure was. *What the hell kind of power was Harry packing?* It seemed to come from a ring with a huge glowing stone on his left hand. *Was this part of the planetary parade stuff?*

He raced after Harry, regardless. He pulled moisture from the air, creating a thick mist that curled in front of him, and sent it after Harry like it was an octopus, the tendrils writhing and snaking as they reached for him. He was at the threshold to the room with the treasure when it caught him, and he fell in a heap, cursing.

Reuben advanced on Harry, tightening the mist's grip, but a glowing red light like a laser beam shot through the murk and Reuben ducked. The beam hit the wall, boring a hole through it the size of Reuben's head.

What the actual...

The mist vanished and Harry slammed the door open with a blast of energy, wood splintering everywhere as he strode inside. In seconds he emitted a cry of fury and returned to the corridor, his eyes wild, his entire body glowing with a peculiar red light as he pointed his finger at Reuben.

Fearing his head was about to be blasted off his shoulders, Reuben threw himself into the closest room as a ray of red light struck the doorframe. He was outmanoeuvred, no doubt about that, but it seemed that Avery and El had escaped with the treasure. He was preparing to attack when an explosion rocked the corridor. Poking his head beyond the doorway, he saw a huge, gaping hole in the ceiling and no Harry.

Avery arrived with El and the treasure in El's living room, then promptly announced, "I'm going back."

El was trying not to be sick after witch-flight, and after a few deep breaths said, "Not to the same room! He could be there."

"I'll aim for the corridor where Reuben was. Are you sure you'll be okay?"

"I'll be fine. Go!"

Avery summoned air and envisaged the corridor where she'd last seen Reuben. In seconds she was there, staring at blackened walls and smelling ozone. She ran to the junction of the corridors, and went slap-bang into Reuben's chest. "Shit!"

"Ave!" he grasped her arms. "You did it?"

"Done. El's fine. Where's Harry?"

He pointed up. "Blasted through the ceiling like some fucking demolition man. Come on."

He raced along the corridor and she followed, wary of using witch-flight again. She could end up in the middle of a fight with her back to the enemy, and besides, she didn't want to leave Reuben alone.

When they finally reached the ground floor, they both stopped in their tracks. The reception area was a disaster zone. The displays were shattered, their objects strewn everywhere, the counter was damaged, and a large smear of blood marred the floor.

"There are no bodies, Ave," Reuben said, running in the direction of the rear entrance. "That has to be good."

But when they finally reached the car park, they both skidded to a halt. Hunter, still a wolf, was standing over Briar's body, hackles raised and teeth bared at Harry, who stood transfixed a short distance from the entrance. Alex guarded Mariah, who was bound within writhing runes, an outstretched arm pointed at Harry.

"Harry, back off!"

For a moment, it seemed Harry would fight, and then he saw Reuben and Avery arrive. He enveloped himself in a cloud of thick black smoke, a crack of thunder coming from its midst, and in seconds he had gone.

Avery's ears were ringing, but she was relieved to see that her friends looked fine—except for Briar. Reuben cast a worried glance at Briar, and then turned to race after Harry.

Avery grabbed his arm. "Let him go. He's using magic I've never seen before. Let's not risk anything else. Alex, are you okay?"

"Battered, but happy we've got Mariah," he said, standing over her struggling body. "Although, I have no idea what we're going to do with her. But Briar..."

Avery was already running to her side, where Hunter nudged her with his nose and licked her face. Briar was horribly pale, but she was alive. Her clothes, however, were scorched, as was her hair. Avery placed her hand on Briar's forehead, uttering a healing spell. Briar's eyelashes fluttered, and with relief, Avery looked into Hunter's glowing yellow eyes. "She'll be okay, but we need to get out of here... to El's, for now. I'll take her first and come back for you. Grab your clothes."

He padded across to the far corner and Avery stood, noticing for the first time that there was glamour over the car park. She felt as if they'd made enough noise to raise the dead, but the windows that overlooked the space were still dark, and it seemed no one else had noticed a thing—yet. She joined Alex and Reuben, who were deep in conversation.

"Have one of you put a veiling spell over this place?"

"I did," Alex told her. "The last thing we wanted was locals running here to see what the hell was going on. But we need to find somewhere to take Mariah."

"Are we calling Newton?" Reuben asked.

"Not until we're well away from here. Avery, can you transport Mariah without breaking my binding runes?"

Avery shook her head. "I would hate to risk it."

"Then leave her to us." He flashed Avery a weary smile. "I'll be in touch."

Fifteen

El paced her flat as she waited for Avery and the others, wondering what was taking so long.

She eyed the crates full of gold coins that gleamed in the lamplight and couldn't help but shudder.

Ever since Nancy had called it blood-soaked gold, she couldn't think of it any other way. The deaths that had occurred in order to obtain this would have run to the hundreds, if not thousands. All the men who died trying to ship goods to Cornwall, only to be wrecked on the coast. The men who died trying to transport it off the beaches, through passages and caves, waging private wars and fighting with excise men. Blood-soaked didn't even come close. It was a bloodbath. Not to mention, Cruel Coppinger's gang had been worse than most. And on top of those deaths would have been the additional deaths or heartbreak of their widows, daughters, fathers, sons, and mothers. After all, smuggling was sometimes a family affair—dark, ugly, and rife with risk.

Suddenly, El wanted the gold out of her warm, comfortable apartment that was blessed with light and life. The treasure seemed to pulse with malevolent intent. *How could she have ever thought it exciting?*

Whirling blackness heralded Avery's return, and with a shock, El saw Briar at her feet. "Briar!" she cried out, racing over and crouching at her side. "What happened?"

"I have no idea! When me and Reuben found the others in the car park, it had already happened. I'm going back for Hunter."

Within seconds she'd gone again, and El shook Briar gently, murmuring her name. But Briar was unconscious, horribly still, her breaths shallow.

El made her comfortable, placing a pillow under her head and a blanket over her, and with a quick spell, she lit the fire in the grate, sending it blazing. Then she ran to her spell supplies, choosing a few gemstones she knew had healing qualities.

By the time she'd grabbed those, Avery and Hunter were manifesting on her rug. Hunter barely acknowledged El, instead sitting at Briar's side and holding her hand. "She looks awful," he murmured.

El exchanged a worried glance with Avery, and then settled on Briar's other side. "Did you see what happened?"

"No. Well, sort of." He tore his gaze away, and El saw that his eyes were ringed with yellow fire—a sure sign of his anger and agitation. "She sent me inside to warn you they'd arrived. By the time I got back, she was trapped in some sort of lightning strike."

"A *what*?"

"It was like this white light over the car park, crackling with energy. It was very odd. Alex hit Mariah with a ball of magic and it went away, but Briar hit the ground."

Avery crouched behind Briar's head and lifted it, and El felt underneath, her hands coming away streaked in blood. "Shit! I hadn't seen that. Okay, I have herbs that we can use to make a poultice, and a spell to bolster her healing. I'm not as good at healing as Briar is, but I can certainly help."

"Me too," Avery said. "And perhaps we call Eli?"

"Of course!" Relief swept through El. "Yes, but let's stabilise her first." It was then that she noticed Hunter sitting awkwardly, blood seeping through his jeans. "By the Gods! What happened to *you*?"

"Harry and a pane of glass. Don't worry, I took a chunk out of his leg." He snarled. "I'll take a bigger one when I see him next."

El felt she'd abandoned all of them in keeping watch on the pile of gold, and she glared at it. "And all because of that!"

"But we got it," Avery said, a note of triumph in her voice. "And Mariah."

El was heading back to her magic supplies, but that pulled her up short. "What?"

"Alex has her bound in runes in the carpark. They're moving her now."

"Where to?" El felt her panic mount. "They can't bring her here! And what the fuck are we going to do with her?"

Avery regarded her calmly. "We leave that with them and focus on Briar."

Reuben drove the museum van along the lane to his house, checking regularly on Alex in the back.

"Everything okay?"

"Everything's fine, except for the fact that Mariah is shooting daggers of hate at me with her eyes." He clambered up behind Reuben. "Are you sure about this?"

"Not really. Locking a woman in my cellar is not something I've ever aspired to do. It's sort of creepy." He glanced over his shoulder, seeing the runes binding Mariah glowing in the dark. "I amend that. It's super creepy. What the hell were you thinking, Alex?"

"I was thinking that she was attacking Briar and that I was next, and I needed to stop her, moron! I don't normally plan on kidnapping women, either. And besides, she's a bloody killer, and has seriously injured Briar."

Reuben felt an ugly wave of panic roll though him. "She'll be okay." *She has to be.*

Once alone in the carpark, he and Alex had realised that they hadn't got a car to use, as no one had planned on taking a captive. The only thing they had accommodated for was the treasure. They had improvised and stolen a museum van, using glamour to disguise the lettering on the side, and a spell that ensured no one would take any notice of them as they passed down the quiet roads of White Haven. Alex had waited until they were on the edge of town before calling the police anonymously and then Newton, and the sounds of police sirens had quickly followed.

Reuben continued, "Seriously. What are we going to do with Mariah? Kidnapping is an imprisonable offence, and I'm way too pretty to go to jail." He frowned at Alex. "And so are you. Besides, if you get imprisoned, Caspian will swoop in on your missus."

"Thanks for that reassurance, Reu, you gigantic tit of a man. I thought you said he was moving on."

Reuben shot Alex a guilty smile. "He is. But even so, with you gone…"

"I'm not going anywhere, and neither are you!"

Ignoring Alex's agitation, Reuben pulled onto the huge, circular driveway in front of his house, and then headed for the road than ran around the back toward the old stables and his garage, finally stopping at the side door. "This is the closest door to the cellars. There are some big rooms down there with sturdy doors, and we can make up a bed and ward the whole place with spells."

He exited the van, opened the door to his house, and then opened the van's rear doors. Real fear as well as fury had settled in Mariah's eyes now, and despite everything that Mariah had done, Reuben felt like shit.

"I hate this, Mariah," he said to her. "But this is your fault, and for now, I'm going to have to live with it. I am your karma—and karma is a bastard."

Alex had already pulled her to the rear doors, and he leapt out. "I'll take her feet, and you take her head. Just avoid the binding runes."

"And if I can't?"

"They'll give you an unpleasant buzz. Just like they're giving Mariah now."

Mariah was of average build and height, and they lifted her easily. Reuben guided them along the passage, down the stairs, and through the meandering cellar rooms. It was tricky, and they bumped into walls and shuffled through places until Reuben guided them into a room in the middle of the area, pushing open a door with his hip.

"Let's put her on the floor, for now."

They lowered her down, and Alex checked his runes again. Reuben saw them flare as he reinforced them, and Mariah winced.

"How long will they last?" Reuben asked Alex.

"As long as I need them to. But she'll need to eat and drink at some point." He stared at her. "I can adjust them to be around her ankles and wrists. Secure her to a wall, perhaps."

"But we can't keep her down here forever."

"Of course not. We need to think over our options. And we haven't got many."

"We have more than we had an hour ago. I'll go get my kidnappers kit—you know, blankets and shit. You'll be okay for a while?"

"I'll be just fine."

Newton surveyed the gigantic mess of White Haven Museum's reception area and raged silently. *This was supposed to be easy. In, out, with no one the wiser until the next morning.* But the place was a bloody disaster zone. And he had to pretend to know nothing. Well, to the other team, at least.

Normally, this wasn't his jurisdiction. This was theft, not murder, but with weird blast marks over the walls, a crater in the car park, and a hole in the floor between the basement and the ground level, everything indicated that this was clearly *not normal*. He'd had to wait impatiently for the call to come in, pretending he knew nothing, and then try not to arrive on scene too quickly.

He'd half wondered if he'd get called in at all. Alex had been brief on the phone, so the details were lacking, but just as he was beginning to doubt, his superior called him, and dutifully he called Moore and Kendall. His new sergeant couldn't keep her eagerness out of her voice.

She was currently examining the wall, properly dressed in her white coveralls, and she looked over at him. "What could cause these scorch marks?"

He swallowed. "Blasts of energy...*magic*. I've seen it before."

"Magic!" She sprang upright. "Witches? Wizards?"

"Perhaps. Many things have magical abilities. Let's take a stroll through the building and let SOCO do their thing."

Moore shot him an amused look, but said nothing as Detective Johnson, a big bear of a man with a huge, bushy beard who had been called in first, approached them. "Thanks for coming, Newton. It looks like there was a fight, so I suspect a couple of gangs arrived at the same time."

Johnson was competent, but hated complications, especial paranormal ones. Newton glanced around the space, trying not to give too much away. "Why don't you tell us what you have so far."

"Excellent." His head bobbed. "None of the exhibition halls are disturbed...well, apart from the one with a hole in the floor, but the exhibits are undamaged. The fight took place here, the car park, and the basement. And someone attacked the security guard."

That was unexpected. "Is he okay?"

"Fine, just shocked. Says he can't remember a thing." He nodded beyond Newton and his team to the first exhibition hall as he walked to the door to the basement. "We found him in there."

"And definitely no bodies?" Newton asked, following him down to the stairs, his sergeants in tow.

"No. But," he grimaced with annoyance, "there are plenty of scorch marks on the walls, so God knows what caused those." He shot Newton a dark look. "I'll leave you to work out that one."

"No problem. And do we know what's been stolen?"

"The museum director has just arrived—very upset," he added in an undertone. "It seems it was the treasure that was in the paper today."

Newton tried to look suitably shocked. "Ah! That was fast work, then."

Newton observed the marks on the corridor, hoping his friends were okay, but Johnson grunted as he rounded a corner and pointed at the ceiling. "That's the hole leading to the exhibition hall above. And the room the treasure was in is the last one on the right. The director is in the room opposite. I thought you might want to have a word."

Kendall spoke up. "I thought they had more security in place than just one guard!"

Johnson looked at her as if noticing her for the first time. "You're not normally on this team!"

"She starts today," Newton said, realising it was already after midnight. "And that's a good point. What about security?"

"In addition to the guard, the place is fully alarmed, but it was fried. And there's a security patrol who said they heard and saw nothing. And," he grunted again, "the security cameras are fried, too."

Relief swept through Newton, but he again looked annoyed. "That's the trouble with the paranormal—it undermines everything we normally use."

Arriving at the room the museum director was waiting in, they found a woman sitting on a lone chair looking rumpled, tired, and utterly shell-shocked. She was surrounded by boxes and unused exhibits.

Johnson introduced them. To any member of the public, Newton's team was referred to as a Special Operation, as they liked to keep the word *paranormal* out of it. "This is Ms Natalie Hughes, the museum's director."

Natalie rose to her feet, surprising Newton with her height, and shook his hand. She was almost as tall as him, in her forties, he estimated, with blonde hair and blue eyes, and a very firm handshake. "DI Newton. I'd like to say this is a pleasure, but it really isn't. I don't understand what's going on! Who did this?"

"It's too soon to know that, I'm afraid, but obviously we'll do everything we can to find them, and your treasure."

"But the scorch marks," she persisted. "What's caused them?"

"Probably a flamethrower," he suggested, thinking that was a terrible lie. "Not a usual weapon to use, but all thieves have their preferences. Once we've completed our investigation, we'll have a better idea. You're sure only the treasure was stolen?"

"It seems that way. Oh, and a van from the car park."

"A van?" Newton didn't know if that was good or bad, but he kept his face neutral. "Okay. Sergeant Moore will interview you, while I take a good look around with Sergeant Kendall. You can go home as soon as that's done."

She looked horrified. "Absolutely not! I have to stay!"

He shook his head. "No. You'll only get in the way. You can come back when we're done. And besides, the museum will be closed tomorrow."

"But—"

He turned away before she could finish, knowing Moore would go through it all, and instead led Kendall out.

"Right Kendall," he said with a smile once they were out in the corridor. "Time to get you acquainted with our processes."

Sixteen

Avery studied Briar, still lying unconscious on the bed they'd made for her on the floor in front of the fire, and said, "Eli will be here in minutes."

El tightened her grip on Briar's hand. "I'm not sure it will do any good! He hasn't got magical abilities like us!"

"But he is a healer," Avery insisted, "and I think we need all the help we can get."

"Agreed," Hunter said, a growl low in the back of his throat. "Anything he can do is useful."

"And," Avery added, "Eli will dress your injured leg far better than me or El."

"Forget about me. Briar is more important." He was holding Briar's other hand, but for all that his eyes burned with fury, his hold was gentle. "I just need to go out and hunt that bastard down."

"No!" Avery shot back. "I don't know what's going on with Harry's magic, but he's powerful. And I know you're fast and lethal, Hunter, but we can't risk you being hurt again. Besides, Briar would never forgive us." She reached forward and squeezed his shoulder. She had wondered if their relationship was waning, but there was no doubt about Hunter's feelings right now. "Let's make a better plan first."

She and El had just cast several healing spells, and Avery had tried to do what Briar did and feel her energy levels, but Avery was nowhere near as competent, and felt she was stumbling around in the dark.

"I'm going to make a drink," El said, rising to her feet and heading to the kitchen. "I need some tea to take my mind off things. What the hell are the boys doing?"

"What they have to," Avery mused, hoping Mariah hadn't escaped and that nothing was going horribly wrong. "As soon as Eli is here, I'll go to Reuben's place and see what's happening."

"There's no need to wait," El reassured her. "Go now. I'm as anxious as you are to see what's going on. And while you're there, see if we can hide the treasure there, too. I don't want that stuff here." She glared at the crates still in the middle of the floor. "I hate it."

"All right. Hunter, promise me not to do anything yet!"

He grunted. "I suppose I can wait for now. I'll track better when my leg is healed, anyway. But I'm not waiting long!"

"Don't worry, neither will we."

In seconds Avery was standing on Reuben's drive, and unaffected by his barrage of protection spells, she used magic to open the front door. Inside, however, the house was very quiet. She explored the ground floor, and seeing the open door leading to the cellar, she headed down, relieved to hear voices ahead.

Bare light bulbs illuminated the space, and she progressed through rooms and past open doorways, before finally finding the right one. When she stepped inside, she groaned.

"You've got to be kidding me!"

"Bloody hell, Ave!" Reuben said, whirling around. "You nearly gave me a heart attack!"

"I think *I'm* having one right now! What the hell are you two doing?"

"Making a magical prison, of course!"

Alex wasn't speaking, because he was concentrating on completing the cage constructed with blazing runes in the corner of the large, dusty, and damp room. The walls were made of brick, and the floor was packed earth, but in the corner was a rudimentary bed on which lay Mariah, still bound in runes. She was smeared in dirt and her hair was unkempt, but her eyes were wild as she glared at Avery.

Avery groaned again. "This is a nightmare."

Alex finished his spell and turned to her. "I know, but what choice have we got? If I release her now, we'll end up fighting again."

"But we have to let her go at some point!"

He nodded. "Of course. When we have a plan."

To be fair to Alex and Reuben, they both looked tired and jaded, and Reuben gave her a wry smile. "I didn't want Mariah here, Ave, but what else can we do?"

"You're right. But she'll need the bathroom at some point, and food and water!"

"I can adjust the rune chains," Alex said. "And lift the tongue binding, but only once she's secured in the cage. If I draw on your magic, as well as Reuben's, it will strengthen the cage even more. Are you happy to do that?"

Avery stared at Mariah, hating the fact that she was bound in a cellar and wondering what they'd turned into. In her position, Avery would be angry and scared. But Mariah was dangerous, and had been complicit in several deaths. "I'm not happy about it, but of course I'll do it."

Alex squeezed her shoulder. "Thanks. Let's do it now."

Together they faced Mariah within the rune cage and all three joined hands. Alex started an incantation, and the rune cage blazed with a fiery light. Other runes multiplied and thickened, and she knew Air and Water were being added to Alex's potent magic. Soon the cage was looking like a mesh of chainmail, the runes were so dense, and when Alex was happy, he completed the spell. Then he changed Mariah's personal rune chains, leaving them around her wrists only, and removed the tongue binding. In seconds, Mariah was on her feet, a stream of curses falling from her lips.

"It's pointless, Mariah," Alex told her. "Nothing can leave that cage. None of your spells, curses, or tricks."

"Think you're all so clever, don't you?" Mariah spat. "You sanctimonious fools. You can't keep me here forever! I will get out."

"You'll stay here for as long as we need you to," Alex warned her in a low, commanding voice. "And we'll find the others, too. There's blood on your hands, and karma seeks justice."

Mariah didn't speak, instead launching a series of fire balls and blasts of magic at the cage. Despite Alex's assurances, Avery retreated, but the rune chainmail repelled all of them. With a final glare, Mariah turned away, lay on the cot bed, and stared at the ceiling.

They headed to the far side of the room, conferring in low voices.

"I'll get another chair and a table, and a couple of other things," Reuben said. "I can keep first watch. Regardless of the cage, I don't want to leave her alone."

"That's good. We'll take it in turns," Alex agreed, looking at Avery with a raised eyebrow. "What about you?"

"I'll take my turn, and I'm sure El will, but Briar is still out cold, and we've called Eli in."

"Still unconscious?" Alex asked, eyes wide.

"Her clothes and hair were singed," Avery told them. "What spell was she caught in?"

Alex shrugged. "Hard to say. It was a huge storm cloud of lightning. Briar's quick and strong, so whatever it was must have overwhelmed her." He turned back to Mariah. "We can question her once she's calmed down. We may learn something."

Reuben snorted. "I doubt that. Give me five minutes to get everything sorted, and I'll be back."

He disappeared, and Avery lowered her voice again. "What the hell magic were they using, Alex? Was it some kind of planetary power thing?"

"I don't know, but maybe Cornell will." He stroked her cheek, and she pressed it into his hand, instantly calmed by his touch. All she wanted to do was go to bed and hold Alex tightly, but that wasn't going to happen any time soon.

"This isn't going to be over quickly, is it?"

"I'm afraid not. And at this moment, I have no idea what we're going to do with her." He jerked his head at Mariah.

"We'll think of something. I think we should tell Genevieve." She took his hand in hers. "And we need to tell our team. Oh, and another thing. El doesn't want the treasure in her flat...and I don't blame her. She feels it's cursed. I could bring it here, but I think having Mariah and the treasure in one place is a bad idea. What if we keep it at ours?"

"I think we should rotate it, actually. We can have it tonight, and maybe Cornell will want it, but if we do rotate, El will still have to take her turn!" He shrugged. "What's got into her? El doesn't normally get spooked."

"I don't know. I'll speak to her about it." She squeezed his hand. "I better go. I want to check on Briar. Are you sure about your cage?"

"It will hold." A troubled look flashed across his face. "I've just had a thought. I can't come home with you tonight. I want to stay here, keep an eye on Mariah and make sure Reuben is okay. Maybe you should also stay here, or with El."

She reached up and kissed him. "I'll be fine at home. But be careful. I'll see you tomorrow."

Newton stood on the car park at the back of the museum and lifting his head, inhaled deeply. "Smells of ozone."

"From a spell?" Moore asked.

"Perhaps."

Moore leaned against the wall, hands jammed in his pockets. "Our friends, the witches, were here, weren't they?"

Newton groaned and rubbed his eyes. "Is it that obvious it's them?"

"No. Just to me. They wouldn't have been so destructive, though, so who were they fighting?"

Kendall looked between them, her mouth falling open. "You know who did this? *Witches*?"

"Lower your voice, for the Gods' sake," Newton complained, relieved that no one was close enough to hear.

They'd just been all around the museum, walking through what they thought had happened, and watching SOCO take evidence, but he knew they wouldn't find much in the way of material clues. He needed to speak to the witches to find out the details. But first, he had to come clean to Kendall.

He faced her. "You need to know that I have five good friends who are also witches; they help us with lots of our paranormal investigations. And there are others, too. You'll meet them all soon enough. They were here tonight to get the treasure, because they needed to stop someone else stealing it. Other witches who, we think, want to do bad things with it. They are the ones responsible for all of the recent deaths."

She frowned and looked at Moore. "You know them, too?"

"I do. Not as well as Newton, but they help us all the time with our paranormal issues." He gave her a wry smile. "We need something paranormal on our side when we have to fight it."

Kendall nodded. "That makes sense. But they're not an official part of the team?"

"Not at all," Newton said, "but they are integral to it."

She folded her arms across her chest. "Why aren't you telling Johnson?"

"Because we keep things within our team! Our contacts are ours alone. Johnson doesn't need to know. And trust me, he doesn't *want* to know. He may have started this investigation, but it's ours now. Unfortunately, our remit runs to more than just murders. It involves anything paranormal, and this is firmly in that basket."

"You're saying we get the job done, but the other police don't want the details of how?"

"Exactly. We're doing what they don't want to acknowledge even exists. And besides, we don't interfere with other teams." He studied her curious expression. "What did you hear about us to make you want to apply?"

"That you dealt with weird stuff that wasn't easily explained, and that as odd things happened frequently in Cornwall, they needed a dedicated team. I've had odd experiences, as I told you in my interview. I was intrigued. But," she smiled, "you're right. Everyone skirts around what you do. It's like you exist in another dimension."

Newton and Moore laughed, and Moore said, "And it sometimes feels like it, too."

"So, we sort of operate in the shadows," Kendall said, a gleam in her eyes.

"Yes. Although, reports and results are still expected," Newton said, just so she didn't get the wrong idea.

"Cool! I like it! But it's dangerous."

Newton sighed. "Inez died on the job. Yes, it's dangerous. But we always try to be as safe as possible, obviously."

Moore brought their conversation back to the theft. "At least they didn't kill the guard. I guess our friends got here first. Are they okay?"

"I believe so," Newton said. He checked his watch. "I'll call Alex. But," he shot Kendall a warning look. "We won't formally interview them. This is between us."

Her hands were on her hips, her stance wide. "You're kidding, right?"

"Nope. Their involvement remains quiet. That's the price of their help."

"They've just stolen treasure, from a museum! They can't just get away with it."

Newton massaged his forehead and tried not to shout. Clearly, the intricacies of their arrangement were evading her. "They're not getting away with anything! They're helping us. They stole the treasure to stop someone from doing something bad with it. And actually, this is my fault," he reluctantly admitted, feeling like a fool. "I released the gold thinking it would be a positive thing to do, and that the museum would benefit from adding it to their exhibit. I had no idea I would set this off." He didn't add that Stan had badgered him for days on behalf of the museum.

He glanced at Moore for help, who said, "She needs to meet them. And besides, we have no leads right now. Only what they can give us."

Newton dug his phone from his pocket. "Let me phone Alex and see what I can do—but it won't be tonight. I suggest you both go home. And remember, I'm heading to London tomorrow. Moore, you're in charge while I'm gone."

He wondered whether he should cancel his trip, considering everything that was happening, but meeting Maggie after this seemed an even better idea. And besides, he really needed to get out of Cornwall. The wolf was here.

When Avery returned to El's flat, Eli was there, and surprisingly so was Zee. Both men seemed to take up a lot of space in El's living room, more than the average, human male. It wasn't just their height and build; it was their commanding presence. She was used to seeing them in the pub or the shop, but two of them together seemed to magnify their size.

They were dressed in jeans and t-shirts, their wings hidden in their mysterious way. They turned swiftly at her arrival, hands moving to the swords strapped at their sides, but then relaxed when they realised who it was, and Eli returned to his conversation with El. There was no sign of Hunter, but Avery could hear the shower running, and presumed he was in the bathroom.

"Avery," Zee said. "You've had an interesting night."

"That's one word for it. How come you're *both* here? Not that's it's a problem, obviously."

"We're alone in the farmhouse. Our brothers have gone to France with Shadow. Eli was reluctant to leave me alone after our attack the other night. Although," he shot him an amused glance, "I would have been fine. It's not me they're after. And I was worried about Briar."

They both studied her, and Avery was relieved to see that her colour looked better. "What has Eli done?"

"Mixed some potion or another, and guided El with another healing spell. He doesn't have your magic, but he is pretty good at diagnosing."

"And what was the verdict?"

Eli turned his head at Avery's question. "I think she's had a series of electric shocks. That's why she's singed around the edges." He raked his hands through his hair, a frown creasing his face. "Hunter tells me she was caught in an electrical storm."

Avery nodded. "We believe so...a magical one."

"A lightning strike can kill—even when you're earthed—and Briar was *suspended* in it. But she is an earth witch, grounded and steady in her magic, and the Green Man dwells within her. I think that's what saved her. But she's in shock. I think she needs earth beneath her to help her heal. I've also brought a special tea for when she comes round, and have recommended more gemstones to help her recovery."

El looked at Avery hopefully. "Can you bring in some soil?"

Avery laughed, bewildered. "Sure. I've got some in my potting shed. I can get it now. This night just gets weirder and weirder."

El frowned. "Are the boys okay?"

"They're fine, although Reuben's cellar has become a prison," she said, explaining what they'd done.

Zee whistled. "Herne's balls. That's unexpected."

"And then some."

He shook his head as he looked at Eli. "And there we were thinking our brothers would have all the fun."

Avery sank onto the sofa as exhaustion hit her. "We haven't stopped in hours! I don't think I've ever done so much witch-flight in such a short time."

Zee sat next to her. "You weren't expecting such a fight at the museum?"

"No! I mean, we thought we might run into them, but nothing like what actually happened."

El dropped into a graceful cross-legged position on the rug. "It was far more than I expected. And I still can't believe Alex captured Mariah."

"We have to take turns watching her," Avery said. "Even though she's in a rune cage. I can't believe we're in this situation."

Zee and Eli considered them both, exchanging speculative glances, and Zee said, "Well, we are happy to help. We're not immune to magic, but it doesn't affect us as much as others. We can take watch too if needed. And help hunt the others down."

"Are you sure you want to get involved?" Avery asked. "It's already messy, and could get much uglier."

Zee laughed. "Oh, Avery. You don't know us at all if you think we'd back out at the threat of *ugly*. We all love a good fight—even lover boy, Eli."

"Funny guy," Eli said, mock-offended.

Zee squeezed Avery's hand. "Have a cup of tea with El and rest. I'll fly to your place and get the compost, and we'll get sleeping beauty arranged on her bed of earth. And while I'm gone," he looked up as Hunter limped in, a towel slung low over his hips, blood already soaking through it and dripping down his leg, "Eli can clean up the wolf before he ruins El's floor." He stood and rolled his shoulders. "And then I think I might pay Alex and Reuben a visit."

Zee landed on Reuben's drive just as Newton was getting out of his car, and he regretted startling him.

Newton backed against the car. "Bloody hell! I thought I was about to be attacked!"

"Sorry, Newton. Good timing, though. I can come in with you."

Newton looked at him suspiciously as he folded his wings away and pulled his t-shirt on. "What are you doing here?"

"Avery called Eli to help with Briar, and I thought I'd see what's going on here."

Newton froze. "Briar? What's wrong with her?"

Shit. "You didn't know? She was attacked by Mariah. She's unconscious, but she'll be okay."

"Unconscious!" Newton floundered, and looked as if he was about to get back in his car. "Where is she?"

Zee had forgotten how much Newton liked Briar. It must sting, with Hunter being here. "She's at El's flat and she's safe. Avery, Hunter, and Eli are there, too. She's in good hands."

For a second, it seemed Newton had got his emotions under control, but then he let fly. "Fuck it! Bastard! Shit!" He kicked his car tyre several times, then paced across the gravel, yelling more obscenities at the sky. "Is it that bloody wolf's fault?"

"No. It is solely Mariah's fault."

"I'll wring her fucking neck!"

Zee perched on the low stone wall that edged Reuben's sweeping steps and folded his arms across his chest, prepared to listen. He liked Newton. They'd chatted about football while Newton sat at the bar some nights, and right now, he was a man with a lot on his mind, and he looked exhausted as well.

Newton continued to pace. "I need to question Mariah, and find the others! I need to stop them all!"

"*We* need to, not just you. You have a whole team. And you can't find them now. It's some stupid time of the morning, and Mariah won't talk yet."

"If anything happens to Briar…"

"Don't worry about Briar."

"Don't tell me what I should do!" Newton snapped, rounding on him. "Briar is hurt, and there's a bloody witch in Reuben's cellar! Kidnapped, to boot! What am I supposed to do about that?"

"Nothing. You have your side of the investigation, and we have ours." Zee had no idea at what point the problem had become *ours*. Ever since he'd offered an exhausted Avery his support, he guessed.

"Kidnapping is still kidnapping, no matter that she has killed people and injured Briar!"

"And where exactly are you going to lock her up, Newton?"

Newton glared at him. "Stop being so bloody logical!"

"Why are you even here? You shouldn't be. Don't get involved in this side of things."

"I'm leading the sodding investigation!"

"The police half. Do you trust Alex and Reuben?"

"Of course I do!" Newton looked at him like he'd grown two heads.

"Then you know they'll keep Mariah safe. They won't abuse her or torture her."

"I know they won't! They're not monsters!"

"Exactly. I would imagine they're both freaking out right now. You raging in there won't help."

Newton looked as if the will to live was leaching out of him, and he sank onto the gravel and leaned against his car. "This is a nightmare."

Zee knew Newton wanted to do something. *Anything.* He walked over and sat on the gravel next to him. "You'll stop them—one way or another. Focus on what you can do when you catch the rest of them."

Newton nodded, staring at Reuben's house vacantly. "That's partly why I'm going to see Maggie tomorrow. All of the other crap we've dealt with had a solution, but I wasn't worrying about rogue witches who happen to be real people before."

Zee was pretty sure that wasn't exactly true. Newton had dealt with ordinary people involved with paranormal weirdness before, but he wouldn't debate that now. "You'll work it out. Have you had any sleep?"

"Not really. People," he shot him an annoyed look, "tend to wake me up, reporting attacks."

"Sorry. And you're still grieving Inez. Go home, get some sleep, and enjoy London. I think you need a real break."

"That's what Caspian said, but this is my job!"

"Doesn't mean you can't get away for a night or two. You two should get drunk and get laid. That would make you feel a lot better."

Newton grunted. "I don't want to sleep with Caspian."

Zee bellowed with laughter. "I didn't mean him, but to each his own. If it's any help, I don't think Briar will stick with the wolf forever. He's a good guy, but he's not her forever guy." And he meant it, too. Hunter gave Briar something she wanted right now. She needed something else for her future happiness.

"Are you some kind of agony aunt, now?"

Weird, Alex had said much the same thing. "When the shoe fits."

"Okay. You're right. I'm going home and getting some sleep. Are you sure she's okay?"

"As much as I can be. Eli is confident in her recovery. Any messages for her?"

"Just that I send my best." Newton struggled to his feet, and Zee stood, too.

"Are you okay to drive?"

"I'm tired, not an imbecile," he said as he got into his car. "Tell the guys to be careful—and that includes you."

Zee winked and saluted, watched him drive off, and then turned to the house.

Time to see what a caged witch looked like.

Seventeen

When Caspian arrived at El's flat on Thursday morning, it was to find the blinds down, the lights dim, and the mood sombre.

"I wish one of you would have called me sooner," he complained to El as he accepted a cup of tea. He looked over at Briar, lying unconscious on the bed of earth in front of the fire. The room was too warm for his liking, but it made sense to keep Briar comfortable. "How do you think she's doing?"

El sighed and mussed up her hair. She looked different without her makeup on. Younger, more vulnerable, but no less pretty. "Hard to say. It seems she's sleeping now, more than being simply unconscious. Her energy levels seem better...not that I read them very well."

"She smells better," Hunter said, turning to them. He was sitting by her and looked as if he'd lain next to her all night.

"Smells better?" Caspian asked, confused.

Hunter tapped his nose. "We're good at picking up all sorts of scents. We can smell disease and ill health." He looked at her affectionately. "She definitely has a more normal Briar scent now."

Caspian had never considered that shifters could scent disease before, but that made sense. People trained dogs now to do such things. "That's good news. I can drive to London feeling more optimistic, at least." He studied El's worried expression. "I wish I'd come with you last night."

"I'm glad you didn't, considering your injury. It was tougher than we thought. Besides, we're okay—more or less. Eli worked wonders on Hunter's leg."

Caspian looked around, shocked. "You were hurt, too?"

"Bloody pane of glass sliced through my leg, but Eli used some of his miracle poultice, and it feels amazing." He stretched his leg out with a slight wince, allowing Caspian to see the ragged tear in his jeans and the dried blood on it. "It will just be another war wound. I have plenty."

"Looks like it was deep. I'm glad you're okay. All of you."

"Who phoned you?" El asked him.

"Reuben. He'd just emerged from the cellar after Alex took the second watch. He decided that six o'clock was a respectable time to call." He laughed. "It wasn't. But I was glad to hear from him. It sounds like a mad night."

El gave a very unladylike grunt. "It was. He phoned me about the same time, but it was brief. He was heading to bed."

"I've already called Avery." He winced with guilt as he remembered her grumpy tone. "I think I woke her up."

El sniggered. "If you phoned her before eight, you would have. She is not an early riser!"

"Ah, well. I told her to keep hold of some of the treasure—not to hand it all to Cornell yet. I think that keeping it split up is better than the initial plan of moving it around." He shrugged, unable to explain the sense he'd had of the need to do that. "It's just a feeling."

"Great. That probably means I'm going to have to keep some here, after all. Whatever. How long are you planning on being in London for?" El asked.

"Only a couple of days. Hopefully I'll be back tomorrow night, if not, then Saturday. It depends how quickly Olivia will be around, and what other business Newton has."

El smiled, illuminating her face. "That's so good of you to take him with you. I'm worried about him. He's not really processing Inez's death. He still blames himself! And I know he's frustrated at this investigation."

"I'll be glad of the company. And I've booked us into a good hotel."

"He'll like that, I'm sure," Hunter said, joining them in the kitchen and refilling his mug with tea. "Who wouldn't?"

Caspian shrugged. "Hopefully it will help him de-stress. A bit of luxury should help."

"Costs a fortune, does it?" Hunter asked, cocking an eyebrow.

"Actually no, but it is London, so you pay more for anything half decent. And it's *very* decent. I'll offer to pay, but I doubt he'll accept it."

"Of course he bloody won't!" Hunter said, looking shocked. "He has his pride!"

"I think it's lovely of you," El said, shooting Hunter a warning look. "Sometimes men just need to accept that friends like to be nice, and put their bloody egos aside."

Friends. There was that word again. And El was right about egos. Every single one of his new male friends had very healthy egos. He shrugged. "I guess I'll soon find out, won't I?" He checked his watch. "I was hoping to look in on Alex and Reuben, but I don't think I'll have time. I'm really not sure how I feel about seeing Mariah, either."

El walked around the kitchen breakfast bar and perched on a stool. "I honestly hate what Alex has done, although I accept why he's done it. And I hate that Reuben's house has been turned into a prison! I also hate," she said, her voice rising, "that I will have to take my turn watching her!"

Caspian exchanged a worried glance with Hunter, and said, "I'll take my turn, too, until we think of a better solution. I take it no one has informed Genevieve?"

"I certainly haven't."

"Someone needs to."

"Alex can. It's his bloody fault," El complained.

Caspian had never heard El criticise any of her coven before, so this was worrying. And he never thought he'd hear himself defending Alex, either. "He did what he had to do. It was the right thing."

El glared at both men. "She's a woman trapped in a cellar, imprisoned by two men! What the fuck?"

"She's a witch who nearly killed your friend," Hunter said, his Cumbrian accent accentuated by his tone. "It was the right call. And even more reason for you to go by and check on her. She might like to see another woman. Might even open up to you."

El looked mollified. "Maybe. But doubtful. She hates all of us. And I know Alex and my mad boyfriend are right, but it leaves me feeling so uncomfortable!" She dropped her face in her hands, and when she looked up, she took a deep breath. "I'll have a shower and then I'll go. Hunter, are you okay to stay with Briar on your own?"

"Of course I am. I'll call you if anything happens. You too, Caspian."

Caspian drained his tea. "Thank you. In that case, I'll get on my way, and if I think of anything to help, or learn anything useful at all, I'll call."

El leaned over the counter and unexpectedly kissed his cheek. "Safe travels, Caspian. Come home safely, too. They could still get to you in London. Both of you."

Avery was still lying in bed, even though she knew she should get up and get ready for work. Both cats sprawled on either side of her, as they luxuriated at having more of the bed than they normally did.

Despite the late night and jumbled thoughts, Avery had slept reasonably well, but the idea of getting up and actually facing the day was something else. She'd dozed again after Caspian's call, but now she pondered his request. Splitting up the treasure did make some sense, but part of her wanted to give the whole lot to Cornell. But for the very same reason she hadn't wanted him with them last night, she was also loath to give him everything.

She smacked her forehead with her palm. She really needed to stop being so suspicious. Cornell was helping them, and Claudia trusted him. And she trusted Claudia and Caspian, so she'd do as he asked.

Giving the cats one final fuss, she got up and wandered into the attic, her gaze falling on the crates where she'd left them smack in the middle of the rug last night. Lifting them up with a whirl of air, she placed them on the far side of the room, and draped them in shadows and glamour, as much to hide them from sight as to keep them safe. She really didn't want to look at them, and realised El's distaste had become her own.

By the time she'd showered, fed the cats, and arrived in the shop, it was past nine and Happenstance Books was already open, although devoid of customers. Dan was playing Louis Armstrong on the sound system, and the shop felt like a warm, safe haven.

Dan's expression, however, said volumes. "Herne's balls, Avery, you guys caused a lot of havoc last night!"

"Is it on the news?"

He rolled his eyes. "On the news? Of course it bloody is! The press is at the museum now. And as usual, there's endless speculation!"

"Bollocks," she groaned, clutching her head, and sitting on a stool behind the counter with him. "I'd forgotten about the aftermath."

"Like police and SOCO and all the ordinary trappings of committing crime?"

She looked up at him, shocked, but he was teasing her, a smile twitching his lips. "Piss off. We had to get the treasure before the others did. And we managed it—just about." She explained what had happened and told him how Briar had been injured, but omitted how they had captured Mariah. It made her feel like a monster.

"What aren't you telling me?"

Crap. She was such a bad liar. "It's probably best you don't know. Where's Sally?" she asked, suddenly realising she was nowhere in sight.

"Went for early coffee and cakes. We decided it was going to be one of *those* days. Plus, there's the added bonus of hearing the town gossip. She may have gone via the museum."

Avery sniggered. "Even though it's completely in the wrong direction?"

"She's exploring new coffee shops."

"You two! What would I do without you?"

"Go broke, for one thing, seeing as we keep your shop running. I presume you'll be popping off somewhere today?"

She nodded, sobering. "Yes. I'll head to Reuben's house soon. And I'll take the you-know-what with us."

Dan's eyes widened. "It's *here*?"

"Not for long. I feel it's like keeping a stick of dynamite around."

Dan closed his eyes and pinched the bridge of his nose. "Great. And any news of supercharged stone circles?"

"No. I'll add that to my list of things to find out."

"I might give Dylan a call, anyway. I'm intrigued. And worried. Everything feels cataclysmically charged."

"Thanks. You say the most reassuring things."

"I know. What happens now?"

"Good question." They seemed to have so many things on the go that Avery's head was spinning. "Cornell is working on a strategy to do with planets and correspondences. We think that's what Harry's doing, so we're trying to either use it ourselves or negate his plans."

"Which you think are connected to the ancient stone circles?"

"Yes. Frankly, I have no idea how that's going right now, but we thought the treasure might help."

"I guess you'll need to get some to him today, then. It's tonight, isn't it? The planetary parade?"

Avery groaned as she realised what day it was. "Shit. My week seems to be racing by. I guess I should, then. But I'll have to drive. I have no idea where he lives, so I can't use my preferred method of transport."

"You shouldn't go alone."

"No. I'd better head to Reuben's and see what's happening there first." She stood with a grimace, not looking forward to seeing the captured witch.

Dan was persistent. "What *is* happening at Reuben's?"

"Nothing at all! Will you be okay if I pop out now?"

For a moment he said nothing, just regarded her with a worried frown. "You're hiding something big, I know it. Just be careful, Avery."

El's stomach was churning with worry and anger as she watched Mariah test Alex's gilded rune cage again and again. Sparks flew from where her magic collided with his.

"By the great Goddess, Alex! This is unbelievable!"

"My amazing cage? I know. I've even impressed myself."

She glared at him, furious with his flippancy. "This isn't funny!"

Alex quickly sobered. He looked tired. His hair was pulled away from his face and bound up on his head, revealing a jaw covered in more stubble than usual, and dark shadows under his eyes. "I'm trying to see the positives in a shitty situation. But remind me again, how is Briar doing?"

Alex's comment stung, but it was a timely reminder of what Mariah had done. She didn't answer, instead staring at Mariah again, who finally stopped spell casting and glared at El. "Pleased with yourself?"

El advanced on her, covering the distance between them until she was only a few feet from the cage. Mariah looked grubby and unkempt, but uninjured. "You have brought this on yourself, Mariah! I hate the fact that you're in there, but I hate even more than you have killed people and injured Briar—who, by the way, will be just fine!"

"What a shame. That interfering bitch should have left well enough alone. You all should have!" She looked beyond El to where Alex watched from the corner. "This is something you won't win."

Alex gave a hollow laugh. "Brave words from the witch in the cage."

"I'll find a way to get out." Her gaze slid back to El, her eyes dancing with malice. "You have no idea what you're dealing with."

El was not about to tell her what they did know. Mariah's statement was a probe. And if she did get out, El didn't want her informing the others. Instead, she said, "I know Lowen is probably not feeling too good right now. Half of your team is down, Mariah, and trust me, we're working on the other two."

There seemed to be a flash of pleasure on Mariah's face before she turned her back and lay on the bed, taunting, "You can try."

El returned to Alex's side, and certain of what Mariah's expression meant, mouthed, *There are more of them.*

He nodded, but when he spoke his comment was innocuous. "I'd love a cuppa."

"Do you want me to bring you one down or do you want to stretch your legs?"

"You go," he said, settling back in his chair. "I can manage another hour until I'm sick of the sight of her."

El headed to the kitchen, where she found Reuben dressed only in his board shorts, making coffee and cooking bacon. As usual, his abs were ripped and he had a deep tan, even deeper than normal now that it was summer.

"Hey, babe," she said, kissing his cheek. "I thought you'd be sleeping for hours yet. How are you?"

"Not so bad, considering there's a killer witch in my cellar. How's Briar?"

"Still unconscious, but better, we think. Hunter is with her."

"Good," he said, turning to flip the bacon. "Want some?"

"Yes, please." Reuben seemed to be cooking for ten people. "Are you expecting more guests?"

He winked. "Me and Alex have been busy, and I'm starving. And besides, I expected that you'd drop in. Why aren't you at work?"

She pulled plates from the cupboard. "Zoe is covering for me, and she was able to get her friend, Petra, to help. I can take my turn watching Mariah."

"That's good of you, but we've got this. I know you hate what we've done."

"But I also know you had no choice. It's just a shitty situation."

"And we have no idea when it will end."

They both heard movement behind them, and turned to see Avery striding in from the snug. "Hey, guys. Mmm! Bacon."

"You see?" Reuben said. "I knew I'd need lots of breakfast." He peered beyond Avery, through the open door. "Can I see the treasure?"

Avery nodded. "I didn't want to leave it in my shop."

El looked at it with distaste. "No, of course not."

"I need a favour from someone. I have to take some of the gold to Cornell. I've already phoned him, and he's at home working on a spell. Can someone come with me?"

Reuben gestured to El. "El can. Me and Alex have got this covered."

El shot him a grateful smile, a wave of relief rushing through her. It would be good to spend a few hours with Avery, talking things through. "Thanks. But I will take my turn. It's only fair."

"We both will," Avery insisted. "But we have to do this first."

"Only once you've had breakfast," Reuben insisted as he started plating up. "Can someone take these down to Alex and Mariah?"

"I will," Avery said immediately. She cocked an eyebrow at El. "I'll see if I hate this situation as much this morning as I did last night."

Eighteen

Zee heard the door of The Wayward Son swing open, and saw Moore and a tall, athletic woman with short hair and a heart-shaped face head to the end of the bar where Newton and the witches normally sat. A stir of unease ran through him as he walked over to speak to them.

"Morning, Sergeant. Is everything okay?"

Moore raised his eyebrows. "As well as they can be, after recent events." He nodded to the woman next to him. "I've brought Sergeant Kendall to meet you. It's part of her—" he hesitated, "*induction*, I guess I would call it. Kendall, this is Zee."

Zee shook Kendall's hand, pleased to find a strong grip. She scanned him, taking in his build and bruises. "You've been in a fight."

He grinned. "You could say that." He looked at Moore. "Have you told her about Monday night?"

"I thought I would now, over a pint." He glanced down the bar. "No Alex?"

"He's at Reuben's, taking care of some business." He had no idea what Moore knew, even though he was Newton's trusted sergeant, and he certainly wasn't about to spell it out over the bar. Zee reached for a pint glass. "What do you want to drink?"

"Pint of Doom for me. Kendall?"

"And for me, please." She leaned on the bar, her eyes everywhere.

It was Thursday at lunchtime, so the pub was reasonably busy, and the scent of good food was strong. Simon, the manager, was at the other end of the bar, and he glanced over, his eyes widening with a question. But Zee just nodded. Simon never said much, but Zee knew he understood some of what Alex was about. He was pretty certain he knew nothing about Zee, however, and he was keen to keep it that way. All he'd told him about Monday night was that the farmhouse had been targeted in a robbery.

"This is a nice pub," Kendall observed, taking the pint Zee slid over the bar.

"You haven't been here before?" Zee asked.

"I live near Truro, so no. Moore has told me though that Newton is a regular, and has," she lowered her voice, "good paranormal links here."

"I guess he has." Zee looked at Moore. "I don't remember Inez being given an induction."

"Inez had more paranormal policing experience, but in retrospect, not introducing her sooner was a mistake. I thought that if Kendall met some of our key players, it might help her understand how things work. And," Moore admitted with a sigh, "our morning has been frustrating."

"No leads on last night?" Zee asked.

Moore sat on a barstool, indicating Kendall should do the same. "No fingerprints or indications of where the perpetrators might be. Harry's car was seen on CCTV, but then disappeared. We've picked up nothing since he left White Haven. All we have is Alex's version of events, and the guard's vague memory of being attacked."

"And no sign of Zane, Lowen, or Mariah?" Again, he wasn't sure if they knew that Mariah was locked in Reuben's cellar.

"No. We're chasing down friends and family where we can. In fact, we'll be questioning Harry's wife again this afternoon."

"Is that wise?"

"Wise or not, we need leads. They're hiding somewhere, and someone out there must know something." He grabbed a menu and nodded towards a table in the corner. "We'll grab a seat and I'll update Kendall on your brothers."

Zee groaned under his breath as he watched them settle at the table, knowing that Kendall was going to be looking at him with a great deal more than just idle curiosity later.

Bollocks.

Briar blinked and winced. Everything ached, and something smelled funky. Burnt. *Where the hell was she?*

Alarmed, she lifted her head and focussed, recognising El's living room. Relieved she was somewhere safe, she lay down again, and then wondered what she was lying on. It felt odd, but strangely comforting.

She lifted her hands, saw soil beneath her nails, and groaned in confusion.

"Briar!" Hunter said, and with a flurry he landed beside her and grabbed her hand. "You're awake."

"Hunter! I thought I was alone." She struggled to sit up, and he eased her upright. "What's going on? Why am I on a pile of soil?"

"Don't you remember?" He searched her face. "It's good to see you awake. I was so worried. We all were!"

Hunter's hair was standing on end, and he seemed to be in pain. She could feel it. "You're hurt."

"Just my leg. Eli patched me up. I'll be okay. How are you feeling?"

She rubbed her head with her free hand and then realised she was smearing herself in dirt. "Will you please tell me why I'm at El's place, lying on soil!" She knew she was sounding cranky, but she absolutely couldn't remember why she was there.

"You were caught in some weird magically-generated lightning storm. Don't you remember?"

Real panic started to swell in Briar now. "The last thing I remember is being on the road, outside the museum." She stared at Hunter. "By the Goddess! How much have I forgotten?" She looked around El's dark, warm flat. "Where is everyone else?"

"They're all fine. Don't panic. You were the only one hurt—well, significantly. The soil was to ground you and help you heal."

He patiently explained what had happened, holding her hand tightly within his own strong one. She could feel the callouses from his previous fights. Hunter was always a fighter. It was in his blood. He brooded and strutted and stood up for himself, and anyone he needed to look after, including her. But he had a big, kind heart, and he made her feel safe.

Briar started to well up. "I feel like I've lost a part of myself. I can't remember any of that!"

"You were alone because you sent me inside. I won't leave you again!"

She squeezed his hand. "If I sent you away, it was for a good reason. You say the others are all okay?"

"Yes." He rose to his feet. "I'm going to make the tea that Eli left. He insisted you have it as soon as you woke up."

Briar suddenly realised it felt very late. "What time is it?"

"Almost two in the afternoon, on Thursday. You haven't lost days or anything."

"My shop!"

"Is being covered by Eli and Cassie."

She tried to stand and failed. She felt as if all her strength had been drained, and she realised now what the soil was for. But she needed to be grounded in it properly. That would help more than anything.

"I need to be outside."

"And you will be, soon enough. Tea first."

"But—"

"But nothing!" He walked over to the kitchen, laughing. "You know when you swear at Reuben for not listening to you? You're doing the same."

"Am not! I know what I need!"

"And so does Eli!" He winked. "I'll give you a massage if you behave."

She melted at just the thought of it. Hunter's strong hands gave the perfect massage. "All right, sneaky. And then I'll head out. And then I'll heal *you*!"

"Only if you're strong enough."

He returned with the brew, and she sniffed it appreciatively. "Eli's so good at making tea." She sipped it, feeling it start to energise her already. As her focus returned, she noticed her singed clothing and saw that the ends of her hair were burnt, too. "Herne's balls! Look at me!"

"You're still beautiful," he said, kissing her. "Eli reckoned the Green Man helped you survive."

Briar knew she wasn't invincible, but she had considered herself capable of defending herself against many things. It was shock to find herself like this. But mention of the Green Man did trigger a memory. "I had weird dreams."

"Like what?"

"A searing heat. It was awful. I could feel my skin burning, and then suddenly all I could feel was cool earth and the sound of singing. A gruff voice." She'd been staring into her tea, but now she looked at Hunter. "Eli's right. It *was* the Green Man. It was like he wrapped me in a blanket and sang to me." She smiled. "A weird, earthy song of leaves and roots and damp, dark places." Realisation flooded through her. "He saved me."

"Then I owe him a debt."

"So do I." She wasn't sure she could ever repay the Green Man, but she'd find a way to do something for him. "I'm sorry, Hunter. Last night wasn't how I wanted to welcome you back to White Haven."

He kissed her fingers. "I don't know what I would have done if I'd lost you. I may not see you very often, Briar, but I can assure you that I think of you all the time, and I'm not leaving any time soon. Have you finished your tea?"

She nodded, quickly draining the dregs, her heart already pounding.

"In that case," he said, moving behind her and starting to knead her shoulders, "it's massage time. And then a shower. Actually," he said, kissing her on her neck and sending a thrill of desire rocketing through her, "I'm sure El won't mind if we shower together."

Cassie finished serving a customer, packaging Briar's handmade soaps and candles with care, before waving her out of the shop. Then she heard Eli's phone beep from where he was weighing herbs further along the counter.

He checked it and grinned at her. "Briar's awake."

Cassie was about to restock some shelves, but instead she leaned against the counter. "That's excellent. And she's okay?"

"A loss of memory, according to Hunter. That doesn't surprise me, but it might come back."

She studied Eli, always impressed at his healing abilities and knowledge of herbs, especially because of his warrior build and background. She found him enigmatic. And he was dazzlingly good looking, even with his current bruises and cuts. If she was honest, she had a bit of thing for him, not that she'd ever tell anyone.

Cassie nodded. "She's in shock."

"Her body has had a traumatic experience, and the brain blocks out such things. It's a protective mechanism. But she's strong." He bagged up some more herbs. "I found out that Barak was injured last night, too."

"Oh, no! Is he all right?"

"He was poisoned, but apparently he experienced some kind of healing that came from his father. Latent power he didn't know he had. It seems," he said with a smile, "that our fathers have the power to surprise us, even now."

"Your angel fathers." She watched him, curious as to how much he or any of them would have looked like their fathers.

"Fallen angels," he reminded her.

"They were still angels! Wow. I can't even believe I'm saying that. You guys are fascinating. Most days," she confessed, "I forget your background, and then it comes flooding back. It's so weird!"

"For me, too! Especially when I wonder if he's still out there somewhere, watching."

"But angels don't die, do they?"

"Sure, they do. Just not that easily. Many died after the fall." He continued to work as he talked, a far-away expression on his face. "There was a war...a big one."

Cassie knew this from the occasional comment Eli had made before, but he didn't often talk about his past. She decided to take advantage of it. "But you were born after all that."

He looked across at her. "It was a war that didn't end. It was still happening during my lifetime, and we presume it continued after the Flood. Now, I'm not so sure." He shrugged. "As long as they leave us alone, I don't much care. But enough of that. It's history—ancient history."

Deciding not to push, Cassie asked, "Barak works at Caspian's warehouse, doesn't he?" She had never met him, but had heard about all of them.

"Yeah. For now. That may change, depending on how much work we get. I, however, will remain here."

"Don't you think you'll miss out on where they go and what they do?"

He winked at her. "Nope. Let's face it, it's not like this place is boring. And I keep busy enough."

Cassie knew exactly what that meant. One of his girlfriends had already been by that day, and he'd arranged to see her after work. She'd cooed over his injuries, and Cassie had headed to the herb room to leave them in peace.

"So," he continued, pushing the scales away and settling on a stool, "have you found out more about the stone circles?"

She nodded, slumping on a stool, too. "Ben and Dylan went to King Arthur's Hall on Bodmin yesterday, in the daylight, and found that's been activated, too—if that's even the right word."

"The stones are harnessing energy?"

"That's the only way we can describe it. We talked about it last night, and decided to head to a couple of circles in the south of Cornwall, but interestingly enough, they are not affected."

Eli nodded, his focus distant for a moment before fixing her with his seductive gaze—because it *was* seductive, whether he meant it to be or not. "So, it seems only Bodmin is affected."

"And the two just a few miles away. Maybe it's a residual effect. Dylan and Ben will check the other circles down south today. They want to exclude them all."

"And we would never have known, had you not been investigating?"

"No. It's scary," she admitted. "We still have no idea what might happen. It might be nothing..."

"Or, it could be *something*."

Avery looked at the stone altar in Cornell's garden with surprise. "That's enormous!"

He smiled. "I decided that if I was going to have an altar within a grove, I may as well go big!"

El was strolling around the sacred space, looking impressed. "Wow. Maybe Reuben should have one of these. He's got the room. So have you, Avery!"

Avery shook her head. "I haven't got a grove. And if I was to have a massive stone altar, it really needs to be in the right place, not the middle of my garden beds."

They had arrived at Cornell's house a short time earlier, but a bit later than they had planned. El and Avery had accompanied Mariah to the bathroom, rather than Reuben and Alex. They had an awkward arrangement with closed doors and rune chains, so Avery and El had offered to help. Mariah was sullen and silent, but Avery had the feeling she was grateful to have women with her. Avery closed her eyes at the memory of it. She'd somehow turned into a prison guard. She shook it off and studied Cornell's grove.

It was situated behind his house, which was outside Perranporth, on the edge of a village. Cornell's cottage and its grounds were rustic, and he lived there with his girlfriend, who it seemed was not a witch, although she knew he was. She was currently at work. Cornell had led them up the garden path to his grove, and at the edge of it was a garden shed that doubled as his spell room. *This place suits him*, she thought as she studied him. He radiated a certain wildness from his tousled hair, suntanned and slightly weather-beaten face, and old jeans and t-shirt. She imagined he spent a lot of time outdoors.

"So," Cornell said, eyeing Avery's overnight bag, "how much have you brought me?"

She hefted it and placed it on the altar. "I've filled the bag with it. There was a lot of treasure, and we thought you probably didn't need it all. Plus," she thought she should be honest with him, "we have decided to keep it split up."

He was already opening the bag, and nodded absently. "That's a good plan." He lifted up the coins, and they glinted in the sunshine that struggled through the clouds. "Wow. This really is something."

"What will you do with it?" El asked.

"I'm going to cleanse some of them today, and I have designed a ritual to charge these coins with the power of Saturn. It's like when you charge crystals in the full moon—which I'll be doing tomorrow, too. The other half, I'll leave as they are."

"Why Saturn?" Avery asked, trying to recall what she'd read only a couple of days before.

"It's the planet of boundaries, restriction—discipline. I think we need to fight back, hard, with something that can bind and restrict them."

El frowned. "But Jupiter has powerful positive correspondences. Wouldn't we be better using those strengths?"

Cornell's eyebrows shot up. "You know about planetary correspondences?"

"I'm no expert, but I use them in my work with metals."

He gave Avery and El a wary look. "It's hard to know what to do with the gold for the best, isn't it? I'm planning to fight head-on with whatever our opponents are planning. To fight fire with fire! I've decided to use one of the stone circles on Bodmin tonight, and I need your help." He looked at them both with a hopeful expression.

Avery glanced at El, and then back to Cornell. "We wondered if you might have something planned, and are happy to help, but I'm worried we'll run into the others on the moors."

"It's a big moor," he pointed out. "And they can't use all of the stone circles. Besides, we should see if anything changes tonight. Hemani will come, and I'm going to ask Ulysses, Eve, and Nate, too."

A puzzled frown settled on El's face. "How come you're only asking now? You've been working on this for a day or so."

"I'd hoped to use just me and Hemani—as you know, she likes working with stones—but I think if we're to harness as much energy as possible, we need more witches."

"It might only be us two," Avery warned him. "Alex and Reuben won't be able to get away, and Briar was injured last night. I'm not sure she'll be up to it. And of course, Caspian is away."

Cornell picked the bag up and carried it to his shed, and they followed him in, Avery taking in the well-organised space, and shelves full of magical paraphernalia.

"That's okay," he said, placing the bag on the bench. "That's seven of us—a good, powerful number." He pulled a drawer open and picked up a large polished black oval stone that looked like jet. "We'll be charging this."

"Holy crap!" El said, inspecting it. "It's looks like a massive egg! Where did you get this?"

"Hemani. She's full of surprises."

Avery hated to admit it, but she was confused. "And then what happens?"

"Like any other crystal, it will hold energy—a lot of it." He ran his fingers across his lower lip, worried. "I suspect our rogue members will harness negative, destructive energy, ready to be released at a later date. The solstice, perhaps. This will be part of our counterattack." He gave a dry laugh. "Not that I've worked out the details of what *that* will be yet."

Avery leaned against the doorframe. "We really don't have a clue what's going on, do we? Just vague ideas, based on what Ghost OPS found out."

"At least we know they're planning something, and are trying to prepare a response," El pointed out. "I will be charging all my crystals tomorrow—like many witches will—and I can prepare my weapons, too. There's a ritual I like to use on the full moon."

Avery voiced something that had been worrying her all morning. "What if Lowen returns tonight using spirit-walking? We'll be vulnerable, out in the open."

"If he even can," El reminded her. "The spells and the poppet we used the other night have been reinforced. He should be too weak to do anything. And we might have affected Zane, too."

"Unfortunately," Cornell said, "I don't think we can take anything for granted. And from what you've described of last night, they are using very powerful magic."

"What time do you want us?" Avery asked. "And where?"

"I'll let you know where closer to the time, but let's meet at eleven on the site. It will give us the chance to set everything up."

"In that case," Avery said, digging her keys out of her pocket. "We'll leave you to it, and see you tonight."

It wasn't until they were in Avery's van and driving away that she said to El, "I think I'm going to charge some crystals tonight, too, before we join the others."

"How come?" El said, reaching for the bag of sweets she knew Avery kept in the glove compartment.

"Something Helena suggested the other day. She directed me to Jupiter. I think I should listen."

"All right. Why don't I bring my weapons and crystals to your place, and we'll charge a few things together? If Briar is feeling better, she may want to help. And my shop is covered for the day, so I can work with you all afternoon on the spell."

"Excellent. I can't explain it, but I just feel that it's important."

El offered Avery a sweet and then settled back in her seat. "Great. Now let's put some killer music on and get singing."

Nineteen

On Thursday afternoon, Newton had left Caspian preparing to meet some business associates, as Olivia was still in Nottingham, and after spending a few hours at the Imperial War Museum, was on his way to meet Maggie Milne.

They had enjoyed a pleasant journey to London, chatting for a while about work before settling into a companiable silence. Newton hadn't been sure about travelling with Caspian. It seemed odd. But after his talk last night with Zee, he'd known he needed to get away. He felt like he was losing his reason. His perspective. And he was floundering. He wasn't sure that Maggie could offer any help at all, and if he was honest, felt foolish for even asking, but this was a new situation, and he wasn't above admitting when he needed help. She sounded short- tempered on the phone, abrupt even, and he might not like her, but who else could offer him guidance? He shook his head at the thought. *Bloody guidance! Anyone would think he was Luke Skywalker in need of Obi Wan.*

The good news was that Briar was okay. Zee, of all people, had phoned him, beating Alex to it. And Alex had been cagey about Mariah, just saying that she was fine. Newton's skin crawled with his discomfort over the situation.

He pushed through the door of the curry house in Lambeth and told the woman that came to greet him there was a table booked in Maggie's name. She ushered him to it, and after ordering a beer he sat and waited, perusing the menu. The food smelled amazing. It was an unassuming place, and he guessed Maggie came here often.

Within minutes a woman slid into the seat opposite him. She was of average build with light brown, shoulder-length hair and blue eyes, and she was utterly unassuming. But her stare was keen, and she looked amused as she shook his hand. "DI Newton, I presume?"

"DI Milne."

"For fuck's sake, call me Maggie."

He grinned as she swore. "Ah yes, I'd recognise those dulcet tones anywhere. Call me Newton. I like to ignore my first name." *Except when Briar said it, softly, when she was teasing him.*

"Fair enough." She poured water for herself and Newton, but their beer was swiftly delivered, and she nodded in thanks. "It's good to finally meet you in person after our sporadic phone calls."

"You too. The Nephilim and Shadow speak highly of you."

She snorted. "Fuck off, they do! Christ, they cause me some trouble!"

"Something we have in common," Newton said with a grin, already warming to her. She may be abrupt, but she was very likeable. He glanced around the restaurant. "You're a regular in here."

"Reasonably. You can't beat the Lamb Maas. And it's bloody hot, too."

"Good," he said, putting the menu down. "I'll have that. And plenty of naan bread. And some starters. I'm bloody starving."

Maggie grinned and gestured the waiter over, and once they'd ordered, said, "So, what's on your mind, Newton?"

"Everything!"

"There's not much I can do about your bloody Nephilim and that Shadow madam."

"Not much I can do about them, either. They've racked up quite the body count recently."

"And I thought they saved their killing sprees for me. At least they're the good guys...I think."

"They are," Newton said, finally able to say that after being suspicious of them for months. "Although, their arrival was violent."

She leaned on the table, watching him. "It's a different world we live in though, isn't it? I'm sorry to hear about your sergeant."

There it was. That stab of guilt again. "Thank you. I met your sergeant on Tuesday when he came to the funeral. Her brother-in-law. Well, ex brother-in-law."

"He was surprisingly cut up about it. I guess it's a stark reminder of our mortality—especially when dealing with the unpredictable paranormal." She sipped her beer. "I presume you want to talk about your rogue witches. Something you didn't want to discuss over the phone?"

"Yes, all of that, amongst other things." He stared into her blue eyes, noting the faint lines at the corners. She didn't wear much makeup. He imagined she didn't care for it. She didn't seem a fussy kind of woman. She would appreciate straight talking, so he plunged in. "I'm feeling useless. I don't feel I'm even running the investigation anymore. The witches I work with seem to be taking over. And the thing is, I have to let them! How the hell can I deal with witches who have killed people? I don't have magic! I have a bloody shotgun with salt shells." He stared at her, flustered, but also relieved that he'd now voiced his concerns. "I feel like a bloody failure!"

For a moment she didn't speak, and then she sighed. "I know what you mean. Here we are, horribly powerless without magic or any other paranormal abilities, and yet we're tasked with dealing with it because, let's face it—not many want to."

"Exactly! I had to explain to my new sergeant last night that the other DIs don't give a crap about what we get up to, as long as they don't have to deal with it. Fortunately, my other sergeant gets it."

"So will the new one, eventually." She paused while the waiter delivered their starters and then said, "You're grieving and feeling guilty. That's colouring your perspective."

He grunted as he reached for an onion bhaji. "So people keep telling me. What I need to learn is what I'm supposed to do with all of my bloody witches!"

Maggie broke her own bhaji into pieces and took a bite, chewing thoughtfully. "You haven't been working paranormal for that long, have you?"

"Just the past year, and that came out of my dealing with the White Haven witches."

"How did it start?"

Newton frowned. "Good question. It started with demons in White Haven. Avery—she's one of them—had been given information that suggested there were missing grimoires belonging to the original five witch families of White Haven. She decided to find them, and someone wasn't happy. Turned out to be another witch's wife. She was related to the Favershams, who were behind it all." He shook his head. "Although, I actually came here with one of *them*." He summarised what had happened over the course of the year.

Maggie pushed her empty plate away. "Yes, alliances can change, but that's life. You've had an eventful year."

"Very. The witches have always been in White Haven, but until the last year had kept a low profile. I mean," he struggled to explain, "they still do. But *things* happen now."

"One trigger is all it takes sometimes."

Newton sipped his beer. "I guess so. Perhaps I just didn't see it before. Maybe these odd occurrences slipped under the radar."

"They would have. Like you said, the other police don't *want* to see what you see. You have no choice anymore. Besides," she added, "it sounds like you're being hard on yourself. You deal with things very well. You arrested half a theatre group."

He grunted, thinking about the chaos of Beltane. "And then had to let them go because they'd been cursed! Reams of paperwork for nothing!"

Maggie laughed unexpectedly. "Hey, you have to admit, this makes for interesting dinner chat!" At his bleak expression, she sobered. "What you did then made a difference. You made sure the public was safe—and that *they* were, too. You stopped them from injuring each other when they couldn't control themselves. I've learned to see ourselves as gatekeepers and peacekeepers. We're an important part of dealing with paranormal rule breakers. The acceptable face of it."

"The powerless face of it."

"No, not at all!" She leaned further towards him, resting her folded arms on the table. "To the public, you're not powerless. You provide protection. And like the example I've just given you, that's exactly what you did. Your witches may have been acting behind the scenes to deal with the curse and the perpetrator, but you handled everything else! You legitimise their actions. I do the same here. Bigger team, same shit. *Much* more shit. We have different rules." She leaned back and sipped her beer. "For instance, I fingerprinted Gabe and Shadow's team. Took DNA, the works. I was probably a bit hard on them...after all, it was a shitshow that wasn't of their making. They were the good guys, despite the carnage. They just dealt with it. Much like what happened to you a few days ago."

He nodded thinking of the bloodbath at Gabe's farmhouse. "I did the same—statements and everything. They didn't like it, but they complied. And we have a stack of bodies being processed in the morgue right now."

"Exactly. Every event we document makes a map of the wider paranormal world. So, some people are made to pay for their crimes by alternative means." She shrugged. "I don't give a fuck how they come to justice, as long as someone serves it to them. Most won't end up in prison because the paranormal world doesn't work like that...and prisons are not equipped to handle it, either. You have to change the way you think, Newton."

He fell silent, considering the way justice had been handed out in previous events. The witches had dealt with Gil's wife, and Suzanna, Avery's ancestor. The Nephilim and the witches had dealt with the mermaids—although, he had been forced to blame the deaths the Nephilim had caused on an unknown assailant. A compromise he'd hated back then, but grudgingly accepted now. They had all worked together to deal with the vampires...including the bloody wolf. And it had been a group effort to handle the Empusa, who was banished by the Raven King along with her human conspirators.

Newton finally spoke. "You're right. But I guess civilian deaths—because that's what I call them—make me cranky. I have to face their families and spin them bullshit. I can't tell them that a bloody spriggan killed their loved ones."

Maggie's expression softened. "No. That is the hardest part, of course. You have to tell them whatever makes the most sense."

The waiter took their plates away and delivered their main course, and when they were alone again, Maggie said, "You still run things and have an important job to do. You're still the public face, and the one who keeps your bosses informed. Remember, you're the gatekeeper."

"And it doesn't matter how justice is dispensed," he said grimly. "There's a witch in my friend's cellar right now. Locked up by some bloody spell."

"A bad witch?"

"Yes."

"So let them handle it, but stay involved! Justice will be served, and the public will be safe." She tapped her head. "Mindset. Different rules for different jobs. I have long since accepted most of what I achieve will never be acknowledged by anyone outside of my team. I'm cool with that." She forked up some curry. "I know I make my part of the world a safer place. So do you." She gave him a wicked grin. "I like being a rule breaker as much as I like swearing. It makes me happy. That's why I do it so fucking much."

Newton laughed, feeling suddenly lighter. "You're very good at it."

"Swearing? I know."

"And the job," he acknowledged. "So, I guess I need to love working beyond the normal policing boundaries," he said, before finally taking a bite of curry and thinking how utterly fantastic it was. He needed more beer. Suddenly things started to order themselves in his mind, and a way of working clicked into place as the issues he'd been struggling with for months melted away. "You're right. I need to embrace it."

"Absolutely. You have to own this shit. It's the only way."

Newton gestured for the waiter. "Two more beers please." He turned back to Maggie. "Thank you. Your advice is just what I needed."

"Good, because I have more to share. This is going to be a fun night."

Alex watched Mariah, increasingly worried that she was so still. She hadn't moved for hours, and was lying on her rudimentary bed staring at the beamed cellar ceiling.

He walked over to the cage, relieved to see that she was still breathing. He reinforced his spells before heading back to the corner of the room and settling in one of the old armchairs they'd brought down from the attic. It was getting late, only a few hours from midnight, and just as he was wondering what the others were doing, Reuben entered with two beers. He gave Mariah a cursory glance and then sat next to Alex.

"I thought you'd need a beer," he said, handing him one. "She asleep?"

Alex shrugged. "Seems that way. Unless she's traveling the spirit world right now, rustling up some friends." He'd actually been worrying about that for hours, but the house was well protected, and so far, all was quiet.

"El phoned." Reuben leaned closer so his lips were to Alex's ears. "They'll be joining Cornell and the others at a stone circle tonight."

"What? Why?"

"They're charging crystals."

"I guess Cornell knows what he's doing."

"Briar and Hunter will join them."

"Is she well enough?"

"Seems so," Reuben said, sipping his beer. "Watching Mariah doesn't seem that exciting anymore."

Alex turned toward Mariah and noticed her stir. "I wouldn't be so sure."

She stretched, sat up and looked at them. "Are you planning to starve me to death?"

"Food is on the floor where you left it hours ago," Reuben told her. "One of my best burgers, too."

She grimaced. "It's cold now."

"Tough shit. It wasn't when I gave it you."

She picked up the burger on a plastic plate and returned to the bed. "My, my. Aren't you a delight?"

"I always am. Right, Alex?"

"Always, mate. Are you ready to work with us rather than against us, Mariah?"

She finished her mouthful of burger and wiped her mouth with the back of her hand. "That will never happen. Are you prepared to watch me forever?"

Alex decided to goad her. "We won't need to. I've been debating your fate all day, hoping you'd decide to help us. But I can see it's pointless. I'll call Genevieve tomorrow and we can plan to bind your powers properly. Then you can go free."

She froze. "You wouldn't dare."

"You're too dangerous not to. There are many deaths you're responsible for."

"Not just me."

"You were involved. I think the days following the full moon are the best for binding spells, don't you agree, Reuben?"

"Absolutely, mate."

Mariah gave them a calculating stare. "You could try, I suppose, but you won't be strong enough. You may have noticed that I possess some very potent magic."

"That hadn't escaped me," Alex said, biting back his growing fury. "Especially when you nearly killed Briar."

"She was cocky. You all are!" Mariah stood up, her burger forgotten. "Ever since you found your grimoires, you think you're better than everyone else."

Alex and Reuben stayed seated, and Alex forced himself to be calm. Arguing was better than her sullen silence. "We didn't think that and never have. Some of our magic was bound up in another binding spell that our ancestors were forced into. Having it returned to us was our birth right."

"So, you'll risk losing it again by binding me?"

That was a good question. "We'll have the Cornwall Coven behind us. No one else will lose their power. Just you."

"Genevieve won't allow it."

Actually, they hadn't even asked her, but he wasn't going to tell her that, and clearly neither was Reuben, who merely smirked. "She's only too happy not to have a rogue witch on her hands."

Mariah's eyes narrowed with suspicion. "We'll see. Because if you think this is over, you're stupider than you look." Then she sat on the bed again and resumed her meal.

Reuben pulled Alex from the room. "I think we should cast a circle of protection around her cage. What if she's pulling planetary power and it all goes boom later? In fact, maybe now's the time to use her hair and jewellery."

Alex was about to scoff, but recalling Mariah's self-confidence, and his initial struggle to bind her in runes, he nodded. "All right. I agree to the circle, but we'll save the hair and stuff. That will be useful for the full binding. Bring everything down, and let's get started."

Briar stepped onto Avery's well-manicured lawn, wriggling her toes into its lush freshness. She already felt so much stronger, and after drinking Eli's tonics—one on the hour, every hour, as instructed—she felt almost like her normal self. And of course, constant contact with the earth for most of the afternoon had re-energised her, too.

Avery watched her with a cool, dispassionate gaze. "Are you sure you're up for this, Briar?"

Still wriggling her toes, she said, "Of course. If I wasn't, I wouldn't be here. And Hunter wouldn't let me, either."

Avery huffed. "Like he would stop you!"

"I would have listened!"

Hunter appeared silently out of the darkness, as silent as a human as he was as a wolf. "Like hell you would." He cocked an eyebrow at Avery. "For a little woman, she has a lot of fight in her."

Briar looked pleased. "Yes, I have. So will you both shut up? Remind me, Avery, what are we doing?"

"We are charging amethyst and rose quartz with the powers of Jupiter and Venus, and also charging some of El's weapons."

Avery led them across the lawn to the circular area she performed her rituals in. Her walled garden was a private, quiet space, perfect for working outdoors, and as they approached the area, Briar saw candlelight and El's shadowy figure moving around the prepared circle.

Briar rubbed her head, thinking perhaps she'd missed something after all. "I thought we were doing that with Cornell?"

"That's different," El said as she joined them. "He's charging jet with Saturn's attributes. However, Helena suggested Jupiter was the way to go. Positive beats negative."

"I like it," Hunter said immediately. "You have to undermine the enemy."

"Exactly." Avery beamed at him. "This way, we'll have two strategies. I trust that Helena has pointed me in the right direction.

Briar clapped. "I'm so glad Helena is back with us. You're lucky to have her, Avery."

Avery smiled. "I know. I didn't always see it like that, but I have really begun to appreciate her. She's an interesting character."

"Imagine what she'd be like in flesh and blood!" Briar only wished she had her own ghostly ancestor to help and advise her.

Hunter stared at sky. "Remind me what this planetary line up is, again? Should I be able to see it?"

El finished her preparations. "Only with a telescope, I think." She pointed to a section of the sky. "I believe that's where they are. Amazing, isn't it? It really reminds me of our place in the cosmos. In fact," she spread her arms wide, "if you focus, you can feel the energy gathering."

"Where do you want me?" Hunter asked.

Avery had already stepped into the circle. "Inside here with us. You can join your energy to ours while we carry out the rituals. Is that okay?"

Briar smiled at him, knowing how powerful his wild shifter energy was. "I think you will add an extra something special to the spell."

He grabbed her hand and pulled her into the circle after him. "In that case, let's get stuck in."

Twenty

D ylan pulled into the car park at Hurlers Stone Circles and killed the engine. "I think we should set up on the rise over there. We'll get a good view of the whole site."

"Are you sure this is wise?" Cassie asked, as she grabbed her backpack and exited the van.

"Yes!" He looked at her, incredulous. "This is the night. I'm hoping we see something impressive. This is the biggest and most powerful of the circles, and it's on a ley line."

"And," Ben added, checking his pack to make sure he had everything, "we have the drone."

Dylan grinned, pleased at the modifications he'd made that afternoon. It had taken him longer than expected, but he knew it was the perfect way to get the best view.

"All right," Cassie said, falling into step behind them as they marched across the moor in the darkness, their torches lighting up the dips and rises in the uneven ground. "I'm not entirely sure that this will tell us any more than we already know, though."

"All data is useful," Ben remonstrated, "you know that."

"If I'm honest," Dylan said, thinking of the hours they had spent on this over the past few days, "I'm over stone circles. But what's happening is fascinating and unusual, and we can't ignore it. Besides, if I can get the drone high enough, I may be able to get images of the other circles close by."

For a while, they trudged in silence. The moor felt uncannily still. Even the wind had dropped. The only sounds were the odd hoot of an owl and the trickle of streams.

"All right," Dylan finally said, scoping out the area they'd arrived at. "This should do."

The old mining works were close by, the remaining walls of the pump house dark grey against the night sky and endless expanse of the moor. Cassie spread a waterproof blanket on the ground, and they placed out their camping stools. They'd come prepared for a few hours.

"You did bring the spells, didn't you?" she asked, pausing in her work.

Ben patted the bag across his shoulder. "All here." He gazed across the moor and pointed. "Dylan, can you send the drone over there, too?"

Dylan looked up, puzzled, and saw the uneven stones of the Cheesewring against the stars. "Yeah, shouldn't be a problem. Why there?"

"They're on the ley line, too. They might be affected by whatever's going on."

"Fair enough."

The Cheesewring was a rocky outcrop caused by granite slabs stacked on each other, and was named after the cheesewring tool that was once used to make cheese. A very unsuitable name, Dylan always thought, for such a majestic and unusual formation. It seemed to demean the place, rather than elevate it. Myths said that a giant had formed the stones, part of a contest between giants and saints as to whether the giants should follow Christianity. Of course, Christianity won, it always did in these tales; that was the point of them. They perched on the very edge of the Tor, where the sides fell steeply to the moor and what had been a quarry at the base, but next to the Cheesewring were signs of an old settlement. One of many on Bodmin.

Dylan lifted his thermal imaging camera and panned it across the skyline. "Bloody hell, Ben. I can see it from here. It's like a bloody beacon!"

Ben and Cassie immediately dropped everything and scooted over to look at the screen.

"Holy shit! What does that mean?" Cassie asked, sounding both horrified and excited.

Dylan lowered the camera and looked at his friends. "I have no idea, but this seems bigger than I initially thought. That's not exactly close to the circle." Looking beyond Cassie he saw a light by the old engine room that was now a small Visitor Centre, and pulled both to the ground. "Turn the torch off, now!"

Cassie was the only one with a torch and it had landed under her. For a moment she fumbled, and then said, "It's off. What's going on?"

Dylan rolled to the side and pointed at the old pumphouse. "I saw a light, just briefly, at the head of the old mine."

Ben whispered, despite the distance. "Trick of the eye, perhaps?"

"I don't think so, but maybe I'm just jumpy," Dylan admitted, staring at the spot. "Let's wait."

For a few minutes they lay immobile, and then Ben said, "I saw something at the edge of the building. Get your camera on there, Dylan."

"What if it's the witches?"

"What if it's a bloody spriggan?" he hissed back.

Dylan looked at him, horrified. "Dude! What did you have to say that for?"

"We're too far and too close to the ground to be seen from here," Cassie insisted. "I can barely see the damn building, it's so dark. Get your bloody camera out!"

"All right." Cautiously, Dylan rolled to the side, easing up his camera from where it had been uncomfortably wedged under his stomach. Making sure the screen was facing him, he turned the video on and immediately, three figures sprang into view. "Oh, fuck! There's someone there."

Cassie and Ben squidged close, Cassie so close that he could feel her breath on his cheek as she leaned in. "Men or women?"

"Does it bloody matter? One of them is being supported by the other two."

The figures walked towards the largest stone circle, which could also be seen on the camera, the stones glowing with the orange light.

Cassie groaned. "Remember I told you that Reuben and El hoped they'd bound Lowen? What if that's him?"

"With Harry and Zane?" Ben asked, squinting at the figures. "Mariah is still at Reuben's, right?"

"Right," Dylan said, his heart now pounding. "They must be here to do some kind of rite using the planetary parade."

Ben glared at him. "I thought you said this would be solstice thing!"

"I don't bloody know, do I? They could be planning to use it for both!"

"Stop bickering!" Cassie said. "This is the perfect chance to see what they're doing and record it. This could give our guys the edge. What I'm more interested in right now is where they've come from!" Dylan's eyes had adjusted to the light now, and he could see the stubborn frown on Cassie's face. "There wasn't another car in the car park, so unless they parked in the village and came earlier, what were they doing in the pumphouse? Have they come up from an old mine?"

Ben sounded exasperated. "They're all capped off, you numpty."

Tearing his gaze from the three figures making their way to the centre of the circle, Dylan stared at Cassie. "Are you serious?"

"No. I'm just making up random shit! Of course I'm serious." She jabbed Dylan on his head. "Think. They are hiding somewhere. Zane and Lowen live in Bodmin. Bodmin's stone circles are lit up like a bloody Christmas tree. Beneath us are old mine workings. Probably a warren of them! They're hiding below us. Minions village is close. They can pick up supplies there."

Dylan looked at Ben. "She's right. It's highly possible. Let's face it, they broke into all kinds of caves in their search for Coppinger's gold."

"And," Cassie added, "there are smugglers tunnels below here, too. This is Bodmin! The epicentre of all the smuggling routes." She looked across at the pumphouse. "We need to look in there."

"Are you nuts?" Ben asked. "With them out here!"

They checked the screen again and saw one figure pacing out a circle, the other crouched next to the third figure, who sat on the ground.

"Look!" Cassie said. "They're caught up in their spell! We have time to at least look. I'm not suggesting we head down there or anything!"

"She's right," Dylan admitted. "This is a great chance to see where they came from."

"We can do that in the light," Ben argued. "I am trying to think of our safety. I don't want to end up another one of their victims."

"I'll go, then," Dylan said, seeing the frustration on Cassie's face and fearing she was about to head there on her own. "You can film it. With luck, we'll be back in fifteen minutes."

Ben glared at him. "Great, now you make me sound like a pillock. All right. I'll go with Cassie, and you film. Just be careful!"

Dylan sighed. *Sometimes Ben could be such a pain.* "That's not what I meant!"

"Too late," he said, rising into a crouch. "Come on, Cassie."

"Well, you be careful, too. Don't fall down any shafts," Dylan hissed.

But it was too late. They'd already gone.

El stood in the centre of Stannon Stone Circle, ready to start on the next spell of the night.

Their new Hunt Coven, as she thought of it, just to give it a name, had met on the lane not far from the circle, a few cars marking the spot, and they had trudged across the tussock-filled ground together, with much cursing.

The moor was a forbidding place, even more so at night, with clouds scudding across the almost full moon. The air and earth felt charged with potential. They had worried that they might be late after finally completing the spells at Avery's, but thought that had gone well. They had charged a selection of stones, pirate gold, and weapons with Jupiter's expansive energies, and then had decided to combine a few of the planet's correspondences, too. One of El's swords was at her side now, and it was a comforting presence in the brooding landscape.

Hunter's energy had added an extra dimension to the spell, too. However, he wasn't taking part in this one. He'd already changed into his wolf and was exploring the stone circle. And it was big, so much so that it was hard to see it all in this light. While Cornell completed his preparations with Hemani, the other witches gathered together, talking in low voices as if someone would hear them.

Eve examined the bag of coins that Cornell had brought with him. "Wow! So this is some of Coppinger's gold?"

Avery eyed it warily. "Yes, but there's so much more."

"Plundered from wrecks and earned through bloodshed," Nate said. He picked up a coin and held it up to the moon. "If these coins could talk! I bet the stories would be gruesome."

Eve shuddered. "No, thanks. Fascinating though that history is, I'm glad it's behind us."

"Except it's not," Avery reminded her. "It's having repercussions right now."

Ulysses had also picked up a handful of the coins, and they slithered in his hands. "You know," he said, his deep, rich voice rolling around them, "we're forgetting the power of gold." He looked up sharply. "Or perhaps I am. We know the potential value of these coins, and how rare it is to have so many, but we need to think of it for its spellcasting potential. This is *gold*! How often do we have access to this much of it?"

"Never!" El answered, realising what he was driving at. "I buy it in small amounts to make jewellery with, but nothing ever on this scale."

Ulysses's eyes flashed in the dark. "Exactly. And what properties does it have?"

"Self-confidence, power, inner strength. I combine it with certain gemstones to add to its properties." El shrugged. "I do the same with all my jewellery, whichever metal I use."

"And it's related to the sun—its most powerful correspondence."

"We all know that," Briar said puzzled. "What are you getting at?"

Ulysses looked above them to the whirl of stars and the moon. "Somewhere up there, five planets are aligning. It's a powerful time. Alchemists strived to turn lead, the most mutable of metals, into gold. Not only for the wealth it offers, but for its magical properties."

"Cornell and Hemani are charging it tonight with Saturn's powers, and the jet, of course," Nate pointed out.

"And it's worth doing. But," Ulysses said, looking at the gold in his hand again, "this will be of most value on the solstice. We're thinking too small. We need as much of this as we can get."

"To use as part of the solstice celebrations, you mean?" Avery asked.

"Yes. We don't know what Mariah and the others are planning, but it's something big. We need something equally big to counteract it. We know this...we've talked about it. But forget about the blood on this gold," he said, noticing El's grimace. "We can cleanse it all tomorrow under the full moon, and then use it at Litha. It will provide protection—and a cleansing for us. We'll probably need it."

Nate flipped the coin through his fingers. "You're suggesting that rather than doing a traditional solstice celebration, we add to it?"

"I'm not sure Genevieve will like that," El said. "She doesn't want to be involved in this. Most people don't."

"We have four rogue witches, and another we think might be involved," Ulysses said. "She can't afford to be squeamish now. Bad energy is building. Energy we must banish."

Cornell's voice broke into their conversation. "I'm ready. Bring the gold and get in place. We need to begin."

Without another word, Ulysses hefted the bag up and carried it into the large, candlelit circle, and the others followed.

El nudged Avery. "He's right. I guess it's a good job we have so much of it. Is it secure?"

"It's in Reuben's attic right now. I didn't want to leave it anywhere unattended."

El's stomach tightened. "But Mariah is there."

"Bound in a cage."

"But the others really want it. And we don't know where Harry is. What if they're planning an assault and we've conveniently left both the gold and Mariah in one place?"

Avery gave El's shoulder a reassuring squeeze. "They'll be doing their own rituals right now, I'm sure. We need to trust Reuben and Alex."

Avery hurried to join the others and after a moment's hesitation, El followed. Reuben was much more confident after breaking the curse with Caspian the other night. But, El also knew that deep down, he still doubted himself. She could only hope that in the event of something terrible happening, he would be okay.

Twenty-One

Reuben stepped back from the completed circle of protection they had placed around Mariah's rune cage, and then at Mariah sitting cross-legged within in it. Her eyes were closed, and her hands rested on her knees as if she was doing yoga, but Reuben doubted she was merely meditating.

Candles blazed around the circle, and although the spell was strong, Reuben couldn't shake his unease. He pulled Alex back beyond the doorway again, watching Mariah as he spoke.

"Something's not right, Alex."

Alex's jaw muscles tightened as he watched her. "Her calmness is unnerving."

"She's plotting something."

"The circle and my cage are strong."

"I want back-up. I'm fetching the poppet."

"You made one for her?" Alex looked shocked. "I thought we were saving it."

"I started it, but didn't finish." Reuben saw Mariah's lips silently move. "I'm going to go finish it, and I'll be back down very soon. If we don't need it, then great."

Alex nodded and returned to the cellar, and Reuben raced along the passageway, back into the main house, and past the billiards room that still had the back wall blown out but was secured with tarpaulin. He'd been annoyed that the builders couldn't come until next week, but now he was relieved. He paused to check that all of his spells were in place, and then locked the door and spelled that, too. He knew he was jumpy, and he trusted Alex, but...well, he had a bad feeling he couldn't squash.

When he finally reached the attic, he checked the poppet. This time he'd customised it, making it look more female. As well as stuffing Mariah's hair in it with a selection of suitable herbs, he'd also sewn some hair around her face. Now he cast the spell bestowing the poppet with power, and then placed it carefully in his pocket, along with Mariah's silver chain that Avery had stolen.

The huge crates of gold gleamed in the corner of the room, and Reuben cast them in a shadow spell and then placed a circle of protection around them, too. He felt like a worrisome old woman making so many levels of protection, but the air felt charged with danger. Just as he turned to leave the room, a flash of flame and smoke had him whirling around, hands raised. The first poppet they'd made had been on the corner of the table, but now flames consumed the binding around it and then the poppet beneath. It burned quickly, leaving only ashes and a charred mark behind, as a rumble of thunder rolled overhead. Dousing the remains in water—*the last thing he needed was a house fire*—he raced back down the stairs.

Cassie edged across the uneven ground, constantly glancing to the middle of the stone circle, but struggling to see the figures in the centre. She stumbled and almost fell, and Ben's hand shot out and gripped her arm.

"Watch your step. You could break your neck. There are still massive dips in the ground."

"Sorry." Her heart was pounding, more due to fear of discovery than falling. "You said the old shafts were capped."

"Not that well!"

A light flared, and they both froze, looking to where a candlelit circle flamed in the centre of the largest ring of stones.

"This doesn't feel like when our witches do it," Cassie murmured to Ben as they progressed. "I always feel a sense of wonder when they use magic. Here I'm just scared."

"Honestly," Ben said kindly, "so am I. Now hush and focus on the ground."

Nerves made her chatter. "I wish I had Eli's eyesight. They see as easily at night as day."

"I wish I had his muscles and way with the ladies. Bollocks to his eyesight," Ben grumbled, and it made Cassie giggle.

She focussed. This was not the time to forget the danger they were in.

The dark bulk of Minions Heritage Centre was close; it had once been an engine house for the South Phoenix mine. Most of the building was a wreck now. The roof had long gone, and the windows were open to the elements. Only the lower floor had been sealed in to make the tiny Visitor Centre.

They circled around the back of it, well out of sight of Harry and the others casting their spells, and Cassie said, "I saw this place the other day. The floor is completely solid. They couldn't have come from in here."

"But there's a level below it," Ben said, edging around and pointing to a low, curved doorway on the far side.

They were shielded by a low stone wall now which partially circled the old engine room, and Cassie gasped. The wood sealing the lower window was discarded on the ground. Ben crawled towards it and stuck his head in while Cassie kept a nervous watch. She raised her head above the wall, watching two figures in the centre of the circle lift their arms.

She wasn't sure if it was her imagination, but the air seemed to thicken, and the almost-full moon, which had helped light their way, was obscured by dark clouds. She glanced towards the village, wondering if anyone would notice. *Maybe they didn't care. Or maybe the witches had spelled the whole place.*

She crept back to Ben's side as he emerged and said, "Have a look—just don't go in. There's a huge shaft."

Curiosity overcoming her nerves, she followed his directions and gasped. A narrow shaft was visible in the centre of the small place, and a light shone from its depths. She scooted backwards. "Shit. How far down does it go?"

"Hard to say. I wouldn't want to go down there, though. I bet it's a death trap." He tugged her arm. "Come on, time to go."

They had barely started on their way back when they felt a strange disturbance in the air, and the ground seemed to shift beneath their feet. The stone circles shimmered with light, and energy rolled out in a wave, throwing Cassie and Ben to the ground. A crack in the earth ran from the circle up the hill to where they'd been watching, and she heard a muted cry from Dylan.

Avery felt the power of Stannon Stone Circle reverberate through her, reminding her of the crossroads in Scotland. She'd had no choice in being there, but had summoned Hecate to help. And it was where Caspian had declared his feelings for her.

But tonight, there were differences. For a start, Caspian was now in London, and she was among friends and other powerful witches. For all that she hadn't known what to expect, Cornell's spell had actually been much like any other. They stood within the circle of protection, the coins and a large piece of jet in the centre, and invoked Saturn, feeling the atmosphere charge with an age-old power that could bind and constrain. She only wished she could see the stones around them as Dylan could on his camera. Their power shimmered and stirred, thickening the air within the space.

Cornell was nearing the end of his spell, his words weaving with Hemani's. Their magic felt different to her own, and being so close to Ulysses was even odder. His magic almost made her shudder because it was so similar to that of the mermaids. But one look at his strong profile reassured her. As Cornell and Hemani closed the spell together, a snap of power ran around the circle, and then light flashed through the objects they were charging.

"Done," Cornell said with a smile. "I will store these safely for Litha. When we join with the others, our magic will magnify what we've done tonight, and we'll be able to bind our enemies' power."

As he was speaking, a shudder rocked the ground, almost throwing them off their feet. Briar cried out and fell to her knees, and El was at her side in moments.

"Briar?"

"I'm okay. Something weird is happening…something huge."

Eve looked skywards. "It feels like when I gather energy for a weather spell. It's coming from a distance."

"The south," Ulysses said, pointing across the moors.

Hunter's howl broke the deeper silence of the moors as he raced to join them, and he changed form, appearing naked before them. "I've felt this at Castlerigg—our local circle. The witches would use its energy when they wanted to harness powerful magic." He gave Avery a wicked grin. "Before we banished them."

Hemani looked at the others, bewildered. "But we expected this."

Cornell frowned. "We expected them to charge their gold, but what else are they doing?"

"Something big," Eve said, frowning, as thunder rumbled overhead, "and they're drawing a lot of power to do it. With help, I may be able to disrupt them."

"I'm willing to try," Nate said immediately.

All night, Avery's thoughts had rarely strayed from worrying about Reuben and Alex guarding Mariah. She hated that they were so close to an unpredictable witch, and now she groaned. "What if they're trying to free Mariah? After all, Saturn and Mars have belligerent, aggressive traits."

Cornell straightened as if coming to a decision. "It's possible, and I like Eve's suggestion. We must try to disrupt their spell. I'll lead us, with Eve's help."

"Excellent." Eve looked across at Avery and El. "Maybe you two should go. I can see that you're worried."

Avery felt completely torn. If they stayed, Eve could use their power, but if Reuben and Alex were in danger... She turned to El. "I can take two of us, but," she glanced at Briar and Hunter. "I'm sorry, I can't take you, too."

"That's fine," Briar said, hushing her. "I'll help here. You two go, now!"

Alex watched with horror as Mariah levitated, wild fingers of energy crackling around her.

What was she doing?

He hadn't bound her powers; she still had them. But they were contained within the cage, and so far it had worked very well. But now he wondered if Reuben had been right all along. He'd been pussyfooting around, reluctant to bind a witch's powers, and hoping Mariah would repent. He hadn't even contacted Genevieve to tell her that they'd taken her prisoner. Reuben and El hadn't hesitated when it came to Lowen, and had probably save his life as a result.

Tapping into his cage spell, Alex threw more of his magic into it, swelling the runes with power again, but the walls of the cage began to bulge as the fingers of energy prodded them, testing their strength. He pulled magic from deep within him, battling furiously with Mariah. Suddenly, her eyes flew open, and she stared at him triumphantly as power exploded from her and shattered the rune cage.

Alex staggered back, feeling his own defences weaken, and yelled, "Reuben! I need you now!"

For the moment, the outer circle of protection held, but Mariah was still hovering midway between the floor and the ceiling, caught within a nimbus of crackling magic that now tested the final barrier. Alex knew he couldn't contain her. She was still staring at him, almost through him, and it was terrifying. He was nothing to her, and he knew she would crush him.

"Reuben!"

Perhaps Reuben had been attacked upstairs. Maybe Harry was on the doorstep, breaking down the house's protection.

Alex edged towards the door and threw all his power into the protection spell, relieved when he heard Reuben skid into the room.

"Shit! Your cage!"

"I need your help! Right now!" Alex focussed entirely on Mariah, who was shooting spiky black shards of magic at the weakening boundary. "I can't—"

But he couldn't finish his sentence because Mariah blasted through, and he flew backwards, crashing into the wall.

Hoping the witches were still focussed on their spells, Cassie ran in a weird scuttling crouch across the moor, Ben beside her, and landed in a heap next to Dylan, who lay winded on his back. The crack in the earth ended only feet away, and Dylan was blinking, his hand clutching his eyes.

"Dylan! What happened?" Cassie asked.

"I think I've gone blind!"

"Don't be an idiot," Ben whispered, searching his bag. "You're just dazzled."

"What the hell happened?" he asked, clearly still trying to focus. "The whole screen just blazed with light."

He struggled to sit up, but Cassie forced him down as one of the figures in the circle turned to them.

"Fuck it," she groaned. "I think we've been spotted. We need to run for it."

"I can't see!" Dylan said.

"Stay down," Ben commanded, his voice calm and authoritative. "I found Avery's shadow spell. Cassie, pull everything close. I don't know how far this will cover us."

Cassie was lying on her stomach, but she scrambled to gather everything to her, rolling the blanket's edges in, just as a figure left the circle and started up the hill.

"Ben…"

He lay on the other side of Dylan, a bottle in his hand. "Wait for it…"

Dylan was silent, his hands clamped over his eyes again, but Cassie watched the figure get closer as Ben struggled with the cork.

Barely breathing, she repeated, "Ben!"

The cork pulled loose, and Ben whispered the short trigger spell. With a whoosh something settled over them like ground mist, thickening with every second that passed, until Cassie could barely see her two companions.

But she could see the man striding towards them only too clearly. The moon sailed from under the clouds, illuminating a thin frame and gaunt face with a mean, calculating expression that quickly dwindled to disappointment as he searched the area. *It was Zane.* She recognised him from Avery's description.

He came closer, following the path of the cracked earth, and scanned the rise. Cassie's breath caught in her chest, the pounding of her heart hammering into the ground. She gripped Dylan's arm, willing him to be silent.

A shout had Zane turning around, and he answered, "There's nothing here. Must be a trick of the light."

After one final, suspicious frown, he headed back to the stone circle and Cassie sagged with relief. They waited some time before finally speaking.

Ben whispered, "That was too close."

"Who was it?" Dylan groaned, blinking, and trying to focus.

"It was Zane," Cassie told him, "and we were seconds from death."

It sounded like she was exaggerating, but she knew Zane wouldn't have hesitated. He would have cursed them with something horrible, and she had never been so scared in her life.

"When can we go?" Dylan asked.

"Not bloody yet," Ben said, fumbling for the camera. "We're here until they leave. Let's just hope they don't take all night."

Reuben felt a searing-hot blast catch his arm and spin him around, sending him tumbling backwards out of the room and into the passage beyond. He hit the wall with a thump.

Mariah was surrounded by red and black jagged bolts of energy, but it was her icy, malevolent expression that was even more terrifying as she glared at Alex, hidden from Reuben's sight behind the door.

She cried, "This is what happens, Alex Bonneville, when you aren't strong enough to imprison me!" She raised her hand and pointed.

But Reuben struck first. He pulled water from the damp passageway and fired it at Mariah, catching her completely unawares. She spun around and hit the rear wall, and while she was disorientated, he pulled the poppet from his pocket and fumbled for the chain.

However, Mariah was already advancing, hands outstretched, firing bolts of power at both of them. It seemed to happen in slow motion. He saw fire spearing towards him, but still couldn't find the damn chain, hindered by his injured arm. He rolled out of the way of one blast, and it hit the wall, shattering plaster and brick. She threw another from only feet away, still advancing, unstoppable.

Reuben rolled again, fumbling the poppet as he went, and it fell to the ground as he scuttled backward. He'd lost his chance. Mariah was advancing like the angel of death, and she was going to kill them.

But she hadn't seen what he'd dropped, and the fire that flew from her fingertips hit everything...including the poppet.

It burst into flames and Mariah combusted with a bloodcurdling shriek.

Reuben watched, transfixed, his back to the wall, horrified as Mariah burned.

A final wave of power exploded from her, shattering the lights, and Reuben reacted instinctively, flinging up a shield of water that propelled her into the corner of the room, dousing fire as it went, and finally breaking over her and putting out the flames.

In utter darkness, Reuben threw a witch-light into the cellar, revealing that the only thing that remained of Mariah was a smoking, blackened heap.

Twenty-Two

A very used witch-flight to take them to the base of the cellar steps, and almost fell in the darkness.

"Where the hell are the lights?" she said, almost breathless with worry as she threw half a dozen witch-lights up.

El was bent over her knees, heaving. "You go. I'm right behind you."

"No. You check upstairs. I'll go this way."

El's lip tightened as if she would argue, but instead just nodded, and clutching the wall for support, headed to the main floor.

Avery ran down the corridor, her voice sounding tinny as she shouted, "Alex! Reuben!"

Her hands were raised, energy balling in them, when she heard Reuben shout, "We're okay!"

Relief washed through her, but she didn't slow until she reached the entrance of the room Mariah had been imprisoned in. The stench of acrid smoke and something far worse hit her. "What's happened?"

"Mariah happened," Reuben said, his voice hollow.

Her head whipped around, seeing him leaning against the wall looking bloodied and bruised, his arm hanging limply by his side.

"Reuben! Where's Alex?"

He nodded behind the door, and her heart in her mouth, she looked around it to see Alex slumped on the floor, his t-shirt shredded and smoking, and a horrible burn on his bare skin that spread from his chest up to his neck. He grunted as he looked up at her, his gorgeous eyes in pain, but he struggled to be cheerful. "Hey, babe. How are you?"

She managed to reach his side before her legs collapsed under her. She stroked his face, beyond grateful that he was alive, and then immediately said a healing spell to reduce his pain. "By the Goddess! What happened? Where's Mariah? Did she escape?"

He winced. "Yes and no."

"What do you mean?" Her tongue felt thick in her mouth, and she could barely form sentences, terrified she'd sent El to her death. "I sent El upstairs."

It was Reuben who answered. "Mariah is in the corner. What's left of her, anyway."

"*What*?" Avery spun around, hands raised again and balling with energy, wondering why the other two weren't doing something, and not grasping what Reuben was talking about. Mariah was nowhere in sight.

Reuben limped over to her, pushing her hands down. "You won't need that. Mariah is dead."

"Dead?" She looked up at him, and then with growing horror followed his gaze to the corner of the room and the smoking heap crumpled there.

Using Reuben as a crutch, she pulled herself upright and stepped closer, finally able to discern twisted limbs and burnt clothes fused to flesh. Her hand flew to her mouth.

"Who... How?"

Reuben's arm wrapped around her shoulders and pulled her close. "She did it to herself. In trying to kill me she set fire to her own poppet. She went up in seconds."

For a moment Avery couldn't stop looking, transfixed by Mariah's remains, and then she dragged her gaze away, staring at Reuben again, and taking in his injures. He had a burn down his right arm, red and weeping, and his clothes were bloodied and torn. His face was etched with shock and pain. Looking at Alex again, she saw the same expression on his. Whatever happened in here must have been horrific, and she took a few deep breaths to steady herself and marshal her shattered thoughts.

"Let's get you up to the snug. We can sort this out later."

"Take Alex. I can make my own way up, and I need to fix the fuse box, anyway. She overloaded the circuits."

He was already leaving the room as Avery knelt next to Alex. "I'm sorry. I know you hate witch-flight, but this is the best way."

"No! My legs work," he grunted. "That will just make me feel even shittier. Pull me up!"

Rather than argue, Avery did as he asked, and giving the charred body in the corner one last worried glance, they made their slow way along the passageway and up to the main house, where they met El coming towards them.

"Everything is clear, but... Alex, what happened?" Her eyes widened at the sight of him. "Is Reuben..."

"He's injured, but fine," Avery reassured her. "He's fixing the fuse box."

El nodded. "I'll go find him."

"See you in the snug!" Avery called after her.

By the time they'd made it there, the lamps were back on, and despite the warm night, Avery spelled the fire on, lit candles, and then peeled Alex out of his shirt, finally assessing the wound properly.

"It's ugly, but superficial. What happened?"

"Give me a whiskey and then I'll tell you." He lifted her hand and kissed it. "I'm glad you're okay. What happened at the circle?"

"Lots of weird stuff. That's why we're here." She eased him into a seat. "I'm going to start some rudimentary healing spells, and then head back there. We need Briar here." She faltered. "I can't believe Mariah is dead. This is terrible."

"Avery, I swear it was not our fault. We were trying to keep her contained! Her powers just seemed to magnify, and then exploded. I thought I was going to die. I thought we both were. Reuben saved us."

"The poppet did."

He nodded and winced as he eased back in his chair. "She was an utter bitch."

"Then I'm glad she's dead." She pulled her phone out. "On second thoughts, I'm going to get Eli to help. Briar might still be involved with a spell at Stannon Circle. I'll leave El with you and come back when it's done."

He caught her hand. "Wait. What was happening there?"

"I'll let El tell you." She kissed his cheek, and then left.

Ben was thankful for the waterproof blanket they were lying on, because it was getting cold, and the dew was thick on the grass. All three of them were now shivering, but they couldn't take their eyes off the activities in the centre of Hurlers Stone Circles.

Knowing that Mariah was trapped at Reuben's house, the group deduced that they were watching Harry, Zane, and a seemingly now recovered Lowen. Partway through their ritual, he shook off whatever had hampered him and joined the other two. Something was between them in the circle, but no one had any idea what. Clouds had gathered, and were swirling above their heads in an ever-increasing circle.

Ben could hear their chanting, and it sent a shiver down his spine. This felt evil, dark, and menacing. Nothing at all like when their friends used magic. "I think you're right, Cassie. They must have spelled Minions Village, or someone would be here by now, watching."

"I'd rather not be watching anymore," she confessed. "If we creep away, do you think Avery's spell will follow us?"

"Maybe."

Dylan grunted. "We are not going anywhere." His eyesight had more or less recovered, and he was watching his thermal imaging screen again—just the small one this time. "This is insane."

"Even more reason," Cassie said, incredulous, "that we should leave. We could get caught up in something we aren't prepared for and get seriously hurt."

Ben squeezed closer to Dylan and assessed the growing energy. "Let's edge back, just to be safe. We can still film and watch, but Cassie's right, Dylan. We need more distance."

Grudgingly Dylan nodded and they shuffled backwards, dragging the blanket and bags back with them. Fortunately, the shadow spell followed.

A crack of thunder and a burst of lightning made them flinch, and then the ground rumbled beneath them.

"Do you think we should worry," Dylan said, staring overhead at the swirling energy, "that we're on top of masses of mine workings and we seem to be experiencing an earthquake?"

Ben glanced around, nervous, and then back at the witches. "If they're not worried, I'm not. Keep filming."

Briar was beyond tired, but she gave as much of her power to Eve as she could, and wriggled her feet into the earth, pulling up as much as she was giving, like a conduit.

She felt suspended in time and space, surrounded by a growing vortex of energy that seemed to pull the gathering clouds closer as the earth vibrated with power. At times, she felt as if it might be torn apart. She also felt rather than saw Avery slip into the circle, her cool, clean magic giving everyone a welcome boost.

Briar felt sweat gathering on her brow, the night air cooling it on her skin immediately. Just as she thought she couldn't handle it for much longer, Eve fired their combined magic into the sky like a cannon. The sky seemed to shatter into a million pieces. Thunder exploded, lightning cracked, and the clouds boiled.

And then everything suddenly dispersed like a popped balloon.

The clouds rolled away, and the moon shone down like an eye. Briar felt stripped clean and naked under it as she found herself flat on her back, watching the stars return to the night sky. Groans resounded around her, and she twisted her head, seeing everyone else on the ground, too.

"What the actual fuck?" Nate asked, easing upright. "Eve? What did you do?"

She giggled, sounding on the verge of hysteria. "I thought I should hit it once with everything we had. It seemed to work. But it was Cornell really who directed it."

"Hit *what* exactly?" Hemani asked, also pushing upright. Her long, dark hair had fallen loose and streamed down her shoulders, framing her face.

"Cosmic energy," Cornell said, looking a little more composed that the rest of them.

Briar groaned and sat upright, knowing she'd overdone it. She felt as limp as a doll, but maybe that's because her spirit felt light, too. Hunter nuzzled her hand, and she stroked his thick, dark fur and then buried her face in it. *By the Goddess, he felt good. Warm, honest, and whole.*

As her thoughts settled, she looked across at Avery. Her hair was tangled; in fact, they all looked like they'd been to some mad hippie convention. Everyone appeared to be spaced out. Their clothes were rumpled, their hair was wild, and they each had a faraway look in their eyes as they struggled to return to normal.

Ulysses rubbed his eyes, a curiously childlike gesture for such a big man. "I feel like I've been drugged. I haven't opened up to the universe quite like that before." He squinted at Eve and Cornell. "It's a good thing I trust you."

"And I you," Eve said with an impish grin.

"Thank you—all of you," Cornell said, throwing them a grateful smile. "That was rapidly becoming toxic. I just hope we've stopped whatever they were planning."

"We didn't," Avery said, her voice barely above a whisper. "Mariah broke free of her cage and attacked Reuben and Alex. It sounds as if she was swollen with power." She pointed up. "The power of the cosmos."

"Oh, no." Briar dug her hands into Hunter's fur. "Are they okay?"

"They're alive." Her gaze travelled around the circle of witches, the candles long since blown out. "But they're injured. And Mariah is dead."

A shocked silence fell and then everyone spoke at once, firing questions at Avery. She held up her hand and stopped them. "She killed herself when she hit her own poppet with fire. She burned to death."

Briar closed her eyes tightly as unbidden images flooded her thoughts.

"So, what now?" Eve asked, her euphoria vanished. "What can we do to help?"

Avery looked around at the moors and then up at the moon. "We need to go home, rest, gather our energy, and prepare for whatever is coming, because this isn't over. Not by a long shot."

El couldn't stop her hands from shaking. In fact, she trembled all over, and as she brewed a restorative tea, she took deep, calming breaths and clenched her fingers.

She was in Reuben's kitchen, and she stared out of the window at the sea, watching the moonlight's silky path across the water. It looked so calm, so beautiful, and yet this was turning out to be a horrific night. Reuben was injured *again*, and he'd barely recovered from his stab wound. Now, Alex was also horribly burned across his chest and neck, and Briar, for all her protestations otherwise, was still drained and looked horribly pale.

And Mariah was dead. Her body a mangled, twisted heap in the cellar somewhere beneath her feet. El's toes curled up in revulsion as she recalled seeing her remains. For the briefest second, she had felt fury towards Reuben and Alex for imprisoning her in the first place. If she hadn't been here, then she wouldn't be dead now. But then rational thought returned. Mariah had tried to kill Briar, Alex, and

Reuben. She was a bitch. It was better that she was dead than any of them.

Realising the kettle had long since boiled, she poured the water into a large tea pot, and for a moment just inhaled the rich herbal scents. Chamomile, lavender, honey. If it helped her sleep, she'd drink a gallon of it.

"Do you need help?" Zee spoke from behind her.

She jumped, her heart thumping, and turned, trying to smile. "No. I'm fine."

"You're far from fine." Zee had arrived earlier with Eli. His eyes were kind, and his size and calm demeanour were reassuring. He radiated peace, and she wondered if he did it deliberately or if it was natural. She'd never noticed it before, but then again, she'd never been alone with him. He picked up a selection of mugs and placed them on a tray. "I'm not sure Reuben will thank you for tea."

"He'll do as he's told, for once."

She was intending to put the top on the tea pot, but found she couldn't move, and instead she leaned against the counter, immobile, wondering why her brain didn't seem to be working.

Zee pulled her into a hug. "You're in shock, and I'm not surprised. It's not every day that someone dies in Reuben's cellar...at least, I hope not."

She tried to laugh into his chest, almost sagging against him, but it came out as a sob instead. "It's really, really horrible. And it could have been Reuben or Alex! How terrible am I that I'm glad it was her?"

"I'm also glad it was her, if that's any consolation. If I'd have been here, I would have happily killed her myself."

El was crying properly now, big fat tears running down her cheeks. "I'm just so relieved that Reuben didn't do it deliberately. He'd never have forgiven himself. I already know he'll blame himself as it is!"

Zee continued to hold her, his palm on her head as he pressed her into his chest. "He saved them both. He knows that. He potentially saved the house, too. He doused her in a lot of water."

She struggled out of his arms and looked up at him. "How do you deal with it?"

"Death? It's what we were born to do. Trained to do. It takes a certain mental discipline that I'm very glad you do not have."

She sniffed and wiped her tears away. "I know we've been in fights before, and I've used swords and magic, but it's always been against paranormal creatures. Or our fights were meant to stop attacks. I have never intended to kill someone. None of us have!"

"Of course you haven't. But this situation has been completely different. You were trying to manage it with the old rules, but you need new ones now."

"I don't want new ones. I like the old ones."

He gave a short, sharp laugh. "We don't always get what we want, El. But from what Avery has told us, it sounds like you all dealt with things well tonight."

El nodded. Avery had filled them in on the final spell that Eve and Cornell had cast, dispelling the gathering dark energies. "It wasn't enough though, was it? Lowen has broken free from his binding, if we trust what happened to his poppet."

"Then you'll find another way to deal with him. All of them. At least there's one less now."

"We hope," she said, thinking of Charlie.

Zee moved her aside and picked up the teapot, placing it on the tray with the mugs. "Come on. You need to sit down and get warm, and then head to bed. Sleep will do wonders for you."

He gestured her to move ahead of him into the snug, and giving him another grateful smile, she headed inside and sat on the rug in front of Reuben, wriggling between his legs, squeezing his knee as she sat, and noting that he now had a dressing on his wound.

Eli was just finishing tending to Alex's injury, wrapping a bandage around his chest, half-batting Briar away as Avery watched his every move. "Briar, behave. I've got this. You need to rest."

She pouted. "But I can help."

"Help yourself first." He stared at Hunter. "I don't want to see her in the shop tomorrow. She must rest—all day!"

He saluted. "You have my word that she will stay at home. We'll be leaving once she's had her tea."

"You're being so bossy," she told him, but El could tell she liked being looked after, and she smiled.

Zee had placed the tray on the coffee table and poured the drinks, and he handed El a mug first before distributing the others. As predicted, Reuben accepted his with a grimace.

"I suppose," Avery said with a sigh, "that I should call Moore."

Reuben groaned. "Do we have to do that now?"

"Of course we do. We can't leave her body down there all night."

"I suggest," Zee said, "that you call Newton first. Even though he can't come, he is the one in charge. He needs to know."

"I was hoping to let him enjoy his break in London," she confessed.

"He'll be furious if you don't," Alex said, wincing as Eli finally let him sit back in his seat.

"You look like a bloody mummy," Reuben quipped, nodding at the bandage that also wound around his neck. "At least your pretty face is undamaged. That might help when we're in prison."

Alex just glared at him as a ripple of laughter spread around the room. "Please stop talking about prison. In fact, just stop talking."

Hunter grinned. "You aren't going to prison. She killed herself. Newton will be glad to know there's one less witch to worry about."

"And Moore," Eli added, sitting in front of the fire and helping himself to tea, "will think exactly the same. It will be good training for Kendall, the new sergeant."

Everyone looked up at him, surprised, and Avery asked, "You met her?"

"Moore brought her into the shop. Zee met her, too."

Zee nodded. "They came into the pub for lunch. He was doing the rounds—part of her induction."

El shrugged. "None of us were at work today. Or rather, yesterday." She guessed it must be close to three in the morning now.

Zee seemed to take pity on them. "Let me call Newton. You all look terrible. And besides, I want to chat with him," he said enigmatically as he rose to his feet and headed to the kitchen.

Eli sipped his drink, assessing them thoughtfully. "You *all* need to stay home and rest tomorrow. All of your businesses can manage for a day."

"I'll be okay," Avery said, "but I will sleep late and make sure Alex is comfortable first. I need to keep busy, or I'll go mad."

Alex groaned. "I could sleep all day, actually. I feel exhausted. Maintaining that cage was hard work. I hadn't got nearly enough energy left to deal with Mariah when she broke it."

"Yes, you should." Avery kissed his cheek before turning to El. "I feel we got lucky tonight. Things could have been so much worse."

El nodded, but she still felt unlucky, like a huge weight was hanging over them, and she knew it wouldn't go until the other witches were neutralised. Bound forever. And it didn't help that she felt like she was missing something. Some important part of the puzzle of what they were actually doing.

Zee strode back into the room. "Right. Moore will be on his way soon. Just him and Kendall. No SOCO. Newton says you're all to go home, and Moore can catch up with Alex tomorrow. They can get most of the information from Reuben. Sound good?"

"I'll stay, obviously," El said, trying to rally herself and cheer everyone up. "I can't trust Reuben not to cause trouble. And besides, I want to meet Kendall." *And make sure Reuben didn't do or say anything remotely compromising.*

The others didn't linger, all eager to get to bed, and although Zee and Eli offered to help, El shooed them away, hopeful that the less people were around, the quicker Moore would be. When they did finally arrive, she ushered them down to the cellar before doing anything else, leaving Reuben in the snug.

Moore silently appraised Mariah's body. "Well now. This is tricky. How long was she down here?"

"Barely twenty-four hours," El said, feeling like it was the longest day of her life. She began to say 'they,' but instead carefully explained, "We were hoping she'd repent and help us, but she had no intention of doing that."

Kendall asked Moore, "Are we getting the coroner in?"

"Not here." He looked over at El. "There's a museum van on the drive. What are you planning to do with that?"

El faltered. "I'd forgotten about it. It's how they got her here."

"Then that's how we'll get her out of here."

"What?" El thought she'd misheard him.

"Newton doesn't want you dragged into her death, especially considering the havoc Mariah caused in life. I think the best thing is if we discover her in a burnt-out museum van. Agreed?" he turned his calm, speculative gaze on her.

El's mouth was dry. "You mean put her...remains in the van?"

"And set it on fire. I presume your magic can help us do that?"

Never in her worst nightmares had El thought she'd be doing this. But it would solve many problems. "Er, yes, I guess so."

Kendall looked between them, and finally said, "We're disturbing the scene of the crime?"

Moore didn't hesitate. "There is no crime here. She killed herself, from what I've gathered. Right, El?"

"Yes. She set fire to her own poppet whilst trying to kill Reuben and Alex."

"There you go." Moore tapped his head. "Different rules for paranormal crime, Kendall. She's been brought to justice. If you're uncomfortable with this, then maybe this is the wrong team for you. Although I will admit, this is a *very* unusual circumstance, even for us."

Kendall swallowed. "No. I get it."

El looked at her sympathetically. She was young, fit, and ambitious, and she liked the look of her. To be brought into a new team and have to deal with this must be terrible. She was a police officer, and had no context of what they were about. She tried to smile, but it stuck on half-formed on her face. "I can assure you that this is not normally what we do, and she was a horrible woman."

Kendall straightened her shoulders. "Then let's get this done."

Twenty-Three

C aspian stared at Newton over the breakfast table in the hotel, utterly shocked at his news. So much so that he was momentarily speechless, and forgot that he had his own news to share.

"Sorry," Newton said, looking sympathetic, "I thought I should just get it over with."

"Of course." Caspian put his coffee cup down on the table before he fumbled it and splashed coffee everywhere. "It's just the last thing I expected to hear." He attempted to filter through what Newton had just told him. "You said Reuben and Alex were injured?"

"Burns—chest and arms. But they're okay. The girls weren't there. Neither was Hunter."

He grunted Hunter's name, like it pained him to say it, and Caspian knew only too well how that felt. But Caspian also knew that Avery would be worried about Alex. And furious.

"Damn. We really did pick a bad time to leave."

Newton shook his head and reached for his coffee. "Not really. They handled it, and I know Moore will do a good job. Good training for Kendall, too."

Caspian propped his elbows on the snowy white tablecloth, his chin on his clasped hands, and studied Newton. He looked brighter, more determined. Utterly composed. "I take it you had a good meeting with Maggie Milne?"

"The best," he said, topping up his coffee from the pot. "I've been playing by police rules, Caspian, and Maggie made me realise that rules only take you so far in paranormal policing."

Caspian blinked, thinking he'd passed through some weird space-time continuum, and he was now staring at an alternate version of Newton. "What?"

Newton smiled like the cat who got the cream. "I keep trying to apply normal policing to this under the radar job, but I don't need to. Not all the time, anyway."

"Is your new name Maverick Newton?"

"Call me what you like, Caspian. I don't care."

Despite the news of Mariah's horrific death and his friends' injuries, Caspian couldn't help smiling. "You have shaken off the shackles of the policing world."

"Sort of." Newton reached for his toast and buttered it aggressively. "There are times, obviously, when SOCO and interviews and everything have their purpose. Of course they do. I need information, databases, sources, descriptions...all of that. But what matters is that justice is served, and," he picked up his toast and jabbed it at Caspian, "Mariah has been served justice by her own hand. I'm absolutely fine with that."

"Even the fact that she was imprisoned by your two good friends?"

"Yes. She nearly killed Briar, and they were keeping her safely off the streets and preventing anyone else from being put in danger. I knew that logically, of course, but still struggled with the manner in which they did it. But not any longer."

Caspian wasn't sure what he thought of this new Newton. It was unexpected. He still wore a crisp shirt and suit, but the tie had gone, and he looked refreshed. He was clean shaven, hard-jawed, and a there was a determined glint in his eye. "You've always had a hard edge, Newton," he mused. "Understandable considering you hunt down murderers. But this new attitude has definitely given you an extra something."

Newton grinned, pleased. "Yes, I've decided that I answer to only myself now, and my superiors will have to put up with my unorthodox ways. It feels quite freeing. And also unnerving, to throw out some of those old habits. I used to feel that I had to hand over a legitimate criminal. Tick the box to make it count. Now?" He shrugged. "I still get answers. The problem will get solved, just in a less conventional way."

"The Maggie Milne way?"

"Absolutely."

"But Newton, to be honest, that's already been happening for the last year."

"But I felt *constantly* guilty about it. Maggie pointed out that I don't need to be. Clarity is everything." He hesitated, and then said, "Thanks for the invite. You were right. I needed to get away."

"I'm happy to have helped." Caspian wondered if he was about to charge back home and reclaim Briar, but decided asking that would be far too familiar, and knew Newton wouldn't answer anyway. Instead, he said, "I have news, too. Gabe contacted me to say that they have completed their latest case in France, and they're all okay, including Estelle." Caspian had been unexpectedly pleased to hear that, despite the way in which they'd parted.

Newton's eyes narrowed. "I heard she'd gone to help the Nephilim and Shadow. Unusual timing."

"Estelle does what she needs to do...always has. Anyway," he said, resolving to talk to her more civilly when she returned, "what else are you doing today?"

"Meeting Maggie's SOCO team. It's a side branch of the regular team, dedicated to paranormal policing. I thought I could potentially pick out a couple in our own unit as my primary contacts. And then, I don't know, maybe hang out with you if you've arranged to see Olivia."

"I'm meeting her for lunch in Chelsea. She lives there, apparently. Late lunch, actually. You're welcome to join us." He smiled as another idea struck him. "What if I visit SOCO with you?"

"You mean invite a civilian along?" He looked scandalised. "I'm not sure that's appropriate."

Caspian knew he was joking. "But you're a rule breaker now."

"Oh yes. All right, then. No business meetings today?"

"I wrapped it all up yesterday. And besides, they're boring." He'd been desperate to conclude them early and leave time for more interesting activities in the city.

"That business has made you rich."

"True. But like you said, Newton, all the rules are changing, and I'd quite like to break out of my box, too."

Avery stared at Alex across the remnants of their late breakfast, the warm summer breeze caressing her skin through the open French doors and ruffling the serviettes on the table.

He looked tired and distracted, and he toyed with his bacon and eggs, pushing them around the plate rather than devouring them like he normally would. She wanted to hold him and reassure him like she had in bed, but knew it wouldn't dispel his circling thoughts of the night before.

"Are you sure you'll be okay if I leave you on your own?" she asked him.

Alex looked up. "Of course. I'll probably go back to bed once I've dosed up on painkillers." He sighed. "I'm exhausted. I thought I'd feel better this morning, but I don't."

"Like you said, you used a lot of your energy maintaining the cage rune spell. It will take time for your body to recover."

He pushed his plate away and stared at her. "You were right. I should never have taken her prisoner."

She reached over and clasped his hands. "No. I was wrong. You did the right thing. Mariah was dangerous. Her actions last night proved that. She could have tried to immobilise Briar at the museum, but she didn't. I'm still struggling to understand just why she wanted to kill us, but I guess that doesn't matter now." Her gaze slipped across his neck bandage, the only one visible as the others were under his loose shirt. "I can't believe she injured you so badly."

"It could have been much worse. And besides," he squeezed her fingers, "Eli did a great job. Honestly, it really doesn't feel that bad. And he's coming around to check it later."

"All right." She sighed, and pulling her hands free, collected the plates to take to the sink. "I'll bring you a coffee later."

He smiled, although it didn't really disguise his discomfort. "And a cake. I think I'll need it."

"Of course! Although, finishing your breakfast would be a good start."

He stood, his hand raking through his hair. "I'm going back to bed. Be careful. I don't trust Harry and the others not to try something."

Avery stood, too. "They don't know Mariah is dead yet. What will Moore announce?"

He shrugged. "Right now, I don't care. I just hope he doesn't come for my statement too early." He kissed her and headed upstairs, and Avery watched him go with a heavy heart.

Dan and Sally cornered her when she finally arrived in the shop, Dan wearing another terrible pun t-shirt, and Sally wearing a worried frown.

Sally hugged her, which was becoming a daily occurrence lately. "I am so worried about you!" she declared.

"Make that two of us," Dan said, studying her closely. "You've seen the weird photos of the clouds over Bodmin last night, right?"

"What weird photos?"

"The clouds gathering like an alien spaceship was about to emerge from behind it?"

She grimaced. "I was there. Well, a short distance away from the epicentre, but I know what you mean."

Sally inhaled sharply. "I knew it! What happened?"

"I'm not exactly sure how it started, but we finished it," she said, updating them on their rituals. Puzzled, she asked, "Where are the photos?"

"Online—social media, the news." Dan leaned against the bookcase behind the counter. "All over, really. I saw the reports this morning over breakfast. You know Dylan has been trying to call you?"

"No! When?" Avery pulled her phone from the pocket in her long summer dress, realising she had barely glanced at it for hours. "Shit. Lots of messages."

There was half a dozen, all from Cassie, Dylan, and Ben. She stared at Dan, alarmed. "Are they okay?"

"You can ask them yourself," he said, nodding at the door to the shop as Dylan and Ben entered and hurried to the counter.

"At least we've found one of you!" Ben said, a mixture of relief and annoyance in his voice. "We've been trying to get hold of you—and everybody else—for hours!"

They both leaned across the counter, and up close Avery could see that they looked tired and worried. "Why? What's happened?"

Dylan glanced around to check that no customers were nearby. "Bloody mad witches on Bodmin Moor are what happened! Where were you?"

"Busy on Bodmin too, actually!" She was indignant. Since when was she answerable to Ben and Dylan? And then she realised what he'd said. "You were on Bodmin? Last night? Where?"

"Hurlers bloody Stone Circles, that's where!" Ben said. "Risking life and limb filming those crazy, bloody witches invoking something insane!"

Avery was temporarily speechless, but Sally asked, "You were there? Why?"

Dylan looked at her like she'd gone mad. "Because it was the planetary parade, and the stone circles are gathering energy. We decided to see if anything would change."

"And wow, did we pick the wrong place," Ben said. "Well, actually the right place, I guess."

"Who was there?" Avery asked.

"We think," Dylan looked at Ben uncertainly, "that it was Zane, Harry, and Lowen. Well, no, we *know* it was Zane. He almost found us."

"And would have," Ben added, "if not for your spell."

They were trying hard to keep their voices quiet, but the more they shared, the more excited and animated they became. Avery was desperate for a normal, quiet day, but deep down knew that was impossible.

"And," Dylan said, lowering his voice as he clocked the odd puzzled glance from customers, "Cassie told us about Mariah. She's with Eli today."

"What about Mariah?" Sally asked.

Avery sighed and closed her eyes. This was the conversation she'd been dreading. When she opened her eyes again, Ben and Dylan were staring at her, tight-lipped and wide-eyed, and she looked from them to Sally and Dan. "She's dead."

Sally gasped, hands flying to her open mouth in horror, while Dan just silently mouthed, *Wow.*

"I'll tell you everything later, I promise. Right now, I'm just trying to process things."

But Ben was relentless. "But Reu and Alex were hurt, right?"

She glared at him. "Yes! Pretty much everyone is hurt except for me and El!"

Sally clutched her arm. "But they *are* okay?"

"Yes. Or rather, they will be."

"We have news," Dylan said, trying to regain Avery's attention. "That's why we've been trying to find you." He leaned completely across the counter, so he was only inches away. "We think we know where they're hiding."

All other thoughts evacuated Avery's mind. "What? Where? How?"

"Not here," Ben said, shooting Dylan an annoyed look. "Back room, now."

Alex ended the call after his conversation with Genevieve feeling like shit.

He put the phone on the bedside table and pressed his fingers to his eyes, trying to block out the images from the night before that constantly flashed through his mind. Images of the rune cage that shattered and sizzled as it dissipated, wounding him and his magic like a blow. Mariah's swelling magic that lashed with jagged black and red lightning-like energy. And then her burning body.

He groaned and pressed back deeper into the pillows, and then felt one of the cats settle in his lap, mewling softly. He couldn't help but compare Mariah's death to Helena's experience. At least Mariah had died quickly. Helena was dragged to her death, knowing her fate and powerless to do anything about it.

And the smell. It was still in his nostrils and hair, and he couldn't shower because of his bloody injuries. *Damn it!* Her screams, too, were horrific, but quickly snuffed out. She was gone in an instant. *One horrifying instant.*

When he opened his eyes again, he jumped. Helena was standing at the doorway, watching him with an almost compassionate gaze. He pushed aside his natural revulsion for her. "Helena! You made me jump, and as you can see from my bandages, that hurts!"

She nodded and retreated, and both he and the cat watched her go. He'd never been more thankful for the spell that banned her from the bedroom. He idly stroked Circe while he considered Genevieve's words. He had hoped for support, understanding, and maybe praise, but all he got was a shocked silence, and then a clipped response as she questioned their reasoning. She'd finally said, "I need to think on this."

"What for?" he had asked, alarmed. "It was an *accident*."

"But a witch is dead, Alex."

He was so angry he had wanted to throw his phone across the room. Instead, he'd said, "Well, perhaps you should have been more helpful from the start, Genevieve. You are the High Priestess, after all, and frankly, you've given us nothing."

He ended the call at that, not caring what might have followed.

Screw her. He was right. She hadn't helped, and he sensed, from what Avery had said, that the rest of the council were shocked that she wasn't involved in the Hunt Coven, too.

A knock at the back door made him get up. He pulled jeans on and arranged his shirt carefully over his bandages, leaving it unbuttoned, and padded downstairs. Two figures stood at the back door, visible through the frosted pane of glass, and he knew one of them was Moore from the way the sun caught his short, red hair.

As soon as he opened the door, Moore's gaze raked over him, taking in his injuries. "You're in a bad way, Alex," he said by way of greeting.

"I've been better." He stepped back, ushering them in, and looked at the tall young woman with the pixie haircut next to Moore. "Sergeant Kendall, I presume?"

He held his hand out, and she shook it gingerly, as if worried he was about to spell her.

Moore noticed, and also shook Alex's hand. A big, hearty handshake, as if to reassure her. "I'm sorry to disturb your rest, but I need to update you on how Mariah died."

"What? I know how she died."

Moore tightened his lips, although his eyes held a glimmer of intrigue. "It'll be easier somewhere more private."

Alex led them up the stairs, aware that both of them were looking around with avid interest, which made Alex more uncomfortable. *What the hell was Moore on about?*

"Have a seat, Alex," Moore said, gesturing him to a chair.

Alex sat at the table rather than on the sofa. It felt more formal somehow, and he started to feel sick with worry. Suddenly, he wished Newton were here. "What's going on?"

"Mariah was found in a burned-out van stolen from White Haven Museum in the early hours of this morning. She'd crashed into a stone wall, and she must have punctured the fuel tank. The whole lot went up." He shrugged. "It's easier this way. To have found her at Rueben's home would have been a disaster. Too many questions as to why she was there in the first place."

"And too many questions," Kendall said, "about why Reuben had a van stolen from the museum."

Alex had been so side-tracked by imprisoning Mariah that he'd completely forgotten about the van. He floundered for words. "Er, I guess you're right. That's a good idea. You don't need a statement from me, then?"

"Did you see the van anywhere after it was stolen?" Moore's eyes were wide. "Because it was quite a distance from Reuben's place, and here."

Feeling like a complete idiot as the depth of the deception sank in, Alex said, "No! No, of course not. I didn't see a thing."

"And you scalded yourself with hot water, did you?"

Alex glanced down at his injuries. "Garden bonfire, actually. Got out of control. My own fault...I used too much accelerant."

Moore nodded sagely. "Of course. You have to be careful. Best stick to paper and wood next time."

"What about the press?"

"They were at the scene shortly after we removed the remains. They waited for us to break the news to her family before releasing it."

"They know?"

"Her mother was told this morning. I trust she's informed everyone else." He checked his watch. "It will be on the lunchtime news if you want to watch the statement. I kept it brief. Sad business."

Alex's thoughts were reeling. "Why would Mariah be in a museum van?"

"Excellent question, and one we shall be seeking to answer as part of our ongoing investigation into the museum robbery. Harry has been named as a person of interest. We'll interview his wife again."

"But how did you arrange it all?"

"El was very helpful."

Alex sagged back in the chair, horrified that El, who hated what they'd done, had helped cover it up. He was speechless.

Moore stood up, his hand smoothing his red hair flat, and Kendall stood too, her eyes still darting around the room. Alex was suddenly grateful that they kept all of their magical paraphernalia in the attic. He knew that they knew, but it somehow made him feel better.

"I suggest," Moore said, as he headed for the stairs, "that you be careful for a while. We'll see ourselves out."

As soon as Alex heard the front door shut, he moved to the sofa and collapsed, his legs weak. *What just happened?* He'd expected to be questioned and have to explain things, and although he knew Newton wouldn't press charges, he still thought that he'd have to say something. And El...how could he ever thank her? He needed to phone her, but he couldn't face it right now.

He flicked the news on and was skipping through the channels when the door burst open below and Avery bounded up the stairs, the excited chatter of voices with her. She appeared breathless, Ben and Dylan behind her.

"Alex! I have news!"

Twenty-Four

Newton studied Olivia James across the table, thinking how very good looking she was, and how well she blended into this chic bar in Chelsea.

Her shoulder-length hair was tussled artfully, and her chestnut lowlights were expertly applied. Her clothing was expensive, draping beautifully over her slim figure, but there was nothing uptight about her. She was elegant, yet relaxed, and she had a mischievous smile on her face as she regarded both of them. Glancing at Caspian, Newton wondered if he was slightly smitten. He looked dazed.

"So," she said, her fingers loosely clasping her wine glass, and manicured nails tapping the glass as the moisture caused by her chilled white wine trickled down the stem, "you're looking for black market gold dealers. That's a big market. Tell me more about the objects."

"It's a big, steaming pile of pirate treasure," Newton started. "Lots of it."

Olivia's gaze flicked to him. "How much are we talking?"

"Crates full of it. Hundreds, if not thousands, of guineas and doubloons. Some jewels, too—gemstones, chains. It would be worth a lot of money."

She nodded. "This is related to that theft in Cornwall, isn't it? The museum?"

"Sort of," Newton said, sipping his pint. It wasn't Doom, but it was a decent ale. "There was more than just that. We managed to secure the museum hoard, but they have more in their possession."

Olivia's smile became even broader. "We? My, my, Detective Inspector. You are surprising." She turned to Caspian. "Was that your doing?"

He blinked. "No. Some friends acquired it."

She leaned forward, and her scent wafted across the table. "Other witches, you mean?"

She was a tease, and Newton liked it. Caspian liked it even more. He decided he'd better answer for him. Caspian seemed to have lost his tongue. "Yes. I believe you've met two of them, Alex and El?"

"Oh, yes! At Angel's Rest. They arrived to protect the house with spells. That was an interesting few days. The Nephilim are fascinating!"

Caspian looked surprised. "You went into the Temple of the Trinity?"

"I wouldn't have missed it for a whole season's worth of Louboutins! And if you knew me, you would know that is significant!"

"You didn't wear them in there, though?" Caspian asked, obviously amused, as he shifted his gaze to her feet.

She wiggled her toes that were encased in strappy sandals and smiled. "Of course not. Only steel-toe caps for raiding tombs."

"By the way, I'm sorry to hear about The Orphic Guild's secretary's death," Newton said, recalling his conversation with Maggie about Black Cronos. He was beginning to feel like a gooseberry, and decided to steer the conversation away from Louboutins...whatever they were. Some kind of posh shoe, he presumed.

Olivia's flirtatious manner immediately disappeared, and her grip on the wine glass tightened. "Yes, that was terrible. Poor Robert. Mason is devastated. He's returning today. I'm just relieved that everyone else has survived—well, mostly." She took a deep breath, as if to shake off the memory. "Right. Treasure. Why aren't they just selling it to a museum or a legitimate collector? They'd still make an awful lot of money."

Caspian shrugged. "It's possible they are, but why keep so quiet about it? They're on the run. They've killed people because of it. They clearly want to keep it a secret."

Newton thought of what Zane's mother had said. "Someone suggested that the events associated with the gold—it was acquired by murder and theft for the most part during the smuggling years— would give it some extra desirability."

Caspian nodded in agreement. "A powerful metal associated with death and bloodshed is useful in magic."

"Of course!" Olivia nodded, her eyes taking on a faraway expression before focussing sharply. "Gold obtained by bloodshed leaves a dark, violent stain. That is potent. That much gold with so much dark history has a certain appeal. It isn't just black-market gold dealers you want. It's also an occult dealer, and that," she spread her hands wide and smiled, "is very much my thing."

"Do you know where or how it might be sold?" Newton asked, finally thinking they were getting somewhere. "I'm hoping that if we can't track the witches down, then we can find them this way."

Olivia nodded. "We use Burton and Knight's auction house for the most part, who are the respectable face of occult and arcane objects that are for sale. But there are underground dealers who have far less scruples about where the items come from and what they might be used for. I could make some inquiries, see what information is out there." She smiled. "There are usually always whispers."

Newton's phone buzzed, and murmuring his excuses, he headed to a quiet corner of the bar, half watching Olivia and Caspian flirt, and trying not to smirk. "Hey, Alex. Is everything all right?"

"Not really. It appears that Harry and the others have been working on something much bigger than just accumulating gold and using it in rituals. It looks like they've made new objects—powerful ones. Potentially to use on us, or we think that's what they're planning to sell."

"Perfect timing. Tell me everything you know."

Reuben stared at the TV screen, and then at the people gathered in the snug. All of the witches were there, plus Hunter, Ghost OPS, and Eli and Zee. All were transfixed by the events on the screen.

Dylan had formatted his footage of the previous night's filming, and they had just watched a flare of power around Lowen—or at least they presumed it was Lowen. The firelit circle was full of shadows despite the almost full moon, and although Dylan had zoomed in, they weren't close enough to see details.

"That's when they broke your binding spell," El said, nudging Reuben. She had cleansed the whole house, especially the cellar, and after that had barely left his side all day, clearly worried about him.

Alex grunted. "The power of harnessing the planets' energies, I guess."

"It was about now," Cassie said, "that the clouds really started to gather overhead." She tore her gaze away from the screen. "We thought they were winding down, but they were really just getting started."

"Which would match when we started to feel an increase in gathering energies, too," Avery said, staring at El and Briar.

Briar was sitting next to Hunter on the long sofa, and she shook her head, confused. "But Eve seemed to break up the power that was gathering."

"Yeah," Hunter nodded, "that massive jolt of magic that shot into the sky!"

"It was hard for us to work out what was going on at that stage," Dylan confessed. "We were cloaked in a shadow spell after Zane almost caught us, and I abandoned my bigger screen out of paranoia, worried that the light would reveal us, using only the camera's small screen instead. The thermal imaging definitely showed the stones glowing —"

"Even the quartz path under the soil," Ben interrupted, nodding at Briar.

Cassie pointed to the screen. "Look, there! It's like Harry harnessed another beam of magic, and drew it into the gold at his feet."

"A beam of magic!" Hunter scoffed, leaning forward, elbows on knees as he stared at the screen. "What is this? *Close Encounters*?"

"Hold on," Reuben said, struggling to understand, but thinking the whole pattern of events sounded hugely suspicious. "You three," he looked at El, Briar, and Avery, "were part of some ritual at Stannon Stone Circle that involved charging crystals, but because of gathering energies overhead—the whole big, swirly clouds thing—Eve, what? Manipulated power to dispel it?"

"Yes," El said, frowning at him. "We thought we were stopping what was happening. She drew on our magic."

"Whose idea was it to do that?"

El glanced uncertainly at Briar and Avery. "Eve's?"

"No." Avery stared at Reuben. "It was Cornell's suggestion. He asked for her help. He guided the whole thing." Her eyes widened, and he knew she was thinking exactly what he was. "Are you suggesting we were duped?"

Reuben felt a horrible but certain knowledge settle in the pit of his stomach. "I think it's very possible." A ripple of unease ran around the room. "Think about it. Cornell is insistent on helping, and seems like a good guy. Claudia recommends him, and we trust her. There's no reason not to...she's always been very supportive of us. So, Cornell becomes part of the smaller team. He also happens to be a cosmic witch, and understands harnessing the power of the planets far more than we do. Excellent! Just what we need. He offers to charge some gold and crystals with Hemani's help, and then suggests you take part, too. Did he pick the spot?"

Avery nodded slowly. "Yes. When me and El saw him yesterday he hadn't decided on the place yet, but he said he'd tell us later. And he did. A couple of hours before, telling us to meet him at Stannon Stone Circle."

Alex groaned. "Which is on the north side of Bodmin Moor?"

"Yep," Dylan said, fumbling for his phone. "I'll bring up the map, but from my recollection, it's almost opposite Hurlers." Seconds later, he said, "Shit. It's almost directly opposite, in a straight line. But it's a few miles away."

Almost simultaneously, everyone was either searching on their phones for the map of stone circles, or craning over shoulders to peek.

"Bloody hell," Hunter said, staring at his own phone. "It *is* almost in a straight line! Does that mean something?"

Avery exploded in anger. "Fuck it! He used us! We added to the whole thing!" She jumped off the sofa, almost dislodging Alex, and started to pace at the back of the room, fury radiating from her. "We probably fed power to Mariah!"

"How?" Zee asked. He'd arrived earlier with Eli, who'd changed dressings and checked wounds, and had been absorbing everything silently. "That sounds far-fetched."

"I don't know how!" Her eyes were wild. "But they're all connected! Lowen's binding spell was broken, and Mariah burst out of her cage. I don't know how they're connected, but they are!"

"Maybe," Alex suggested, trying to be calm, "they all performed a spell to connect themselves before any of this happened. They have been laying the groundwork for a while."

"Hold on!" Dylan raised his voice to shush them all. "You haven't seen what happened later. I've fast-forwarded—we were there for ages. After the big burst of power, they kept feeding their spell or whatever in the middle. They started to fashion things..."

Ben interrupted. "Objects of power, from what I could tell. They had a cauldron set up, and a fierce fire under it."

"And moulds," Cassie added. "They were pouring gold into various-shaped things—big and small."

Hunter looked baffled. "In the middle of a bloody stone circle? That sounds insane. What if the weather had been bad, or someone had interrupted them?"

"It's not a crime," Eli pointed out. "And most people would avoid watching weird activities in the middle of a stone circle. It looks like what it is. An occult ritual."

The footage was playing now, and everyone's attention focussed on the images. Dylan was right. They were definitely making some kind of ritual objects. *Bowls, jewellery, chalices, maybe even athames*, Reuben thought, squinting at the image.

"It's a regular little smithy," El said, impressed despite everything.

"I told Newton," Alex said to the room in general, "as soon as I knew the basics. I thought it might be important."

"And of course," Ben continued, "they were close by, like we told you earlier. They came from beneath the old engine room that's now the Visitor Centre."

"So," Eli said, starting to smile, "they are potentially still down there. Perhaps we should pay them a visit."

"You want to go down the mines?" Ben asked, his brow furrowing into one big knot. "Are you nuts? The whole place is riddled with shafts and tunnels. It would be a death trap."

Eli just smiled. "But they are down there."

"*Were*!" Ben reminded him. "It doesn't mean they still are. And it would be a warren! You could easily get lost. Or suffocated. Not to mention, buried alive."

"I'm prepared to take the risk," Eli said with a shrug. He looked at Reuben. "You still have some of the gold, right?"

"We have quite a lot of it. It's still upstairs. I'm hoping they're not planning to steal it."

Alex shook his head. "I doubt that after what happened to Mariah. I reckon they've swallowed their losses." He watched the three witches' activities on the video. "It seems they had enough gold to do what they needed to."

"Do they know that Mariah is dead?" Cassie asked.

"They must by now," Briar reasoned. "It was on the news."

"Not much coverage in a mine," Hunter pointed out.

Avery had finally stopped pacing, but a look of grim determination had settled on her face. "So, what's Cornell doing? Was his job just to dupe us into feeding their spell?"

"We think," Alex reminded her. "We can't jump to any conclusions until we know for sure. It could be a coincidence."

She cocked her head at him. "Coincidence? I don't buy it. And what now? They just disappear with their profits, never to be heard from again? One of them could be selling whatever they made last night, right now!"

"Which is why," Briar reminded her, "Caspian is still in London with Newton."

Reuben nodded. "Waiting for Olivia's contacts to come through with some news." Alex had updated them earlier, but the conversation had shifted once Ghost OPS arrived. He felt sorry for Alex. He still looked in pain, despite Briar's healing and Eli's dressings, and Reuben felt guilty that his own wound had been less severe. "Alex, remind me what Newton said."

Alex winced as he grabbed his beer. "Olivia had a few ideas of who to contact, and suggested they stay in London until she's heard from them. Apparently, it's unusual for these items to be stored for months. There's a quick turnaround, and high profit margins. Of course, Harry or Zane could have their own private buyer already, but Olivia said the biggest market is in London."

"And in the meantime, we need to do something," Avery said, pushing the others. "They're probably still here somewhere."

"The mines!" Eli said, refusing to drop his suggestion. "I'll happily go down there and flush them out."

Reuben snorted. "I thought you were the peacekeeper and healer? Now you want to find them?"

"They hurt good people, killed others, and need to be stopped. They certainly shouldn't disappear into the sunset with lots of money and smug egos. Zee knows that I'm willing to do what it takes when needed."

Zee laughed. "Yeah, pretty boy's bruises came from a very brutal fight on Monday. Eli will fight when he has to. And so will I." He cast Eli a sidelong glance. "We were just saying only the other night that we didn't think our brothers should have all the fun."

"Tonight, then?" Avery said, grim but determined.

"Woah!" Alex said, alarmed. "Who said anything about *you* going?"

"These enemies are witches. Eli and Zee will need help."

Eli looked at Zee, who shook his head, and then gave Avery a crooked smile. "I think we'll be just fine. In fact, you could be a hindrance down there. You stay here and decide what to do with Cornell—and work out what he might be doing. You've still got a solstice coming up." Eli stood. "Come on, Zee. We have somewhere to be."

Undeterred, Avery hadn't finished her argument. "But how will you catch them without magic?"

Eli's grin spread. "Who says we're going to catch them?"

Zee stood, too, slapping Eli on the shoulder. "I suggest we pick up some weapons on the way. And Alex," he added as he headed to the door, "stay at home tomorrow. The pub can manage without you."

With predatory smiles, the Nephilim disappeared, as shouts of "Be careful," followed them out the door.

"Eli is right," El said, turning to Avery and Briar. "What if we've helped Cornell undermine the coven's solstice celebrations?"

"Ha! Undermine? More like blow them up!" Hunter scoffed. "Isn't that a thing where everyone celebrates together? Your whole coven will be there."

"He's right, Ave," Reuben said, trying to reason with her. She was obviously still fuming about not going down the mine. "If Cornell is planning something, that's the time he'll strike. We need our own plan to stop him, and unless he gives anything away this weekend, we've got nothing to act on."

"I agree," Alex said. "And honestly, I don't know what's got into Genevieve, but she was not willing to hear my side of the story earlier. I have a feeling she was thinking on giving me some kind of penance."

"We could show her the footage," Cassie suggested.

"I think we keep it quiet," Reuben told her. "Right now, other than Caspian and Newton, I trust no one outside of this room."

"What about Eve and Nate?" Briar asked. "They have always been good friends to us!"

"Maybe...but let's not assume they still are."

The mood in the room was grim, and El's hand tightened where it rested on his thigh. "Okay, let's be logical about this. We think Cornell manipulated us. Maybe one of us should chat to him this weekend, just to see how he sounds and check that he'll be at the solstice celebrations. Charlie is also under suspicion—we can't forget that. He may well be working with Cornell. I'm sure he'll be there, regardless of his argument with us the other day. Perhaps all this is about dissolving the Cornwell Coven...or restructuring it."

Briar gave a strangled cry. "But there are over thirty members! You can't tell me that they think we'll all just acquiesce to whatever they propose! That's madness!"

Reuben's head hurt. Everything sounded nuts. Personally, he'd never craved power, so he couldn't understand that need in others, or what they would even do with it. He liked freedom and choice; but then again, his choices didn't lead to anyone getting hurt. "Perhaps freedom is what this is all about," he mused aloud. "Maybe, unbeknownst to us, some members have been wanting more freedom to do different magic that Genevieve and the older members have frowned upon."

"What kinds of different magic?" Ben asked. "I thought you all had different kinds of magic, anyway. Different strengths."

Avery had barely sat down when she started pacing again. "But we adhere to certain rules of witchcraft. That we harm none and instead work with nature and the seasons, enhancing lives—our own and others. Improving health and wellbeing. Positive things. Others sometimes choose more selfish paths."

"The Dark Arts!" Hunter teased with a wicked grin.

"Will you behave!" Briar scolded, playfully slapping him. "This isn't funny!"

Alex shuffled in his chair, wincing as he moved. "I keep revisiting that conversation I had with Genevieve. It was odd! Not like her at all.

I wonder if she's being threatened."

Everyone froze and looked at Alex, drinks suspended halfway to lips, hands motionless in bowls of crisps.

"You must be joking!" Reuben finally said.

Briar almost stumbled over her words. "Genevieve? Our High Priestess? The most powerful witch in our coven? No! I don't believe it!"

Alex rubbed his stubble, staring into distance. "Or perhaps she's holding herself back for some reason. Is purposefully not getting too involved. I have no idea why."

Briar shot out of her seat too, also pacing off nervous energy. "Perhaps she's keeping a clear head. Focussing her energy."

"Let's hope so," Avery said. "We just need to figure out what will happen at Litha—and how to stop it."

"Perhaps I should see Genevieve," Briar suggested. "Check if she's okay?"

"No!" Alex said immediately. "It might compromise her, or put you in danger. Let's just leave it. We'll see her on Monday. One way or another, everything will become clear then."

Reuben groaned. He really wanted to go to sleep, just to be able to think clearly in the morning. And he wanted to surf. That always cleared his head. But with bandages on his arm, that wasn't going to be easy. "Stop, please. All of us are shattered. No one is thinking straight. We're in shock, and injured. People we trusted are now compromised. Let's go to bed and meet on Sunday with fresh ideas and clear perspectives."

"Wait!" El said suddenly. "Ulysses said something last night that has stuck with me. We have a whole pile of gold that we're not using, and that's madness. It's the solstice. Sun is associated with gold. It will be our most powerful weapon against whatever Harry and the others are planning. And right now, there's a big, fat full moon outside." She stood up. "We need to cleanse the gold tonight, and then I'm taking it to Dante tomorrow." Her eyes were bright with excitement. "Genevieve uses a staff sometimes, right?" They nodded, and she ploughed on. "I'm going to make a new one out of gold, and then disguise it in wood. And the top will be a huge stone. Amber, perhaps, or citrine. I'll see what I've got."

Reuben looked up at her admiringly. *His beautiful, clever girlfriend.* "That sounds amazing. But will she use it?"

El leaned towards him and kissed his cheek. "She has to." She stared at the rest of them. "I'll talk to her. Just leave it with me, and I'll catch you up on everything tomorrow."

"Do you need help?" Avery asked.

El hugged her. "No. I have a plan. You take Alex home. He still looks knackered."

"Oh, cheers," he said, rising to his feet. "But I won't deny that I am."

"Where are we meeting?" Dylan asked, packing his gear away. "Don't think you're leaving us out of this!"

"To be honest," Reuben admitted, "if not for you guys, we wouldn't know half of what's going on. Do you want to meet here again?"

Avery shook her head, walking over to kiss his cheek. "No. You've done enough, and your home has been invaded, blown up, and almost set on fire." She turned to the others. "Come to our place. I'll be in touch about the time. And bring ideas—it doesn't matter how mad they may seem. Mad might be the best thing right now."

Twenty-Five

Eli circled over Bodmin Moor, Zee a short distance away, scanning the ground for any unusual activity.

The full moon was high overhead, a few clouds scudding across the sky, and it was risky to be flying when the moon was so bright. But Bodmin Moor was a scene of undulating waves of grass, abandoned Neolithic settlements, stunted trees, and silence, even when they hovered over Hurlers Stone Circles. There was no sign of occult activity, and apart from a few bright windows in the houses of Minions Village, that looked quiet, too.

He landed next to the converted engine room and headed to the spot where Ben and Cassie had found the tunnel the night before. It was easy to dismantle the wooden covering, and he peered inside as Zee landed next to him.

"Success?" he asked.

"I've found a hole, if that's what you mean." He could see what looked like a wooden covering on the ground.

"No lights?"

"I think the shaft is covered." He pulled his head from the small gap and looked up at Zee. "Maybe I should go alone, and you should keep watch."

Zee grimaced. "Don't go all Rambo on me, brother. I'm coming, too. We can pull the covering back over."

Eli resisted the urge to flip Zee off. He pushed his sword ahead of him, and folding his wings away completely, wriggled through the hole and dropped several feet onto the ground.

The space beneath the Visitor Centre was larger than it initially looked. Although it was only one square room, the lower, unused floor space must have been part of the workplace at one point. Stone walls edged the space, including the floor, but the roof was made of thick, heavy beams. In the centre was a large, round wooden cover that he was able to lift aside easily, revealing a broad shaft descending into darkness.

"Herne's balls," Zee murmured as he scrambled down next to him. "That looks like it goes down a long way."

Eli wrinkled his nose as the rich scent of must, dampness, and metals hit him. It was pitch black, but their eyesight was good enough to see well. "There's a ladder attached to the side. I hope it holds us."

"It's not wide enough for our wings," Zee murmured. He looked across the shaft at Eli. "So, I'm guessing we're going to trap them down there? Kill them?"

"It's better than the witches trying to bind their magic, surely. And I can't imagine they'd want to apologise and turn their back on their wicked ways, would you? Mariah didn't." Eli leaned over and grasped the metal ladder, tugging it sharply, but it held, just about. "I suggest you wait until I'm at the bottom before you follow." Without waiting for an answer, he swung his leg over the edge and started his slow descent.

It was only when he was partway down that he considered stale air and poisonous fumes, but if he remembered correctly, that wasn't something to worry about with tin and copper mines. And besides, he could see smaller shafts running off in places, and faint stirrings of air brushed across his face. When he finally reached the bottom, he stepped into a pool of shallow water, and saw a passageway running in front of him, long and straight, and well above head height. The walls and roof were rough-hewn, with old beams wedged in place in some sections. It would be easy to get lost down here, even though he had a good sense of direction. He pulled chalk from his pocket and marked the wall, and in a few minutes, Zee arrived next to him.

"It reminds me," Zee said, pulling his sword out, "of that time we entered the emerald mines of Egypt. It all got very messy, and I nearly died."

Eli grinned as he led the way. "Better not make the same mistakes here then, brother."

Caspian eased his finger around his t-shirt's neckline, relieved that he'd changed out of his suit. The pub, The Alley Cat, was hot and crowded, and the corner they were in was dark, lit only by low lights which seemed to accentuate the warmth. The scent of sweat and perfume battled for supremacy, and he sipped his beer and watched Olivia in an effort to distract himself.

Newton was at the bar getting a second round, but Olivia was at another table, leaning forward earnestly as she chatted to a shifty looking middle-aged man with a paunch and greying hair. It was Olivia, though, who held his attention. She really was arresting. Her toned arms gleamed in the soft light, looking silky and smooth, and her upturned, mischievous face as she talked to the man was just asking to be kissed.

Wow. He leaned back in his chair and finished his beer. *Where had that thought come from?* Actually, who was he kidding? He'd been thinking it all afternoon. He was single, and so was she from what he could tell, so why did he feel ridiculously guilty that his thoughts were straying from Avery? *That was easy*, he thought, answering himself. *Because he was a lovestruck fool who needed to move on.* His brain was moving on before his heart had caught up.

As if she was aware of him looking, Olivia glanced back at him, her lips parted in a smile, before she resumed her conversation.

Look away. He finally did, and saw Newton returning with two pints and a glass of white wine. He huffed as he sat. "Is she still talking to that dodgy bloke?"

"She is, which must mean," Caspian answered as he picked up the fresh pint, "that he has news."

"Good. I feel like I'm bunking off, just sitting here drinking."

"It's nearly midnight, Newton! You're allowed to drink in a bar on a Friday night. And besides, new rules, remember? Or rather," his lips twitched with amusement, "no rules."

Newton frowned. "There *are* some rules! I like rules. They're just different ones."

"And besides," Caspian argued, "this is work! With luck, we'll be at an auction in the next few hours, eyeing up whatever Harry and the others have made."

"But then what? We can't buy anything. And what if Harry or one of the others is there? They'll recognise you. And maybe me."

Caspian had been pondering this on and off all day, ever since Olivia had said she could get them into an auction, if one existed. "The objects are made now, and they will be used in whatever way the buyer sees fit. It may not be for anything bad!" he pointed out, surprised at the intensity in Newton's stare. "I only want Harry...or Zane. I doubt Lowen will be here. I was targeted in my own home, and they tried to kill me." He grew angry just thinking about it. "I intend to take them back for *our* kind of justice."

"And how will you do that?"

He wondered how much to reveal, but he had few allies here, and he needed Newton's support. "By using my magic, of course."

"But Harry is strong, you said so yourself. And he has that powerful ring that shoots magic like a bloody laser beam."

"I have a few ideas. Although, you may not like the magic I employ."

"As long as you catch them, I don't give a shit what you use."

Caspian was unsure he would ever get used to Newton's new attitude. "Well, I'll do what I can."

Newton was still staring at him, a speculative look on his face as Olivia returned to the table, looking jubilant.

"Have I interrupted something?" she asked, her smile fading.

"No," Caspian answered, rather too quickly. "You have news?"

"Yes. Sam arranges small, select auctions from time to time. A few weeks ago, he was contacted by a man called Harry Pedrick, who said he had new, powerful objects to sell and a quantity of gold, but warned that he wanted a high price. The auction is tomorrow night." Her eyes narrowed. "Harry is the name of the man you mentioned, right?"

"Right," Caspian said, trying not to look at her tempting lips. "Whereabouts?"

"It will be in rooms on the Embankment. Suitably Machiavellian. Various routes in and out for safety, including one from here. Because he knows me, and I vouched for you, you can go. But," she stared at them intently, "you are not to cause trouble."

"As if we would!" Caspian said, mock-offended. "Will Harry be there?"

"I believe so. I didn't press too much, as Sam started to look suspicious. I said you were a rich businessman who collected occult objects and had used The Orphic Guild for a few years. Happy?"

"Very."

"Good." Olivia picked up her wine glass, took a healthy sip, and beamed at both of them. "And just so we're clear—I will be coming with you!"

Zee was comfortable in the dark, confident in his own abilities and those of his brother, but he had to admit that the mine was seriously creepy.

The path was uneven, and large caverns sloped off to either side. The ground rippled with pools of unknown depth in places, and the constant trickle of water sounded like whispers all around them. The thought of working down here for hours was depressing. They hadn't even travelled that far, and from what he could remember of the moor, they were heading to other abandoned mine buildings slightly to the northeast.

A large pool of water appeared in front of them, forcing a detour to the left. Zee was barely halfway around the pool when the ground crumbled, wood cracked, and a shaft opened up beneath him. In seconds he was falling. Instinctively, and despite the cramped space, he unfurled his wings and braced them on the sides, suspending him above certain death.

"Stop!" he yelled, twisting his head to see Eli lunge for him. "I'm okay. Just wait. The ground is still shifting."

The wall to his left was mere feet away, and his wing was folded awkwardly as he'd twisted to get purchase, but on his right, his other wing was fully extended into the water, the depth uncertain.

"Fuck," he muttered. "The bastards set a trap."

Eli was a few feet behind him still, watching the ground, and he gingerly poked forward using his sword. "This feels solid."

Zee stared into the darkness below, his feet swinging. "I can see the shaft's edges. It's not that big."

"Big enough to have killed a human," Eli pointed out. "Only your wings saved you."

Eli used his hands to knock the remaining wood and earth away so the edges of the shaft could be seen clearly. "They fitted a rotten piece of wood over it and covered it with dirt. Sneaky shits."

"And now they've probably heard us," Eli said. "I'll jump over you and pull you out the other side. Let's hope there's not another hidden shaft."

Eli retreated a few feet and then ran, jumping over the shaft and Zee, landing safely a few feet away. For a moment he froze, as if expecting the ground to give way again, but then exhaled, eyeing Zee with relief. He lay on his stomach and extended his arm. Swinging slightly to ensure a better grip, Zee grabbed Eli's hand, and within seconds was hauled over the side.

Zee gripped his arm tightly. "Thanks, brother."

"Let's take it slowly."

They hadn't progressed far when there was an almost imperceptible change in the light, and he threw a hand out to stop

Eli. "I see something up ahead."

Eli had paused to stare into the darkness of another passageway on the right, but now he turned and spoke barely above a whisper. "Good. I'm already over this."

They continued silently, the passage widening until they finally stood on the threshold of a huge cave, the floor sloping upwards where it narrowed at the roof. A fire crackled on the raised ground, and candles and lamps illuminated what looked to be a camp, a shaft rising above it. But no one was in sight.

Backs pressed against the cave wall in the darkness, they both scanned the area. Someone had to be here somewhere, but no doubt his shout earlier had warned them of their approach.

Eli pointed to the ceiling high above them and slowly unfurled his wings before rapidly ascending into the darkness, keeping well away from the firelight. Zee circled the cave, edging up the rising ground and sticking to the shadows as he approached the campfire.

Out of the darkness, a fireball was hurled towards him, and Zee dived to the ground and rolled, sword in hand. Seconds later more fireballs followed, and he rolled again and again, finally leaping to his feet and ducking behind a pile of fallen rock. A strange sensation started in his feet, and his head buzzed, and he realised someone was trying to use a spell on him. He'd never been more thankful for his angel blood. Magic never really worked on them, and he felt the effects quickly dissipate. He focussed on the cave. It seemed that the attack was coming from two different directions, and he darted out, trying to draw their fire to allow Eli to attack from above.

Old mining tools and huge, man-sized metal buckets were strewn across the floor, and he ran between them, stopping for seconds only as he made his way up the slope. His speed was advantageous, the powerful blasts of energy missing him constantly.

A cry came from above as Eli swooped down and hauled up a wriggling man, magic flowing from his outstretched hands. He tried to attack Eli, but couldn't twist around enough. Another fireball flew from the darkness, and Eli swooped to avoid it with the still screaming man in his firm grip, as Zee ran full tilt up the slope to draw the second person's attack. He finally arrived in the camp area and dived behind a large metal container that had tumbled over on the remains of an old track.

Fireballs and bolts of energy were now zinging around the cave, threatening to bring the roof down. Another wild cry came from above, but ended abruptly as a man's head crashed to the floor in front of Zee, followed by his body. Blood splattered everywhere.

There was another enormous crack of power aimed at the roof, and this time a huge section broke off, rock crashing to the ground. Zee lunged out of the way, and then watched with horror as the way they had entered was sealed off in massive slip of rock.

Debris rocketed around the cave, and Zee extended his wings and flew to the spot where the magic had come from. But another blast of magic sent him whirling up and out of range, the power dislodging yet another chunk of rock. The whole cave was in danger of collapsing.

"Can you see the other witch?" he shouted to Eli, desperate to catch their attacker before they lost their chance.

"That way!" Eli pointed to a narrow passage opening at the rear of the cave, almost hidden by a spur of rock. He swooped out of the way of another falling block of stone. "But—"

Before he could finish, another massive blast saw the narrow entrance below collapse, effectively blocking them from chasing him.

"Fuck it!" yelled Zee. "He got away!"

"We have a more pressing problem, brother! The roof's collapsing, and we're sealed in."

An ominous crack zigzagged across the roof of the cave and Zee frantically whirled around, looking for a way out. Their only option was the shaft leading back up.

"This way!" he yelled to Eli as he soared to the opening. The shaft stretched above them, and reducing his wingspan, he flew upwards, relieved to see Eli follow.

But the shaft was faring no better than the cave below. Cracks were running up the sides, and rocks crumbled away, bouncing off his shoulders and catching in his wings. He reached the top and found it sealed with a slab of stone. He grabbed the remains of a rickety ladder, and within seconds, Eli was next to him.

They examined the slab above them, noting it rested on a lip of rock, but the shaft was wider than the slab, and Eli said, "If we can pull that free, everything above it should fall, and we should be able to get out."

"But we risk being caught in the rock fall."

"And if we don't try, we'll be stuck here." The rumblings of falling rock continued below, and dust billowed around them, despite how far they were above the cave. Eli grunted and coughed. "You know how we said we should spend our quiet evenings drinking beer and playing games on the console? We should have stuck to that plan."

"This was your idea!" Zee reminded him.

"Yeah, well, remind me what a dumb idiot I am next time, and tell me to stick to seducing women and healing wounds." Eli pulled his short dagger out. "If I gouge out the rock on this side, and you work on that side, we should be able to release it."

Zee nodded and balanced precariously, his feet and wings wedged against the wall to steady him. Together, they worked fast. As the rock broke up, they kept hacking, Zee thankful for the spells that made the blades abnormally strong.

With an immense crack, the slab started to slide free, and flattening themselves against the walls, they both gave it a final pull. With an ominous rumble, the stone plug plummeted past them, almost carrying them with it. A rush of rock and earth followed, seemingly never ending, until finally it stopped and fresh air rushed around them. There was another shaft above, narrower certainly, but he could see the night sky.

Zee hauled himself up, hands and arms pressed against the sides, crab-walking his way to the surface, and finally threw himself onto the grass at the top. Seconds later, Eli rolled next to him, and they stared up at the full moon.

"I was beginning to wonder," Eli admitted, "If I'd see that again."

Zee eased upright, and found that they were still on Bodmin Moor, but a distance away from the engine room. And there was no sign of a fleeing witch anywhere. The ground still shook beneath them, and he hauled Eli to his feet. "Congratulations on the kill. Another one down, two to go."

Twenty-Six

B riar stared at Eli in disbelief. "*You* killed Lowen?"

"It must have been him. It certainly wasn't the skinny-faced guy that Dylan filmed." He nodded at Cassie, who was also listening, mouth and eyes wide open.

They were in Charming Balms, Briar's shop, early on Saturday morning, and there were currently no customers. Hunter had tried to persuade her to stay home, but she'd missed enough days of work already. Plus, she had fully recovered from Mariah's attack, and she enjoyed making her soaps, candles, lotions, and balms, seeing her regulars, and catching up on chat. It soothed her, and provided a sense of satisfaction and achievement.

Now, however, she just felt sick. "You beheaded him?"

"Yeah. Little bastard tried to hit me with those magic blasts," he wiggled his large hands, "and he was targeting Zee. I'd had enough." He leaned on the counter and sipped his coffee. "I thought you'd be pleased."

"I think it's bloody brilliant," Hunter said, grinning and raising his cup in salute. He'd come into work with her, promising to take her out to lunch.

Eli returned his grin. "I knew you'd understand."

"I *am* pleased," Briar confessed, feeling horribly guilty. She pressed her hands to her eyes. "I just thought we'd stop them with less violent means."

"Then you were deluded," Eli said, but not unkindly. "And that's because you're a nice person."

When she opened her eyes, he was looking at her with concern, Hunter already voicing his agreement. "But that's what is so loveable about her."

"I agree with Briar," Cassie said, "but I have to say that I'm really relieved he's dead. I didn't like watching them on Thursday night. They were scary. I think Zane would have killed us if he had seen us."

Eli grimaced. "Well, unfortunately, he's still out there. The little shit ran off down another passageway and then blocked it. And there was no sign of Harry."

"But," Hunter said, "one less enemy is a good thing. I think I'll head to the moor, look around, and try to pick up a scent."

Briar rounded on him. "No! It's too dangerous!"

"I'm just going to look, as my wolf! I'll keep away from people."

Eli stood up, stretching his enormous frame. "It's a good idea, but be careful. We opened a shaft up last night, and then called it into the police when we got home. We were worried someone might not see it and fall in. It was a *long* way down."

Briar exchanged a nervous glance with Cassie. "It sounds like it was horrible."

"Fascinating, actually. There's all sorts of abandoned equipment down there. It's probably buried under earth now, though. Far too unsafe to go in again." He rolled his shoulders. "I'll get started on that batch of balm we need. I used a lot on Alex and Reuben."

Cassie slid off her stool. "I'll help. And besides, I want the details."

They headed for the herb room, and Briar turned to Hunter. "I know I can't talk you out of going, but please be careful."

He pulled her into his arms as he leaned against the counter, a seductive look in his eyes. "Of course. I've got a few days left with you yet, and I don't intend to be injured for any of them." He kissed her, his hands in her hair, and she sighed into him, loving how his hands felt on her bare skin. He set her on fire. The doorbells chimed and she pulled away, feeling hot and bothered, as Stan, the town's pseudo-Druid came in.

He smiled indulgently. "Sorry to interrupt young love! Just doing my rounds. It's the solstice parade later today!"

Briar wriggled out of Hunter's arms. "Of course! We'll watch it, won't we?" She nudged Hunter.

"'Course we will. And we'll be at the beach later. I love a good fire!"

"Excellent!" Stan beamed, his eyes sweeping around her shop that she'd decorated with sunflowers and summer garlands. "Lovely job in here as usual, Briar. See you later, then!"

As soon as he'd gone, Briar admitted, "I'd almost forgotten the parade!"

"I think it's excellent timing. We need a night off from chasing bloody witches. The sooner I get to the moor, the sooner I'll be back. And I'm still holding you to lunch!" Kissing her again and leaving her breathless, Hunter sauntered from the shop, and Briar hoped that he was right. They needed a stress-free day. Hopefully one without further bloodshed, too.

Alex had decided to go to work, eager to get out of the house. He was feeling much better as his wound had healed well, thanks to Briar and Eli.

However, Jago, his chef, out of sympathy for his injuries, had made him an enormous breakfast sandwich on crusty bread. It was overloaded with bacon, eggs, tomatoes, and sausage. The meal looked delicious, but also made him feel like a twit, because he'd stuck to his story about using too much accelerant on the fire in the garden.

"There you go, Alex," he said, placing it on the bar. "You look a bit peaky! That'll pick you up. Has Avery not fed you lately?"

"Of course she's fed me! I can cook, too, you know!"

"Well, you look bloody terrible. Are you sure you should be here?"

Alex was indignant. "Yes, thank you! And actually, I feel much better!"

Jago folded his arms across his large chest, resting them on his well-fed belly. "Just checking. Don't get tetchy! I know you get up to some interesting things out of work."

Alex paused as he reached for his sandwich, looking at Jago suspiciously. *What did he know?* But Jago just winked, and Alex decided to ignore him as he took a bite of the admittedly magnificent brunch. Jago was incorrigible.

Jago headed back to the kitchen, and Zee grinned at Alex. "I think he's on to you."

"I hope he's bloody not. Or at least not the unfortunate incident with you-know-who, anyway. I'd lose staff."

"Yeah," Zee said lowering his voice, "it has been a violent week for all of us. I'm just glad Shadow and my brothers are okay."

Alex finished his bite of sandwich. "When are they coming back?"

"Monday, I think. They're enjoying France while they can. Estelle is there, too."

"So I gathered from Caspian." An unexpected figure entered the pub as they chatted, and Alex frowned. "Cornell's here."

"Your suspected collaborator?" Zee asked.

"Yep. What does he want?" Alex brushed crumbs from his chin and smiled at Cornell as he reached the bar. "Hey! I didn't expect to see you here. You're a long way from home."

Cornell smiled, leaning against the counter as he took in the pub and then Zee. "I'm looking for Avery, but she's not in her shop, and her staff don't know where she is."

Interesting. Sally and Dan usually knew everything.

"She's probably stretching her legs around town. What do you need her for?"

Cornell looked uneasily at Zee. "I was just after some more of that stuff she loaned me the other day." His eyes widened meaningfully.

The gold that they had no intention of giving him.

"Ah, that! You can talk in front of Zee. He's a good friend," he said, introducing them, before lying. "We haven't got it anymore. It's the with the police now."

"Police!" Cornell looked appalled. "Why?"

"Avery was really uncomfortable having it around the house with all of the bad luck it's caused, and no one else wanted it, either. The police have it somewhere safe now."

Cornell's eyes flashed with anger, but he quickly controlled it. "That's unfortunate, but I understand."

"What did you want it for?"

Cornell shrugged, obviously trying to appear casual. "Just preparation for Monday night. I'll manage without it."

Alex nodded, looking as sympathetic as possible. "Yeah, it was a sudden decision. Sorry. You've heard about Mariah, I assume?"

Cornell blinked, and his lips tightened. "Yes. Unfortunate."

Alex had liked Cornell. He was of a similar age, easy going, and he'd thought he was trustworthy. Now he found himself careful of everything he said. He lowered his voice. "I'll be glad when all of this is over, won't you? Thanks for your help on the moor the other night. Avery said you were fantastic."

He relaxed and smiled. "It was good to be able to help. Anyway, I'll leave you to it, and see you on Monday night."

Alex leaned forward. "I'm glad you're on our side. It could be a tricky night. You said you have a few things prepared?"

"Yes, absolutely." He nodded as he stepped away from the bar, unwilling to be drawn into further conversation. "Sorry, must go now. Thanks, Alex." He gave Zee a troubled look, and then left the pub.

"I wonder," Zee mused, "if he is on their side, whether he's spoken to Zane and knows about Lowen?"

"He certainly seemed to be interested in you." Alex watched Cornell glance through the windows at them before he left. "I reckon he has." He let out a long sigh. "Fuck it. Life just gets more and more complicated."

"Not for much longer. It should all be over by Monday night."

"It better be," Alex said darkly. "I'm just worried what else he wanted to prepare for Litha." He pushed the remainder of his sandwich away, his stomach churning. "I can't eat this."

"Excellent. I'm starving." Zee's eyes lit up as he grabbed the plate. "And as far as Monday goes, you better make sure you have a few things lined up, too."

Avery was glad that the working week was finished, and she could relax. Or try to. Despite knowing that Lowen was dead, she was only too aware that Harry and Zane were still out there plotting something, no doubt with Cornell, and maybe even Charlie. And there could even be others involved.

Knowing Cornell had come looking for her had been unnerving, and she was relieved that she'd spotted him from the back of the shop and made her escape before he saw her. Sally and Dan were only too happy to lie for her.

And now she was sitting on a blanket on the sand dunes with her friends, watching the end of the parade as the participants streamed onto the beach, the fire already blazing in the dusk, desperate to relax and forget the recent events.

Alex nudged her. "You're supposed to be having fun!"

Startled, she turned and smiled. Alex's dark hair was loose, and stubble kissed his jaw. She stroked his cheek, thinking how relieved she was that he hadn't been badly injured. "Sorry. Miles away."

"I get it. But we've reached the end of the week and we're all okay, so let's enjoy it." He reached forward into the picnic hamper for the wine bottle and topped up her glass. "Here you go."

She accepted it with a smile as El said, "More easily said than done, Alex." She was holding a half-empty beer bottle, but her eyes swept the crowd before resting on her friends. "I'm jumpy, and I can't shake it."

Hunter was stretched out on the blanket, gazing at the sky that was suffused with pinks and purples, but he rolled to his side and propped up on his elbow. "I found three scents today in the centre of the big circle at Hurlers, and their path to the Visitor Centre, but they were faint after so many days. I certainly didn't find anything further afield."

Reuben nodded. "Zane must have exited somewhere else. Or he's still down there, in another cave. They must have a few bolt holes."

"I hope that Zee and Eli blocked him in and he rots down there," Briar said, pouting. "But I doubt we'll be that lucky."

Avery was startled. It was unlike Briar to voice such things, but they had all been pushed to their limits this week.

Hunter leapt to his feet, extending his hand, a mischievous look in his eye. "Come on, Briar. Time to dance."

"Dance?" Briar looked up at him, wide-eyed.

"Yes!" He grabbed her hand and gestured down to the crowd below. A group of local musicians had set up close by, and the sounds of acoustic guitars and tribal drumming was carrying across the sands towards them. Already a few people were dancing around the fire. "That looks fun, and it's just what we need!"

She gave him a wry grin and allowed him to pull her to her feet, and Reuben did the same to El, saying, "Wolfman is right. It's time to party!"

Within seconds, Avery was alone with Alex, and he leaned in and kissed her. "They're right. Let's join them."

"But I feel a bit guilty. People have died this week! And Newton and Caspian are still in London. Who knows what they might be facing tonight at that underground auction!" Newton had called to let them know what they would be doing that night, and now she couldn't stop worrying.

"They're grown men, perfectly capable of looking after themselves. And although I'm worried, too," he confessed, "Caspian is powerful, and Olivia is there. It's time to unwind!" He stood up and looked down at her, a warm, inviting look in his eyes.

She clambered to her feet, almost stumbling in the soft sand, and thought the fire and the dancing did look fun. The parade members were dancing too, and the fire jugglers had set up to entertain the crowd. He was right. She needed to let go, so she took his hand and let him lead her down to the beach.

Twenty-Seven

The room the auction was being held in was more like a cave, and Newton studied it suspiciously.

The ceiling was vaulted, the walls were made of stone, and there were several passages that led to it, as well as a couple of other rooms that led off from it. He felt like he was in the middle of a spider's web, and he wasn't the spider. Olivia, however, stylish in a dress and heels, looked at ease, and Newton presumed she'd been here many times before. She had given a password to the man who guarded the narrow entrance on a side street, and he had ushered them through silently. She had then led them down winding stairs to a subterranean passage. Newton assumed all of the entrances were similarly protected.

Caspian looked wary as he scanned the room, no doubt, like Newton, looking for Harry. However, studying the dozen or so people who were there for the auction, Newton wasn't sure that Caspian being there was a good idea. If Harry turned up and saw Caspian, it might provoke him to violence, and in such a small, enclosed space, there could be bloodshed. But he reminded himself that a few people here could be paranormal in some way, and would therefore be able to look after themselves. He had to let the night unfold as it may.

All three of them were at the back of the room, but while Olivia and Caspian were seated, Newton loitered by the wall, watching the last few stragglers enter the space. A long table had been set up with nibbles and wine, and another table and podium were at the front.

Sam, the man Olivia had spoken to at the club, was already up there, chatting to another man with dark, slicked-back hair and a pale face.

Sam raised his gavel and smacked it down, drawing everyone's attention. "Thank you, ladies and gentlemen. The room on the right is now ready, and you may look at the items for auction. No touching, please. And no drinks or food as you examine the lots." His eyes hardened. "All rule breakers will be thrown out."

The group murmured and nodded as they made their way to the room, Olivia and Caspian included. Newton hung back, still studying the exits and hoping that Harry, or maybe Zane, would show. He knew what they looked like, but was confident they wouldn't know him. So far, however, there was nothing untoward happening.

Within a few minutes, Caspian returned, a grim look on his face, and headed to Newton's side. "There are quite a few powerful objects in there, and I think I know which ones are Harry's. There are gold rings inset with gemstones, amulets, chalices, and a couple of pendants, and all reference a combination of planetary correspondences. None of them are particularly ornate, but the power they hold is impressive."

"Dangerously so?"

"No more so than any other object there. It's not the power they possess that's the problem...it's what you choose to do with it." Caspian's eyes narrowed as he surveyed the room. "I think a few people were busy on Thursday night making objects to sell. This auction is called Cosmic Alchemy. But only Harry's wares seem to have old, blood-soaked gold included."

"You can tell the difference?"

"Feel it, more like. He's done something palpable to enhance it."

Olivia joined them, a smug smile on her face. "Harry will be here. All the makers are. They agreed to answer questions about their goods. Sam thought it added a level of authenticity—and may raise prices."

Caspian nodded. "Excellent. He won't expect to see me."

Newton eyed Sam with new respect. He was chatting to a slender woman with a blunt, blonde bob. "Of course. It's like an art exhibition, with the artist strolling among the punters." Newton saw movement at the rear exit and looked across Caspian's shoulder. "Talk of the devil..."

Olivia casually looked around. "The man with grey-streaked, shoulder-length hair?"

"The very same," Newton said, watching in case Zane would appear next to him. "I think he's alone. He's talking to the man with slicked-back hair."

"Jeremiah," Olivia supplied. "Sam's right-hand man. He'll also be running the auction. Sam won't stick around for long."

Caspian had deliberately not looked around, keeping his back to Harry. "Any idea which way he came in?"

"From The Alley Cat, I think," Olivia said. "Sam owns the bar, as well as this place. It's convenient for him to come and go, and one of the staff most likely escorted Harry here."

Newton shook his head. Talk about an underground lifestyle. *Bloody dodgy occult dealers.* In an effort to get his bearings, he asked, "And we're under the Victoria Embankment Gardens, right?"

"Yes. Not far from the tube station."

"Where is Harry now?" Caspian asked.

"Heading into the lots," Newton told him.

Caspian turned to Olivia. "If he sees me, he might run. Which way is he likely to leave?"

"Probably through the bar. No doubt he'll celebrate afterwards—if he has a good night's sales. What are you thinking?"

"That I should wait there. It will be dark, crowded, and noisy. I can glamour him, and we can manoeuvre out to the street safely."

Newton was worried. "Can you glamour another witch?"

"It's tricky, but I can do it. Especially if I catch him unawares." He gave Newton a grim smile. "We have few options here, Newton. Grabbing him on the street might be even messier."

Newton huffed. "All right. But let's be as discreet as possible."

"I'm not an idiot! I'll see you in the bar. Just make sure Harry doesn't decide to go elsewhere!"

Newton breathed a sigh of relief as Caspian left, thinking that the plan was shaky, but the best available given the circumstances. "Right. Olivia, maybe I should ask a few questions to appear to be a genuine bidder?"

Olivia shook her head. "Not that there's anything wrong with your Cornish accent, but it may raise suspicion. You sit tight. I'll ask the questions. I'm your guide here anyway, remember?"

And without waiting for his consent, she pushed him into a chair and left.

Caspian managed to find a free booth in one of the cellar bar's rooms, and settled in with a pint.

It felt like he was waiting for ages. A couple of people pointedly looked at him as he was taking up a table alone, but he told them he was expecting friends, and then said a spell to deter anyone else from coming close.

After almost two hours of him reading on his phone and endlessly surfing the internet courtesy of the bar's free wi-fi, Newton texted to say they were at the bar getting drinks. Caspian downed the last of his now warm pint and found Newton, who greeted him with relief.

"He's at the far end with Olivia, about to get a round in to celebrate."

"He did well?" Caspian asked, searching through the crowd for them before he approached.

"Very. Made a bloody fortune. Can you glamour him from here?"

"Unfortunately not." Caspian spotted Harry, his back to him as he chatted to Olivia and leaned on the bar. "Wish me luck."

Before Harry could even look around at his approach, Caspian sidled up to Harry and said the spell to seal his tongue. He then stepped in front of him, staring into Harry's bewildered gaze as he started to glamour him. As soon as he saw Caspian, his eyes widened with fury and he fought to speak. He dragged his stare away as Caspian tried to maintain eye contact.

Shit. Harry was strong. Very strong. Before Caspian could even register what was happening, Harry raised his hands and sent a bolt of power out, catching Caspian directly in the chest and propelling him across the room, where he smacked through a table and crashed against a wall.

But that was the least of his worries. Harry didn't care who saw him. He sent another bolt of magic at Caspian that he managed to deflect. It hit the ceiling and brought down a chunk of stone, and the bar erupted into chaos.

Bouncers started to move in, but Harry grabbed Olivia, snaked a hand around her neck, and using her as shield, pushed her in front of him as he headed to the exit. Newton was closer and charged to intercept him, but Harry sent him crashing through a screaming group of customers. Caspian struggled free of the table's wreckage, his head pounding from where it had struck the wall, and ran after Harry.

It was impossible to get close. Harry was dragging Olivia with him, and continued to throw jagged bolts of searing-hot magic around him. The walls were blasted and blackened, tables were smouldering, and the bouncers were throwing people aside to get to them. Uttering spells to confuse and bewilder the bouncers, Caspian saw a couple stagger away. Harry, however, kept running.

But as Caspian had suspected, there were more than just normal customers in The Alley Cat. He felt magic swell around him, whether to attack or defend he couldn't tell. A man who looked like a member of the staff was at the far end of the pub raising a protection spell designed to seal them in. Harry, however, had spotted him, and was launching an attack. Olivia saw her chance and wrenched free from Harry's grasp, and Caspian hurled the biggest spell he could in such an enclosed space. It picked Harry up off the floor in a whirl of arms and legs, and Caspian raced after him, propelling him through the man at the exit and up the stairs. Customers were diving for cover, and Olivia scooted through them, following Caspian. He hoped Newton was close by.

The next few minutes were a blur as Caspian fought off attacks to immobilise and trap him, and keep Harry in sight. Arriving on the street, he found Harry already rounding on him.

"Harry! Don't do this!" Caspian pleaded, his arms raised as he threw out a wall of protection. "You're in enough trouble! And you have a family to think about. Come quietly! There's been enough bloodshed."

Harry almost snarled at him, and Caspian realised that his tongue-binding spell had gone. "There will be far more before this is over!"

"But what is this all about? It makes no sense! You made a lot of money tonight. Isn't that enough? You have a name now—you can make more goods to sell."

"Not if you bind my powers, Caspian, and I'm not letting anyone do that." Harry straightened, throwing his shoulders back. "The coven needs a change, and we will bring it—one way or another."

He struck again and Caspian counterattacked, but Harry fled. Cursing, Caspian summoned air, reappearing in Victoria Embankment Gardens. It was late and there was little traffic about, and even fewer people, fortunately. He saw Harry racing along the road, heading for the Embankment Station. Caspian had no intention of losing him. Trees lined one side of the narrow street, and he uttered a spell that splintered several of them, and branches crashed to the ground, trapping Harry beneath them.

Caspian didn't stop. He sent wave after wave of magic, bringing more branches down and making a massive cage around Harry until it was virtually impossible to see him beneath the tangle of branches and leaves. He ran, heedless of whoever might be watching, desperate to finally capture him. The events in the pub were a disaster, but if he could contain him now, it would all be worth it.

Just as he was closing on him, something hit him from behind and he fell, sprawling forward on the hard ground. He rolled onto his back, just in time to see the man from The Alley Cat hurl a spell at him. Tree roots sprang from the ground, binding his arms and legs, and the advancing man uttered another spell, igniting the roots and trapping him within a flaming binding. Caspian did the only thing he could. He summoned air, and vanished.

Newton skidded to a halt at the end of the road, watching in horror as Caspian was suddenly trapped in flames.

The man standing over him was focussed so entirely on him, he hadn't seen Newton. Beyond he spotted Harry, struggling out of the mass of branches. Hearing footsteps, Newton turned and found a group of men running towards him.

Olivia tugged at his arm. "This way."

She pulled him down the street and made a sharp turn, zigzagging back and forth across narrow lanes, before running down a flight of stairs and through a door into another narrow passage.

"Olivia! Where are we going? We left Caspian behind! And that bastard Harry will escape!"

She shut the door behind them and led Newton onwards. "Unless you want to end up being questioned by Sam's men for hours— which won't be a pleasant experience—shut up and keep moving."

"But I'm the police!"

"Your authority means nothing to them."

"But what about you? He knows you!'

"I'll worry about that later." She took a bewildering number of turns, and then fled down another long set of steps. A rumble of something came through the walls, and beyond that noise, Newton thought he heard footsteps.

Olivia finally halted in front of a door with an emergency bar fitted across it. She hit it forcefully, trying to get through. It didn't budge. "Newton! Help!"

He smacked it down, and put his shoulder to it, hitting it again and again, and they finally fell forward into a tube station.

"Charing Cross," Oliva muttered as she grabbed his arm and pulled him along.

They emerged onto a platform with a train on it. She dragged him into the car just as the door slid closed. As the train pulled away, Newton saw a man race onto the platform, looking around wildly. *Their pursuer*. But he was too late. The train was moving too fast to be caught.

Newtown was furious with himself. "We left Caspian behind! Injured! And that bastard looked to have escaped his trap."

Olivia sat down as the tube rattled through the tunnels. "Didn't you see? Caspian vanished."

Newton immediately reached for his phone, glad to find that it was still in his pocket. Within seconds, Caspian answered his call, sounding breathless.

"Thank the Gods," Newton said, sagging back into his seat. "Are you okay?"

"Slightly singed, but at the hotel. You?"

"On the tube. Be back soon. And you better break into the mini bar."

Twenty-Eight

A lex handed Caspian a beer, noting the tight line around his eyes and grim set of his mouth that not even the Sunday afternoon sunshine could dispel.

The witches had gathered in Avery and Alex's garden, along with Hunter, Newton, and Ghost OPS, for what felt like a council of war. He and Avery had debated about asking Ulysses, Hemani, Nate, and Eve to join them, but in the end decided against it. They were all too wary of inviting anyone else, and they would have had to disclose their worries about Cornell.

Caspian and Newton had relayed the events of their weekend, and Newton looked as subdued as Caspian as he sat at the wooden table, distractedly watching Reuben flip burgers and sausages at the barbeque.

Alex and Avery had started the day feeling buoyed by their fun night at the solstice celebrations. Unfortunately, now they just felt lame for celebrating while their friends had battled Harry alone.

"So," Avery said, frowning, "Harry pretty much admitted that he wanted to overthrow the coven?"

Caspian nodded. "Yes. Said it was time for a change, and he was going to deliver it. It all sounded very ominous. Of course, I didn't mention Cornell." He was staring at the table, his fingers rubbing the grain, but he finally lifted his head and stared at the others. "He was strong, but I almost had him. If only that other bloody witch hadn't interfered."

"You did well," Newton told him. "It was chaos in that club. It was a success to even follow him out the bloody door. And Olivia was amazing."

Caspian's face brightened with a rare smile. "No wonder Shadow and Gabe like her. She's reliable and resourceful."

"She saved my skin," Newton admitted.

"So," Avery persisted, "they'll try to take over the coven. Either bind or injure Genevieve, maybe the older members, too. Force the rest of us to comply."

"Or just kill those who disagree," El pointed out. "It seems they don't care about that."

"Exactly. So, we have to stop them—by any means necessary."

Cassie shook her head. "I don't get it! Why not just leave this coven and form their own? It's not like anyone is begging them to stay."

"But there's power in numbers," Caspian told her. "And the Cornwall Coven is large. To splinter off would make them weaker. Even though we know they're powerful individuals at the moment, they aren't as powerful as all of us together. And we wouldn't tolerate them setting up their own coven if they continued to use it for violence."

"Come on, guys!" Hunter said, trying to cheer them up. "Two of them are dead now. You know they're planning something for tomorrow night. We know they know that you know. But they *don't* know you suspect Cornell, and maybe Charlie. You need to keep it that way. You have a special Hunt Coven, and you haven't met for days. The solstice is *tomorrow*! You need to meet and lull Cornell and his cronies into a false sense of security. You need to lay a decoy trail."

"What?" Ben said, alarmed. "That sounds like gobbledygook!"

Hunter gave a feral, not quite trustworthy grin. "You said that the old fella's place was big?"

"You mean Rasmus?" Briar nodded. "Yes, he has woods and extensive grounds in Newquay."

"You should drop me off close by and I can circle the place. Harry and Zane will be up to no good somewhere around there, surely. I can keep an eye on them. Wasn't Cornell working on a plan for the solstice?"

"In theory," Alex said, "but of course we don't trust him now."

"But you need to make him think you do. Then you do something different."

Briar nodded again. "He's right. We pretend to go along with it, but instead plan something using the spells and crystals we charged on Thursday night...the cosmic ones that Cornell doesn't know about."

El grinned. "And the gold staff I made yesterday with Dante. It needs a few finishing touches, but is otherwise done."

"But," Reuben said, coming to the table with a plate of sausages, "that would leave our team—the Hunt Coven—sitting ducks. The ones who aren't betraying us will be left unprotected."

"Who do we really trust in that group?" Caspian asked. "I trust Nate, Eve, and Ulysses. I'm not so sure about Hemani, and we know we can't trust Cornell. As for the wider group, Charlie is definitely a suspect."

"I think you're right," Alex said, unexpectedly agreeing with Caspian. It helped that he hadn't given Avery any lingering looks since he'd arrived. *Maybe he was really trying to move on, after all.*

"Two meetings then, tonight," Avery said. "We tell the team that you've been gathering information. Be honest about finding Harry, but losing him. You pretend you're more injured than you really are, Caspian, and we pretend that so are Reuben and Alex. We end the meeting, but," she grinned, "the others will know to return a short while later for the *proper* meeting, and we update them on what's really happening."

Cassie stared between them all. "That's Machiavellian!"

Avery looked gleeful. "I know! But it's necessary. Caspian? You're the lead on this. Perhaps you should arrange it."

"Absolutely. I'll phone them now and we'll meet at mine, tonight at seven. I'll forewarn the ones we trust—and hope it doesn't backfire. But we need to decide on a proper counterattack."

"Our collaborators could help with a new plan," Reuben said. "They might have some great ideas."

"And," Briar suggested, "let Cornell take the lead on the fake plan. Maybe debate it for a while, and then relent."

"Then he will leave, thinking he's misled us all!" Avery said. "But we keep our knowledge of Lowen's death a secret."

"And keep your real plan simple!" Hunter added. "If Harry and Zane are on the grounds, I'll find them." A calculating look swept across his face. "What if you say that Reuben and Alex are far too unwell to attend the solstice at all? They could be on the grounds with me! Then you guys will be inside."

"A pincer attack," Dylan said, nodding. "Brilliant!"

"And Genevieve?" Alex asked, thinking of how odd she sounded the other day. "We have to get her involvement, or it won't work."

"I'll call her," El said. "I need to tell her about the staff anyway, and arrange to give it to her." She turned to Caspian. "By the way, I've been meaning to mention that I spoke to Shadow. Most of them are staying in France, but Barak and Estelle are returning tomorrow. Will she be at Litha?"

Caspian looked startled. "She's coming back? I guess she will be, then."

"Perhaps you should call her."

"If I trust her," Caspian said darkly, but he didn't elaborate, and it seemed no one wanted to push it.

As they talked and their plans took shape, Alex started to relax again. *This could work.* He'd be more than happy to play injured while stalking around Rasmus's grounds with Hunter and Reuben. He didn't like leaving Avery in there without him, but she'd be with the others.

"At what point do we intervene?" Avery asked, taking a handful of crisps to nibble on.

"I think," El said, slowly and thoughtfully, "we have to be intuitive. We have to decide when the time is right! Or rather, Genevieve does."

"Ultimately," Alex said, "although they're strong and have a plan, there are more of us. If Cornell thinks he's duped us, then he'll let his guard down. We can do this. But we can't leave stragglers. This ends tomorrow. I'm sick of looking over my shoulder."

"I'm sick of my house being blown up!" Reuben said, ferrying the rest of the food from the grill to the table and taking a seat. "Come on guys, tuck in!"

Newton had been listening and watching, but now he asked, "And what about me? How can I help?"

"And us!" Ben said. "We'll do anything."

"There's nothing you can do," Briar said, reaching for a plate. "You have to just keep your distance."

The members of Ghost OPS groaned, but Newton just nodded. "As long as you serve justice, I'm okay with that. But if there's anything I can do, just call me. In fact, call me anyway, so I know it's over."

"Right." Caspian stood suddenly. "Time to convene the coven for tonight. Just save me some food before Reuben scoffs the lot."

So far, the coven meeting was going well, and Avery was trying her best to be as friendly with Cornell as she possibly could, whilst also looking as worried as possible.

They were gathered in Caspian's dining room, which had a large oval table in it—antique, of course—and Caspian had apologised profusely for not gathering them together sooner. "I really am sorry," he reiterated, looking pale and sweating slightly. He'd made himself a herbal concoction that was enough to make him unwell temporarily. "I had a lead on Harry and needed to capitalise on it."

Eve's dark eyes were worried. "But that's what we're here for! To help. And you didn't tell us about Mariah, either!"

"To be honest," Avery said meekly, "we didn't know how to broach that! Kidnapping another witch was extreme, and led to a few arguments. And then, of course, she died. As awful as Mariah was, that was a terrible thing to happen."

Eve glared at her, and Avery inwardly grinned. Eve's performance was Oscar-worthy. She had suggested to Caspian that they show discord within the group to fool Cornell even more.

Cornell's lips were pressed in a tight line. "Agreed. And how did you find out about Harry?"

"I have contacts in London who are involved in the occult-dealing scene," Caspian explained. "They informed me of the auction, and I realised that some of the objects were Harry's. It was quite a shock, I can assure you. Unfortunately, he got away."

"Very unfortunate," Nate agreed. "And you don't look well."

"No. I was injured, and am not at my best. Nevertheless, I'll do what I can tomorrow. Which brings me to tomorrow's plans. During our—" he hesitated, "*argument,* Harry revealed that he is intending to overthrow the coven. I presume he is still working with Lowen and Zane, and maybe Charlie. How do we stop them? Cornell, you're the cosmic witch. How do we use the spells you've prepared?"

Cornell licked his lips, his eyes widening as he looked around the table at the attentive faces. Ulysses, as was his usual manner, was listening and not saying much. Nate and Eve were still playing their part of discontents, and Hemani...well, it was hard to say what Hemani thought. She did, however, look worried.

"As you know," Cornell said, starting tentatively, "I have, with your help, charged a large piece of jet with Saturn's binding energies, and combined some of Mars's correspondences in there, too. Two powerful planets. I'll take it tomorrow and suggest to Genevieve that we use the power of the coven to build on the energy within it to fight. Genevieve can harness a huge amount of power, and we can dispel any attack."

"But," Eve said, frowning, "if Harry, Zane, and Lowen are working outside our circle—or aren't even there—we may be wrong about their means of attack. How can this affect them?"

"Because we'll use it as part of our circle of protection." Cornell smiled. "Honestly, it will work—won't it, Hemani?"

She looked troubled, her eyes darting around the table. "Yes. But I still feel that on the solstice, the power of the sun is the strongest of all. The gold charged with positivity will be a force for good. I think bringing more negative energy into the space will be a bad idea."

That was surprising, Avery thought. *Maybe Hemani wasn't on Cornell's side, after all.*

Avery pushed back. "But fighting fire with fire—if you know what I mean—is usually a good idea."

"Are we going to utilise the gold?" Hemani asked.

Cornell nodded. "Yes! Of course. I'm taking that, too. I've cleansed it of its negative energies. It's just a shame, Avery," he looked at her with disappointment, a hint of reproach in his voice, "that you gave the rest to the police."

"Yes, Avery," Nate said, rounding in her. "What was that about? The sun, the solstice—it all relates to gold!"

Avery shuddered. "It had a horrible feel to it. Even when I cleansed it—admittedly before the full moon. None of us wanted it, so now it's locked in police vaults, somewhere safe."

Ulysses shook his head and sighed. "Maybe consult with your team next time, Avery."

Avery hoped Ulysses was acting, too. "I will, of course."

Eve tutted as if Avery was a silly child, and angled away from her, instead focussing her attention on Cornell. "Walk us through this, Cornell, and the spell we should use. And let's hope Genevieve sees reason soon."

The rest of the meeting passed in a blur of spell discussions and how they would convince the wider coven to help. Avery was glad when it was over. The atmosphere felt charged with anger and resentment towards her and her decisions. When everyone finally left, she walked to the window looking on to the back garden, startled when Caspian returned, grinning.

"That went really well!"

"You think so?"

"Cornell was positively preening, and Eve in particular looked really put out with you." He leaned against the frame, watching her. "Cornell thinks he has the upper hand. At your expense."

"I think Hemani's on our side. She looked troubled by some of Cornell's suggestions, but she went along with his explanations."

"With luck, we can count on her helping us tomorrow, then." He checked his watch. "The others should be returning soon."

Avery mirrored his actions, leaning against the other window frame and cradling her gin and tonic. She studied Caspian's pale face and his singed hair. "Are you sure you're okay? Last night sounded awful."

"I'm fine. I got out of that trap quickly. My hair was the worst casualty. I'm glad my herb concoction is making me look so awful."

Avery had noticed a coolness towards her from him over the last times they'd met. An unwillingness to meet her eyes. He was more business-like now. She wasn't sure she liked it. "Have I upset you in any way, Caspian?"

He'd been looking at the garden, but now his head whipped around to stare at her. "No! Why would you think that?"

"You just seem a little distant, that's all."

He gave a short laugh and stared into his drink. When he answered, he sounded embarrassed, almost apologetic. "No. There's no problem with us, Avery. I still admire you as much as I always have. But we're friends, nothing more, and I think I've finally accepted that." His eyes met hers, his expression almost painful in its honesty. "So, this is me not mooning over you any longer. I'm moving on—as your good friend, Reuben, told me to."

She was momentarily speechless. "Reuben?"

"It seems," he said, looking sheepish, which made him look younger, "that my feelings have not gone unnoticed by others, which is quite embarrassing."

Avery felt unsteady on her feet, and was glad she was leaning against the frame for support. "I had no idea. I hope he didn't threaten you!"

"Of course not! He said it as a friend, and I accepted it as such." He looked out into the garden again, the thickening twilight casting the lawn and borders in shades of purple. "He's a good man. So is Alex. I am determined to keep them—and all of you—as friends."

Avery felt unexpectedly bereft, but she had to admit, also relieved. This was a new stage in their relationship. A good one. She felt a surge of love for Reuben, for once again confounding her with his behaviour. "Reuben is very lovely," she said, blinking back a few sharp tears. "I'm glad we're still friends. I promised to find you someone, but I failed."

He laughed. "I'm a grown man, and don't need your help. I must admit that I rather liked Olivia...not that I'll be seeing much of her in future, I'm sure. Now, I just need to make amends with my sister." The sound of cars outside broke into their conversation, and he gave her a wry smile as he headed to the door. "Right. Time for part two of our meeting."

She was glad of the silence, needing to compose herself. That had been an unexpected conversation. Reuben had never, ever intimated to her that he knew anything about Caspian or his feelings for her. Neither had El, for that matter. But he was Alex's best friend, so no doubt they'd talked.

Eve burst in on her thoughts as she bounded into the room. "Avery! You sneaky cow!"

"Oscar winner!" she shot back. "You made me feel very uncomfortable in that meeting!"

Eve rushed over, her dreadlocks streaming from her colourful head scarf, and hugged her, enveloping her in patchouli. "We fooled him!"

"Do you think so?"

Eve stepped back, holding Avery's shoulders. "I *know* so! We spoke on the drive. He said something about it being a shame that we couldn't trust you as much, and that your judgement was failing. I agreed, of course."

Avery almost reeled at Cornell's deception. "Bastard!"

"I know."

Nate entered the room with Ulysses and Caspian, grinning broadly. "I've got to admit, I thought you two had gone mad," he said, looking between Avery and Caspian, "but it seems not." His smile faded. "I always liked Cornell. Now I'm just pissed off at him. He's been corrupted by the others. Hemani, though? I'm not so sure."

"Us either," Caspian confessed. "I think we can trust her."

Ulysses gripped Avery's shoulder in one large hand and squeezed. "It's too soon to celebrate. What's our plan? I trust we have one!"

"Take a seat," Caspian said, urging them to the table once again, where he'd placed a few bowls of crisps and some biscuits. "Let's outline our ideas first, and then hear yours. I'm sure we're stronger together."

As Avery took her place at the table, she allowed herself to feel a glimmer of hope.

They could do this.

Twenty-Nine

Avery studied Sally's worried face and repeated for what felt like the millionth time, "Honestly, we'll be okay!"

Sally's hands fidgeted with the cups she prepared on the kitchen counter while she waited for their early morning coffee to brew. "The whole thing sounds scary!"

"We'll have almost a whole coven working with us. Far more than they'll have with them."

"But they're so strong! And ruthless!"

Dan threw his arm around Sally's shoulders and gave her a gentle squeeze. "Have a little faith in your friends, Sally."

She glared at him. "I have every faith! It's the others I worry about."

Avery leaned against the fridge, holding the bottle of milk she'd just extracted. "I'm nervous too, but," she couldn't help but giggle, "it was a lot of fun to deceive Cornell at the meeting. Well, the first meeting. Eve was amazing!"

"Let's just hope he really swallowed it," Dan said, easing Sally out of the way to pour the coffee. "I must admit that I enjoyed the town's solstice celebrations."

Avery smiled. "It was fun. We weren't out too late, but we did dance around the bonfire for a while. I thought I might see you both!"

"We were in the town watching the parade," Sally said, "and didn't really hang about at the beach for long. The kids were overtired, so we whisked them home. As usual, the costumes were amazing. Stan and the council do a great job."

"I spotted you on the dunes," Dan confessed as he handed Avery her coffee. "But I decided not to bring Caroline over. Soon, though."

"Anyone would think you're ashamed of us!" Sally exclaimed. "You don't even bring her into the shop!"

"Not ashamed! Just laying firm groundworks before building on it."

Sally rolled her eyes. "That is such a boring metaphor. Where's the romance?"

"There's plenty of romance! I like her. I don't want all this subterfuge and witchyness to put her off, that's all."

Avery frowned at him. "You don't think she'd approve?"

"Oh, no. She's into myths and folklore, like me, loves the past and White Haven witchy vibes, but the reality is something else, right? There's a dark, dangerous edge beneath things sometimes. Especially now. I just want to protect her from it a bit."

"See!" Avery said to Sally. "He *is* being romantic. He's protecting her from me!" She glared at Dan.

"That's not what I meant, and you know it! You've got to admit, things are tricky right now. And the papers are full of it!" He leaned back against the counter and looked at Avery. "Did you hear? They found Lowen's body."

Avery nearly dropped her cup, instead spilling the coffee so that she scalded her hands. She immediately muttered a spell to heal them. "Bollocks! When?"

Dan rolled his eyes. "Don't you ever watch the news? Someone reported that there'd been a shaft entrance collapse. Concerned as to what had triggered it, they sent a man down on a rope and found a body. A headless one!"

Avery gasped. "Shit! But I guess it's better that they found his body than him being lost forever. Do they think it's suspicious?"

"The report said the police thought he'd hit disused machinery in the mine, and he was decapitated by the force of the fall. I guess

Newton dealt with it."

"He never mentioned it!" Avery thought back to their conversation with him on Sunday. "He was in London. I guess Moore handled it, with Kendall, their new sergeant. They covered up Mariah's manner of death, too." She groaned. "Last week seems a million years ago now. So much has happened."

"Perhaps you shouldn't be in the shop today," Sally told her. "Focus on tonight."

"No." Avery shook her head. "We did a lot of work yesterday, and we're prepared. Today I just need to keep busy. We won't even be at Rasmus's until the late evening. El will speak to Genevieve today." She drained her coffee and smiled at her friends. "Come on. Best faces forward. It's time to open the shop."

Reuben leaned against his car, shading the lowering sun from his eyes with the back of his hand as he surveyed the area surrounding Rasmus's land, Hunter and Alex next to him.

Rasmus lived in a large house on the edge of Newquay, nestled within woods and fields. His land was ringed by a mixture of stone walls and fences, although a public footpath ran through some of it. An area of woodland was completely secured from the public, however; the area reserved for their rites.

"Where's the best spot to be?" Hunter asked, following his gaze.

"A lane runs through the edge of the wood, if I remember correctly," Reuben said. "I can pull in there under the trees, and we can proceed on foot."

Alex had been staring at his phone, but he now looked up. "According to the map, there are a few footpaths running through there. We need to decide where Harry and Zane are most likely to mount their attack. It has to be in there somewhere."

"I agree," Reuben said, nodding. "The fields are far too open, even at night. And over there," he pointed to the right, "is the road leading to Rasmus's drive. It's a good mile further on."

"Big place, then," Hunter said, opening the car door. "Not so big for me, though. I can cover that amount of ground easily. Better get going. They could be there already."

Hunter's eyes were already kindling with yellow light, and it was obvious he was anxious to hunt.

"All right, wolfman!" Reuben teased.

He drove them another half a mile until they came to a place where they could pull off the road and into the woods, and using magic, they concealed the car. The twilight was thick with birdsong and whirring insects as they made their way through the undergrowth, eventually stumbling onto a proper track.

Hunter pulled his clothes off and handed them to Alex, who put them in his pack. "Right, I'm off. I'll find you soon." In seconds he shifted and loped beneath the trees.

Reuben turned to Alex as they continued along the path. "You still want to spirit-walk?"

"If needed, but I'll try scrying first. Between me and Hunter, we should be able to find where Harry and Zane are. I think we get as close to the Rasmus's boundary as possible, and I'll set up a circle to work inside."

"I worry about you spirit-walking outdoors," he confessed, noting the red mark that stretched down Alex's neck and under his t-shirt, the remnants of his injuries caused by Mariah. "I know you'll be within a protective circle, but it still seems risky."

Alex smiled, but it was weak, and Reuben knew he was worried, too. "Lowen is dead, so there shouldn't be anyone else spirit-walking. And if there is...well, I'm prepared. I'm just worried about the girls."

Reuben picked up the pace. "Then let's make sure we give them plenty of support."

El strolled through the many covens gathered behind Rasmus's house, greeting everyone she passed, some with a simple nod, chatting to those she knew better, all the while trying to decide who they could rely on.

There was a general air of excitement for the night ahead, and excited chatter as they gathered on Rasmus's broad patio before the celebration started. Briar and Avery were close by, also mingling with the others as they tried to get a feel for the night. Caspian was talking to Jasper, his dark head bent close and an urgent expression on his face. No doubt he was sharing some of their concerns about the night ahead.

El watched Genevieve talking with Rasmus, her staff in hand, hoping she was finalising the plans for the night. Their meeting that day had gone well. Genevieve was highly sceptical of Cornell's betrayal, although she had finally relented that his actions were suspicious. She had agreed to use the staff El had made, and it was now disguised well, looking just like her old one. The trap—they hoped—was set.

Cornell appeared out of the crowd, interrupting Genevieve and Rasmus's conversation. He looked excited, eager, and Genevieve certainly greeted him warmly enough. But the conversation was short as she finally cracked her staff on the stone slabs, simultaneously releasing a pop of magic and a plume of smoke.

She called out, "Attention everyone!" She paused, waiting for the crowd to turn to her. She looked as commanding as usual with her dark hair bound elaborately and wearing a sweeping cloak. "In a few minutes we will start the procession to the clearing. We will each carry a candle—they are on the table over there, so make sure you collect one—and then we will raise our temple around the altar and commence our celebrations." She hesitated for a moment, her expression darkening, but then she forged on. "There are notable absences tonight. For those who are not aware, I must share that Mariah Rowe and Lowen Gaskill are dead, and their other coven members have left us, our greater coven. Zane and Harry will not be joining us tonight." A murmur ran around the group, and El watched their expressions. It was clear that some knew, but others looked shocked and upset. Genevieve raised her hand. "We also have coven members who are sick and unable to come. Reuben Jackson and Alex Bonneville of the White Haven Coven send their apologies, and are celebrating quietly at home.

"So, tonight will be different, because we fear there will be an attack upon our coven, and we must be prepared to counter it." She paused, and another ripple of alarm ran through the crowd. "It seems the Looe and Bodmin Covens wish to break away from us. I have no issue with that. We are all free to do as we choose. But news suggests they may wish to destroy the Greater Coven completely, and attempt to bind our power. We must work together to stop them."

El watched as the witches absorbed the news. Some looked shocked, others frightened, and many stoic as they nodded, their postures showing hardened resolve. Charlie, she noted, just scowled.

A young witch called Mina, who El remembered as being part of Jasper's coven, stood next to her. She had been trampled by the fey during Samhain the previous year, and El knew Jasper protected and nurtured her. Now she looked terrified as she turned to El. "Bind our powers?"

El nodded and tried to look as confident as possible. "We believe it's possible. But if we stand together, we will defeat them."

Mina swallowed and nodded as Genevieve continued. "I value all of you, and wish to keep this coven as it is. A powerful, supportive, working group. I hope you do, too. We will begin with our usual Litha celebrations, but once those have ended, Cornell is leading us in another rite. If we are correct in our assumptions, the attack will start at midnight. We will repel it together, fighting them with their own magic. Please don't be alarmed. Lend me your power, as you always do."

Cornell looked at her, obviously surprised. "But I—"

Genevieve smiled and cut off his protestation, her hand resting on his arm as she addressed the coven. "Yes, Cornell will lead, but as your High Priestess, *I* will gather your magic." She turned to him.

"Powerful though you are, Cornell, the power flowing through me will be greater still."

El held her breath as his eyes widened, and then he beamed. "Of course. That would be excellent."

El didn't dare look at the others for fear she would give herself away, but she sighed with relief and felt the charged stones in her pocket. *With luck, this would work. It had to.*

Alex found a tiny clearing on the edge of Rasmus's land, surrounded by a thicket of scrubby undergrowth, and bathed in dappled shade from the slowly rising moon. He raised a circle of protection, sealing him inside, and first turned to his scrying mirror, leaving Reuben to prowl Rasmus's land cloaked in the shadow spell.

For a long time he saw nothing, and Alex was almost ready to give up, when he saw a ripple of movement pass across the glass, and like a veil had been pulled back, he saw Zane and Harry close to a stone wall. *Rasmus's perimeter.* They were testing the protection, and several times he caught a flash of white light respond to Harry's attempts to break it. He was using his ring again, and after numerous attempts, he almost heard the crack as the section of wall crumbled to dust and they headed inside.

Alex lifted his head, confused. He had expected them to work outside the grounds, not break in. As agreed earlier, he connected to Reuben psychically, something that wasn't easy, but was the best way of sending a mental image of the place, and immediately felt Reuben's response. *Good.* He turned back to the mirror and passed his hand across it. He needed to see if there was anyone else involved, and if there wasn't, he would head into the grounds, too.

Briar felt the atmosphere change as Genevieve brought the celebration to an end. It had been an uplifting occasion with the candles lit before them, and the altar in the centre was covered in a white cloth and decorated with summer flowers, more candles blazing amongst them.

With the temple raised around them, their magic was palpable as they celebrated the turning of the season, the longest day of the year, and the inexorable turn towards the winter. They had turned deosil around the circle as they invoked Cernunnos and the Goddess, hands held, but behind the celebration, Briar felt the twist of fear. Before their final words had died away, they heard a shout.

Zane's voice resonated around them. "Genevieve, your time as the High Priestess has come to an end. Walk away willingly, and we will let you keep your magic. Should you resist, we will bind your magic forever."

Genevieve froze, her eyes searching the darkness around their circle, and everyone turned with her, cloaks and clothes rustling. No one dared speak. Cornell looked grim, but Rasmus leaned forward and whispered to Genevieve. She swung around, staring to the south.

"Zane! Show yourself if you challenge my leadership. Subterfuge does not become you."

Zane stepped out of the woods, and a torch flared in his hands, the flames for a moment masking his features. Then he held the torch to the side as he stepped forward so they could see him clearly.

Briar shuddered.

His sharp, pale face was stern, his blond hair swept back from his face, and his lips twisted into a cruel sneer. He was dressed entirely in black, his cloak sealed with a glinting, gold clasp. "Here I am, Genevieve. I ask you once more to step aside as High Priestess and allow me into the circle."

"You presume that others want your leadership. What if they don't?"

"You presume that they want *yours*!" He smirked as he addressed the rest of the coven. "Genevieve has restricted your actions for too long. Bound us in old-fashioned practices that serve no purpose in today's witchcraft. I will bring change. Renewal. Modernity. Who is with me?"

"Not I!" Rasmus replied loudly. "You are not welcome here. Leave my property!"

"I would never expect you to join me, Rasmus. Nor would I want you to. You are old and have nothing to offer the new ways. Nor could your magic keep me out." His gaze ran around the circle that was still frozen in shock, and Briar summoned her magic, ready for what may come. "As for leaving, I will go when I have what I came for. The coven."

Briar wasn't sure what they had been expecting, but it certainly wasn't this overt attempt to take over.

Caspian spoke up next. "I certainly will not join you, Zane. I have seen the magic you employ lately. I will have no part of it."

Zane moved closer. "Ah, Caspian. Such a changed man since your father was killed. Weaker now. I would not want you in my new coven, either."

Claudia stepped out of the line of witches to face Zane. "You're a bigger fool than I thought if you wish to discard age and experience. It brings wisdom and greater power."

"With age comes fear and monotony. You're already boring me. But you are right about your power." His smirk grew and he opened his arms wide, the torchlight flaring into a column of flame. "I have a proposal. Those who wish to join me are welcome, but those who do not will lose their powers, because I shall bind your powers to mine. Yes, you heard correctly," he said, prowling the circle as a collective gasp ran through the coven. "I will take the magic of those who oppose me and they will be cast from the coven forever. If you choose to join me, then your powers will be safe. It's very simple. Cast out those who oppose me and protect yourselves, or I shall take *all* of your power."

Real fear ran through Briar, despite all of their plans. This was so much worse than they had imagined. But it was clever. To divide and sow discord with threats. Already, there were whispers and shuffling around her.

Genevieve cracked her staff on the ground, and a shudder ran through the earth as their protective circle flared. She drew herself upright, and with the power she wielded, she looked magnificent. "Silence! Zane Roberts, you are challenging an entire coven by yourself? You are truly foolish. It will be *your* magic that is bound. Not ours."

Zane ceased his pacing and planted his torch in the ground. "I am not alone, and I have prepared well for this moment. While you sleep and dream, wasting your magic on petty rituals, we have enhanced our power. We can defeat an entire coven...and will." He appealed to the wider group again. "Join me now, or lose your powers forever."

Ulysses shocked everyone when he laughed, his voice booming out, and the shuffling and whispers that had started again suddenly stopped as Ulysses addressed the coven. "I see the fear in some of you —the debate you have as to whether to stay or go. But you are fools if you waiver now. Zane and Harry—who is hiding out there, somewhere—have no intention of letting you keep your powers. They will bind them at some point...if not tonight, then soon." He looked back to Zane. "Liars. Cowards. Death dealers. Mariah and Lowen are dead because of your foolish plans, as are many others. Death is also your fate." He turned back to Genevieve. "Enough."

"Well said, Ulysses. You have your choice, witches. Whoever wishes to leave may do so now, but he spoke the truth. Who among you will go? Or will you all stand and fight, and instead bind the powers of those who threaten you?"

Briar caught Avery and El's worried glances before they surveyed the others, and although there were frightened faces, no one budged. And no doubt Zane, Harry, and Cornell wanted this, despite Zane's offer. An attempt at a total power grab would be cleaner and easier— especially with Cornell, the double agent.

"Excellent," Genevieve said, turning back to Zane. "You have your answer. Now *you* have a choice. Go now, or you will lose *your* powers."

Zane shook his head. "You will regret this, Genevieve. All of you will."

He extended his hands, and his robes fell back, revealing large, golden bracelets inset with gems around his wrists. They crackled with power—hot, angry, red bolts of power that he directed at their protective circle.

While they talked, Cornell had been swiftly preparing, and now a pile of the gold coins gleamed around a waist-height stone pillar, on which rested the large jet gemstone.

Genevieve shouted, "Cornell, begin!"

Thirty

Reuben hung back in the shadows, watching Zane begin his attack, and wondered where Harry was.

He had found the place where they had entered Rasmus's grounds easy enough, but finding them was trickier. No doubt Harry was veiled in a spell. Zane, however, was now cocky, and the bracelets allowed him to wield great power. But Harry would be feeding that... somewhere.

Reuben watched the coven respond to Zane's threat, and was glad to see that El and his friends were all right. But should he attack Zane now, or stay out of sight and find Harry?

Harry. He must find Harry.

He dropped back into the trees again and within moments, Hunter was next to him, pushing his huge head against his hip. Reuben always forgot how big he was when shifted to his wolf. Hunter nudged him again, his eyes glowing like tiny suns, and leading the way through the trees, Reuben followed, his excitement mounting.

Suddenly, Hunter stopped, paw raised, nose lifted as he stared straight ahead. Reuben stared too, at seeming blackness. If Harry was there, he was well protected. Reuben dropped to his knees and dug his hands in the earth, connecting with the cool ground. He sent his awareness out, feeling for a change. And then he felt it. A focus of power a short distance away. And heat. Harry must be next to a fire, but Reuben couldn't even see a glimmer of it. But the longer he focussed, the clearer Harry's power became. It was like a black hole of energy, pulling everything into it.

He turned to Hunter, who lifted his lips in a silent snarl. *Time to spoil the party.*

Reuben raised his hands and blasted the area with wave after wave of magic, and the wall of protection around Harry shimmered, becoming visible for the briefest of moments. He just had time to see a fire and Harry standing over it, arms raised. Harry lifted his startled face, glancing around wildly, before he vanished again.

No matter. Reuben had found him now, and digging into his pockets for the stones he'd brought with him, started to mark out Harry's perimeter, just as he felt a pulse of power erupt from Harry's circle.

Shit.

Alex's scrying mirror shimmered like a ripple in a pool, and suddenly a blinding light pierced the darkness. It was Harry, next to a fire. Beyond that were Hunter and Reuben in the undergrowth, barely visible, but the fire and Harry vanished in a blink.

Alex focussed on Zane, and was rewarded when he saw him blasting the Cornwall Coven's circle of protection until that vision vanished too, and Alex sat blinking in the darkness.

Despite his best efforts, he could see no one else on Rasmus's grounds. He shivered, realising the temperature had dropped, and looking up through the tangled branches, saw the starlight blinking out as clouds rolled in. A crack of lightning pierced the sky, and magic thickened the air.

Alex quickly rose to his feet and shouldered his pack before dissolving the circle. He could do nothing more from here. It was time to join Reuben and stop the attack.

Avery followed Genevieve's lead as she joined Cornell's incantation.

Cornell was in the centre of the circle, Genevieve next to him, and in front of them was the large jet gemstone on a stone pillar. His hands were cupped around it, several inches from the surface, energy dancing between his palms and the stone.

The entire coven had drawn close and were holding hands now, repeating Genevieve's incantation, their power building as they did so. The candles were behind them, lining the circle of protection, and as they spoke, the flames flared higher and higher until it seemed as if they were in a glowing chamber, with a shimmering dome of white light above them.

Zane was motionless beyond the circle, his arms raised to the sky. Avery was struggling to concentrate, wondering what he was doing, where Harry was, and how Alex and Reuben were faring.

As the incantation grew louder and their power magnified, Avery felt a sudden weakening, as if she were no longer giving her power, but something was drawing it from her.

Suddenly, a force hit their shield with a crackle of red light, and power rippled over them. Angry, binding power. Avery looked up with shock and met El's eyes. *They were too late.* Genevieve hadn't acted quickly enough. The circle was holding—but only just. The tide seemed to have turned as strands of red energy blossomed from the polished oval of jet, reaching towards the witches. Simultaneously, red light erupted from Zane's outstretched hands, connecting with their shield. In seconds, it shattered.

It was as if a scorching desert wind howled around the coven. The fingers of red light hit the witches, and Avery felt a jarring pain in her chest.

Their power was passing directly back to Zane.

Reuben had just finished placing the charged stones around Harry's circle when Alex emerged from the shadows beneath the trees.

"Success?" Alex asked him in a low voice.

"Well, the stones are in position, but his spell is already underway."

"I saw Zane. He's attacking the coven right now. Do you need me? Because—"

"Go." Reuben faced Harry's circle and raised his hands. "I can manage. In fact, this will be my pleasure. You tackle Zane. And take Hunter with you." He glanced down at the wolf and grinned. "I have a feeling you'll have more fun there."

Briar felt the earth tremble beneath her as the assault intensified.

The red binding power was trying to pierce her very core, but she dug her feet into the earth, drew on its power, and pushed back. She felt scorched by the heat of the spell, but deep within her, the Green Man offered his cool, rich, earthy magic, and she wrapped it around her like a cloak.

She glanced at their trusted team, and saw their eyes harden as they fought to regain control. Then she noticed Hemani's confusion, and realised she was fighting for control as much as they were. However, many in the circle were utterly blindsided. Some fell to their knees, and she cursed their own stupidity. They should have warned more of them so they could be prepared. It was useless setting a trap when most people had no idea what was happening anyway.

Real panic hit Briar then. For all their planning, they were far too late. Pinned in position from the assault, she watched Cornell. His eyes were closed, his face lifted to the sky as his connection to the jet gemstone continued. *They had to break it.*

Suddenly, Genevieve's staff blazed into light, and she cracked it down hard on the jet. It exploded, pieces ricocheting outward, striking Cornell hard and lifting him off his feet. He landed on the altar with a crash, upending flowers and candles, and splintering the table into pieces.

Instantly, the grasping red fingers of light vanished, and chaos erupted.

Alex skidded to a halt at the edge of the clearing, just as the jet exploded. He watched with horror as most of the coven dived to the ground to shield themselves from the shards of stone, but some witches were already responding.

Caspian was battling Cornell, who was desperately trying to attack Genevieve. Caspian gave him no ground, sending spell after spell at him, but Cornell fought back with a startling amount of power. Estelle ran to Caspian's side to join the fight. Charlie's wife, Hannah, was hurrying to support Cornell, and she hurled a bolt of fire at Caspian. But Avery intercepted her, catching Hannah unawares with a powerful whirl of air that sent her hurtling across the clearing. Charlie rounded on Avery immediately, but El was already responding with a spell of her own, and she hit Charlie square in the chest, throwing him into the candles. Robyn, the other Polzeath Coven member, was striding through the confused witches towards Genevieve, but Ulysses intercepted her, and within seconds they were fighting, spells zinging back and forth between them.

Hunter didn't hesitate, and with an enormous, bloodcurdling howl, he bounded into the circle to help the witches.

But Alex held back, scouring the scene for Zane. For seemingly endless moments, he couldn't find him. And then a figure struggled in the undergrowth, limbs becoming clear, as Zane tried to get to his feet. The explosion must have hit him.

Alex blasted him backwards into the bushes, and then sent a powerful binding spell. Runes multiplied in the air as they soared across the clearing, wrapping around Zane's limbs. But Zane threw them off as if they were nothing, and leaping to his feet, he sent a jagged bolt of red, binding power at Alex. Alex dived to the ground, throwing up a protective shield as he did so.

Zane covered the space between them quickly. His eyes were hard and his lips were twisted in a sneer as power snapped between his raised hands, and Alex knew he was going to throw everything he had at him.

Reuben cast the spell he'd been practicing all day, and the stones he'd placed around Harry's circle exploded like dynamite.

Powerful magic rolled outwards like a tidal wave, obliterating Harry's protective circle. It caught Harry in its path, throwing him into the air and against a tree. He was completely stunned, his head lolling toward his chest. Reuben didn't bother with spells. Before Harry could begin to respond, Reuben ran over, lifted his head, and with great satisfaction, punched him. Harry's head snapped back, instantly rendering him unconscious.

Reuben bound him quickly using the rope he'd brought with him, sealing the knots with spells, and then he spotted the ring that had shot power like a laser beam. It blinked on Harry's finger, the red gemstone swirling with power. There was no way he was leaving it on Harry's hand. Hoping nothing weird would happen if he touched it, he pulled it off and slipped it in his pocket, then turned to the scattered remnants of the circle.

The fire still burned, but the flames were stuttering. Harry's magical objects, however, were still vibrating with power, although the powerful beam of magic that had projected into the sky had gone. Reuben threw the objects into his bag and sealed it shut with a protection spell. He immediately felt their power mute. He then put out the fire with a jet of water he pulled from the air and kicked earth over it. Then he turned to Harry, satisfied to see that he was still out cold.

He summoned air as Avery did, struggling to wield it as efficiently, but finally manoeuvred it under Harry's body. It was time to find the others.

Avery was surrounded by battling witches. It was clear now who was siding with who. All of Charlie's coven were fighting against her friends, and she had to duck and roll and strike back hard to avoid being hurt. *At least her magic was responding now.* For several horrifying seconds, it had felt like they'd failed.

In the centre of the circle, Genevieve stood firm within the madness. She whipped her staff around and cracked it against the ground. Bright yellow light blazed from it, the stone at the head as blinding as the sun, and a rush of healing, bright, and positive magic pulsed across the clearing. Avery felt it strike through her, leaving her breathless as the power of Litha banished the ugly, binding magic.

Claudia looked horrified at Cornell's actions, and ignoring everything around her, hurried to Caspian's side to reinforce his attack on Cornell.

Genevieve raised her voice and shouted, "Bring our attackers before me! Those who will join me, do it now!"

The harried group of witches who weren't fighting struggled to Genevieve's side, all linking hands. A large group, however, had rounded on the Polzeath Coven and Cornell, and using a combination of spells, herded them before Genevieve's blazing staff. Many of them were bloodied and limping. Hunter hadn't held back, and he dragged Cornell into the clearing by his ankle, blood dripping everywhere.

Despite being injured, all of their enemies still fought to break free, and Ulysses raised his voice and began an eerie song that sent prickles up Avery's spine. He was using his Siren voice to spell them into submission.

Hunter had retreated, but he released a sudden howl, whipped around, and raced back to the clearing, just as Avery looked up in horror to see Zane attacking Alex, who was struggling to repel him.

Avery raised her hands to respond, but Hunter was already there. He leapt across the remaining space between them, flattened Zane, and ripped his throat out.

Avery didn't know whether to be horrified or relieved. But as Alex staggered to his feet, she decided she didn't care that Zane had just been killed in the worse way possible. He deserved it. She ran to Alex's side.

"Alex! Are you all right?"

He ran his hand across his face, smearing dirt into his sweat. "I'm okay. I probably look worse than I feel." He looked down at Zane's spreadeagled, bloodied body, and grimaced. "Better than him, anyway. Thanks, Hunter."

Hunter just looked at him with ferocious yellow eyes and his lips curled back. Avery was convinced he was laughing. She was very glad he was on her side.

Avery pointed towards Genevieve. "She needs us. Come on."

He shook his head. "I need to check on Reuben."

But as he finished his sentence, Reuben emerged from the trees with Harry, and they ran to help him.

"Well done, mate," Alex said, examining Harry's unconscious body. "You okay?"

Reuben grinned. "Better than okay. Punching this idiot has just made my year."

Avery and Alex accompanied him as he dropped Harry into the centre of the circle with the others, and threw the bag of magical goods and the ring in too.

Avery stood between Reuben and Alex, clasping their strong hands, and as they connected to the rest of the coven, she felt power radiate through her. Avery slowed her breathing and focussed. Genevieve gathered herself, one hand on the staff, one hand in Claudia's. Rasmus was on her other side, one hand also resting on the staff, his other holding his daughter's hand.

While they composed themselves, Avery studied the disgraced witches clustered in the middle. Charlie, his wife, Hannah, and Robyn, the third coven member, Cornell, and Harry. They had all been bound one way or another with a variety of spells, some with silvery ropes of light, others writhing with fire ropes, and all looked dazed by Ulysses's Siren spell. Cornell looked the most distressed, his face beaded with sweat.

The silence that had fallen after the fight was eerie. Of the Cornwall Coven, some of the witches were angry, some tearful, while others could barely look at those in the middle. Mina, Jasper's young witch, clutched Jasper's hand tightly, and she saw him give her a reassuring smile. Hemani looked grim and preoccupied, Oswald too appeared distressed, but he seemed to draw strength from Ulysses. Eve and Nate stood together, watching Genevieve. El and Briar seemed uninjured, but Caspian once again looked ill. A streak of blood grazed his cheek, but Estelle stood composed at his side, his uncle and cousins next to her.

Genevieve broke the silence and addressed the witches huddled in the centre. "You have all tried to subvert the will of this coven. You tried to grasp power that does not belong to you, and that you do not deserve. Three of you are now dead. The rest of you will have your powers bound forever."

Cornell almost screeched, "No! Anything but that!"

Genevieve stared at him pitilessly. "You have left us no choice. You betrayed your coven leader, and your fellow witches."

"Then let me die." He stared at Hunter who stood beyond the circle. "Let him kill me as he did Zane!"

"No!" Claudia shot back. "There will be no easy escape for you." She turned to Genevieve. "Let's do this now."

Genevieve gripped her golden staff that radiated light and said, "Join me now in the incantation. This will not be pleasant, and will take time and concentration, but as you followed me before, please follow me now." She began the spell in her commanding, clear voice, and they repeated it after her.

Spools of light blossomed from the gemstone in Genevieve's staff, and much like the angry red light that had earlier sent searching tendrils into the witches, this light pierced the witches gathered in the centre. As the words they repeated grew louder and stronger, the light weaved around each individual, binding them within a cage of light, and sinking into them. As the binding took hold, the witches in the centre struggled, panic etching across their faces.

Avery felt horrible.

She had never wanted to bind anyone. But she never wanted these witches to be able to use their magic against anyone, either. And it seemed the rest of the coven thought the same. Many witches had tears in their eyes as the spell grew in strength, and the whimpers of the witches caught in the middle were awful to hear.

Avery wanted to close her eyes, but didn't. She had to see this through, for the sake of all those who had died. Her gaze fell on Zane's bloody body outside the circle, and she renewed her resolve. *This was the only way.*

The spell seemed to take an eternity. Genevieve was methodical and unrelenting, and soon the witches were bound within a fine mesh of power. With one final line, Genevieve cracked her staff into the ground once more, and a scream that seemed to come from everywhere and nowhere shattered the night.

The light dimmed, the bindings vanished, and Genevieve said, "It is done. Break the circle, and let them leave."

The outcast witches scuttled to their feet. Cornell immediately raised his hands to invoke a spell, but nothing happened. He stood, stunned and silent, but then looked at Genevieve. "You can't just leave us like this!"

"You gave us no choice. You tried to take our magic."

He stuttered, "You misunderstood…"

"I misunderstood nothing. And neither did anyone else here. Your actions were clear, as were those of your conspirators."

A myriad of emotions passed across Cornell's face, and it looked as if he would speak again, or maybe even physically attack someone. But then he looked at Zane lying dead on the ground, and walked away. Charlie's eyes were downcast throughout the scene. He roused Harry, and with Hannah's help, dragged him to his feet as Robyn followed Cornell, looking just as shocked.

Rasmus took a deep breath and addressed the coven. "I'll escort them out. Isolde, will you help me?" He turned to his daughter and Drexel, the other Newquay Coven members, and they hurried forward to usher the disgraced witches from the grounds.

In silence, they watched the witches depart, and then Genevieve spelled a fire into the centre of the clearing. "Let's sit together and finish our solstice celebrations. We should try to end the night with some measure of peace."

Thirty-One

C aspian found a spot on a bench next to Estelle.

It was a good half an hour after the binding spell took place, and the atmosphere in Rasmus's clearing had started to feel like normal again. Together the coven had gathered chairs, benches, and logs, righted the smashed altar, and placed out the food, and they now gathered around the fire in small groups, talking quietly.

Estelle looked at him warily as he sat down, and he said, "I'm glad you're back, and survived the Dark Star Astrolabe. And thank you for helping me, too." She turned her gaze to the fire, remaining mute, and despite her help earlier, he knew he needed to apologise if he was to stand any chance of repairing his relationship with her. "I'm sorry we argued last week. I was disappointed that you chose to go to France, but I hope you gained some perspective. Freedom."

Estelle took a deep breath and nodded. "I'm sorry, too. I didn't anticipate that events here would get so bad." She lifted her head and studied the Cornwall Coven. "I loathe having to represent us at the council meetings, but this group does serve a purpose. It certainly served one tonight." She finally looked at him. "You hit a nerve."

"I did?" He struggled to remember his words, and then sighed. "Barak."

"Barak." She repeated his name softly, and a light that Caspian didn't often see sprang to her eyes. He studied her profile, noting the softened lines and relaxed posture. He was tempted to blame the firelight, but perhaps it was something else.

When it became clear she wouldn't elaborate, he said, "He's a good man. I like him. At least you picked someone who isn't already in a relationship."

She arched an eyebrow, a wry smile twisting her lips. "Out of the many things I get wrong, at least I did that right. Not that I'm sure of what will happen yet."

He smiled too, and felt a rush of affection for his often-annoying sister. "You have a tan, and you look well. Very well. France must suit you."

"It was more than just France. But it helped."

"You didn't argue with Shadow?"

"Everyone argues with Shadow! It's inevitable."

He laughed, and then summoned his courage. "If you wish to leave the company, then you should. I don't want you to go," he rushed in as she looked at him in shock, "but I know only too well how the family business traps us. I too am aiming to do a little less."

She leaned forward, elbows on knees and stared at him. "What's happened to you?"

"The realisation that my life is horribly narrow in some respects."

"Ah. The White Haven witches."

"Don't say it like that. They're my friends. And besides, I am not our father, and have no intention of living my life like he did. Not anymore."

"I think he did a number on both of us." She stared at the fire again, and then said, "I won't leave, but I will reduce my hours and responsibilities. I like working with the Nephilim. It was fun to be doing something different."

Caspian felt an inexplicable need to hug her, but knew she wouldn't appreciate it. They had never been that type of family. "Of course. We'll talk about it tomorrow. Or whenever you're ready."

"Tomorrow will be good."

Caspian looked across the circle, noting Briar sitting close to Hunter, his arm around her shoulder. El sat next to Reuben, watching him talk animatedly to Alex and Avery, and Nate and Eve were there, too. He suddenly wished to hear about how Reuben had trapped Harry.

"Go on," Estelle said, nodding to them. "Go join them. I'm going home."

"You can't stay longer?"

"I only arrived back at midday. I think I need my own bed and my own space." She rose to her feet, and Caspian stood with her. She gave him an enigmatic smile and then headed over to Genevieve to say her goodbyes. Caspian hurried to his friends.

Briar shuffled over on the log she was sitting on and patted it. "There's room for one more."

He smiled as he settled next to her. "Thank you. I've come to hear Reuben and Alex's news."

Reuben laughed. "Exploding stones and a good punch are my news!"

"You *punched* him?" Caspian shook his head. "No magic?"

"Oh, there was a lot of magic. Those charged amethysts worked well. When I released their energy, they exploded Harry's protection with such force that it threw him into a tree." He rubbed his fist. "It felt good to punch the bastard after all the trouble he's caused. But it was thanks to Hunter's nose that I found him at all."

Hunter nodded. "He'd disguised himself well, but he didn't think about his scent. I half wish I'd have ripped his throat out, too."

Briar grimaced. "That's a horrible thing to do."

"Horrible, but sometimes necessary," Eve said.

Hunter's eyes were hooded as he looked across at Zane's body, now covered with a blanket. "I'm sorry, but when he stood over Alex, swollen with power, I lost it. I didn't want to give him a chance."

Briar cuddled into his side. "I know. He would have struck you both if you hadn't acted first." She looked at Alex. "Are you okay?"

Alex looked grubby. Dirt was smeared across his face, and twigs and leaves were still tangled in his thick hair. *And yet, he still looked a handsome bastard*, Caspian thought resentfully.

"I'm fine," he said. "But Zane was crazy with power. When I arrived, the circle was already broken, and he was in the bushes. How much power did he absorb?"

"Too bloody much," Nate grumbled, his soft Geordie accent sounding stronger with his anger. "I was afraid we'd made a big mistake. I thought Genevieve was working against us."

"Me too," Avery confessed. She looked very beautiful in the firelight. Her red hair was in a loose, messy bun, tendrils trailing around her face, and her eyes sparkled, but Caspian pushed those thoughts aside, focussing only on her words. "I managed to speak to her after the binding. She said she was waiting for the right time. She wanted to draw Cornell and Zane in completely. And reveal the others." She looked across at Claudia, who was staring into the fire. Lark, her other coven member, was leaning against her. "Poor Claudia. She's been utterly blindsided by Cornell's betrayal."

"At least Lark wasn't involved," El said. "Although, Lark saw Cornell as an older brother. Thank the Gods he didn't drag her into this."

"And you were right about Charlie," Eve said to Avery. "His whole coven being involved is a shock, though."

"It's not surprising his wife was involved, really," she mused. "But Robyn was an unexpected twist."

"But how the bloody hell," Nate asked, "did Harry and Zane persuade them to become involved, anyway? It's madness, going up against a whole coven!"

"Charlie knew Zane as a child, and Lowen," Reuben reminded them. "And Zane's mother said he was always eager for control."

Caspian shrugged. "Power is an intoxicating lure to some people. No doubt he offered to share the magic he was trying to steal from us. I doubt he would have, though." He gestured to Zane's body. "Has anyone called Newton? He'll be anxious to know what happened."

"I have," Avery said. Her nose wrinkled with distaste. "We'll move his body soon to the public woods. His death will be recorded as a wild animal attack. I must admit that I'm glad it's all over."

"Me too," Eve confessed with weary smile. "The Cornwall Coven will feel quite different for a while with three missing covens, but things will settle down eventually." She looked up, staring beyond Caspian's head as she finished speaking, and turning around he saw Hemani approach.

"Am I interrupting?" Hemani asked in her calm voice, although her eyes looked wary.

"Just chatting," Avery said, smiling and edging closer to Alex to make room for her. "Come and join us."

"I wasn't sure if I'd be welcome," she admitted, wiggling into the small space. "I have a feeling you didn't quite trust me."

"Sorry," El apologised. "We wanted to, and thought we could, but after the events at Stannon Stone Circle, we weren't sure if you were involved with the others. And to be honest, we don't know you as well as the witches who were helping us."

Hemani nodded. "I get that. Our coven does have a tendency to keep to themselves."

"We met again last night," Avery confessed, "and didn't invite you. I'm sorry for that. But I'm very pleased you weren't a part of that nastiness."

Hemani gestured to where her other three coven members were sitting together. "I am going to ensure that we mingle more in future. The value of trust and friendship after the events of the last few weeks has become even clearer now." She sighed. "I also trusted Cornell. I liked him, and admired his magic. It's devastating, actually."

"Why don't you ask them to join us now?" Reuben suggested. "I'd like to meet them all properly. You should get your uncle and cousins to come over, too," he said to Caspian.

Caspian laughed. "I think they all feel out of sorts, actually. They liked Zane and Mariah—Father's old support act. I think they feel betrayed too, but more because they weren't invited in." He looked across at his uncle's sharp face as he talked to Oswald. "Everything changes, doesn't it?"

"Change is good. Well, most of the time," Hemani said, smiling. "And yes, I will. Thank you, Reuben. I'll get them now."

She hurried away to gather her coven, and as they rearranged themselves to make room for the newcomers to join them, Caspian reflected on his own intentions. The solstice had indeed brought change, and he was very curious as to where it would all lead.

It was after the lunchtime rush in The Wayward Son on the following day, when Alex was finally able to take his own break. He settled in with half a pint and a burger on a small table in the courtyard, and within minutes, Zee had joined him with his own food.

It was a hot day, and Zee was wearing old jeans and a worn t-shirt that revealed his tattooed arms. He pulled a chair out. "Do you mind if I join you?"

"Not at all," Alex said, waving for him to sit. "I've been trying to catch up with you all morning. Shouldn't complain that we're so busy, though."

"Marie is good. She's covering for me now that it has finally gone quiet." He chewed a chip thoughtfully. "So, how was last night?"

"As mad as we thought it would be." Alex updated him on all their news. "Zane was wearing gold cuffs inset with gems, and Harry had an enormous ring. Both wielded incredible, dark power. We think they fashioned them from the pirate gold."

"And made the other things to sell?"

"Yep. They planned it for a long time, and it was all for nothing in the end." It was horrible just thinking about it, and Alex shook it off. "How's the house now that your brothers and Shadow are back?"

"Bloody noisy," he complained. "I had the whole place to myself on Sunday night. Eli spent the night with one of his women, and I could play whatever games I like and watch movies, all without anyone complaining once. Now it's mayhem again." He raised his eyebrows and gave Alex a wicked grin. "Shadow and Gabe are a couple now."

Alex nearly spat his mouthful of burger out. "Really? Since when?"

"Since the last few days. France worked wonders, and it's about bloody time! There was so much sexual tension between them, it was unbelievable. And now Barak is all loved up, too."

Alex put his burger down before he choked on it. "You're serious? With who?"

"Estelle!"

"Holy shit. I didn't see *that* coming." He studied Zee's ruggedly handsome face. "And you're still single?"

"And liking it that way, so don't you dare try and match me up!"

Alex held his hands up. "No way! That's Avery's job."

Zee laughed. "Anyway, we're having a party. Big bonfire, barbeque, the works. It's short notice—tomorrow night. Can you make it? We've asked Caspian and Estelle, Ghost OPS, and Newton is coming, too. It seems that Shadow has talked Gabe into it." He winked. "She could probably talk him into anything right now."

"That," Alex said, "sounds great. Avery can't wait to look around your place again."

"Cool. Ash is asking Reuben today, too. Should be a full house."

Zee took another bite of his burger and Alex frowned at his wide-eyed, nonchalant expression. "Is there another reason for this party?"

"So suspicious!"

Alex refused to be put off. "So there is!"

Zee smiled. "Not really. But with all of this double-crossing business and subterfuge that we've all experienced lately, we thought it would be good to really cement our friendships. After all, in this strange paranormal world we live in, that's sometimes all you can rely on."

Alex raised his glass in agreement. "I'll drink to that."

Thanks for reading *Chaos Magic*. Please make an author happy and leave a review.

I have also written a spinoff series called White Haven Hunters. The first book is called *Spirit of the Fallen*, and you can buy it here.

If you enjoyed this book and would like to read more of my stories, please subscribe to my newsletter at tjgreen.nz. You will get two free short stories, Excalibur Rises and Jack's Encounter, and will also receive free character sheets of all the main White Haven witches.

By staying on my mailing list, you'll receive free excerpts of my new books, as well as short stories, news of giveaways, and a chance to join my launch team. I'll also be sharing information about other books in this genre that you might enjoy. Read on for a list of my other books.

Author's Note

Thank you for reading *Chaos Magic*, the ninth book in the White Haven Witches series.

This wraps up the storyline that started in *Vengeful Magic*. There are many stone circles in Cornwall, and there really are nine on Bodmin Moor, as well as the remnants of many mines. The Visitor Centre at Minions Village really does exist, too, but I have taken liberties with its construction.

There are more White Haven Witches stories to come, and although I'm not exactly sure what the next one will be about yet, there's still plenty more English and Cornish myths to explore. The next book should be released in August 2022.

If you'd like to read a bit more background to the stories, please head to my website, www.tjgreen.nz, where I blog about the books I've read and the research I've done on the series. In fact, there's lots of stuff on there about my other series, Rise of the King, as well.

Now for the thanks I owe everyone who helped me produce this book.

I decided to run a competition in my newsletter and Facebook group, TJ's Inner Circle, to name the group of parapsychologists. I had some fantastic suggestions, and ended up narrowing it down to eight that had the final vote. Ghost OPS won by a big margin! Thank you Margaret Meyer for your awesome suggestion!

Thanks again to Fiona Jayde Media for my awesome cover, and thanks to Kyla Stein at Missed Period Editing for applying her fabulous editing skills.

Thanks also to my beta readers—glad you enjoyed it; your feedback, as always, is very helpful!

Finally, thank you to my launch team, who give valuable feedback on typos and are happy to review upon release. It's lovely to hear from them—you know who you are! You're amazing! I also love hearing from all of my readers, so I welcome you to get in touch.

If you'd like to read more of my writing, please join my mailing list at www.tjgreen.nz. You can get a free short story called Jack's Encounter, describing how Jack met Fahey—a longer version of the prologue in Call of the King—by subscribing to my newsletter. You'll also get a free copy of Excalibur Rises, a short story prequel. You will also receive free character sheets on all of my main characters in White Haven Witches—exclusive to my email list!

By staying on my mailing list, you'll receive free excerpts of my new books, updates on new releases, as well as short stories and news of giveaways. I'll also be sharing information about other books in this genre you might enjoy.

I encourage you to follow my Facebook page, T J Green. I post there reasonably frequently. In addition, I have a Facebook group called TJ's Inner Circle. It's a fab little group where I run giveaways and post teasers, so come and join us. https://www.facebook.com/groups/696140834516292

About the Author

I grew up in England and now live in the Hutt Valley, near Wellington, New Zealand, with my partner, Jason, and my cats, Sacha and Leia. When I'm not writing, you'll find me with my head in a book, gardening, or doing yoga. And maybe getting some retail therapy!

In a previous life I've been a singer in a band, and have done some acting with a theatre company—both of which were lots of fun.

Please follow me on social media to keep up to date with my news, or join my mailing list—I promise I don't spam! Join my mailing list here.

For more information, please visit my website, as well as Facebook, Pinterest, Goodreads, BookBub, TikTok, and Instagram.

Other Books by TJ Green

Rise of the King Series

A Young Adult series about a teen called Tom who is summoned to wake King Arthur. It's a fun adventure about King Arthur in the Otherworld!

Call of the King #1

King Arthur is destined to return, and Tom is destined to wake him.

When sixteen-year old Tom's grandfather mysteriously disappears, Tom will stop at nothing to find him, even if that means crossing over into a mysterious and unknown world.

When he gets there, Tom discovers that everything he thought he knew about himself and his life was wrong. Vivian, the Lady of the Lake, has been watching over him and manipulating his life since his birth. And now she needs his help.

The Silver Tower #2

Merlin disappeared over a thousand years ago. Now Tom will risk everything to find him.

Vivian needs King Arthur's help. Nimue, a powerful witch and priestess who lives on Avalon, has disappeared.

King Arthur, Tom, and his friends set off across the Otherworld to find her. Nimue seems to have a quest of her own, one she's deliberately hiding. Arthur is convinced it's about Merlin, and he's determined to find them both.

The Cursed Sword #3

An ancient sword. A dark secret. A new enemy.

Tom loves his new life in the Otherworld. He lives with Arthur in New Camelot, and Arthur is hosting a tournament. Eager to test his sword-fighting skills, Tom is competing.

But while the games are being played, his friends are attacked, and everything he loves is threatened. Tom has to find the intruder before anyone else gets hurt.

Tom's sword seems to be the focus of these attacks. Their investigations uncover its dark history, and a terrible betrayal that a family has kept secret for generations.

White Haven Hunters

The fun-filled spinoff to the White Haven Witches series! Featuring Fey, Nephilim, and the hunt for the occult.

Spirit of the Fallen #1

Kill the ghost, save the host.

Shadow is an overconfident fey stranded in White Haven after the Wild Hunt is defeated on Samhain.

Gabe is a Nephilim, newly arrived from the spirit world, along with six of his companions. He has a violent history that haunts him, and a father he wants answers from—if he ever finds him.

When they get into business together with The Orphic Guild, they're expecting adventure, intrigue, and easy money.

But their first job is more complicated than they imagined.

When they break the fey magic that seals an old tomb, they discover that it contains more than they bargained for. Now they're hunting for a rogue spirit, and he always seems one step ahead.

The fight leads them in a direction they never expected.

Gabe can leave his past behind, or he could delve into the darkest secrets of mankind.

Shadow has no intention of being left out.

Shadow's Edge #2

As Shadow and Gabe become more involved with The Orphic Guild, they find out that the occult world is full of intrigue, and far more complicated than they realised.

Especially when it seems that someone wants the same thing that they do—The Trinity of the Seeker.

Cause for concern?

Absolutely not. If anything, Shadow is more committed than ever, and relishes pitting her wits against an unpredictable enemy.

And Gabe? When they find instructions that could enable him to speak to his father, he and the Nephilim are more than ready to fight.

Join Shadow, Gabe, and Harlan as they race against an occult organisation that is as underhand as they are.

Dark Star #3

A race against time to find a stolen arcane artefact turns out to be far more dangerous than they ever expected.

When an ancient relic is stolen from the Order of the Midnight Sun, Shadow and Gabe are hired to track it down, pitting them against a new enemy.

The search leads them across the country and tests their resources— and their faith in each other, as fey and Nephilim discover that this world is as tricky as the life they left behind.

Harlan, desperate to help, finds himself at war with JD, and suddenly alliances are under pressure. No longer able to trust The Orphic Guild, Harlan is faced with a dilemma that forces him to make choices he never envisaged.

Enjoy magic, mystery, intrigue, and the occult? Then you'll love the White Haven Hunters. Buckle up for the ride!

Printed in Great Britain
by Amazon